Elizabeth Lowell

—❦—

ELIZABETH LOWELL

Only His

AVON BOOKS • NEW YORK

To Maggie Lichota
who understands risk, romance
and the deft art of editing

AVON BOOKS
A division of
The Hearst Corporation
1350 Avenue of the Americas
New York, New York 10019

Copyright © 1991 by Two of a Kind, Inc.
Inside cover author photograph by Phillip Stewart Charis
Published by arrangement with the author
Library of Congress Catalog Card Number: 91-91763
ISBN: 0-380-76338-9

First Avon Books Printing: July 1991

AVON TRADEMARK REG. U.S. PAT. OFF. AND IN OTHER COUNTRIES, MARCA REGISTRADA, HECHO EN U.S.A.

Printed in the U.S.A.

RA 20 19 18 17 16 15 14 13

THE "ONLY" FAMILY

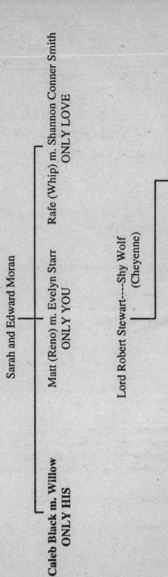

Sarah and Edward Moran

Caleb Black m. Willow
ONLY HIS

Matt (Reno) m. Evelyn Starr
ONLY YOU

Rafe (Whip) m. Shannon Conner Smith
ONLY LOVE

Lord Robert Stewart----Shy Wolf
(Cheyenne)

Wolfe Lonetree m. Jessica Charteris
ONLY MINE

1

THE man looked dangerous.
Dark, strong, unsmiling, he filled the hotel doorway. Leashed power radiated from his stillness. When he moved, the muscular coordination of his body was predatory rather than merely graceful.

Dear God, Willow Moran thought as she watched the man stride closer to her across the lobby of the newly built Denver Queen hotel. *This can't be Caleb Black, the God-fearing military scholar Mr. Edwards found to take me to my brother.*

Willow's dismay didn't show in her hazel eyes or her posture. She didn't back away so much as an inch despite the sudden frantic beating of her heart. The War Between the States had taught Willow that when a girl couldn't run and couldn't hide, she stood her ground with as much dignity as she could muster . . . and a two-shot derringer hidden in a special pocket of her skirt.

The knowledge of that cold steel weight lying between folds of silk comforted Willow now as it often had in the past. Gripping the small gun, she watched the dark stranger draw near. What she saw of him at

1

close range didn't comfort her at all. Beneath the shadow of his broad-brimmed, flat-crowned black hat, an icy intelligence watched the world from eyes the color of whiskey.

"Mrs. Moran?"

His voice was as intensely male as the thick mustache and black beard stubble that heightened rather than blurred the strong planes of his face. Yet the voice itself wasn't harsh. It was deep, smooth, potent, like a midnight river flowing to an invisible sea. A woman could drown in that dark voice, in those tawny eyes, in the power that seethed beneath the man's controlled surface.

"Yes, I'm Mi—er, Mrs. Moran," Willow said, feeling heat stain her cheekbones as she spoke the lie. Willow Moran she was. Mrs. she was not. "Have you come to take me to Mr. Black?"

Willow's voice was too husky, almost breathless, but she could do little about that. It was difficult enough just to force air past the sudden tightness in her throat as the stranger's masculine impact flooded over her in a dark, compelling tide.

"I'm Caleb Black."

Willow forced herself to smile. "Forgive me for not recognizing you. From Mr. Edwards' description, I expected a somewhat older gentleman. Is Mr. Edwards with you?"

There was a very faint emphasis on the word *gentleman* that most men would have missed, but not Caleb Black. His mouth shifted into a curving line that only a charitable person would have called a smile as he jerked a thumb over his shoulder.

"Out in those mountains, Mrs. Moran, a *gentle*man is less use than a handful of spit. But I wouldn't expect a fine southern lady such as yourself to understand that. We all know the importance you Virginians place on elegant manners." Caleb looked past her toward the wide doorway at the far side of the lobby. "Eddy and the Widow Sorenson are waiting for us over there."

A faint flush rose beneath Willow's translucent skin, a combination of embarrassment at her own accidental rudeness to him and anger at Caleb's intentional insult to her. She hadn't meant to demean him with her careless tongue. The long journey from her ruined West Virginia farm might have hardened the muscles of her five Arabian horses, but it had turned her own brain to pudding.

Unhappily Willow admitted that she deserved at least some of the bleak appraisal in Caleb's whiskey eyes, eyes which at the moment were lingering with faint contempt on the fit of her clothes. The dress had been tailored for her in 1862, before war had wholly ravaged her family's farms and fortunes. New, the dress had more than allowed for each curve of Willow's budding body. Four years later, Willow's curves had become more pronounced. The cut of the dress had stayed the same. As a result, the blue-gray silk pulled across her breasts and fit tightly around her waist.

Yet it was Willow's only silk dress. She had worn it because she expected to meet a gentleman who would appreciate her gesture toward a more gracious time. She hadn't expected an unshaven gunfighter who would note only the bad fit of her clothes. Her chin came up slightly as she faced the man who so obviously didn't like her.

"The war is over, Mr. Black."

"And you lost."

Willow closed her eyes, then opened them. "Yes."

The husky admission surprised Caleb, as did the sudden darkening of Willow's hazel eyes. Surprise at finding that his quarry, Matthew "Reno" Moran, had a wife was giving way to the suspicion that the young woman with the tight dress and frankly sensual mouth was not quite what she represented herself to be. Reno's *woman*, surely. But his wife? Probably not. Nothing Caleb had learned about Reno since he began hunting him indicated that Reno was the marrying kind.

Caleb looked Willow over again, taking his time, watching the color rise once more in her cheeks. The blush piqued his curiosity. Females like Willow couldn't afford emotions or pride, yet it was apparent she had both.

Not for the first time, Caleb wondered what her so-called husband was like—what kind of fine southern gentleman could both seduce an innocent like Caleb's sister Rebecca and inspire such passion in an experienced young thing like Willow that she was willing to pursue her missing man to the heart of the untamed West.

With a shrug that made muscles shift and coil beneath the dark trail clothes Caleb wore, he dismissed his own curiosity. It didn't matter that Willow was probably a Miss rather than a Mrs. Nor did it matter what the elusive Matthew "Reno" Moran was like. Caleb had been looking for his sister Rebecca's seducer for eleven months.

When he found Reno, he would kill him.

"Shall we go?" Caleb asked. "Or have you changed your mind about finding your . . . husband, is it?"

Cool golden eyes looked at Willow's left hand, which was slender and without a ring. She flushed guiltily. She hated having to lie, but her brother's letters had made it clear that he was living in a wild, uncivilized place. A young woman travelling alone in such a place was at risk. A wife, on the other hand, had a husband's protection. Even an absent husband was enough to give other men pause.

"Yes," Willow said, clearing her throat. She met

Caleb's eyes with a combination of embarrassment and defiance. "My husband. Have you heard of him by any chance?"

"A lot of men change their names when they get west of the Mississippi. Even honest men."

Willow's eyes widened. "How odd."

"Most people don't think honesty is odd."

The cool contempt in the words stung Willow. "That isn't what I meant."

Caleb looked from Willow's burnished blond hair to her delicate patent leather shoes peeking from beneath the long silk skirt. "I've never met a man called Matthew Moran. Did he have a nickname?"

"If he did, he never mentioned it."

Caleb's eyes narrowed. "You're certain?"

"Quite."

"How long have you been . . . married?"

Caleb's inflection made it clear that he doubted Willow was married. His eyes repeated the message. Willow fought against the tide of color she felt rising in her cheeks. She truly hated to lie, but the war had taught her that survival required doing things she hated.

"Does it matter?" Willow asked.

A sardonic smile curled one corner of Caleb's mouth. "Not to me. You just look a little young for marriage. Barely out of rompers, in fact."

"I'm twenty," she said distinctly. "Many women my age already have children."

Caleb grunted. "How old is your husband?"

"Twenty-five," Willow said, eager to tell the truth wherever possible. "Matt is the youngest of my—that is—" she corrected quickly, "he's the youngest of five sons."

After a brief, reassessing silence, Caleb lifted a black eyebrow and offered Willow his arm. She ignored the mockery implicit in his polite gesture, for she was certain Caleb was not a man whose actions were ruled by politeness. Despite that, she placed her fingertips on his sleeve in a graceful gesture that had been drilled into her in the years before the war had ended all need for gracious manners.

"Thank you, Mr. Black," Willow murmured.

The slight drawl and contralto huskiness of her voice brushed over Caleb's nerves like a caress. The warm, gentle weight of her fingers sent heat rippling through his body. He hardened with a violent rush that shocked him, for he had never allowed himself to be at the mercy of his own lust. It angered him that his body responded with such primitive eagerness to Willow's haunting voice and alluring curves.

With too much interest for his own comfort, Caleb wondered if Willow would come to a man with honest passion or if Reno's "wife" was simply a cold, pretty whore who would open her legs for any man who had a piece of silver in one hand and his hunger in the other. Caleb had no use for whores, including the traditional one.

Across the lobby a short, stocky man stood up slowly and gestured toward them. His suitcoat was of a dull broadcloth, his shirt was boiled, and like many men in the West, his pants had formerly been part of a military uniform.

"There's Mr. Edwards," Willow said.

"You sound relieved," Caleb observed.

"Mr. Edwards spoke very highly of you."

"And you think he was lying."

Willow stopped walking. Automatically Caleb stopped as well, missing the gentle pressure of her fingertips on his forearm.

"Mr. Black," Willow began, then faltered when his bleak, whiskey-colored eyes focused on her. She took a breath and began again. "I have apologized for offending you. I truly meant no insult. Your appearance surprised me, that's all. I was expecting a man twice your age, a scholar of military campaigns, a silver-haired, old-fashioned—"

"Gentleman?" Caleb interrupted.

"—God-fearing man," Willow finished.

"What makes you think I'm not?"

"I don't think you're afraid of anything," she retorted, "including God."

Caleb's mouth shifted again, into a true smile this time, a smile that changed the hard lines of his face. Willow's breath caught. When Caleb smiled, he was as handsome as the devil was reputed to be. Impulsively she touched his arm once more, smiling in return.

"Could we start over again?" she asked softly.

The seductive bow of Willow's lips sent a shaft of hunger through Caleb that was almost painful. His body's savage response to another man's fancy woman made Caleb furious. The curve of his mouth changed, becoming thin and hard as the blade of the long knife he wore at his belt.

"Save the long eyelashes and soft smiles for your *husband*, southern lady. Every time I look at your fancy dress and silky yellow hair, I remember how many men died on both sides of the war to keep you in the luxury you think you deserve."

The contempt in Caleb's voice froze Willow. In truth she was not southern, not rich, not spoiled. But telling Caleb that would do nothing to arouse his compassion and could easily prevent him from accepting the job she was offering him. If he knew that she had no money to pay him until she reached her brother, Caleb might very well turn his back on her.

That would be a disaster. Mr. Edwards had made it clear that Caleb was one of the few men in the West—and the only man in the raw little city of Denver—who could be trusted with Willow's life, her virtue, and her valuable-blooded horses.

Without a word Willow turned away from Caleb and walked toward Mr. Edwards. She didn't notice the admiring looks and masculine murmurs that followed her progress through the lobby. It had been so long since she had thought of herself as a woman that she was out of the habit. To Willow her body was something she fed, bathed, and clothed in order to make it work. After her father had gone off to fight, leaving Willow alone with her fragile mother, it had been Willow who had struggled to see that the home farm provided the food that kept the Moran women alive.

Willow might have been oblivious, but Caleb noticed every approving look she drew. His cool, raking glance chastened more than one eager male. Caleb told himself that he wasn't being protective of Willow's non-existent virtue; he was merely guarding his ticket to the elusive Reno's funeral. Any one of the tough young men lounging around Denver's newest hotel would have been happy to earn fifty Yankee dollars for leading the lovely young Willow into a land so remote that most of its rivers, canyons, and mountain peaks had no names.

"Mr. Edwards," Willow said in a low voice, "it was good of you to arrange this meeting."

Eddy smiled, took her hand, and bowed over it before he turned to introduce her to his companion, a plump woman of thirty with black hair, red cheeks, and vivid blue eyes.

"Mrs. Moran, this is Mrs. Sorenson. Rose, this is the young woman you've been hearing so much about for the past three weeks."

Willow looked startled. "Three weeks? But I've been in Denver less than three hours!"

Eddy grimaced. "Since the darned telegraph went

in, loose talk travels so fast it makes a man dizzy. We've been hearing about a beautiful southern lady and her five blooded horses since you climbed on the stage in St. Joseph and tied your horses on behind."

Rose stood and took Willow's hand in her own calloused ones. She patted gently. "Pay no mind, Mrs. Moran. Out West a body don't have much to talk about but rumors. Anything outside the ordinary sets us to buzzing like a kicked-over beehive."

Willow saw the kindness in the other woman's face, and the lines of sadness as well. It was a sadness Willow had seen in her own mother's face, after war and widowhood left her with nothing to look forward to but the illness and death that soon overtook her.

"Don't worry, Rose," Caleb said, coming up behind Willow. "Any girl who is chasing a handsome young stud like Matthew Moran all over God's creation must be used to being the butt of gossip."

Rose's laugh sounded suspiciously like a giggle. Smiling, she held out her hand to the dark man who towered above her.

Though Caleb had been careful to stay out of Rose's bed since he had introduced her to Eddy a few months before, Caleb still enjoyed seeing Rose when he came to Denver. He admired the widow's combination of grit and humor, and the way she had managed to keep all five of her young children and raise them without a man to support her. If the discreet contributions of a few men had helped in the three years since Rose's husband had died, Caleb didn't think less of Rose for it. The money went to her children's care, rather than to silks and fancy horses.

Caleb swept off his hat and bent over Rose's fingers with the grace of long practice. The courtly ease of his gesture silently told Willow just how little Caleb respected her. The man had excellent manners, yet he had never once removed his hat in her presence, much less bowed over her hand in greeting.

"I thought you said you didn't know my br—husband," Willow said, her voice as cool as the silk folds of her skirt.

"I don't."

Willow's dark amber eyebrows lifted. "Then how do you know Matt is handsome?"

"I've never known a girl to chase an ugly man unless he was rich. Is your husband rich?"

"No," she said instantly, thinking of the gold strike Matt had found and was trying to protect. "He hasn't a dime."

But Caleb wasn't listening. He was turning away from Willow, offering his hand to Rose's escort. "Hello, Eddy. Glad to see you back on your feet. I thought that green-broke stud had been the death of you."

"Damn near, er, darn near was," Eddy said, taking Caleb's hand gingerly and then sitting down with obvious relief. "My right hand and leg are still kinda numb. Next time I'll let you shake the kinks out of that horse."

"No thanks. If I were you, I'd unload that stud the same way you got him—in a poker game. He has a flashy golden hide," Caleb's glance went to Willow's hair, "but he's mean as a snake underneath. Even if he throws yellow colts, you'll never be able to trust them. Bad blood is bad blood, no matter how pretty the wrapping."

Willow told herself that Caleb wasn't insulting her, he was simply making conversation about a horse. She was still telling herself that when Caleb turned away and made such a prolonged fuss over seating Rose once more that Eddy started to struggle to his feet to assist Willow.

"Please don't get up," Willow said in a low voice

when she saw Eddy's difficulty. She sat down quickly. "I'm quite capable of seating myself."

"Thank you, ma'am." Eddy sighed and muttered unhappily, "Since that stud threw me, I'm a damned poor excuse for a man."

Willow smiled and spoke too softly to be overheard, wanting to spare Eddy's pride. "The quality of a man doesn't change due to age or injury. You have been the soul of gentleness and helpfulness to me."

Caleb's acute hearing caught every word Willow said. He gave her a narrow look, but saw only compassion in her expression, rather than the flirtatious sidelong glances of a woman bent on seduction. Frowning, Caleb took the last chair in the informal lobby grouping. He had expected Willow to wait imperiously to be seated like the spoiled southern lady she was. Instead, she had seated herself and at the same time graciously eased Eddy's embarrassment at the injuries that kept him from leaping to his feet and aiding her. Reno's fancy woman was turning out to be a surprise.

Caleb didn't like surprises. He had seen too many men die with a look of surprise on their face.

"Did you have any trouble coming West?" Rose asked, turning expectantly toward the younger woman, obviously eager for conversation.

"It was quite an adventure," Willow admitted with a rueful smile. "Matt's letters mentioned the Mississippi, but until I stood on its banks at sunset and saw it burning like a great golden sea, I never realized how big the river really was, or how powerful. When we crossed the next day, it was like riding an unruly horse."

Rose shuddered. "I recollect it. Scared me near to death when I crossed it years ago, and my husband waited until low water. If you crossed in May, that devil river must have been brawling along."

"It was. Trees bigger than wagons were being tossed around like jackstraws. When one battered old oak crashed into the ferry, some horses were knocked overboard, but we were close enough to the far shore that they swam to safety."

Silently Caleb remembered his own crossing of that great, roiling barrier called the Mississippi. He had been only five, but the size of the river had thrilled him more than it had frightened him. Echoes of his own exhilaration came to him both from his memories and from Willow's husky voice telling him that she, too, had gone eagerly into the river's wild embrace.

"How was the stage ride?" Rose asked. "I been thinking of going East, but I swore I'd never walk it again and I 'spect I'll be dead before a railroad makes it this far West."

Willow hesitated, then admitted, "The coach bucked and lurched, the driver cracked his whip and swore constantly, and the noise of the wheels was enough to wake the dead. In fact, after a few days on the stage I began to wonder if Hell wasn't served by the Holladay Overland Mail & Express Line."

Rose smiled. "It must have seemed strange to a gently raised girl."

"Not as strange as all that land and no trees," Willow said. "Not one tree. The stage stations were dug into hillsides and roofed with sod. Matt had told me about it, but I thought he was exaggerating."

Eddy laughed even as he looked at Willow and shook his head. "Don't say I didn't warn you, Mrs. Moran."

"Oh, you did," Willow agreed. "When I found your name in my father's, er, father-in-law's correspondence and wrote you about finding Matt, you were most discouraging."

"Must be every bit of six hundred miles from St.

Joseph," Eddy said. "That's a long, hard trip for a young woman alone."

"It's a long ride for anyone, but I had my horses. My stallion Ishmael is more comfortable than any stage seat. When it wasn't raining, I rode. Some of the passengers had it much worse than I did. They had no horse to ride and no money to pay for extra overnight stops to rest from the ride. I met several poor souls who were making the trip in half the time I took."

"Why didn't you wait for your man to come and get you?" Rose asked. Then she half-laughed, half-smiled, and flushed. "Lord, listen to me! I'm sorry, Mrs. Moran. I'm so hungry for news of anything east of Denver I forget my manners. Lots of folks that come here don't want to talk about what they left behind, or why, or even what their name was back home."

Before Willow could answer, Caleb said coolly, "Don't fret about pretty manners, Rose. Mrs. Moran is such a fancy southern lady that she doesn't expect much in the way of polish from people out here."

"Caleb Black!" Rose said, astonished. "What's got into you? You're not the kind to care which side a man fought on, long as he had grit enough to fight. And your manners are better than any man's—East, South, or North! Leastways, they used to be good." She turned toward Willow and patted the younger woman's hand. "Don't mind Cal. He's just funning you. He don't hate southerners. My goodness, Eddy is from Texas!"

"Wouldn't matter if Cal did hate southerners," Eddy said. "Mrs. Moran's a Yankee gal. West Virginia, the part that declared for the North."

Caleb gave Willow a narrow-eyed look. "Then why did you tell me you lost the war?"

Willow told herself that she shouldn't answer, but

it was too late. She was already talking, her words as clipped and cold as Caleb's had been.

"Our farms were in the border area," Willow said. "When Johnny Reb came calling, we were called Yankees and everything that could be eaten or carried off was. When Yankees came calling, we were called Johnny Rebs and everything that could be eaten or carried off was. During the war my father was killed and my mother died of a broken heart. All but five of our horses were stolen or 'requisitioned' by one side or the other. Our crops were burned and our trees were cut down. We lost our farms one by one until nothing was left, not even a kitchen garden. Tell me, Mr. Black—in what way was I on the winning side of that glorious war?"

"So that's why you come West," the widow said quickly, trying to interrupt the fierce currents of emotion she sensed between the tired young lady and Caleb Black. "You'll feel right at home in Denver, dear. Lots of folks out here just walked away and left it all behind them like a snake shedding old skin. That's what the West is for, starting over when everything else goes wrong. Are you and your husband going to take up ranching?"

Willow dragged her glance away from Caleb's bleak, whiskey-colored eyes and focused on Rose. She would like to have told the amiable widow the whole truth, but Matt's letter had been quite blunt about not trusting anyone with the map he had sent. Most people were decent and honest in their day-to-day lives, but a gold strike tested even the best friendships. That was why Matt had written home in the hope of finding one or more of his brothers to help him dig gold. When the letter arrived, the Moran brothers had been scattered from London to Australia.

Willow, however, had been available.

"Whatever Matt does," she said finally, hating to lie even by omission, "I hope to raise horses. Ishmael is a fine stallion. My four mares have been bred with equal care."

"Where will you settle?" Rose asked.

"I haven't decided. The homestead laws allow a woman to—"

"Homesteading!" Eddy interrupted. "Mrs. Moran, you can't be thinking of homesteading. You're much too fine a lady to ruin your hands working this stubborn western land. You let your man take care of you."

"You're very kind," Willow said, "but I'd rather depend on myself. Men are so easily distracted. Wave a flag in front of them, or whisper about gold or adventure, and off they go, leaving their women to fend for themselves and the children the men were so eager to create in the first place."

Rose gave Willow a startled look, then laughed aloud. "Ain't it just the God's honest truth! My Joe was as good a man as they come, but when a neighbor set off into those devil mountains four years ago, sure he would find gold, Joe went along and never mind the four little ones hanging on my skirts and the one waiting to be birthed. The neighbor come back coughing blood. My Joe never come back at all."

"I'm sorry, Mrs. Sorenson," Willow said, her voice low. "It was hard enough for me with just Mother to take care of. I can't imagine what I would have done with four children and a babe, too."

"Oh, 'tain't all bad, dear. Men are notional creatures, but charming all the same. Life without them would be a poor thing to live," the widow said, smiling at Eddy. "No one to hold the yarn while I wind it into balls. No one to fix a stubborn pump so I can wash my hair. No one to walk out with when the moon is full and the air smells of lilac. No one to smile when I come into a room." Rose laughed softly. "And no one to run to when thunder comes and scares the living daylights out of me."

An odd yearning went through Willow as she saw the way that Rose and Eddy looked at each other. It had been a long time since Willow had dreamed of sharing her life with anyone. Even then, she had been too young to understand what such sharing truly meant. At sixteen, a girl knew little of life except an impatience to get on with living it.

But the war had come, Steven had been killed, and Willow had learned that life was an endurance contest with no winners, just survivors.

"You'll get over the war," Rose continued, patting Willow's hand. "Your man will get you with child and you'll forget this foolishness about homesteading and taking care of yourself. The good Lord knew what He was doing when He made woman for man."

Caleb leaned back in his chair. "Save your sympathy for someone who needs it. All Mrs. Moran needs is a guide to get her to Matthew Moran."

"Will you do it?" Eddy asked.

"Might as well," Caleb said with an appearance of indifference. "I'm heading for the San Juan country anyway."

"Good," Eddy said, relieved. "I would do it myself, but that damned stud . . ." He looked Caleb in the eye. "I'm glad word caught up with you. I wasn't sure whether you were down to Yuma or up to Wyoming Territory."

"The emptier the land, the faster gossip travels," Caleb said. "I was hunting with Wolfe Lonetree when a tinker came to camp and said you needed me to guide Mrs. Matthew Moran to her husband."

"Lonetree, huh?" Eddy grunted. "No wonder word

got to you so fast. If a bug crawls anywhere in the territory, that halfbreed knows it." Eddy pulled out his watch and squinted at it. "Rose, if we don't get to the dining room, some young fiddlefoot will take our table." As he pocketed the watch once more, he looked at Willow with shrewd, dark eyes. "Now that you've met Cal, are you satisfied with the arrangement, Mrs. Moran?"

After a barely perceptible hesitation, Willow nodded, for she didn't trust herself to speak. Her unhappiness would have been clear in her voice. Yet it wasn't Caleb's competence as a guide she doubted, nor was it his innate honesty. It was his effect on her that made her hesitate. He made her intensely aware of herself as a woman, yet at the same time he made no attempt to conceal his dislike of her. The combination was disconcerting.

I'm just tired, Willow reassured herself silently. *A warm bath and a night of sleep will make all the difference in the world. I've come too far to turn back because of a rough stranger who makes me feel like a clumsy girl. Besides, there's nothing to go back to. Mama was right. The dreams she and Papa had died with the land. I can't go home again. I can only try to find a new home and build a new dream.*

"Mrs. Moran," Eddy said, rising slowly, "I leave you in good hands."

"Thank you. If I can ever repay your kindness—"

"Nonsense," Eddy interrupted firmly. "Your husband's father sold me the best horse I ever owned. Saved my life more than once. If I can help his kin, I'm happy to do it."

Eddy adjusted his coat over the pistol he wore and bowed over Willow's hand before turning to Caleb. "I'd tell you to be careful of the little lady, but if I didn't think you would be I'd never have mentioned your name to her. And if I hear anything about a drifter called Reno, I'll be sure to let you know."

Caleb shot a sideways glance at Willow. She didn't react to the nickname, which meant that she was a fine actress or she knew her "husband" only as Matthew Moran.

"You do that, Eddy." Caleb turned to Rose, bowed over her hand, and said, "Take care of him, Rose. And keep him off that damned yellow stud."

Silently Willow and Caleb watched the couple leave. Despite Eddy's effort to conceal his stiffness, it was apparent that he was in pain.

"Will he be all right?" Willow asked softly.

"As long as his old enemies don't find him until he heals up, he'll be fine."

"Enemies?"

"Eddy wore a lawman's badge in some bad places. A man who does that makes enemies." Caleb turned his bleak, golden glance on Willow. "Where are your horses?"

"At the livery stable down the street."

"Leave them there. I'll provide you with a horse that won't quit the first time the going gets hard."

"That's very kind of you, but—"

"I'm not a kind man," Caleb interrupted roughly, "I'm a practical one. Where we're going, a delicate, nervous, over-bred horse will be a hell of a lot more trouble than it's worth."

"My Arabians are well-bred, not over-bred, and I'll put them up against anything you own for stamina."

Caleb said something harsh under his breath. "Where in the San Juan country do you want to go?"

"The part with mountains."

"Ma'am," Caleb said dryly, "there's no part of the

San Juan country that doesn't have mountains. Which peak did you have in mind?"

"I'll tell you when we get there."

"Southern lady, if we take your fancy horses, we won't ever get there at all."

2

BEFORE Willow could respond, there was a commotion from the direction of the dining room. In the spreading silence of the lobby, a man's voice boomed out.

"You and your second-hand woman can just wait for the next table, old man. In fact, you can damn well wait until me and my friends are finished eating. I don't want that slut sitting in the same room with me."

Appalled, Willow turned and looked toward the dining room. An instant later she realized that Eddy and Rose were being confronted by four young men, all of whom wore pistols. A murmur went through the crowd as people backed away from the confrontation. Willow sorted out a few of the muttered words, something about gunmen and Rose refusing to let Slater's kid brother stay at her boarding house.

Caleb heard the mutterings, too, but he already knew what was going on. He had known since the back of his neck had tightened in an age-old warning of danger and he had spun around to see trouble closing in on his friends. If Eddy had been well, Caleb simply would have walked over to act as an unofficial referee, ensuring that the kid's friends didn't interfere with whatever happened between the old lawman and the young outlaw.

But Eddy wasn't well. He was injured and Johnny Slater knew it. Eddy knew it, too. He had a choice—he could let Rose be insulted or he could try to draw his pistol with his injured right hand. He might attempt a left-handed draw, even though the gun butt was facing the wrong way. No matter which hand, he quite likely would die before the gun barrel cleared the holster.

"No!" Rose said urgently. She stepped in front of Eddy, turning her back on the young tough who had insulted her. "You can't even hold a fork, much less a gun!"

Before Rose finished speaking, Caleb's big hand closed on Johnny Slater's shoulder, spinning him around.

"You've got a bad mouth, kid. Folks around Denver are tired of listening to it. Now you can apologize to Mrs. Sorenson and drag your freight out of town or you can go for one of those fancy guns you're wearing."

Surprise turned to dismay when Johnny measured the dark promise in Caleb's eyes. It was one thing to yell across twenty feet of crowded room at an injured man who could barely draw a gun. It was another to face a man belt buckle to belt buckle, a man who was neither injured nor afraid, a man who didn't give a damn about Kid Slater's reputation as a gunman with a fast draw and a vicious older brother to back him up.

Johnny Slater began sweating. He looked quickly to his friends, only to discover they were watching him with arms folded, clearly expecting him to take care of the interruption himself.

"Make up your mind, kid," Caleb said.

The cool impatience in Caleb's voice made Johnny flinch slightly. His hand crept closer to his pistol, hesitated, crept again. He looked into Caleb's eyes again and froze.

Caleb made a sound of disgust. "Your older brother may be a real curly wolf, but you're pure coyote. Apologize to the lady, Kid Coyote."

"I'm damned if I'm going to apologize to a—"

Caleb slapped Johnny before he could finish the sentence. The open-handed blow was so quick it was almost invisible. It rocked Johnny's head on his shoulders, sending his fine hat flying. Before Johnny realized what had happened, it was too late. Caleb was slapping him with slow, measured motions, blows that humiliated as much as they hurt; but it was the contemptuous words that hurt most of all.

"Kid Coyote, sneaking around," Caleb said. "This is for every man you ever shot in the back." *Slap*. "For every woman you ever insulted." *Slap*. "For every baby you ever stole candy from." *Slap*. "Now take off your guns, Kid Coyote."

"What?" Johnny asked, shaking his head, unable to believe what was happening to him.

"Take off your gunbelts and drop them on the floor."

Johnny reached for his first gunbelt with hands made clumsy by a combination of rage and fear. "You're a dead man, whoever you are! My brother will kill you for this!"

The first gunbelt hit the floor.

"Any time Slater feels lucky," Caleb said calmly, "you tell him to ask for Caleb Black."

The second gunbelt hit the floor.

"If people don't know that name," Caleb continued "tell your brother to ask for the Man from Yuma. As for you, Kid Coyote, you'd be smart never to wear a gun again. Those who live by the sword die by the sword. And you'll die, kid. If I see you wearing iron anywhere, anytime, I'll draw down on you and kill you where you stand. Hear me?"

Sullenly, Johnny nodded.

"It's the only warning you'll get and one more than you deserve." Caleb turned away and faced Johnny's friends. He looked at each one for a long moment, memorizing the faces of his new enemies. Caleb recognized one of them, a bounty hunter and claim jumper from the San Juan mountains. "Shuck those irons, boys."

More gunbelts thudded to the floor.

"You're running in bad company, but it's a free country. Don't know how you stand the smell, though." Caleb tilted his head toward the street. "Get out."

Radiating frustrated anger, Johnny and his friends left. Not until the door closed behind the last gunman did a ripple of excited talk run through the crowd, speculations and surmises spoken back and forth, another incident added to the growing legend of the Man from Yuma.

Willow made no sound at all. She simply let out her breath and withdrew her hand from the leather-lined pocket of her silk dress where the derringer had lain cold against her palm.

After a few moments people went back to doing whatever they had been doing before Caleb had called Johnny Slater's bluff. Everyone except Willow walked in a wide circle around the discarded gunbelts and the big man whose eyes were the clear, burning gold of a mountion lion's eyes—or an avenging angel's.

Caleb turned to Rose. "I'm sorry you had to hear that filth," he said simply.

Rose tried to speak, smiled tremulously, and managed to whisper, "You're a good man, Caleb Black.

There will always be a place set for you at my table."

Caleb smiled and touched the widow's pale cheek with a gentle affection that astonished Willow.

"Thanks," Eddy said simply to Caleb. "I owe you."

Caleb shook his head. "You're the best thing that ever happened to Rose. That's all the payment I need."

"Johnny will backshoot you some day," Eddy said matter-of-factly. "You should have killed him when you had the chance."

"There were too many women in the room to start shooting. A wild shot . . ."

"You're not a wild shooter."

With a shrug, Caleb began picking up gunbelts. "Johnny is a foul-mouthed polecat, but he hasn't killed any of my kin. He insulted Rose and I insulted him. As far as I'm concerned, that's the end of it."

"An eye for an eye," Willow murmured, watching Caleb. "Is that your Western code?"

He straightened and turned toward her with swift, predatory grace. "Not my code, southern lady. God's. 'And if any mischief follow, thou shalt give life for life, /Eye for eye, tooth for tooth, hand for hand, foot for foot, /Burning for burning, wound for wound, stripe for stripe.'"

The intensity in Caleb's voice made Willow shiver. "What about forgiveness?" she asked. "What about turning the other cheek?"

"That's a luxury for city folks who have enough policemen to take care of scum like Kid Coyote. Denver doesn't have that much law yet. Where I'm taking you there's no law at all. If a man turns his other cheek, he gets slapped again, harder, until he either fights or stops calling himself a man. Out in those mountains a man takes care of himself because no one else will do it for him."

"And a woman?" Willow asked unwillingly. "What does she do?"

"She stays in town," Caleb said bluntly. "If she can't do that, she finds a man tough enough to protect her and the kids she'll bear him. That's the way it is out here, southern lady. Nothing fancy. You kill your own meat, you dress it, you cook it, you eat it, and then you go out and hunt again." Caleb looked at Willow through narrowed eyes, stepped closer, and said too softly for anyone to overhear, "Still want to search for your . . . husband?"

Willow looked at the big man looming over her, his eyes like hammered metal and his hands full of weapons. Her first impression of Caleb Black had been correct.

He was dangerous.

Then Willow remembered the brush of his fingertips against Rose's cheek. Caleb was as hard as a whetstone, yet he was also a decent man. She would be safe with him. She knew it with an inner certainty she didn't question.

"Yes," Willow said.

Caleb looked surprised for a moment, but all he said was, "Get ready to ride. We leave in an hour."

"What? But it's dark and—"

"One hour, southern lady. Be at the livery stable down the street or I'll come and drag you out of your room."

ONE hour and three minutes later, an impatient knock sounded on Willow's hotel room door. She froze in the act of fastening one of the many stubborn buttons on the bodice of her riding habit.

"Who is it?" she asked, pausing as she pushed a button through a small buttonhole in the heavy wool.

"Caleb Black. You're late."

The voice was as low, compelling, and darkly masculine as Willow had remembered. A tiny shivering feeling uncurled in the pit of her stomach. The sensation surprised her, for she had never been afraid of men.

Then Willow realized she wasn't really afraid of Caleb. He simply was unlike any man she had ever known, which made it impossible for her to predict what he would do next. Or how she would react. His ability to make butterflies flutter in her stomach simply by talking to her through a closed door was disconcerting.

"I'll be out in a few minutes," Willow said, her voice unusually husky.

"You'll be out in thirty seconds or I'll come in after you."

"Mr. Black—"

Whatever Willow had been going to say ended in a husky sound of shock when she heard a key scraping in the lock.

"I'm not dressed!"

"Twenty seconds."

Willow didn't waste time arguing. Her fingers flew over the buttons. Even so, she barely had managed to close the bodice halfway over her breasts by the time the door opened. When she saw Caleb's wide shoulders fill the doorway, for an instant she was too shocked to move. The fine lawn of her camisole and its delicate embroidery of flowers were revealed, as was the velvet shadow lying between the full curves of her breasts.

Flushing to the roots of her golden hair, Willow grabbed the edges of her bodice and held them together. Beneath the tide of embarrassment, a flash of fury burned along her high, slanting cheekbones.

"Get out of my room!"

"Don't get your back up, fancy woman," Caleb said

as he closed the door behind him. "You've got nothing I haven't seen before."

Shocked, Willow said the only thing that came to her mind. "How did you get the key to my room?"

"I asked for it. Which one of these carpetbags is going with you?"

For several moments Willow struggled to keep her composure. Caleb might not have much regard for her modesty, but he was making no attempt to take advantage of her. He had looked at her unfastened bodice with complete disinterest. She should have been relieved that he considered her married and therefore out of bounds.

Instead, Willow found herself more than a little irritated by Caleb's lack of interest in her as a woman. The irrationality of her response only made her more angry.

"I'm taking all my luggage," Willow said tightly.

Caleb shook his head. "Pick one."

"But—"

"There's no time to argue," he interrupted impatiently. "We're leaving now and we're traveling light. There's a storm coming on. If we get out of here quick enough, we stand a good chance of having our tracks wiped out before anyone realizes we're gone."

Willow remembered Johnny Slater's threat of revenge and frowned. "Do you think Slater's brother will try to follow us?"

"Jed Slater and anyone else wanting a free woman and expensive horseflesh. That's a lot of men, and none of them the kind who go to church on Sunday."

"Mr. Black, I am not a 'free woman.'"

He shrugged. "Fine. You're an expensive woman. Which bag are you taking?"

Willow didn't trust herself to speak. She went to the smaller bags, grabbed a few items from each and stuffed them in the large carpetbag.

"That one," she said tightly.

Caleb picked up the bag and turned away, not permitting himself so much as a sidelong glance at the intriguing gaps in Willow's bodice. The single swift look he had taken when he walked into the room was more than enough. The soft curves and seductive shadows of her body had made him harden in the space of a breath. It had taken a maddening amount of self control not to brush aside her hands and lower his face to her breasts, finding out for himself if she was half as sweet to his tongue as she was to his eyes.

"Southern lady," Caleb said without looking around, "we—"

"My name is Willow Moran."

"—aren't going to a ball," he said, ignoring her interruption. "That fancy riding outfit of yours is as useless as a four card flush. When that long, flapping skirt gets wet, it will weigh more than you do. Wear something else."

"Such as?"

"Pants," he said succinctly.

Willow blinked. He was indeed a practical man.

"That's impossible," she said, as much to herself as to Caleb.

"Indian women do it all the time. We're not riding down country lanes. We're going over some of the roughest land God made this side of Hell. Last thing you need is yards of cloth flying and flapping and catching on every branch."

"I'll just have to do the best I can. I don't have anything else suitable."

Against his better judgment, Caleb glanced over his shoulder at Willow. The single lantern in the room was reflected in his eyes, making them look like they burned.

"Then at least take off the petticoats," he said bluntly.

"I can't. They're sewn into the seams of the riding skirt."

A spatter of rain hit the hotel window. Thunder rumbled distantly. Caleb looked at the black shine of water on the glass, shook his head, and opened the door. A quick glance assured him that no one was in the hall. With a curt gesture he indicated that Willow should precede him through the door.

"What about the rest of my luggage?" Willow asked.

"It will be waiting at Rose's boarding house when you get back."

Without another word Willow walked past Caleb into the dark hall, trying not to touch him on the way by. It was impossible. He left very little room when he stood in a doorway. The renewed realization of Caleb's size sent a flush to Willow's cheeks and more of the odd, shimmering sensations racing from her breastbone to her knees.

The few hall lights had been put out recently, leaving behind the smell of smoldering wicks.

"Left," Caleb said in a low voice that carried no farther than Willow.

She turned left, wondering where she was going, for the hotel lobby lay to her right.

"Mr. Black, where—" she began.

"Quiet," he interrupted swiftly.

A look over her shoulder convinced Willow that it was the wrong time to ask Caleb questions. Wearing the same dark trail clothes he had earlier, he looked like a huge shadow following her. He made no more noise than a shadow, either. If it hadn't been for the gleam of his eyes and the occasional shine of metal where his jacket had been tucked out of the way behind his gun holster, Caleb would have been nearly invisible.

Uneasily Willow turned around and stared into the

darkness ahead of her. She walked slowly, carefully, trying to make her steps as soundless as Caleb's. The rustling of petticoats beneath her heavy wool riding skirt defeated her.

"Wait," Caleb said softly.

Willow stopped walking as though she had run into a cliff. She felt the brush of Caleb's body, then the warmth of him radiated against her as he leaned down, putting his mouth next to her ear.

"I'll go first," he said. "The stairs are narrow and uneven. Put your hand on my shoulder for balance."

Before Willow could answer he brushed by her, turned his back, and waited. Hesitantly, she put her hand on his shoulder. Even through the wool jacket and shirt, she felt the vital heat of Caleb's body. She drew in her breath swiftly. She hadn't been this close to a man since her fiancé had gone off to war.

But Steven hadn't affected her like this, her heart racing and her knees going suddenly weak.

When Caleb moved without warning, Willow stumbled and reached out blindly for support. He turned and caught her with the same lightning swiftness that had been Johnny Slater's undoing. The feel of Caleb's hands pressed around her waist, digging into her, supporting her, was as unnerving as the speed and power of his body. When he bent to whisper in her ear, Willow couldn't force herself to breathe.

"If you can't even walk without tripping in that damned thing," Caleb muttered roughly, "I'll take my hunting knife and cut the cloth off at your knees."

Instinctively, Willow's hands went to Caleb's upper arms as she braced herself against his strength.

"You—you surprised me, that's all," she whispered. "When you moved."

Caleb stared down into Willow's face. It was no more than a pale blur in the darkness. He was grateful. If he couldn't see her eyes, she couldn't see the hunger in his. She smelled of lavender and sunshine. Her slender waist felt good in his hands. Too good. It was all he could do not to knead her tender flesh while he drew her hips against his thighs, easing and teasing the hunger that lay rigidly against the dark cloth of his pants.

Abruptly Caleb released Willow, grabbed her carpetbag, and turned his back on her. There was a pause before he felt a small hand settle lightly on his shoulder once more. The heat of her touch went all the way to his heels. Silently, savagely, he cursed his unbridled response to Reno's fancy lady. Caleb knew he would be suffering the torments of the damned before he pried the secret of Reno's hideout from Willow.

But pry it out he would. There was no other way to bring down justice on the man who had abandoned Rebecca to a lonely death days after she had given birth to her lover's child, a child that died within hours of its mother's death.

In the months since Rebecca had died, Caleb had redoubled his efforts to run Reno to ground. Nothing had helped. When Caleb came to isolated settlements or campfires and asked for information, he was always too late or too early or Reno had never been there at all. Bribery hadn't worked. The Mexicans and Indians, settlers and prospectors simply stopped talking when Caleb brought up Reno's name. Reno might have been a heel when it came to seducing virgins, but he had always given a hand or a dollar along the trail whenever either was needed. Anyone who hunted Reno was on his own.

Caleb had hunted Reno relentlessly. The search was made more difficult by the fact that Reno didn't keep to well-travelled ways or make predictable rounds of the lonely settlements. Reno was after

Spanish treasure—gold. He had a lone wolf's taste for high country and forgotten Indian trails leading through a maze of stone canyons and icy granite peaks. Caleb thought gold hunters were fools, but shared Reno's taste for the untouched high country. In fact, if it weren't for the cold-hearted seduction and abandonment of his sister Rebecca, Caleb suspected he would have liked Reno. But Rebecca was dead and Reno would die for it.

Life for life.

"Stairs," Caleb said, his voice low and cold.

Willow felt Caleb's shoulder dip, then dip again, telling her that he was descending stairs. Carefully, she tested the way ahead with the toe of her riding boot, trying to find where the floor ended and the stairs began. The hard sole of her boot defeated her. Caleb went down another stair, pulling her fingers free of his shoulder.

"Wait," she whispered, "I can't tell where the stairs begin."

She sensed him turning toward her with his unnerving swiftness.

"Hold this," he said.

The carpetbag was thrust into Willow's hands. An instant later she was snatched from her feet.

"What are you doing?" she gasped.

"Quiet."

The savage whisper silenced Willow. The world shifted and spun around her. She hadn't been picked up and carried since she was a child. The feeling of helplessness was startling, particularly in the dark. She turned her face against Caleb's muscular chest and hung onto the bag until her fingers ached, wishing she could hang onto him instead. After a few steps, Willow's fear of falling diminished. Caleb went down the badly made stairs with the absolute certainty of a cat. Sighing deeply, she let out her pent-up breath and loosened her grip on the carpetbag.

The warmth of Willow's sigh was like a brand on Caleb's chest. He clenched his teeth against the temptation to stop and find her mouth with his own, testing the depths of her sweet feminine heat. When he reached the bottom of the stairs he set Willow on her feet abruptly, took the carpetbag, and turned away from her without a word.

Willow let out another long, shaky breath and tried not to remember how it had felt to have Caleb's powerful arms around her back and beneath her knees, holding her. She also tried not to remember how good he had smelled, a masculine compound of wool and leather and the storm wind sweeping down from the mountains. With hands that wanted to tremble, she smoothed her riding habit and wondered what had happened to her customary calm. She had faced down armed soldiers with less trembling than she was experiencing now.

The side door of the hotel opened and closed behind Willow with only a few creaks. The alley smelled of garbage and slops. The wind smelled of woodsmoke and cold rain. She gathered her long wool skirt as best she could and stepped forward. A barrage of rain raked across her face. She wished she had something more useful to keep off the cold water than the tiny green hat that went with her riding habit.

Caleb used the back door into the livery stable, ushering Willow inside with open impatience. He had no great hope that their departure would go unnoticed for long, but they would need all the head start they could get if they eventually were going to lose any followers. No matter how staunchly Willow had defended her Arabians' endurance, Caleb doubted that the fine-boned, elegant animals he had glimpsed behind stall doors would be able to keep up with the big Montana horses he owned.

Jed Slater and outlaws like him also owned tough, long-boned horses that were grain-fed and ready to run the legs off any ordinary horses ridden by town posses or angry cowhands. Since Caleb had little hope of outrunning the outlaws, or hiding the tracks of his own two horses and Willow's five all the way to the San Juans, somehow he would have to outsmart—or outshoot— the men who would inevitably follow.

And there would be many such men, renegades drawn like flies to honey by the prize of expensive horseflesh and a woman with hair the color of the sun.

The fragrance of lavender drifted over Caleb as Willow moved past him into the stable. He tried not to notice. He failed. With a muttered curse he reached for the matches on the ledge by the door. When the lantern was lit, he crumbled the burned match between his fingers before letting it fall to the dirt floor.

Horses nickered and stretched their heads over stall doors, scenting the familiar presence of humans. With murmurous greetings, Willow went to her Arabians, touching them reassuringly. Caleb watched the horses with their delicate heads, sharply pricked ears, and unusually large, widely spaced eyes. Grudgingly, he admitted to himself that the animals were beautiful. Well-trained, too. As Willow began leading them from the stalls, they followed her without hesitation or shying at the flickering shadows cast by the lantern.

Even the stallion was gentle, though spirit visibly ran through him like lightning through a storm. His sorrel coat flashed red-gold fire at every motion of his body. A clean white blaze went from forehead to muzzle. A single white stocking marked his right front leg. When he moved, it was as though on springs, energy rippling with restrained power, coiled strength waiting for release. Centuries of intense, careful breeding ran through the stallion, apparent in each well-defined muscle and clean line of bone.

"That's one hell of a stud horse," Caleb said finally. "It will be worth your life to ride him out of Denver."

"Ishmael is as gentle as he is strong."

Caleb grunted. "It wasn't his manners I was talking about. That stud is enough to tempt a saint into mortal sin, much less the kind of men we'll see on the way to the San Juans. Every outlaw and renegade Indian in the territory will take one look at your stallion and start seeing himself in the saddle."

There was nothing Willow could say. She had noticed on the stage ride that the farther west she came, the more interest her horses excited. Yet she could no more let them go than she could cut off her own fingers. She loved her horses. They were all she had of her past and her only hope for a secure future.

In silence Willow finished leading her four mares from their stalls. Two of the mares were sorrels as fiery as Ishmael. Two were bays with shiny brown bodies and sweeping black manes and tails. All four of the mares moved with the liquid grace of cats.

Any one of them would have been worth killing for.

"Mother of God," muttered Caleb, looking at the five sleek animals. "Getting those horses to the San Juans without attracting every outlaw between here and Hell will be like trying to sneak dawn past the night."

Saying nothing, Willow bent and checked each horse's hooves for debris or loose shoes. The Arabians made it easy for her. No sooner had she touched a fetlock than a hoof was presented for her inspection. When she was finished, she ran a brush over Ishmael's glossy back and slid the saddle blanket into place without ruffling any hair.

When Caleb saw Willow reach for the sidesaddle,

he was tempted to stop her. A sidesaddle in rough country was hard on the woman and harder on the horse. No matter how accomplished a rider the woman was, her weight was always off-center on the horse's back.

Yet Caleb watched Willow finish saddling her mount and said nothing, because it suited his purpose to be silent. Anyone posted to watch the stable would duly report that a woman wearing a long riding skirt and using a sidesaddle had left the livery stable in the dead of night. The men who followed would be asking about a woman in fancy clothes riding a clumsy saddle that was rarely seen west of the Mississippi.

But Willow wouldn't be using that sidesaddle after a few days—not if Caleb had to drag her from it and slice the leather into pigging strings with his big hunting knife.

Caleb led his own two geldings from their stalls. Both animals were ready to travel. He lashed Willow's carpetbag to the pack saddle, tied a tarpaulin over everything to shed rain, and led the horses into the wide aisle between stalls. Ishmael's nostrils flared at the presence of the two big geldings, but his ears remained erect. He was curious rather than hostile.

Deliberately Caleb shook out a dark, finely woven poncho right under the stallion's nose. The sudden snapping of cloth didn't bother Willow's horse. Caleb pulled the poncho on, then ran his palm down the stallion's glossy, muscular neck. The flesh beneath was as hard as his own. The Arabian might look elegant, but it was the elegance of lightning rather than the elegance of a rose.

When Willow was done saddling Ishmael and roping the mares together for easy leading, Caleb walked over and checked each animal's hooves. They permitted his handling with only a few restless motions. When he finished, he tested the strength and tightness of the sidesaddle's girth on the stallion.

"Satisfied?" Willow asked.

"With that contraption?" Shaking his head, Caleb pulled on buckskin roping gloves that were worn and supple. "Glad it won't be my butt banging on that useless leather."

With a cool sideways look, Willow started to lead Ishmael past Caleb to the mounting block. His hand shot out and closed over the reins, stopping her.

"There won't be any mounting blocks on the trail," he pointed out. He bent and laced his fingers together, then looked up at her with clear topaz eyes. "Go ahead, honey. You've been wanting to step on me since you first laid eyes on me."

The deep voice and lazy smile sent quicksilver sensations through Willow. She smiled almost shyly in return and stepped into his hands as though into a stirrup.

Unlike a stirrup, Caleb was alive. And powerful. He lifted her weight with obvious ease. Willow's right leg, covered with petticoats and heavy wool cloth, hooked around the off-center horn of the sidesaddle, helping to hold her in place on the shallow leather seat. The horn, plus the single stirrup on the left side, was the only purchase offered by the sidesaddle, which had been invented for fashionable turns around a park rather than for serious riding.

"Thank you," Willow said, looking down into Caleb's eyes.

"Don't thank me. I'm leading you into the worst night of your life." Caleb turned away, then stopped and looked over his shoulder at her. "Don't you even have a decent hat or riding coat?"

"I was going to buy what I needed tomorrow."

He hissed a word beneath his breath.

"My riding habit is warm," Willow said. "It was made for winter."

"In West Virginia."

"We had snow there."

"How often, how deep, and did you ride all day in it?" Caleb asked sardonically.

"It's raining now, not snowing."

Without a word Caleb pulled off his poncho and held it up to her. "Put it on."

"That's very kind, but I couldn't take your—"

"*I told you I'm not a kind man*," Caleb interrupted in a voice that was just short of a snarl. "Put the damned thing on before I stuff you in it like a pig in a poke."

Mutinous hazel eyes glared at Caleb for a long moment before Willow took the poncho, pulled it over her head and down her body. Cut like a jerkin with riding slits, the poncho had fit Caleb's wide shoulders and lean hips very nicely. It was far too big on Willow.

"Lord, you're a little bit of a thing," he muttered.

"I'm five feet, three inches and I was the tallest girl in our valley."

"Damn small valley."

Caleb pulled a leather thong from his pocket and cinched in the poncho around Willow's small waist. Then he rummaged in his big saddlebags until he found a long wool muffler.

"Bend down," he said.

Willow leaned down to Caleb. Even though she was mounted, she didn't have to bend far. He was an unusually tall man. He wrapped the muffler securely around her head, tied the ends beneath her chin, and tried not to smile at the picture she made with her clear skin and red lips and his slate-colored muffler making her eyes gleam like smoked crystal.

Abruptly Caleb turned away to his own horse. He untied a heavy leather vest from behind his saddle. The vest was like everything else he owned—dark, unadorned, and made of the best quality material. Combined with his long-sleeved shirt of thick wool, the vest would keep him warm enough for the time being, if not exactly comfortable. He put on the vest, tied the mares' lead ropes to the pack saddle, and mounted his tall horse with the casual grace of a man born to the saddle.

"Do you have gloves?" Caleb asked curtly.

Willow nodded.

"Put them on."

"Mr. Black—"

"Try my Christian name, southern lady," he interrupted. "We're not real formal out here."

"Caleb. I'm hot."

The corner of his mouth turned up. "Enjoy it, Willow. It won't last."

Caleb urged his horse out of the barn and into the rain-lashed night. Immediately his pack horse followed, though no lead rope joined it to the saddle horse. After a brief hesitation, the mares followed. Ishmael nickered softly, distressed at being separated from his mares.

"It's all right," Willow said encouragingly to the stallion. "It's all right, boy."

Yet she was slow to rein the horse toward the barn door. Ishmael had no such reluctance. He trotted out into the stormy darkness, snorting at the cold whip of rain.

It's got to be all right, Willow told herself, gasping as slivers of icy rain scored her cheeks. *Because if it isn't, I've just made the worst mistake of my life.*

3

Before they had gone three miles, Willow's riding skirt and petticoats were soaked through. Wet cloth rubbed against her legs at every movement Ishmael made. Caleb set a hard pace through the storm, wanting to get as far away from Denver as possible before the rain stopped washing away the tracks of seven horses headed south on the treeless, well-beaten track that ran along the massive front range of the Rocky Mountains.

Alternately trotting and cantering, walking only when the land became uneven beneath the horses' driving hooves, Caleb led Willow through the night and the icy, intermittent rains of early June. After the first several hours he no longer checked over his shoulder every few minutes. The Arabian mares were keeping pace with his mountain-bred horses, which meant that Ishmael wasn't far behind. The stallion would follow his mares into the mouth of Hell itself, a fact which Caleb had counted on.

What surprised Caleb was that Willow managed to ride Ishmael with grace despite the handicap of flapping skirts, awkward sidesaddle, and storm. Yet no matter how well Willow rode, Caleb doubted that she was comfortable. He certainly wasn't. Cold rain dripped constantly down his face and under his collar. Though his torso remained reasonably warm beneath layers of wool and leather, water was seeping down into his boots. His legs were cold. They would get colder before they got warm.

Caleb didn't dwell on his own discomfort. He had known before he began the ride that it would be hard, long, and uncomfortable. In fact, he had counted on it. Outlaws were lazy men, more interested in their own pleasures than anything else. They would be slow to stir from their warm beds and the women they had rented along with the rooms.

As Caleb and Willow pressed on through the night, the storm gradually abated. Distant lightning still flared, but the thunder that followed was so far away as to be barely a grumble. Rain still fell, but the wet veils were being torn apart by gusts of wind. Soon there would be no more rain to dissolve the sharp edges of the hoofprints that stretched back in the night behind the seven horses like a twisted ribbon.

The land pitched up again in one of the many long folds that stretched out from the granite wall of the mountains. Caleb didn't let his big gelding fall back into a walk, but instead touched him with the brass cavalry spurs that were a legacy of his brief, turbulent stint as an Army Scout in the New Mexican campaigns of the War Between the States. Even while still in the Army, Caleb had filed off the sharp rowels of the regulation spurs, much to the anger of his superior officer. It was just one of the many ways Caleb had defied regulations that made no sense to him. A horse gouged by sharp spurs was a nervous horse, and a nervous horse was useless in a battle, a fact which Caleb appreciated even if the inexperienced lieutenant who led them had not.

"Come on, Deuce. Shake a leg," muttered Caleb as a gust of wind drove cold fingers of rain across his face.

The big horse obligingly picked up the pace to a fast trot. It was the least comfortable of a horse's gaits for the rider, but it covered the most territory for the least effort on the part of the horse.

When Ishmael increased his speed to match that of the mares in front of him, Willow bit back a groan. In the sidesaddle there was no easy way to lift her weight or post as there was when riding astride with two stirrups. She could tighten her leg around the saddle horn and simultaneously lift up her body by standing in the single stirrup, but the posture was awkward and very hard to maintain. The alternative was to have her backside meet the saddle nearly every time one of Ishmael's four feet hit the ground. Not only was that hard on her, it was hard on the horse as well.

Willow grabbed the saddle horn with both hands, uncurled her right leg, and lowered it until she was riding astride. The relief was only temporary. The saddle had been constructed to carry weight off center, which meant that the horn was impossibly placed for riding astride. Even worse, there was only one stirrup on which to balance a rider's weight. Despite that, at a trot Willow's awkward posture was easier on Ishmael than having his rider bumping up and down with every step.

Unfortunately, due to the sidesaddle's peculiar construction, riding astride wasn't easier on Willow. She soon had a stitch in her side from the unnatural posture forced on her by sitting astride in a sidesaddle. She took her mind off her difficulties by fishing out a small tin of candies from time to time and putting one of the potent peppermints in her mouth. The flavor made her think of summers past, warm and sultry, the sun a burning benediction in a hazy, silver-blue sky.

By the time the wind finished tearing apart the storm clouds, Willow was certain dawn couldn't be far away. She was so certain that when she saw the position of the moon she thought they must have somehow turned around in the darkness. Bracing herself on the padded horn, she looked for the Big Dipper. It wasn't where it should have been at dawn. In fact, it wasn't even close.

Dawn was at least four hours away. Perhaps even five.

Dear Lord, isn't Caleb ever going to let the horses rest? Even the stage animals were changed at regular intervals, and they had no saddles rubbing them.

As though Caleb sensed Willow's silent question, he reined in Deuce to a walk. Willow let out a sigh of relief and resumed a normal position in the side-saddle once more. Normal, but not comfortable. The sensitive skin of her inner thighs was chafed from the knees up. The cold, wet fabric of her riding outfit irritated her more than it protected her.

After a time Caleb pulled Deuce to a stop and dismounted. Willow didn't wait for an invitation. She slid off Ishmael in a tangle of wet fabric. Her feet hit the ground with enough force to make her wince. She wasted no time groaning, for she had no way of knowing how long the rest stop would be.

Working as swiftly as her cold hands would allow, Willow began unsaddling Ishmael. When she finished, she upended the saddle on the wet ground, draped the saddle blanket over it, and began rubbing down Ishmael with a handful of grass. Warmth rose in waving sheets of steam off the stallion's back where the saddle and blanket had rested, but other than that he showed no sign of the hard ride. Moonlight didn't reveal any raw spots on his back. Nor did he flinch away from her vigorous rubdown.

"I'm glad we had all those miles from West Virginia to toughen you up," Willow said softly to Ishmael as she worked over him. "I'd feel terrible if my awkward riding rubbed sores on you. The good Lord knows that my clumsiness is rubbing sores on *me*. The stage might have been uncomfortable, but at least it kept out most of the rain."

Sighing, Willow thought of the long ride from the Mississippi. For the first time she understood what a luxury it had been to be able to go from stage to horseback and then back to the stage again, depending on the weather.

Ishmael turned his head, nickered softly, and lipped the cold cloth of Willow's riding habit.

"Go ahead. Eat the useless thing," she muttered. "I can't be much worse off without it than I am with it."

After a taste, the stallion lost interest in the fabric.

"I don't blame you," she said, sighing.

"Don't tell me your fancy saddle rubbed a hole in that stud's hide after only a few hours."

Startled, Willow gasped. She had heard no sound to warn her that Caleb was approaching. After giving him a sidelong glance, she returned to rubbing down her horse.

"Ishmael's hide is just fine," she said.

"How about yours?" Caleb asked, looking at the wet, heavy folds of cloth clinging to Willow's legs.

She said only, "Excuse me, I have to check on the mares."

"They're fine. The little sorrel with two white feet had a stone in her shoe, but it hadn't been in long enough to do any damage. I wouldn't ride her for a day or so, though, just to be sure."

"That's Penny, and thank you for checking," Willow said, absently wiping off her cheek on her arm as she groomed the stallion. "I'll ride Dove—the other sorrel—when we switch horses."

The lock of hair that had been draped wetly across Willow's eye soon slithered back. She rubbed her face against her arm again. Again the lock moved, only to slide back a few moments later. A gust of wind raced over the land with a husky sound. Shivering, Willow gave a final swipe to Ishmael's muscular back before she turned away and picked up the saddle blanket. She shook it out thoroughly before she placed it dry side down on the stallion's back once more.

Caleb watched with eyes made dark by the moon-shadow of his hat brim, impressed despite himself by the fact that Willow was caring for her horse before she cared for herself. When Willow reached for the sidesaddle, his long arm snaked out. He took the saddle and swung it into place on Ishmael's back. Despite the fact that Caleb used only one hand, the weight of the saddle landed as delicately as a feather on the stallion.

"You're stiff," Caleb said curtly. "Walk around. We'll be riding soon, and we won't stop again until just before dawn."

"I see," Willow said, sighing unconsciously.

He hesitated, then added, "Coffee in my canteen. No cup, though."

She heard the subtle challenge in Caleb's voice and knew what he was thinking. No *southern lady* would share a canteen with a strange man. Her mouth turned down in an unhappy smile as she wondered what Caleb would think of her if he knew she had spent more than one night during the war on her hands and knees in a ravaged kitchen garden, grubbing for anything that had been overlooked by soldiers, so hungry that she ate carrots without washing them, simply rubbing the gritty loam off on her skirt.

"Coffee sounds like heaven," Willow said simply.

"The canteen is on my saddle." Caleb secured the sidesaddle's cinch with a few expert motions. "Watch out for Deuce's hindquarters. He's not mean, but he's not used to flapping skirts."

Willow carefully gathered the soggy folds of her clothing. The first few steps she took were painful. Gradually her cold-stiffened muscles warmed, making her progress easier. The chafed areas of her legs burned, but there was no help for it until the cloth dried. Even then, the abraded skin would hurt every time her leg rubbed against saddle.

"Hello, Deuce," Willow said in a low, soothing voice as she approached Caleb's big gelding—from the side, not the back. "I'm not an Indian or a panther sneaking up on you. I'm just a girl who would cheerfully peel you with a dull knife for a chance to get at the coffee in your rider's canteen."

Deuce watched her with half-pricked ears, obviously unimpressed by any threat she might represent. Willow kept talking as she stuffed loose cloth between her legs and clamped them together so that her hands would be free to work over the leather thongs that tied the canteen's strap to the saddle. Her gloves were more hindrance than help. She struggled to remove them. The leather was as wet as she was and almost as stubborn. Finally, she set her teeth in the fingertips and tugged one by one. Reluctantly, the cold leather separated itself from her hands. She pushed her gloves into a wet pocket of her riding skirt.

The thongs proved to be even more stubborn than Willow's gloves had been. The cold, damp wind made her fingers clumsy. Finally she gave up trying to free the canteen strap from the saddle. She simply unscrewed the lid, held the canteen at the length of its strap, and drank. After the peppermint she had just finished, the coffee tasted as raw and black as the night. There was one difference, though, and it was the only one that mattered. The coffee was almost warm.

"Ahhhhh," Willow sighed as she felt the liquid warmth slide down her throat.

"Most women don't like it so strong."

Willow jumped, almost dropping the canteen. "Do you make a habit of sneaking up on people?"

"Better that than the other way around."

Ignoring Caleb, she took one more swallow, then another before she looked back at the tall man who loomed over her like the night itself.

"Do you want some?" Willow asked.

She held out the canteen as far as she could while it was still tethered to the saddle. He took the canteen, drank, then gave her a penetrating look before he raised the canteen to his lips once more and drank deeply.

"Take some more," Caleb said when he handed the canteen over to Willow again. "It's not hot, but it's better than the wind."

The rough velvet darkness of his voice brushed over Willow's nerves like a caress. She took the canteen with both hands and raised it carefully to her mouth. Putting her lips where his had been was surprisingly intimate. She told herself that it was impossible to taste him on the metal rim, but an odd shiver of pleasure went through her anyway.

Almost reluctantly Willow capped the canteen again. As she went to wrap the strap around the saddle horn once more, the wind gusted, freeing a bit of skirt from between her legs. Cloth slapped lightly against Deuce's left front leg. The gelding snorted and shied away, yanking the canteen from her grasp and sending her stumbling. More cloth flapped, making Deuce shy again so violently that his head swung hard against Willow's chest. She went to her knees and stayed there, fighting for breath.

Caleb's big hand closed around the gelding's bridle before the animal could shy again.

"Easy son," he said calmly. "Just a bit of feminine frippery. Nothing to get your water hot over." Caleb looked at Willow, who was struggling to her feet, encumbered by her heavy, wet riding habit. "Useless as teats on a boar hog," he muttered. "I told you Deuce wasn't used to skirts, didn't I?"

Willow nodded but said nothing. She was too busy trying to get back the breath that the horse had knocked out.

"Are you all right?" Caleb asked abruptly.

Eyes closed, she nodded again, still unable to speak.

Suddenly the earth was jerked from beneath her feet. With a startled sound she opened her eyes and clung to the first thing she could reach—Caleb.

"Take it easy," he said, holding Willow high against his chest with one arm and wrapping her skirts around her legs with the other. "I'm just getting you out of Deuce's way before you scare him into running off and leaving me afoot."

Willow opened her mouth but no words came out. Being held close and upright against Caleb was quite different from being carried like a child in his arms. Even as she reflexively threw her arms around his shoulders to keep her balance, she realized that she was pressed against Caleb's strong body from her neck to her knees. The sensation was dizzying, making it almost impossible for her to draw a complete breath.

"C-Caleb?" she said huskily, feeling a curious weakness uncurling in her body. "It's all right. Put me down. I can walk."

The breathless hesitation in Willow's voice went through Caleb like lightning through a storm, bringing the dark thunder of desire in its wake.

"You're lucky to stand up in that damn fancy outfit. For two cents I'd . . ."

Caleb bit down on the words he wanted to say about ripping the flapping cloth off Willow and stuffing her into his spare shirt and pants. He would have to truss her like a turkey for the oven in order to keep his clothes on her much smaller body. But then, why bother? He had been wanting to see her naked ever since he had glimpsed the taut perfection of her breasts rising from folds of fine lawn.

And then Caleb admitted that the wanting had begun sooner than that. It had begun the first instant he had seen Willow watching him with wide, anxious eyes and a spine straight with the kind of pride that wouldn't back down for any man.

She's just a fancy woman, Caleb reminded himself grimly, remembering the flush that had burned on Willow's cheeks when she had described Matthew Moran as her husband. *A fancy woman chasing after her fancy man. No better than she has to be, and maybe a damn sight worse.*

Trying not to think what Willow would look like without any clothes at all, Caleb took a few more long steps before he lifted Willow to Ishmael's back and dumped her there unceremoniously. When she reached automatically for the reins, the fine skin of her hands glowed like pearl in the moonlight.

"What happened to your gloves?" Caleb demanded.

Willow reached into the lefthand pocket of her riding habit, the pocket that didn't hold the derringer. She found only one glove. Without a word she removed the wet leather and began working it over her hand. When she was finished, she picked up the reins once more.

"Where's the other glove?" Caleb asked impatiently.

"Somewhere between here and Deuce."

With a word that made Willow wince, Caleb backtracked. Finding a black glove on dark, wet earth in the middle of the night wasn't easy. Swearing steadily, he pulled out a sealed tin of matches and struck one. Shielding the flame against the wind, he searched until his fingers were singed. Then he struck another match. Four matches later he found the glove where it had been trampled into the ground by Deuce. The realization that it could just as easily have been Willow's soft flesh caught beneath the gelding's big hooves put the finishing touch on Caleb's temper. He snatched up the lacerated glove, snapped it against his thigh to get rid of the mud, and stalked back to Willow.

"Thank you," she said in a low voice.

"Stay away from Deuce," Caleb snarled. "He's a man's horse."

Willow nodded and fumbled with her muddy glove, hoping Caleb wouldn't notice that her hands were trembling. She told herself that she was simply cold and tired and hungry. And a little bit angry, as well. Certainly she wasn't hurt by Caleb's surly lack of manners.

Without another word, Caleb turned and stalked off to where Deuce waited. He went into the saddle with the casual, powerful grace of a mountain lion and touched the gelding's flanks with the spurs. Instantly, the horse broke into a canter. Caleb held the pace for thirty minutes, then reined in to a walk. Ten minutes later he urged the big gelding into a slow trot, then a fast one.

The pattern held all through the cold, long hours of moonlight—canter, walk, trot, walk, canter, and no real rest. Willow did what she could to spare Ishmael, but there was nothing she could do to spare herself. At first she checked the position of the Big Dipper every time the horses shifted into a walk, then less often. It was simply too discouraging. The stars were barely moving across the black arch of the night. At times she would have sworn they were going backward.

After several hours Willow ignored the taunting stars. She no longer really noticed the difference between walk and canter. Trotting was increasingly painful. Grimly she tried to ease Ishmael's burden, but her stiff, cold muscles lacked their customary resilience and coordination. When Ishmael stopped, the change of motion nearly threw her from the saddle. She blinked, checked the stars, and realized that even the longest night had an end. Pre-dawn light was silently stealing the stars from the eastern sky.

Wearily, Willow pushed still-damp locks of hair away from her face. She realized that Caleb had led them off the well-travelled track to a low, narrow crease between folds in the land. A brook no wider than her hand gleamed in the strengthening light. Thickets of streamside willow bushes grew lushly, as high as a tall man, offering both shelter and concealment. Obviously, Caleb was more interested in the latter quality. He began picketing the horses one by one downstream from the camp, giving them access to both water and the random patches of grass that grew between clumps of brush.

Only when Caleb approached Willow with a picket rope and stake in his hands did she realize she was still sitting like a lump on Ishmael, too dazed even to dismount.

"Get to work, southern lady. You hired a guide, not a personal slave. See if you can find some dry sticks, but don't try to build a fire. Sure as hell you'd send up a signal that could be seen all the way back to Denver." Caleb jerked his thumb at one of the pack saddles he had taken off Trey, his second horse. "There's coffee, side meat, and flour over there. Can you cook?"

Numbly, Willow nodded.

"Then get cracking," he said. "When the sun tops that hill, I'm drowning the campfire. Whatever isn't cooked by then we eat raw or go without."

Willow started to dismount, only to discover that her right leg wouldn't cooperate. It had gone to sleep. Using both hands, she lifted her leg over the horn and gritted her teeth, for pain returned as blood flowed freely once more.

With narrowed eyes, Caleb watched. He had known the ride would be hard on Willow, but he hadn't known how hard. He barely resisted the urge to lift her off the horse and carry her to a bed within a streamside thicket. But it had taken longer to find a safe camping spot than he had expected. Unless she worked alongside him, their only food would be cold jerky or hardtack and even colder stream water. He could survive on that indefinitely—he had often enough in the past—but he doubted that Willow would last two days on that diet. She was so tired her skin looked transparent.

Abruptly, Caleb lifted Willow from the saddle. When her feet touched the earth, he felt her knees buckle. He caught and held her, breathing in the faint hint of lavender and rain that she wore like an invisible veil. In his memory he tasted peppermint again, a freshness that had both startled and aroused him when he had realized its source was her lips touching the canteen's rim just before his.

"Can't you even stand up?" Caleb asked, his tone clipped, almost harsh.

The whiplike quality of Caleb's voice stiffened Willow's spine. She pushed away from him and began working over Ishmael's saddle girth with clumsy hands.

"Go gather kindling, southern lady," Caleb said, brushing her hands aside. "I'll take care of your stud."

The nickname was like a slap. For an instant Willow felt like lashing out in return, but she lacked the energy. In any case, at the moment Caleb was able to give better care to her stallion than she was, and her horse's well-being mattered more than her pride.

Without a word Willow turned away from Caleb. She headed for the most dense thicket she could find, pushed inside, and kept going until she could see nothing when she looked over her shoulder but greenery. Only then did she begin struggling with the intricate fastenings of her long skirt. She peeled wet cloth and matted petticoats down her legs and prayed Caleb was gentleman enough not to follow her.

By the time she finished she was shivering. Even so, it was painful to drag the heavy divided skirt back up legs chapped raw by repeated rubbing against wet cloth. Taking small steps, walking awkwardly to spare her sensitive inner thighs, Willow began gathering twigs and small dead branches from the thicket. As she worked, her body slowly warmed and became less stiff.

By the time she had gathered a small pile of wood and emerged from the thicket, Caleb had finished picketing the horses. He was sitting on his heels beneath an overhanging screen of shrubbery, peeling shavings of dry wood from the inner bark of a small downed cottonwood. His wickedly sharp hunting knife was as long as his forearm. The blade flashed and gleamed like water in the vague pre-dawn light.

Willow dropped her double handful of twigs on the ground beside Caleb and turned away. With a barely stifled groan she knelt next to one pack saddle. A few minutes later she had found everything she needed to make biscuits and bacon. When she looked up, Caleb had just finished suspending a small coffee pot from a tripod of branches. Beneath the pot was a fire so tiny he could have covered it with his hat. What little smoke the fire made rose up and was dispersed by the screen of willows. Unless someone rode close by—and downwind—there would be no way to know that anyone was camped in one of the many deep creases that scored the land.

The secrecy of the camp both reassured Willow and made her uneasy at the same time. Caleb's care said more than any words that he expected to be followed. Even if he hadn't expected it, obviously he felt that anyone he met in the wild land was as likely to be enemy as friend.

The message of the hidden camp was repeated in the expression on Caleb's face. Lighted from beneath by small flames, black shadows licking and shifting over his hard features, his eyes were feral with reflected fire and his mouth looked like it had forgotten how to smile. There was nothing of comfort in him for a young woman too tired to hold her eyes open and too cold to take a breath without shivering.

I've survived worse, Willow reminded herself silently. *Besides, I didn't hire Caleb for comfort, I hired him to take me to Matt. I've got nothing to complain about on that score. We must have come forty miles last night. Sooner started, ʲooner finished, as Papa used to say.*

Willow mixed dough in the cast iron frying pan until the dough was the right consistency to clean the pan's black surface. Then she stood stiffly and carried meat, dough, and pan to the tiny fire.

"May I use your knife?" she asked.

Caleb glanced up sharply. Willow's voice was hoarse, either from lack of use or from the damp chill of the long night.

"The side meat," she explained, not understanding the intensity of his look.

"Sit down," Caleb said roughly, lifting the pan from her hands. "I'll take care of it."

Gratefully, Willow sank to the ground and stretched out, caring little that the earth beneath her was wet and cold. The ground was blessedly motionless and supported her without any effort on her part.

She was asleep before she took two breaths.

When Caleb looked up from slicing meat, he thought Willow had fainted. He came to his feet in a rush, then knelt at her side. The skin of her throat felt cool beneath his fingers, but her pulse was steady and deep and her breathing was regular. He shook his head, divided between irritation and reluctant approval of her stubbornness.

"Fancy woman or not, you're no quitter," he muttered.

Glancing up from time to time, Caleb resumed slicing meat into the frying pan. As soon as the coffee water boiled, he added grounds and put it back over the fire to cook. When the coffee was finished, he cooked the meat, stacked it on a piece of bark, and added the biscuit dough to the pan.

While the biscuits cooked, he began systematically cutting thick, dark willow canes as big around as his thumb from the living thicket. He peeled the bark, poured the coffee into his canteen, filled the coffeepot again, and put it over the fire to heat. When the water boiled he added a handful of shredded bark and set the pot aside.

"Willow, wake up."

Caleb's voice was low yet clear. She didn't respond. He leaned over and shook her shoulder gently. There was no response. The cloth beneath his hand was cold and wet. He glanced up at the sky, wondering if there was time to dry her skirt over the fire. A second was all it took for him to conclude that he couldn't take the risk. The sun had already risen, which meant people would be up and stirring along the trail. There were no settlements along this part of the mountain range. Any sign of smoke would be like a beacon pointing toward their camping area. Willow would have to sleep wet.

Caleb put out the fire before he turned toward Willow once more.

"Wake up, honey," Caleb said, shaking her a little less gently.

Slowly, Willow's eyes opened, but she wasn't truly awake. Wide and dazed, her eyes were flecked with gold and green, silver and blue. Her eyelashes were a tawny darkness that emphasized the hazel beauty of her eyes. Against the gleaming pastel dawn, she could see only the silhouette of a flat-crowned hat pushed back over a thatch of very dark hair.

"Matt?" she whispered, reaching up to touch him. "Is it really you? It's been so long and I've been so lonely. . . ."

Caleb's expression hardened when he heard Willow call out to her absent lover.

"Wake up, southern lady," he said coldly. "I cooked breakfast for you, but I'm damned if I'll feed it to you." Impatiently, he pulled Willow upright and shoved the canteen of coffee into her hand. "Drink."

Automatically Willow obeyed the hard edge of command in Caleb's voice. The coffee was just short of scalding. She swallowed, blinked back tears, and drank again, eager for the strong flavor and life-giving warmth. As she swallowed, she felt the streamer of heat uncurling all the way to her stomach. Shivering with pleasure, she drank more.

"Now eat," Caleb said, taking the canteen from her.

Willow took the bacon and biscuit that were shoved

into her hands and looked at them without interest. She was too tired to go through the motions of chewing. Sighing, she started to lie down again.

"No, you don't," Caleb said, pulling her upright. "Eat or you'll be so weak tonight I'll have to tie you on your horse. And that's just what I'll do if I have to, southern lady."

A single glance told Willow that he meant every word. She sighed and looked longingly at the canteen he had placed beyond her reach.

"More coffee?" Willow asked hopefully. Her voice still sounded hoarse.

"After you eat."

"I'm not hungry."

"You will be after your stomach gets the message that food is available."

Willow knew Caleb was right, but that didn't make the food look any better to her. The first few mouthfuls were the hardest. After that, her appetite improved until she was matching Caleb bite for bite and licking her fingers with surreptitious, delicate greed. He smiled slightly and piled more bacon and biscuits in her hands. She murmured her thanks even as her teeth sank into the crisp bacon. The bottom of the biscuits was like fry bread, tender and crisp from the residue of bacon fat in the pan. She had tasted nothing more delicious, not even the tender carrots she had gleaned in a frenzy of hunger from a ravaged garden.

Finally Willow could eat no more. Before she could ask, the canteen of coffee appeared beneath her nose.

"Thank you," Willow said softly.

She closed her eyes and inhaled the hot fragrance of coffee from the open canteen. The sensual pleasure she took in the scent was as clear as the dawn stealing over the land. After she drank, she sighed and smiled.

Caleb's body clenched against a painful shaft of raw desire. The temptation to bend over and lick the sheen of coffee from Willow's lips was so great that he had to look away.

"I'm sorry," she said, nudging his hand with the canteen. "I didn't mean to be greedy."

Caleb took the canteen, glanced down at the metal neck, and thought of the soft lips that had so recently touched it. With a searing, silent curse he capped the canteen without drinking and stood up.

"I'm going to take a look around."

Willow barely heard him. She was stretched out on the ground once more, asleep between one breath and the next.

Caleb climbed silently up the side of the gully, stopping just short of the top. Setting aside his hat, he eased up until he could see over the land. Nothing moved but the brilliant flood of dawn. Withdrawing as quietly as he had come, Caleb went back to the bottom of the crease. It was the work of only a few minutes to cut springy, leafy branches and cover them with one of the tarpaulins that had kept the supplies dry.

Willow didn't awaken when Caleb lifted her and set her on the wilderness bed. Nor did she awaken when he lay down beside her and covered both of them with a blanket and another tarpaulin. She simply sighed and curled closer to the warmth that radiated from his big body.

Angrily, Caleb remembered how Willow had reached for him and huskily called another man's name. But as he looked at her wan face and the rain-tarnished gold of her hair peeking out from beneath his wool muffler, Caleb remembered what she had said about the war . . . living on a strip of land raided by both sides, no man to help her, and an ailing mother to care for. Under the circumstances, Caleb wondered if he could condemn Willow because she had become a fancy lady in order to survive. Other women rented out their company for less reason than survival.

And some foolish girls, like his sister, gave their virtue and their lives for a handful of smoothly spoken lies about love.

"You were luckier than Rebecca," Caleb said in a low voice as he watched Willow. "You survived. But when you sold yourself to my sister's seducer, you sold yourself to a dead man."

Satisfaction curled through Caleb at the thought that never again would Willow wake up in Matthew Moran's bed and softly call his name.

4

CALEB awoke at the first rumble
of thunder. Clouds like great clipper ships were raking across the sky above the ravine. Slate-bottomed,
white-topped, glittering with occasional lightning,
the squall line raced before the wind.

"Just as well I didn't try to dry that skirt," Caleb
muttered, yawning. "Sure as God made little green
apples, we're going to get wet all over again."

Willow didn't answer, except to make a muffled
sound of protest when Caleb's warmth was replaced
by a cold gust of wind as he rolled out of bed.

"Up and at 'em, fancy lady," he said, pushing his
warm stocking feet into cold, stiff boots. "This storm
will give us a few safe hours of daylight on the trail."

Still asleep, Willow pulled the blanket more tightly
around herself, trying to preserve the remaining
warmth. One of Caleb's big hands wrapped around
the thick wool. With a single motion of his arm, he
pulled the blanket and tarpaulin off her.

"Get up, Willow."

As he spoke, Caleb moved away from the bed he
had shared with her. He didn't trust his response if

61

she turned toward him sleepily and called another man's name again.

What do you care if Reno's fancy woman can't keep her bedmates straight?

Caleb had no answer for the question he asked himself. He only knew that, wisely or foolishly, he did care. He wanted Willow. All that kept him from trying a bit of seduction was the chance—admittedly small, as far as he was concerned—that she actually was married to Matthew Moran. But that slight chance was enough to hold Caleb in check. Stealing some passion from a man's fancy woman was one thing. Adultery was quite another. No matter how willing the woman might be, no matter how many men she might have had before him, Caleb would no more knowingly commit adultery than he would go back on his given word.

The problem was to determine if the girl in question was indeed married. The solution to that problem occupied part of Caleb's mind as he climbed up the side of the ravine and looked out over the land.

No one was near. Three miles away, a horseman was headed north on the informal road that ran along the front of the Rockies. A wagon was also headed north, its mules moving smartly in a futile effort to outrun the weather. Nobody was visible heading south.

Caleb waited ten more minutes. Nothing else appeared along the track but cloud shadows skimming over the land. Between the clouds, a hawk floated in a piece of sky so blue it made Caleb's eyes water to look at it. Sunlight the color of molten gold poured over the land. The light was hot and clean, slicing through the damp chill near the ground like an incandescent sword.

From the ravine below came the soft nickering of a stallion calling to his mares. Caleb smiled and stretched, savoring the peace of the moment and the clean scent of sunlight and earth. It was so still he could hear slight ripping sounds as the horses cropped grass. Then a gust of wind came rushing over the land, bending grass and willows alike, whispering and murmuring like an invisible river as it caressed everything between cloud and earth.

The soft-talking wind awakened Willow. For an instant she thought she was back in West Virginia, a child asleep in the meadow while her family's horses cropped grass all around her. Then she remembered that the meadow was gone, the farms were gone, and she was no longer a child. She awoke in a rush, sitting straight up in the dappled shade of the thicket. She didn't remember falling asleep. She certainly didn't remember lying down on a mattress of limber branches covered by a tarpaulin.

"Caleb?" she called softly.

No one answered.

Anxiously, Willow stood up and pushed out of the tiny clearing in the thicket, ignoring the protests of her stiff body and chapped legs. A quick look assured her that the horses were still picketed downstream, their coats gleaming in the sun as they stretched their necks to get to the last bit of grass within reach of their picket ropes. Willow listened intently, but heard no movements that might have come from a man gathering twigs or seeking the privacy of a dense thicket.

But then, Caleb had never made much noise no matter what the circumstances.

Making as little noise as possible herself, Willow sought the center of a downstream thicket, struggled out of and then back into her clammy skirt, and went to check on her horses. The Arabians were moving well and no stones were caught between steel shoes and hooves. Ishmael's back wasn't tender. Nor was he tired. He had enough energy to pretend to be startled by her appearance. He snorted and shied like a colt, then stretched out his neck and fluttered his nostrils in a soft nicker, asking her to share in the play.

"You old fraud," Willow said softly, rubbing the stallion's nose. "You knew who it was all the time."

Ishmael nudged her chest playfully. Willow winced. She was still a bit sore from Deuce's hard head.

Willow glanced at Caleb's horses, but stayed away from them. She didn't want to feel the rough edge of his tongue if she spooked the geldings with her flapping yards of skirt. After a final stroke to Ishmael's velvety muzzle, Willow began gathering twigs for the fire she hoped Caleb would allow them to have.

When Caleb came back from reconnoitering the area around the ravine, he found Willow awake and sitting by a pile of reasonably dry twigs.

"Is it safe to have a fire?" she asked with unconcealed eagerness.

"A small one."

"On this side of the Mississippi, what other kind is possible? There aren't any trees."

"Wait until we get in the mountains. You'll see trees until you're sick of them."

He watched Willow stack twigs for the fire. When she was finished, he removed half and set them aside. Only then did he strike a match and coax a wavering flame from the damp fuel. As soon as the fire caught, Willow got to her feet stiffly. She managed not to groan as she bent over and reached for the coffeepot.

"Drink what's inside before you use the pot," Caleb said.

She lifted the lid and looked. The liquid was dark, but not nearly as dark as Caleb's usual brew.

"What is it?"

"Willow-bark tea. Good for—"

"Aches and pains and fevers," she interrupted, grimacing. "Tastes like sin itself, too."

The corner of Caleb's mouth lifted slightly. "Drink up, honey. You'll feel better."

"I don't want to be greedy," Willow said, looking at him with an unspoken plea. "How much of the tea is for you?"

"None of it. I'm not a soft southern lady."

"Neither am I."

The irritation in Willow's voice increased Caleb's smile. "That's right. You're a fancy northern lady."

"I'm not a fancy lady, either," she retorted, "South or North."

Caleb's cool golden glance raked over Willow, taking in her finger-combed hair and her rumpled, clammy clothes.

"I reckon you aren't," he drawled. "Bet your fancy man would be surprised to see you now."

"Matt isn't a fancy man any more than you are."

"Oh, yes. I forgot. He's your . . . husband."

The flick of contempt with which Caleb emphasized the last word made Willow blush. Futilely, she wished she could keep from blushing every time she was forced to confront her lie about being married. Yet Matt's letter had been quite clear about the necessity: *Don't let Willy sweet talk her way into coming with you, boys. I know she always had a yen to wander, but out here an unmarried woman is considered fair game for every man's attentions. We've got better things to do than stand guard over our pretty little sister.*

With a rather grim pleasure Caleb noted the telltale red stain on Willow's cheeks. Wondering if now was the time to press her, he hooked his long index finger into the watch pocket of his pants. It wasn't a watch he touched. It was the locket Rebecca had given him when he had finally badgered her into telling him the truth about the identity of the man who had planted a child within her and then abandoned her to bear his bastard.

And to die of childbed fever hours before the baby's own death.

All that remained of Rebecca's life was a name—Matthew "Reno" Moran—and the locket with pictures of Reno's dead parents inside. If Willow was Reno's wife, surely she would recognize his parents. But if she had lied, she wouldn't recognize the photos.

"Been married long?" Caleb asked, his voice neutral.

Frantically, Willow tried to decide if it would be better to have been married a long time or a short one.

"Er . . ." She bit her lip. "No."

"Then I guess you don't know your husband's parents."

Willow brightened, more sure of her ground. "Of course I know them. I've known them for years."

"Neighbors, huh?"

She hesitated, then decided to keep the lies as close as possible to the truth. "Not really. Matt's folks, ah, took me in when I was young. They're the only parents I remember."

Caleb smiled sourly. Willow wasn't much of an actress, which helped him. He supposed most men just looked at her full breasts and narrow waist and didn't notice the tide of guilt that climbed her cheeks with each lie. Men could be real fools when presented with a sweet smile and a woman's curving body.

"It's a good thing, knowing your husband's parents," Caleb said. "Makes for an easier marriage all around."

Willow made a neutral sound and raised the soot-covered coffeepot to her lips, preferring the bitter flavor of the medicinal tea to the taste of any more lies.

Thunder cracked, chasing after lightning made invisible by the brightness of day. Shuddering, Willow lowered the coffeepot.

"There's more," Caleb said without looking up from the fire.

"How do you know?"

"There's always more bitter medicine than a fancy lady is willing to swallow."

If it hadn't been for her recent lies, Willow would have objected to Caleb's comment. As it was, she just raised the pot to her mouth and drank until nothing was left. He watched her from the corner of his eye while he added a few more twigs to the fire. When they caught, he added more fuel until the flames were steady and hot, yet the fire was still no bigger than his hat.

They cooked and ate breakfast in silence. Gradually, Willow realized that the unpleasant tea had worked. She was still stiff, but she no longer had to bite back sounds of pain when she bent her right leg. All too soon breakfast was over, the camp was packed up, and Caleb was saddling his horse. This time Deuce acted as pack animal and Trey bore Caleb's greater weight.

"Will that stud of yours resent being tied behind a gelding?" Caleb asked.

"I don't think so."

He grunted. "We'll find out quick enough. Which one of the mares is strongest?"

"Either of the sorrels. They're Ishmael's daughters. Saddle Dove, the one with only one white sock."

Caleb saddled Dove and boosted Willow aboard. Though she said nothing, her face visibly tightened as she settled into the sidesaddle once more. Caleb knew that the tea had helped, but no medicine was going to take the discomfort from Willow today, unless maybe it was a shot of Taos lightning.

"Want some whiskey?" Caleb asked.

Willow blinked. "I beg your pardon?"

"Whiskey. It's a good pain killer."

"I'll keep it in mind," Willow said dryly, amused despite the aching of her body and the burning of her inner thighs each time her damp clothes rubbed against flesh that was already abraded. "For now, I think I'd better stick to willow-bark tea."

"Suit yourself."

Thunder crackled again as the clouds overhead joined to shut out the sun. Rain began to fall as Caleb swung onto Trey and took the lead. Deuce trotted off obediently, leading four Arabians. Ishmael snorted and jigged unhappily for the first few miles, then settled down to the indignity of being led by a gelding through a driving rain.

Except for the watery light of late afternoon, the ride was a repeat of the previous night's endurance contest. Trot, canter, walk, trot, and then trot some more for good measure. Willow barely noticed when the gray of day merged with the black of night. On Caleb's command she ate cold bacon and biscuits, drank cold coffee, dismounted and walked to spare the mare and restore her own circulation, then mounted and resumed the torment once more.

As the hours wore on, fatigue battled with pain for control of Willow's body. She thought she could become no more uncomfortable when a cold wind sprang up and she began to shiver. The ice-tipped wind howled down from the slopes of mountains she had glimpsed only once, from Denver, their peaks swathed in storms and their flanks rising like fortresses flung across the western sky. But even those ramparts were invisible now, concealed within the frigid night and storm.

Shivering, Willow hunched down over the saddle horn and hung on, bending her head beneath the icy wind. She was so dazed by cold and fatigue that she didn't realize the horses had stopped until she felt herself being lifted from the mare's back. Her wet, heavy skirts slapped across Caleb's face.

"Caleb?" she asked hoarsely. "Is it dawn?"

"Not by a long shot, but I've had enough of this goddamned foolishness," he said roughly.

Willow didn't answer, for his words didn't make sense to her.

The ravine Caleb had chosen for camp was deep enough to baffle the wind. Part of the bank had an overhang that offered shelter from the fitful storm. A huge cottonwood log reflected back the heat of the fire that leaped and burned beneath the overhang, making the earth steam. Transfixed, Willow stared at the unexpected warmth and beauty of the flames.

"Lift up your arms," Caleb said curtly.

She did, and felt the wet weight of his poncho being peeled from her body. That puzzled her, for at first she didn't remember putting on the poncho. She forgot her puzzlement when she realized that Caleb was unbuttoning the bodice of her wet riding habit. Automatically she pushed at his hands. It was futile. She might as well have pushed at the invisible mountains.

"What d-do you think you're d-doing?" she demanded through chattering teeth.

"Keeping you from a dose of lung fever," he said grimly, yanking off the riding habit without regard for laces or buttons. "My poncho can't keep you warm in this kind of storm, not when you start out with wet clothes that are too thick and too heavy to get dry from the heat of your body alone. You're such a little thing."

Willow looked at the firelit face of the man who was peeling off her clothes as impersonally as he would have peeled bark from a log. His face was wet, dark with beard stubble, and set in grim lines. His wool shirt and leather vest were black with rain.

"You m-must be f-freezing, too," she said.

Caleb's only answer was a grunt of disgust. He drew his belt knife and did what he had been wanting to do since he had first seen Willow dressed in the unwieldy clothes. Steel sliced through stubborn cloth as he stripped folds of wet wool and useless petticoats away from her long legs. When the tip of the knife flicked against metal, Caleb paused long enough to examine the contents of the special leather pocket sewn into Willow's skirt.

The twin-barrelled derringer looked tiny in his hand. He hefted the gun, saw that it was fully loaded, and set it within Willow's reach on the cottonwood log. Then he resumed wielding the long-bladed knife with a casual skill that would have been breathtaking under other circumstances, but neither he nor she had breath to spare at the moment—Willow was too busy shivering and Caleb was too busy trying not to notice the transparency that wetness brought to her fine cotton pantelets.

But Caleb would have to have been blind and more saint than man not to notice the elegant lines of Willow's legs and the lush golden nest at the apex of her thighs. The fine lawn of her camisole was even more transparent, revealing the fullness of her breasts and the rosy peaks tightly drawn against the cold. The temptation to take off his own wet clothes and warm Willow from the inside out was so great that it shook Caleb. He set his jaw and wrapped Willow tightly in the softest of his heavy wool blankets.

"Stay here while I take care of the horses," he ordered.

Willow wouldn't have argued even if she could have. The heat from the fire burned against her face almost painfully, but it was the warming of cold skin that hurt, not the flame itself. Even in winter when she and her mother had hidden in the root cellar from soldiers, Willow had never been this chilled. Huddled so close to the fire that her hair and the wool muffler steamed, she was grateful for every golden whip of flame.

By the time Caleb returned from picketing the horses, Willow had quit shivering. She had managed to suspend his heavy poncho from a dead branch near the fire. Steam rose from the wool in silver wisps. She had unwrapped the wet muffler from her head and draped the wool over the cottonwood log as well. The remains of her riding habit were also drying.

Caleb gave Willow a sharp glance but said nothing as he dropped an armload of wood near the fire.

"They're wet, so feed the branches in one at a time," he said.

He began rummaging in the canvas sack that held frying pan and food, trying not to notice the silken gleam of Willow's naked arm as she reached toward the pile of broken branches. When the blanket slipped off her arm, he also tried not to notice the graceful curve of her neck and shoulder. When the blanket slipped even more, he tried not to look at the soft rise of her breasts and the transparent veil of lace that enhanced rather than concealed Willow's alluring femininity.

The fire that hissed and licked over the wood was no hotter than Caleb's thoughts. Using a knife as long as his forearm, he sliced bacon with a swift savagery, wanting only to get out of camp and find Willow some decent clothes.

Willow watched in fascination as the wicked blade flashed like lightning, leaving behind a pile of evenly sliced meat. She had never seen such skill.

"You're very good with that knife."

Caleb's mouth curved in an ironic smile. "So I'm told, honey. So I'm told."

Uncertainly, she smiled in return.

"Make yourself useful," he said without looking up. "See if the coffee water is hot."

The coolness in Caleb's voice made Willow remember his cutting comments about not being her personal slave. Shifting the blanket to allow movement, she came to her knees and leaned toward the coffeepot. A lock of her long, bright hair fell forward as she bent over. The curling ribbon of hair came dangerously close to the flames. Before Willow could realize anything was wrong, Caleb's hard arm had yanked her over onto her back in a tangle of blanket and legs.

"Don't you know better than to bend over a fire with your hair loose?" he said scathingly. "I swear, fancy lady, you're more trouble than a fox in a hen house."

"I'm not a fancy lady, my hair is too wet to burn, and I'm tired of you belittling me!"

Caleb looked at the angry hazel eyes so close to his and the soft lips trembling with outrage. The rest of Willow was trembling, too. She was furious at his contempt and was making no effort to disguise it.

"You're tired, period," Caleb said, releasing Willow abruptly. "As for the rest, wet hair burns just fine and I'll stop making comments about your uselessness when you start being useful."

With unnerving swiftness, he stood and went to the place where the pack saddles were. A few moments later he returned with a blue wool shirt that was so dark it was almost black.   The shirt was cut in the cavalry style, with a wedge-shaped front opening that could be unbuttoned down either side. Most of the shirts Willow had seen made like that had sported shiny brass buttons. Caleb's did not. Buttons of dark horn gleamed dully in the firelight.

It occurred to Willow that nothing of Caleb's was bright or shiny. Saddle, bridle, clothes, spurs, even the gunbelt he wore—not one item had any of the silver conchas or other decorations men often used to catch the eye. She doubted that it was lack of money that kept Caleb's gear plain. Nothing that he owned was second class or shabby. All of it helped him to pass over the wild land without attracting any more notice than a shadow.

"I know it isn't very fancy," Caleb drawled, holding out the shirt to Willow, "but it will save you having to pretend modesty when the blanket slips."

Not understanding what Caleb meant, Willow followed the direction of his glance. The blanket had slipped until only the taut rise of her nipple prevented the cloth from falling completely away from her breast. With a gasp, Willow snatched up the blanket with both hands and turned her back to the fire. Golden light flickered and danced caressingly over her skin, making her look as though she were a carving made of luminous amber.

Caleb's fingers tightened around his shirt. He dropped the piece of clothing on Willow and went back to work on dinner, trying to forget the sensual promise of her breast and the elegant beauty of her back rising from the dark folds of his blanket. But he couldn't forget. He could only remember again and again.

Angry because he couldn't control his thoughts—much less the hard, unruly response of his body—Caleb cooked bacon in a silence that wasn't broken even when Willow awkwardly began preparing biscuits one-handed. The other hand was fully occupied hanging onto the blanket to make certain it stayed wrapped around her waist and legs. His shirt fit her like a greatcoat, with the neck sagging down to reveal the delicate lines of her collar bones and the hollow of her throat.

Between shirt and blanket, Willow was largely successful in keeping herself covered. The moments when the blanket opened to reveal curving legs and velvet shadows were few, but they went into Caleb like knives, reminding him of the beauty that lay concealed beneath wool folds.

After dinner, Caleb added more wood to the fire, threw a tarpaulin down on the ground, and turned to Willow. She watched him warily, sensing that he was angry and not knowing why. A more experienced woman would have known the source of Caleb's raw temper, but Willow wasn't experienced. All she understood was that Caleb was riding the fine edge of his self-control.

"Can you use a shotgun?" he asked abruptly.

"Yes."

Caleb's long arm reached past Willow to the big log, where he had placed both his repeating rifle and his short-barrelled shotgun within easy reach. Willow flinched in the instant before she realized that he wasn't going to touch her. His mouth tightened at her retreat, but he said nothing as he lifted the shotgun. With the quick, expert motions of a man who has done something countless times before, he pulled the shotgun from its protective buckskin scabbard.

"Take it."

Willow took the shotgun. Despite its shortened barrel, it was heavy, but she had been expecting the weight. She braced herself and made certain that the barrel didn't cover anything but the night sky. Caleb nodded with satisfaction. Her actions told him more clearly than any words that she had handled a big gun before.

"It's loaded," he said curtly.

She smiled oddly. "Not much use otherwise, is it?"

"Do you know how to reload it?"

"Yes."

He tossed a small box into her lap. "Forty shells.

If any are gone when I get back, I better see a carcass or blood on the ground."

"Get back? Where are you going?"

"There's a settlement a few miles away. I want to find out if anyone's on our trail."

"How could they be? We've done nothing but ride in darkness and rain."

Caleb looked at Willow through narrowed golden eyes. "Everyone in Denver knew we were headed into the San Juan region. Everyone with the sense to tell up from down knows that the San Juans are south and west from Denver. The country is damned empty, but that doesn't mean it's easy to move in. There are only a handful of good passes and all the trails lead to them."

He waited expectantly. Willow said nothing.

"There are only two good ways to get where we're going," Caleb continued, his voice rough. "One is out of Canyon City up a branch of the Arkansas River over a pass and down to the Gunnison River. That gets you to the northern edge of the San Juan country. Or you can go about seventy miles farther south down the front of the Rockies, then cut through the Sangre de Cristo range and pick up the Rio Grande del Norte around Alamosa and head northwest. That brings you to the southeast edge of the San Juans."

Caleb waited again. Willow watched him intently but offered no comment.

"Are you listening to me, fancy lady?" he demanded impatiently.

"Yes."

"If I know where we have to go, so does anyone who wants to follow us," he said impatiently. "So which route should we take—Canyon City or Alamosa?"

Willow frowned as she visualized again the map that had come with one of Matthew's letters and now lay within the lining of her big carpetbag. Canyon City had been mentioned. So had Alamosa. So had other cities. None had been preferred. All had been suggested as possible routes, depending on where the Moran brothers started from. Matt had knows that his letter probably would have to be forwarded to wherever his brothers had gone, so he had shown routes to the San Juan country beginning everywhere from West Virginia to Texas and California to Canada.

But Matt hadn't shown where his gold mine was. He had simply marked five mountain peaks in the San Juan country and trusted his brothers to find him.

"Matt lives on the western watershed of the Great Divide," Willow said slowly. "The Gunnison is the major river draining the part of the watershed where Matt is."

Caleb grunted. "That river drains a lot of country. Canyon City is closer to the northern watershed of the Gunnison, but the Alamosa route takes lower passes."

"Shouldn't we just go the quickest way?"

"Hell of an idea," he said sardonically. "If I had a fortune teller's crystal, I'd know just what to do. But I don't, so I'll go on down south a bit and see if anyone knows what the passes are like between here and there." Caleb turned away, talking as he went. "Let the fire go out. I've picketed Ishmael up the ravine and the mares below us. You hear anything stirring up the horses, you grab that shotgun and fade into the nearest thicket. I'll signal before I come in."

"How will I know it's you?"

As Caleb turned back toward her, his right hand moved to his back pocket and then to his mouth with a swift precision that Willow found unexpected in such a big man. Suddenly a haunting chord was breathed into the night, a harmonic shivering as eerie as the howling of a wolf. The harmonica vanished with the same speed that it had appeared.

Before Willow could speak, Caleb had been swallowed up by the night. She heard the hoofbeats of two horses fading down the ravine, then silence.

After a few minutes the normal sounds of the night resumed, small scurryings and insects rasping. The crackle of the fire seemed very loud, the flames too bright. Gingerly Willow pulled branches back from the fire. Flames shrank, then vanished but for occasional incandescent tongues flaring over coals. In time, even those died to bare gleams against the ashes.

Willow curled up on the tarpaulin, the shotgun next to her, her head resting on the sidesaddle. Despite her reluctance to let down her guard, she quickly fell asleep, too exhausted to fight the needs of her body any longer.

5

CAREFULLY Caleb guided his horse through the blustery pre-dawn landscape, knowing that a settlement was nearby and men might be about. It was doubtful anyone would be stirring in this weather, but he couldn't afford to take chances. He had no intention of going all the way to the nearest settlement, but he had to reach Wolfe's home without attracting attention.

Thank God that Wolfe isn't the sociable type, Caleb told himself as he rode along a small watercourse that led to the log house. *I won't have to worry about him having talkative company staying over.*

No light showed in the window of the log house. No one was moving around the corral or outbuildings.

"Looking for someone?"

The voice was cool, clipped, and came from behind Caleb.

"Hello, Wolfe," Caleb said, holding his hands where they would be clearly visible in the rising light of dawn. "Friendly as ever, I see."

There was the sound of a gun being uncocked.

"Hello, Cal. Couldn't tell if it was you, Reno, or some other oversized white man."

Caleb smiled. "Could have been an Indian."

"Not damned likely. Indians have better sense than to be abroad on a night like this." As he spoke, Wolfe walked out from the cover of a tall cottonwood. He moved with the lithe, silent stride of a man accustomed to surviving in wild country. "Get down and stay for a few days, *amigo*. Deuce could use the rest, from the look of him. So could Trey."

"So could I. Can't do it, though."

Silently, Wolfe watched Caleb with eyes as dark as obsidian. In full sunlight Wolfe's eyes were indigo, betraying the British heritage of his father. At night, however, he looked every bit his Cheyenne mother's son. At all times he was a man other men walked carefully around.

"Getting close to Reno?" Wolfe asked finally, his voice neutral. He had met both Caleb and Reno separately, and liked both men. He didn't know why Caleb was hunting Reno. Caleb had never said and Wolfe had never asked.

"Right now I've got other cattle to brand. I left a woman in a ravine a few miles north of here. She needs dry clothes."

"Might her name be Willow Moran?" Wolfe asked mildly.

Caleb hissed a curse. "Word travels too damned fast."

"A lot of folks were glad to see Johnny Slater get his comeuppance." Wolfe's smile was like an unsheathed knife. "Kid Coyote. Hell of a moniker. He'll never live it down. He's gunning for you."

"If he's lucky, he won't find me."

"He'll find you if you go up through Canyon City," Wolfe said flatly. "He's lying in wait at the trailhead with half of Slater's bunch. The other half is raising dust for the Rio Grande.''

''You certain?''

''They left a man at the crossroads. Ask him. Then ask him about the bounty Jed Slater put on your head. Four hundred Yankee dollars for the man who brings in your scalp. One thousand dollars for the man who brings you to Jed Slater alive.''

''Son of a bitch.''

''Need another gun?'' Wolfe asked. ''I've got nothing better to do since Jessi's guardian wrote and told me no one would be coming this summer.''

For a moment Caleb was tempted. Wolfe was good with any weapon, including his fists, and had the ferocity of the Scots and Cheyennes combined. But as nice as it would be to have Wolfe guarding his back, Caleb couldn't risk it. If anyone beside himself knew that Reno and Matthew Moran were the same man, it would be Wolfe Lonetree. If Willow found out that Caleb was after her fancy man, she wouldn't lead Caleb anywhere close to Matthew Moran.

''I appreciate it, but it's not necessary,'' Caleb said. ''There's more than one way to skin a cat.''

''A mountain pass isn't a cat. You might sneak by Slater's gang on the Rio Grande del Norte, but you won't have a chance in hell going through Canyon City.''

''There are other passes.''

Wolfe's black eyebrows rose. ''Not many white men know about them.''

''My daddy was with an Army survey party in the fifties. There are other passes.''

With a shrug, Wolfe changed the subject. ''Is that stud of hers half what rumor says?''

''Prettiest piece of horseflesh I've ever seen,'' Caleb said simply.

''Pretty isn't much of a recommendation for a horse

or a woman," Wolfe said dryly.

"That stud is a lot tougher than he looks. Gentle and quick, too. Make a hell of a trail horse."

"How's his stamina?"

"He's keeping up. So are the mares."

"Leave the Arabians with me. They'll only slow you down, especially in the high country."

"Willow wouldn't leave them in Denver. Doubt that she'll leave them here, but I'll offer. You better pray she doesn't take me up on it. Having those horses would bring Slater's outfit down on you like a rash."

Wolfe smiled. "I'd take it as a personal favor."

Shaking his head, Caleb chuckled. That was one of the things he liked best about Wolfe—the man was a fighter to the marrow of his bones.

"What about the girl?" Wolfe asked. "Is she holding up all right?"

"She's like her horses," Caleb admitted. "Game little thing. Once I get her some dry clothes and a decent saddle, she'll make it through the passes."

"Then it's true? She's actually riding a sidesaddle?"

Caleb grunted. "It's true."

"Be damned. I haven't seen one of those since I was in England," Wolfe said.

"If I never see another one again, it will be too soon. Pure foolishness."

Wolfe smiled gently. "Maybe, but those English ladies looked like beautiful butterflies perched on the backs of their big Irish horses."

"Hell, if I'd known you felt like that, I'd have brought the damned thing to you. Your shirttail cousin could have used it the next time she visits you."

"Lady Jessica Charteris prefers to ride bareback at a dead run." The amusement faded from Wolfe's voice as he continued, "In any case, the last letter mentioned a marriage. I don't think Jessi will be coming to America to plague me again."

Wolfe looked away, measuring the increasing light rather than confronting the surprising sense of loss he had felt when the letter had arrived telling of Jessica's pending marriage.

"Better leave your horses under cover here," Wolfe said. "Slater's man might have heard that you visit me from time to time. He'll be looking for tracks from seven horses, not two, but . . ." Wolfe shrugged and said no more.

Caleb dismounted, tied his horses back in the thick brush that surrounded the runoff from Cottonwood Springs, and walked alongside Wolfe toward the cabin.

"When Jessi rode with you, did she have anything better to wear than an outfit with flapping skirts and more petticoats than a tree has leaves?"

Wolfe's smile flashed. "How about buckskin pants and a buckskin shirt made for her by my aunt? Last time Jessi was here she also sweet-talked me into buying her some of those Levis that all the Forty-Niners and Fifty-Niners wore. Had a hell of a time finding a pair small enough. Same for the saddle."

"Sweet-talked you, huh? I'd like to meet that girl. Is she the kind that would get on her high horse if I borrowed her clothes and saddle and let another girl use them for a few weeks?"

"Doubt it. Besides, even if she brought her damned blue-blooded husband here, she wouldn't shock a bloody peer of the realm by appearing in public wearing pants and riding astride."

The contempt in Wolfe's voice when he spoke of Jessi's future husband didn't surprise Caleb. Other than the headstrong young Jessica, Wolfe had little use for the British aristocracy that was one-half of his heritage.

"In that case," Caleb said, "I'd appreciate the loan of her clothes."

"Take them. She'll never use them again. Anything else? Don't be shy. Hell of a lot better to get it from me than to go into Canyon City for supplies and have the Slater bunch down on you like a hard rain."

"I'd been counting on picking up supplies in Canyon City," Caleb admitted.

"Name it and you've got it."

"Food for us and grain for the horses, if you can spare it," Caleb said. "Grass is fine for a time, but where we're going, the horses will need the kind of stamina that only grain gives."

"Food is no problem. Will a hundred pounds of grain be enough?"

Caleb let out a relieved breath. "Thanks, *compadre*. Can you spare a blanket or two? Unless this storm breaks, it will be damned cold in the first pass."

"I've got something better than blankets. Sleeping bags."

A half-disgusted, half-amused sound was Caleb's only answer.

"Jessi insisted," Wolfe continued, ignoring his friend. "After the first night on the trail, I stopped complaining. No matter how much you thrash around, no cold air gets in."

Caleb cut a sideways glance at Wolfe. "Getting newfangled in your old age, aren't you?"

Wolfe smiled, for there wasn't a day's difference in their ages. Both men had turned thirty in late April. "I like my comforts. I'm not an Old Testament sort like you."

For an instant, Caleb remembered Willow's words: *An eye for an eye. Is that your Western code?*

"I'll settle for old-fashioned blankets." Silently, Caleb fished a gold piece from his pocket. "If this doesn't cover it, just—" he began.

"Put it away before you make me mad, you stiff-necked son of a bitch," Wolfe interrupted.

Caleb gave the other man a slicing, sideways look, but put the coin back in his pocket.

They walked in silence to the door of the cabin. The interior was dark, cool, furnished with a western flavor. The instant the door closed behind them, Wolfe turned toward Caleb and started talking about the one thing he and Caleb had never discussed after the first time the issue came up—a man called Reno.

"I'm glad you'll be too busy to hunt Reno for a time," Wolfe said quietly. "You never said what you wanted with him and I'm not asking. None of my business. But I'm telling you something, Cal. If you ever find Reno, be damned sure you've got a good reason to draw on him, because a second after you do, both of you are likely to be dead."

Caleb said nothing. Beneath the dark brim of his hat, his eyes were expressionless.

Wolfe looked at Caleb's hard face. "You hear me, *amigo*? You and Reno are too well matched."

"I hear you."

"And?"

"So be it."

ISHMAEL's ringing whinny brought Willow awake with a pounding heart. Slanting sunlight streamed into the ravine, but she took little notice of its beauty. Grabbing the shotgun in one hand and the blanket in the other, she raced for cover, making as little noise as possible. When she could go no deeper in the dense thicket she turned around and crouched, motionless, straining to see what had disturbed her stallion.

A ghostly sound slid through the silence, echo of a wolf's wild cry.

After a minute Caleb rode into sight, leading Trey.

It took a moment for Willow to realize what was different about the pack horse—Trey was wearing a riding saddle rather than the familiar pack saddle. Two bags of corn were roped over the saddle and a thick bedroll was tied on behind. A sheepskin jacket was lashed on top.

"Anything bother you?" Caleb asked when Willow emerged from the thicket.

"Not until a minute ago, when Ishmael scented you."

"That's why I came in upwind, to give you warning." Caleb dismounted, stretched, and began stripping gear off Deuce with quick, almost angry motions of his hands. "No one is around. While I rub down Deuce, make coffee over the smallest fire you know how to build."

Willow started toward Trey, wanting to help Caleb, who looked tired. At a curt gesture from him, she retreated.

"Work on the fire, fancy lady. Flames don't care about flapping skirts or blankets. My horses do."

When Caleb was finished with Deuce, he went to work on Trey. The scent of grain carried downwind to the four mares when he took the bags off the saddle. The Arabians nickered eagerly. He untied one of the fifty-pound bags of grain, lifted it easily, and went from horse to horse, pouring a small mound of grain for each one. The mares' dainty muzzles and delicate greed reminded Caleb of their mistress stealing every last taste of bacon from her fingertips with tiny, secret licks of her tongue.

The thought sent a surge of desire through Caleb. Ruthlessly, he shunted it aside and concentrated on what lay ahead—trails and passes, storms and sunlight, endurance and exhaustion, Slater's bunch and Willow's fancy man.

With a grimace, Caleb rubbed the back of his neck

and headed for the campfire. It burned hotly, making the coffee bubble and seethe. Willow knelt nearby, wearing his shirt rolled up to her elbows and the blanket wrapped around her hips. She had braided her hair and tied it with narrow strips of lace ripped from her petticoats. Dressed as she was, there should have been nothing appealing about her.

But when Willow came to Caleb and knelt beside him, her hands full of fragrant food, it was all he could do not to pull her into his arms. He should have been too tired to feel desire, but the proof of his ability was stretched hard against his pants.

With a savage word, Caleb reached for his coffee cup.

"Caleb?" Willow asked uncertainly, not understanding the bleak intensity of his eyes.

"The passes are open, so long as you don't get caught in a storm. Slater's gang divided up. They're waiting for us somewhere along the Rio Grande and the Arkansas both," he said flatly.

What he didn't say was that Slater had also put a bounty on Caleb's head, enough hard cash to make every outlaw between Wyoming and Mexico sit up and rub his hands with greed.

"What are we going to do?"

Caleb's bleak, golden glance fell on the sidesaddle. With an angry motion he grabbed it and chucked it into the small stream that ran alongside camp. Her torn riding habit followed.

"Caleb! What in heaven's name are—"

"They're looking for a girl fool enough to ride sidesaddle into the Rockies," Caleb interrupted in a cold voice, looking into Willow's startled hazel eyes. "I don't know any girl that foolish. Do you?"

Willow's mouth opened, but nothing came out.

"Good," Caleb said, nodding curtly. "They're looking for a girl stupid enough to wear fancy, flapping clothes that never dry out from rainstorm to rainstorm. I don't know any girl that stupid. Do you?"

Lacing her fingers together, Willow said nothing.

Caleb grunted and continued. "They're looking for a girl stubborn enough to try and sneak five fancy horses past every damned outlaw between here and hell. I don't know any girl that stubborn. Do you?"

"My horses go with me," Willow said instantly. "That was part of our bargain, Caleb Black. Are you going back on your word?"

The instant the words were out of her mouth, Willow wished she could call them back. But it was too late. She had said them and now she must face Caleb's wrath.

"I've never gone back on my word to anyone, not even to a spoiled southern lady who is no better than she has to be," Caleb said icily.

Without looking away from Willow, he yanked the ties of the thick bedroll and unrolled it with a snap of his wrist, revealing the clothes that had been packed inside. He grabbed a fistful of buckskin, denim, and cotton flannel.

"Start with the flannel longjohns," Caleb said in a cold voice. "Then put on the buckskin pants. Then the Levis. On top, wear—"

"I've been dressing myself for years," Willow interrupted. "I can tell top from bottom."

Caleb stuffed the clothes into her outstretched hands. "There's a hat and jacket for you inside Wolfe's sheepskin jacket. He didn't have a slicker for Jessi. Sorry."

"What about you?"

"Wolfe and I both hate slickers. They only work if you're sitting inside a tent."

Curiosity finally overcame Willow's caution. "Who is Wolfe? Is Jessi his wife?"

"His name is Wolfe Lonetree. Jessi is his step-mother's cousin or some such."

"Where does he live? I'd like to thank him personally."

"I doubt that you'd have much to do with him."

"Why not?"

"His daddy was a British blueblood, but his mother was the daughter of a Cheyenne shaman."

"A medicine woman?" Willow asked eagerly.

Caleb looked down at her through slitted eyes. He saw only curiosity rather than the contempt many people had toward a man of mixed blood.

"I never asked him," Caleb said finally. "Why?"

"She would know the healing plants of the West," Willow explained. "I've recognized some that are the same as back home, but not many."

"You'd take an Indian's word about medicine?"

"Why not? They've lived here longer than I have."

"You're the damnedest southern lady I've ever met."

"Probably because I'm not a southern lady," she retorted.

Caleb smiled slightly. "Couldn't tell it by the drawl. Listening to you is like licking honey off a spoon."

"Just because I don't have a voice like a gravel-bottom river—"

"You can insult me some other time," he said, cutting across her words. "We've got better things to do right now."

With quick motions, Caleb tossed the blankets Wolfe had given him onto the tarpaulin, set his saddle in place as a pillow, and crawled into the makeshift bed.

Willow looked around and saw no other blankets. "Where is my bed?"

"Same place it was last night." He lifted the blankets, indicating the empty half of the tarpaulin. "Right here."

She looked as shocked as she felt. "I slept next to you?"

"You sure did."

"But I—I don't remember it."

"You were so tired you wouldn't have noticed if a buffalo crawled in and snored in your ear," Caleb said. "Now you can sleep next to me and stay warm or you can sleep alone and get cold. Your choice, fancy lady. Either way, put out the fire after you've changed your clothes."

Before Willow could think of a suitable answer, Caleb pulled his hat down over his eyes, shutting her out. Within moments his breathing changed, slowing and deepening.

Willow watched Caleb for a while longer, seeing the even rise and fall of his chest with each breath he took. He seemed to be asleep. Even so, she considered retreating into the brush to dress, but was reluctant to drag the wonderfully dry clothes into the dripping willow thicket. Besides, it would be chilly away from the cheerful leap of flames.

"Caleb?" she whispered.

He didn't answer. Nor did he stir.

Abruptly, Willow made her decision. Moving slowly and silently so as not to awaken Caleb, she took off her boots and she set down the clothes on the strip of tarpaulin he had left empty. Easing the longjohn bottoms from the tangle of clothes, she turned her back and let the blanket she was wearing open. Fumbling slightly, she pulled the ribbons that fastened the pantelets around her waist. The thin cotton fluttered down her legs and heaped around her ankles beneath the blanket. She stepped out of the frail cloth and managed to pull on the longjohn bottoms without dropping the blanket entirely.

It wasn't easy. Whoever had been the previous owner of the underwear was somewhat smaller than

Willow. What should have been a loosely fitted garment covered her like a second, supple skin. The long-sleeved top was as snug as the bottom. The result wasn't uncomfortable, simply unexpected.

For Caleb it was breathtaking, especially as Willow had tired of wrestling with the blanket and let it drop in order to pull the top of the underwear into place. When she finished, she ran her hands over the soft, warm flannel and made a sound of pleasure. Caleb set his teeth against a groan. He would have given a great deal to have his hands running over the same fabric and to hear Willow murmur with pleasure in response to the touch.

Grimly, Caleb closed his eyes and rolled onto his side, making no noise as he turned his back on Willow. She didn't notice his change of position when she bent to the new clothes once more, for she was entranced by the feel of the buckskin pants. They were softer than velvet and supple as the wind.

With a murmuring sound of pleasure, Willow ran her palm over the pants before pulling them into place over the longjohns. Again, the fit was close without being uncomfortable. The top, with its rain-shedding fringe and laces down to her breasts, was as soft as the pants and fitted her just as lovingly. Like the underwear, the buckskins were fragrant with the rose petal sachet that had been tucked in the folds. She took a few tentative steps, feeling as though she might float away without the accustomed weight of skirt and petticoats. The freedom of movement pants gave her was almost startling.

Mother would have an attack of the vapors if she saw me in pants, Willow thought with a combination of amusement and sadness. *But beggars can't be choosers.*

Besides, the pants are warm and they cover as much of me as a skirt would. They just don't cover it in quite the same way.

All that remained were the Levis and the wool lumberman's jacket with its big checks of blended red and black. The Levis were looser than the other clothes, as was the jacket. The derringer fit so nicely in one of the jacket's large front pockets that Willow left it there. The fly front fastening of the Levis baffled her for a moment, then her fingers went to work over the stubborn steel buttons. Finally, she shoved her arms into the jacket's sleeves. The jacket had been made for a man rather than for a woman, which meant that the buttons were on the wrong side. Both Levis and jacket had been worn enough to make them flexible.

Willow picked up the pearl-gray, flat-crowned, wide-brimmed hat that had been rolled among the clothes. A few strokes of her hands pushed the hat back into shape. She put it on her head, fastened the chin strings, and wished she had a mirror.

"Just as well I don't," she muttered softly. "My hair must look like river weed."

The warmth of the clothes seeped into Willow, making her realize how long it had been since she had been dry. Almost fearfully, she glanced up at the sky. No clouds were overhead, but that was no guarantee that it wouldn't rain later on. By the end of daylight, clouds could easily pour down from the peaks in one squall line after another.

Wind blew with a long, lonely cry, reminding Willow of the icy night she had endured. Sparks leaped up from the flames. Quickly she pulled apart the fuel, and the fire guttered and died. As she banked the few coals in ashes, she regretted the loss of warmth. She looked at the narrow strip of tarpaulin that remained and realized all over again what a big man Caleb Black really was. The thought was daunting, but not as dismaying as the idea of lying down on the cold, wet ground in her dry clothes.

Making no more motions than necessary, she removed her hat, jacket, and Levis, lowered herself to the tarpaulin, and eased beneath the blankets. The feel of Caleb's body so close to her own was unnerving at first, but when he showed no awareness of her, Willow relaxed, enjoying the warmth that radiated from him. With a long sigh she fell asleep.

It took Caleb a lot longer, but he, too, finally slept. As was his custom, he awoke periodically, listened to the small sounds around him, and fell asleep once more. At one point, somewhere between waking and sleeping, he found himself with his arm around Willow, her head snuggled against his shoulder and her arm flung across his chest. Smiling, he eased the blanket higher, pulling it over their heads, shutting out the light, creating a world whose only inhabitants were himself and the girl who slept so trustingly in his arms. As Caleb fell asleep once more, the scent of rose petals curled around him, residue of clothes once worn by British aristocracy.

The last time Caleb awoke, the ravine was filled with the slanting golden light of very late afternoon and Willow was tucked against him spoon-fashion. Both of them were lying on their left side. His arm was around her waist, holding her close. The warm weight of her hips nestled intimately in his lap had a predictable effect on his body.

Motionless but for the heavy running of his blood, Caleb told himself all the reasons why he would be a damned fool for sliding his hands beneath Willow's clothes and finding out if her nipples tightened half as much in response to a man's caressing hands as they did in response to cold rain. None of the reasons for keeping his hands in his pockets sounded as good in the sleepy, intimate twilight beneath the blankets as they had in the full light of wakefulness.

Slow down, soldier, Caleb advised himself savagely. *She may be married. And even if she's not, she's a woman alone in a mighty empty land. I'm not going to have her saying that I took advantage of her. If she wants me, she'll have to look me in the eye and say so in plain English.*

Before his body could overrule his brain, Caleb rolled out of the inviting, rose-scented nest of blankets. Willow murmured sleepily and rolled over, seeking the warmth that had been so close a moment before.

"Wake up," Caleb said as he stamped into his boots. "This isn't a fancy hotel. You want breakfast, you'll have to stir your hind end for it."

Hazel eyes opened and watched him from beneath long, thick lashes. She yawned, curling her tongue like a kitten, then sighed. Dense amber lashes fluttered down once more.

"I mean it, southern lady. When I get back from looking around, there better be a fire laid and fresh water in the pot. Your stud could use a grooming. If you don't have a currycomb in your fat carpetbag, you'll find one in my saddlebag."

"Good morning to you, too."

Willow waited until Caleb stalked out of sight before she threw off the blankets, pulled on her boots, and began arranging twigs for the fire. The new freedom of movement offered by pants kept surprising her at odd moments.

The air was warm, stirred only occasionally by a breeze. Hidden birds sang through the ravine, falling silent only when Willow went to the narrow stream. There were clouds overhead. Some of them had slate bottoms, but not all.

"Maybe it won't rain tonight," Willow said wistfully to herself.

The rustling of leaves in a curl of wind was her only answer. With a sigh, she made her pilgrimage to some dense brush, where she discovered a drawback of her new clothes. Unlike her pantelets, the longjohns were sewn together at the crotch. That would have caused no particular inconvenience for a man wishing to relieve himself; for a woman, it meant shucking out of every stitch of clothing. Grumbling, Willow bared her backside to the playful wind.

By the time Willow got back to camp, she was still grumbling under her breath about dealing with men's clothing and a woman's body. She was tempted to light the fire, but didn't. If Caleb had wanted that done, he would have said so. For herself, Willow had lived in fear for too many years to be careless about starting fires that advertised her presence to anyone within sight or scent of the smoke.

Willow began putting the camp in order, shaking out and rolling blankets, stacking small pieces of kindling close to the fire, and getting fresh water. When that was done, she found Caleb's currycomb and went to work on the horses. Deuce and Trey welcomed the attention without a fuss, for there was no flapping cloth to worry them now. Ishmael, as always, was a gentleman. She was hard at work on Penny, one of the little sorrel mares, when the Arabian nickered and looked over Willow's shoulder. Only then did she realize that Caleb was standing a few feet away, watching her with unblinking golden eyes.

Abruptly Willow wondered what he thought of her dressed in buckskins like an Indian, her hair loose and tumbling down to her hips. But if Caleb noticed the change of clothes, he said nothing. Nor did he stare at the legs she had never before revealed in such a way to any man.

"Did my horses give you any trouble?" Caleb asked, wondering if Willow had even thought to check on his animals.

Relieved that he was going to accept her clothes without comment, Willow answered cheerfully.

"Trey and Deuce were as gentle as could be while I curried them. They held up each foot in turn and didn't try to lean on me while I cleaned their hooves."

Caleb's eyes widened a fraction as he realized that she had indeed cared for his horses. That was almost as much a shock as the instant he first had seen her wearing buckskins that fit her like a pale shadow, revealing every womanly line of her body. He was beginning to think that wearing pants had been a bad idea—for his comfort, not for hers.

Nor was the top she wore any better. It cupped her breasts as lovingly as a man's hands.

"A freight wagon is headed south, going at a good clip," Caleb said after a moment. "Wind is from the west. If we keep the fire small, nobody on the wagon will smell it. And about moonrise, with a cold wind coming down off the peaks, we'll be glad for a canteen of coffee and a hatful of cold bread."

Willow flashed a smile. "Can we have coffee now, too?"

The corner of Caleb's mouth turned up almost unwillingly as he admitted, "I was looking forward to it myself."

When Willow was finished with the horses, she took her camisole and pantelets and washed them in the tiny creek with a sliver of soap taken from her personal baggage. Carefully, she shook the garments out and draped them over the cottonwood log near the fire, knowing that the thin fabric would dry quickly.

In silence, Caleb stacked bacon and frybread on plates made from a slab of cottonwood bark. Willow finished pouring coffee into the canteen, sat, and began eating. As she reached for a chunk of frybread, Caleb brought out a small pot of honey, one of the many small luxuries Wolfe had thrown into the pack.

"Honey!" Willow cried softly.

"No call to go getting fresh," Caleb said, deadpan.

When she realized what he meant, she blushed and said, "Caleb Black, you know very well I meant what's in that pot rather than you."

"I'm hurt."

"And I'm Salome of the Seven Veils," she muttered.

Caleb glanced at the nearly transparent lawn camisole and fine cotton pantelets that were draped over the cottonwood log to dry.

"Looks more like two veils from here."

Willow said only, "Honey, please."

"How can I resist when you ask so nicely?" he said, surrendering the clay pot.

She made a sound that was almost a giggle. His answering smile made her feel as light as fire. For a shivering instant, Willow felt almost at home again, the home that existed only in her memories and dreams—firelight and her parents and her brothers' masculine teasing, and Matt's affectionate deviling of the younger sister who worshipped him.

Silently, Willow tipped the jar and dribbled a tiny stream of honey over the bread. The thick liquid shimmered like captive sunlight as it was slowly absorbed into the bread. She licked up stray threads of sweetness before she sank her teeth into the unexpected treat. The complex flavor of honey spread through her mouth. Without realizing it, she made a small sound of pleasure at the back of her throat. It had been three years since she had tasted the sundrenched richness of honey.

Caleb watched from the corner of his eye, telling himself that she wasn't doing it on purpose, licking her lips and sending that quick little tongue out to scoop up stray drops of honey. She wasn't putting on a show for him. She was simply enjoying the honey with a sensual intensity that aroused him as much as seeing her in nearly transparent underthings had.

If Willow had been teasing him, Caleb would have had no difficulty ignoring or accepting her invitation, depending on how he felt at the moment. But she wasn't issuing invitations, which put him at a real disadvantage. He wanted her. She didn't want him.

Or if she did, she was keeping it under her hat better than any woman he had ever met.

Maybe she really is Reno's wife. Not every man buys his woman a ring.

Then why does she blush like a kid caught stealing apples each time the word husband *is mentioned?*

There was no answer but the obvious one—Reno wasn't Willow's husband.

Absently, Caleb fingered the locket he carried safely within his watch pocket. Then he looked at the angle of the sun. Three more hours of daylight. Less if a storm came. But it didn't look like it was blowing in the right direction for a storm. A few showers here and there, maybe, but nothing like it had been last night or the night before.

With a reluctance he didn't understand, Caleb pulled out the locket, flicked it open, and studied the two pictures inside. From what Willow had said, she was more familiar with Reno's parents than she was with her own. All he had to do was show her the locket. If she recognized the photographs, she was Reno's wife. If she didn't, she wasn't. Cut and dried.

Show it to her. Find out if she's available.

What if she isn't?

The question went into Caleb like a knife, telling him how much he wanted the woman with the golden hair and the laughter to match.

Thou shalt not covet thy neighbor's wife.

It was easy enough to say. It had been easy enough to obey, before Caleb had met Willow. Now he wasn't certain he could obey the letter, much less the spirit, of that ancient law.

What you don't know won't hurt you, right?

Wrong, fool. What you don't know can—

"What's that?" Willow asked, interrupting Caleb's thoughts.

He turned toward her with a suddenness that made her flinch.

"I'm sorry," she said quickly. "I didn't mean to startle you."

Caleb looked from Willow's clear hazel eyes to the twin golden ovals of the locket lying open in his palm. Two unsmiling faces stared back up at him. With a casualness that cost a great deal, he held his hand out so that Willow could see the pictures.

"Just a locket," he said, watching her intently.

Willow bent forward at the waist and rested her fingertips on the pad of flesh at the base of Caleb's thumb. He responded to the light pressure by tilting his hand, giving her a better view of the pictures.

The man had an unremarkable face, light eyes, dark hair, a mustache, and the most outstanding pair of ears Willow had ever seen. The woman had an unremarkable face, light eyes, dark hair, no mustache, and the second most outstanding pair of ears Willow had ever seen. Surreptitiously, she glanced at Caleb, wondering if the couple was related to him. She saw nothing of them in the lines of his face, in the shape of his eyes, in the curve of his mouth.

And most especially, nothing of them in his ears.

She cleared her throat, swallowing the laughter that lurked just at the edge of her control, and murmured, "Birds of a feather . . ."

A corner of Caleb's mouth lifted in a hard curl. "Yes, I thought the same thing when I first saw the pictures."

"Then the people aren't, er, related to you?" Willow asked carefully.

"I was going to ask you the same thing."

Willow's hands went to her head, lifting her thick, heavy hair away from her ears. "What do you think?"

Caleb thought he would like to take a gentle bite or two, but he said only, "What about your husband?"

Fighting a guilty tide of color, Willow looked away. "Matt's ears are as flat as mine."

"Not his parents, either, huh?" Caleb said, making his voice light, as though he was teasing her.

Golden hair flew as she shook her head emphatically. "No. I've never seen those people before in my life."

"Sure?" he asked, smiling a slow, lazy kind of smile.

"Do you think I'd forget those ears?"

He laughed softly, feeling much better about life than he had when he awakened lusting after a woman who might have been another man's wife.

"No, southern lady, I don't. Those are the damnedest ears I've seen short of a Missouri mule."

Willow wondered at the honey-licking satisfaction in Caleb's smile and voice, but couldn't help responding to it. She laughed softly, pleased that she had somehow slipped past his reserve for a few moments. Not until Caleb's hand curled over hers did she realize that her fingertips were still resting on the hard flesh at the base of his thumb.

A shiver of awareness coursed through Willow, startling her. Instinctively, she pulled back. Sensing both the response and the wariness, Caleb released Willow's fingers with a caressing motion that emphasized his strength and his restraint. Now that he was reasonably certain of her marital status, he was willing to conduct a careful campaign of seduction, one that would end with her pleading for him in no uncertain terms.

That wouldn't happen today or maybe even the day after tomorrow, yet happen it would. The hunter in Caleb was as certain of his ultimate success as he was that he would find and kill the man called Reno.

The man who was *not* Willow's husband.

"Better get your Levis on, honey," Caleb said, standing and pulling Willow to her feet in the same motion. "We've got a long, hard ride ahead before we'll be shed of Slater and his bunch."

6

SHADOWS had already flowed down from the invisible peaks by the time Willow stood next to Ishmael, looking uncertainly at her new saddle. The stallion hadn't objected to it. In fact, other than a flaring of his nostrils at the unfamiliar scent, he hadn't seemed to notice any difference.

Willow did. When she bent to pick up the saddle for the first time, its unexpected weight startled her into letting it drop. Caleb reached past her, lifted the saddle one-handed, and secured it on Ishmael's back.

"Up you go."

Willow looked up from the leather-clad hands held out for her use as a stirrup. Caleb's whiskey-colored eyes were watching her with a masculine speculation that startled her. Then he blinked, banking the passionate fires she sensed burning beneath his self-control.

"Shouldn't I learn how to mount alone?" Willow asked, her voice husky.

Black eyebrows lifted. Caleb shrugged and stepped aside. "Suit yourself."

Willow held reins and mane in her left hand, lifted

103

her left foot up—way up—to the stirrup and grabbed the saddle horn with her right hand. Halfway up she stopped, remembering that she would have to swing her right leg over the stallion's rump instead of over the saddle horn. A judicious boost from the flat of Caleb's hand prevented her from dangling like an ornament from the stirrup.

"Thank you," Willow muttered as she settled in the saddle, flushed from the tactile memory of his big hand on her bottom.

"My pleasure," Caleb said gravely.

He hid his smile as Willow raised her left foot out of the stirrup. If he heard the swift intake of her breath when his hand closed around her ankle to move her leg back from the stirrup, he didn't show it. "I'd better let this down a few notches. I've never seen Jessi, but she must be an even smaller tidbit than you."

The red in Willow's cheeks deepened as she thought of the snug fit of the first two layers of her clothes. "I'm not small," she muttered.

Smiling, Caleb ducked beneath Ishmael's neck, gently removed Willow's right foot from the stirrup, and let it down two notches, though he knew very well one notch would be enough. When he was finished, he fitted her foot in the stirrup with a care that was just short of caressing.

"Stand up, honey."

Willow obeyed.

Caleb slid his hand along the leather beneath her bottom, testing the clearance between saddle and woman. There wasn't enough room for his hand to move freely. It could, however, move.

At Caleb's intimate touch Willow inhaled sharply as she went up on her tiptoes in shock. "Caleb!"

"Yes, I see," he said blandly. "I'll have to take the stirrups back up a notch. Sit down again."

Slowly, Caleb removed his hand and began working over the stirrup leather again. Willow stared down at him. She could see only the black brim of his hat. Gradually, her heartbeat settled down and the feeling of not being able to breathe diminished. She took a rather ragged breath and tried to forget the staggering instant when she had felt his big hand sliding between her legs, sending unnerving sensations radiating up through her body.

Forgetting was impossible.

"Stand up again."

"I'm sure the stirrups are just f-fine," Willow said almost desperately.

Her low, shaken voice was as arousing to Caleb as the soft weight of her bottom pressed against his palm had been. He wanted to feel her again, to curl his hand around her heat and rock against her until she moaned.

But she wasn't asking him to do that. She was asking him *not* to touch her.

"Suit yourself, fancy lady," he said, turning away. "Just don't come whining to me if you raise welts on your soft bottom because your stirrups are the wrong length."

Before Willow could think of anything to say, Caleb swung onto Deuce with a quick, almost savage motion and reined the big black around on his hocks. They followed the ravine due west until the opening became too narrow. It was full dark when they emerged from the crease in the land. A brilliant moon shimmered overhead, alternately veiled and unveiled by wind-driven clouds.

Willow could see just enough of the constellations between the clouds to know that Caleb was heading west rather than south as he had since leaving Denver. She stood in her stirrups and peered ahead, trying to catch a glimpse of the stone ramparts she had never seen fully from top to bottom. Night and clouds defeated her.

Ishmael broke into a quick canter, following the horses in front of him as Caleb led them into the cover of another low ravine. Willow adjusted to the new pace without thinking. Riding astride was easier on her, especially when Ishmael trotted or scrambled up and down steep slopes.

After the first few hours, Willow was able to keep her balance automatically, as though she had always ridden astride. Caleb had been correct about one thing, however. The saddle was indeed harder than Willow's bottom.

Suddenly, Caleb's horse came toward her from the darkness ahead. When the two horses were side by side, Caleb bent over until his lips were so close to Willow's cheek that she felt the warm rush of his breath.

"I smell a campfire up the draw. I'm going to scout a way around. Hold onto Trey until I get back. And don't let Ishmael start hollering if he scents other horses."

After handing over the pack horse's lead rope, Caleb vanished into the darkness.

Willow waited with increasing uneasiness, feeling the minutes move with the slowness of ice melting on a cool spring day. Just when she was certain something had gone wrong, Caleb materialized in front of her as silently as the night itself. At his gesture she followed him back down the draw, retreating from whatever lay ahead. A hundred yards later Caleb turned his horse and came alongside Willow.

"Trouble?" she asked very softly.

His hand snaked out, pulling her even closer. He spoke with a bare thread of sound that couldn't have been heard a foot away.

"Two men with dirty clothes, clean guns, and fast

horses. They were bragging about what they're going to do with all the money they get from selling your damned fancy horses."

One of them had also been wondering if Willow would be worth breaking to a different kind of saddle, but Caleb wasn't talking about that. All that had kept him from drawing on the man right there was the fact that the sound of shots carried, and he couldn't be sure there weren't other gunnies camped nearby.

"Are they part of Slater's bunch?" Willow asked.

"Doubt it. They were northern men. Slater is as southern as cotton." Caleb listened for a moment, then continued. "There's another draw a few hundred yards over. We'll have to dismount so we don't skyline ourselves. Can you walk in the dark without tripping over shadows? There's no wind to mask any noise we make."

"I sneaked past more than one soldier boy," Willow said. "I got caught once. I never got caught again."

Caleb thought of what might have happened to a girl caught by soldiers and felt a cold rage congeal in his gut. He wondered if that was why Willow had become a fancy woman—once lost, no matter how, a girl's virginity couldn't be regained. And after the first time, no man could know how many men had been there before him, so a girl might as well make the best of a bad situation. More than one widow had.

With quick motions, Caleb ducked out of the shotgun sling and settled it over Willow so that the weapon hung muzzle-down. A single motion would pull it into firing position.

"It's loaded," Caleb said tersely. "Any man gets close to you, blow him straight to Satan. Hear me?"

Startled, Willow whispered, "Yes."

There was a whisper of sound as Caleb took the thong off his revolver and slid it in and out of the holster, making certain that the gun wouldn't hang up if he had to draw quickly. He reined his horse toward a place which showed as a narrow shadow across the moonlit land. Holding Deuce to a walk, Caleb rode with his hand on his belt gun and his eyes searching the land. Behind him, the sounds of six other horses lifted into the darkness. A lazy breeze stirred, but it wasn't nearly enough to cover the beat of so many hooves against the land.

Like trying to sneak dawn past the night, Caleb thought savagely.

He cast a bleak look at the sky. The clouds weren't getting any thicker. The moon wasn't getting any dimmer. And the crease in the landscape they were descending into was narrow and barely four feet deep.

As Caleb dismounted, he slipped his repeating rifle from its scabbard. Carrying the rifle in his left hand, he walked forward noiselessly. Deuce followed without urging. Roped together as they were, the mares had to walk so close together that they were all but stepping on one another. Inevitably, they made more noise than a horse walking singly would have.

It seemed to Willow that half the night had gone by before Caleb abandoned the inadequate cover and came back to lift her onto Ishmael's back.

"Do you want to keep the shotgun?" he asked in a low voice.

"Yes, please. If you wouldn't mind . . . ?"

"I'll get its scabbard."

A few minutes later Caleb led the horses off in a northerly direction at a brisk walk. When they were beyond possible earshot of the two men, Caleb touched Deuce with spurs. He held the pace at a canter as long as the land and the illumination permitted. As moonlight waned beneath a thickening lid of clouds, he dropped back to a fast trot. Only when the land pitched up steeply did he allow the pace to slacken.

Not once did he dismount to rest the horses. Before dawn came, he wanted as much land as possible between Willow and the two men who had lounged at ease around their small fire, listening to the night with senses honed by years of living beyond the law.

As the dark hours wore on, Willow clung to the saddle numbly, balancing herself with saddle horn and stirrups, trying to move with Ishmael rather than against him. The first, faint sign of the darkness lifting had never been more welcome. Eagerly, she watched each hint of the coming transformation of night into day. When Caleb reined aside and led them to a small creek, she almost groaned with pleasure at the thought of hot food and a chance to stretch out full length on the ground. Dismounting, she braced herself for a few moments against her patient stallion before she began to walk slowly toward a nearby thicket.

Caleb watched the stiffness of Willow's movements and considered stopping for more than the few minutes he had planned. Then he remembered the muscular, racy lines of the horses picketed near the gunmen's campfire and knew he couldn't take the chance. Those horses were deep-chested, long-legged, and in top condition, able to run all day. His own horses had hard days of riding behind them.

After Caleb put Willow's saddle on one of the sorrel mares, he stripped the gear from his own big horses and switched riding saddle for pack saddle. By the time Willow returned, he was ready to ride once more. When she saw they weren't going to camp after a long night of riding, she had to bite her lip against a protest.

Willow's first effort at mounting failed. Before she could try again, Caleb lifted her into the saddle.

"The only way we can hope to stay ahead of those two men is by riding longer hours than they do," he explained as he mounted his own horse.

"Do you really think they heard us going by?" Willow asked.

He looked into her hazel eyes, trying to measure her strength. Dawn showed the dark smudges beneath her eyes, silent testimony to her exhaustion.

"Two horses might have sneaked by that campsite, or maybe even three," Caleb said finally. "But seven? Not a chance in hell. Along about first light those men will be casting around for our trail. Shouldn't take them more than ten minutes to find it. The ground is damp, just right to hold tracks. Seven horses leave a trail a blind greenhorn could follow. Those men aren't greenhorns. They'll be able to track us at a dead run."

Willow looked at her horses and knew what Caleb wasn't saying. Without the Arabians, they would have a much better chance of evading any pursuit. Leading extra horses slowed the pace as well as churning the land with tracks.

"Our only chance of staying in front of anyone trailing us," Caleb continued, "is to ride and keep on riding and pray that a good storm comes along to wash out our tracks."

Shifting in the saddle, he reached back into a saddlebag and pulled out a dark bandanna that had been tied around the remains of their last meal. "Here's what's left of our bread and bacon," he said, tossing the knotted cloth to her. "Eat when you have the chance. There's fresh water in the canteen on your saddle."

"What will you eat?"

"Same thing you will when that's gone. Jerky."

Before Willow could say anything more, Caleb

touched his horse with spurs and set off at a hard trot.

The transition from night to day was so gradual that Willow couldn't be certain when one ended and the other began. The clouds had thickened to the point that sunlight threw no shadows. All that was visible of the mountains were low ridges lightly clad with pine and wholly capped by clouds.

The land rose and the clouds lowered until no more than a thousand feet separated the horses from the bottom of the mist-shrouded sky. Rain fell occasionally, but never enough to blur the signs left by the passage of seven horses as they pressed higher and higher into the first range of the Rocky Mountains.

Gradually, trees became more common on the hillsides. These weren't the cottonwoods Willow had become accustomed to seeing scattered along the stream courses, but evergreens lifting their elegant arms to a gray sky that was almost close enough to touch. The tracks the horses left beneath the trees would be more difficult to follow. The realization comforted Willow, but not much.

Apparently, it didn't comfort Caleb at all, for he kept up a hard pace, letting the horses rest only infrequently despite the steepness of the route. Centuries of pine needles softened the impact of hooves on the ground, giving a silence that was almost eerie to the horses' passage. Other than the creak of saddles and the occasional snort of a horse, the only noise was a distant, fitful rumble that could have been repeated thunder or the sound of a waterfall carried by an unpredictable wind.

And once, Willow was certain she heard gunshots.

As the land rose, the air became colder and more restless. The wind strengthened into a steady moan. Willow tightened the chin string of her hat and settled more deeply into the saddle, hunched against the cold. Through the trees she caught glimpses of land falling steeply away. The horses were breathing deeply now, working hard even at a walk. Finally, they topped out on the shoulder of a mountain whose upper half was swathed in opaque veils of mist and rain.

Caleb pulled a gleaming brass spyglass from one of his saddlebags and looked out over their backtrail. Willow reined Ishmael in next to Caleb. Her breath came with a surprised gasp when she realized how much of the backtrail they could see from their vantage point. The land was as empty as the wind. No smoke rising from the forested areas. No wagon roads or clear trails through the meadows. No buildings or tilled fields. No tree trunks or stumps with the mark of a steel axe upon them.

"What's that?" she asked finally, noticing a dark thread over lighter meadow grass a thousand feet below.

"Seven horses flattening the grass," Caleb said grimly. "Even if those two gunnies can't track worth sour apples, they'll find us at every meadow we had to cross. We'll be damn lucky to avoid the Utes, too. Usually I don't have any trouble with them, but usually I'm not trailing a chief's ransom in horses behind me."

"I didn't realize . . ." Willow said. Her voice trailed off in dismay. Nothing in her previous experience had prepared her for a land so little traveled that tracks were like signal fires burning until a heavy rain came to put them out.

Caleb put the glass down long enough to look at the worried face of the young woman who was standing so close to him that he could hear the slow drawing and exhalation of her breath. In the gloomy morning light, her eyes were almost silver, with only a few hints of the warm splinters of gold and brilliant blue-green he had come to expect. Her lips were a soft rose, the same shade of pink that wind had teased from her cheeks, and her braids were the color of the absent sun. He wondered how her hair would feel spilling over his naked skin.

With a silent curse at his unruly desires, Caleb collapsed the spyglass and urged his horse forward again. The route he chose took them through forest much of the time, skirting meadows and the gentle, parklike clearings that Willow found so unexpected in such a wild land. Around them, shrouded in clouds, the land rose more and more steeply with each mile. Creeks fell away downslope in a racing white froth.

After a time it began to rain in earnest. At first, Willow welcomed the downpour as a means of blurring their tracks, but soon realized that rain was making their passage much slower and more difficult. Riding through a storm in gently rolling countryside was one thing. Riding through a storm in a steep-sided, stone-bottomed landscape was quite another.

The heavy wool jacket Willow wore repelled most of the water, but eventually it become as wet as her Levis. Water ran off the brim of her hat onto the saddle. Low-sweeping evergreen branches added their lot to the miserable going, shedding sheets of water at the lightest touch. From time to time the ghostly, slender trunks of aspen trees appeared among the dark evergreens. The aspen leaves were light green on top, silver underneath, and trembled at every touch of rain. In many cases, the trunks grew so close together that Caleb avoided the groves whenever he could, knowing the packhorse and mares would come to grief in the tight spaces between trees.

A cold wind came wailing down the slope, tearing apart the clouds. Willow barely noticed, for the trail had become very steep as they worked around the shoulder of a mountain. Way down below and to the left, there was a stream. It was invisible beneath the shroud of rain, but Willow was certain a stream had to be there. The sheets of water washing down off the mountain guaranteed it.

Without warning the clouds parted ahead. Sunlight streamed over the land, setting ablaze the countless drops of rain clinging to the forest.

Caleb glanced up, but had little heart for the beauty of the land. He knew what was coming next, and he knew Willow would fight it. But he had no choice. He had known this moment would come since she had refused to leave her horses in Denver and refused again to leave them the night he had seen Wolfe Lonetree.

Grimly, Caleb urged his horse forward to the edge of a parklike clearing in the forest. There were many such places in the Rockies, some so high that tundra rather than grass grew. Watching the land for movement, Caleb waited for Willow to come alongside. Across the park, deer watched in return. After a few minutes of alert scrutiny, the graceful animals resumed browsing along the opposite edge of the park.

Green, shimmering with raindrops, bright with a crystal ribbon of water winding through its lush center, the grassy basin was so beautiful that Willow made a sound of pleasure when she reined in next to Caleb. Then she looked up from the grass to the mountain tops finally free of clouds, and she froze.

The mountains were overwhelming. Lashed by snow, swept by wind, naked in their bleak granite heights, the peaks dominated sky and earth alike. She had never seen anything to equal them in her life.

"It's like seeing the face of God," she said in a shaking voice.

The emotion in Willow was echoed in Caleb's eyes. He loved the mountains in a way he loved nothing else, a soul-deep feeling of belonging to them and they to him. But he understood the Rockies as deeply as he loved them. The mountains were special to man.

Man was not special to the mountains.

Caleb dismounted and systematically began tying the mares' lead ropes around their necks, releasing them from the relentless tugging at their halters.

"Does Ishmael have a favorite mare?" he asked.

"Dove. The sorrel you've been leading."

"Get down. I'll saddle her for you, unless you think Ishmael won't follow us at all unless he's on a rope."

"I don't understand."

"I know you don't." Caleb's mouth flattened. He didn't like what he was going to do, but that didn't change anything. It had to be done. "Your Arabians are tough and quick and well-trained. Now we're going to find out if they're smart. If they are, they'll follow without a lead rope, no matter how tired they get or how rough the trail. If they aren't smart . . ." He shrugged. "So be it. I'm not getting us killed for any horseflesh, no matter how fancy."

"Surely the storm washed out our tracks," Willow said urgently. "We'll be able to keep ahead of anyone following unless they know the area as well as you do."

"I doubt if they do, but whether or not they know the high, little-used passes just doesn't matter."

"What?"

"It doesn't matter," Caleb repeated flatly. "We're through leading horses. It's too damned dangerous. From here on out the trail gets rough."

"*Gets* rough?" Willow's voice was faint, appalled.

"That's right, southern lady." He fixed her with a fierce, tawny glance. "What we've been over so far is a few lumps set in the middle of a lot of valleys and parks. Nothing special. A horse can lose its footing, go down, get scuffed up some, get up, and go on its way." Caleb took off his hat, whipped his fingers through his hair, and yanked the hat back into place. "It's different where we're going. Up ahead it will be worth your life to lose your footing. There are places where you could scream for a long time before you hit bottom."

Willow turned away and looked at her horses. The altitude and the days of hard riding had told on all of them. They were thinner, less alert, and they grazed hungrily on any grass within reach. The Arabians were strong and willing, but they were being ground down. So was she, even though she had done little more than hang on.

Saying nothing, Willow looked back to the park and to the magnificent, uncaring peaks blocking out the sky wherever she turned.

"Is there really a way through them?" she whispered.

"Yes. It isn't obvious from where we are, but it's there just the same. Finding the route isn't a problem. Getting to it before we're overtaken by those two gunnies is."

Wide hazel eyes searched Caleb's face. "Don't you think the rain washed out our tracks?"

"Maybe. Maybe not. Depends on how good at tracking they are. It's not something I want to bet your life on."

Willow closed her eyes, trying not to show how much her composure was costing her. She would have argued with Caleb, but she knew there was no point. She had refused to leave her horses behind. Now she had to live with the result of her refusal.

At least there was an abundance of natural food around. Even if the Arabians wouldn't follow without being led, they wouldn't starve. She and Matt could come back for them.

Willow clung to that thought as she dismounted. "I'll get Dove."

Caleb watched from beneath his hatbrim while Willow moved among her mares, touching first one and then another, talking to them in a low voice, stroking their warm, sleek hides. He had expected Willow to pitch a fit over his order, but she hadn't. She had looked at the peaks, looked at him with eyes that made him ache, and then she had climbed down from her stallion and gone about doing what must be done.

It took only a moment for Caleb to switch the saddle to Dove's back. Despite the altitude and hard trail, the mare had enough energy left to lip playfully at Caleb's coat sleeve. He smiled and pushed the soft muzzle out of the way, only to have it return again. While he cinched the saddle snugly in place, Dove snuffled over the thick, wooly pelt that lined his shearling coat.

"You're like your mistress," he said, rubbing the mare's velvety muzzle. "Small but game."

"I'm not small," Willow said behind Caleb's back.

He turned and caught her chin in the palm of his hand, tilting her face up gently toward him. "If Ishmael won't follow, do you want to ride him instead of Dove?"

Willow knew what Caleb was asking without actually putting it into words: If the horses wouldn't follow, which one did she want to save?

She closed her eyes. For a moment her long lashes quivered against her cheeks as she fought for control of the tears that burned behind her eyes.

"I—yes," Willow said huskily, turning away without meeting Caleb's eyes. "Ishmael."

"It would be better that way," Caleb agreed. "There are wild horses around. The mares won't be alone for long. Some stud will drive his herd up here for summer grazing. He'll take care of your mares. Ishmael would try, but he's paddock raised. He doesn't know about high-country snow and mountain lions."

Willow nodded but said nothing.

Caleb held out his hands, making them into a stirrup. "Time to go."

She wanted to tell him that she could mount without his help, but the words would have taken too much effort. She put her foot in his hands and swiftly found herself in the saddle.

The park was well behind them before Caleb reined in at a small creek and looked back to see how well the Arabians were following. His mouth flattened when he saw that Willow was riding sixth in line, keeping the loose mares between her and the pack horse, leaving Ishmael to bring up the rear.

Silently, Caleb admitted that the mares were following well enough, but that didn't make him like Willow's position far down the line any better. His concern was somewhat eased by Ishmael's transformation. Being taken off the lead rope had agreed with the stallion. He was walking like a horse on springs, ranging from side to side when the trail permitted, scenting every breeze, and generally acting for all the world like a wild stud overseeing his herd. Any thought a mare might have had of dragging her feet vanished when Ishmael laid back his ears and offered to nip the laggard's rump.

As the mares caught up with Caleb, they ranged alongside his horse, drinking thirstily. He fished a handful of jerky from his saddlebag and handed it over to Willow.

"When we leave here, ride right behind me," Caleb said. "The men trailing us could catch up any time between now and sunset."

Biting her lip, Willow looked at her mares.

"Don't worry," Caleb said. "That red stud of yours will keep the mares in line. That's one hell of a horse.

Any other flat country horse would be dragging his tail by now. Not that one. He's still got lightning in his eyes and thunder in his hooves. Be interesting to breed him to one of my Montana mares and see what we get."

Willow looked at Deuce and Trey. A small smile played around her lips. "Uh, I don't know how to tell you this, Caleb, but your Montana horses are geldings, not mares."

Caleb shot her a look of disbelief, then laughed out loud. The flash of humor in her was as unexpected as the resilient spirit in the Arabians. He leaned forward and tugged gently at one of her golden braids.

"How do you know the difference?" Caleb asked, grinning. "Do tell, honey."

Willow laughed and blushed at the same time.

The sound of her soft laughter blended with the murmuring creek and the sighing wind, becoming part of the beauty of the wild land. Something twisted within Caleb, something very close to the emotion he had felt the first time he had seen the distant peaks of the Rockies and known that he had been born to live among them.

Slowly, Caleb released the golden rope of Willow's braid, letting it slide between his fingers, wishing he had taken off his riding gloves so that he could feel the silky texture of her hair. When he spoke his voice was deep, almost rough.

"If you fall behind trying to keep your mares following me, I'm going to come back and get you. Then there will be blazing red hell to pay."

Before Willow could answer, Caleb touched his big horse with spurs and headed across the meadow at a canter.

The land rose steeply again at the far side of the park, forcing the horses to climb until Willow was certain that her head would brush the clouds. The pace slowed to a walk. Willow found herself looking uneasily over her shoulder, half expecting to see riders on dark horses.

Noon came and went unnoticed. The shoulder of land they were climbing was so steep that Caleb was zigzagging upward in long sweeps. Even the Montana horses were breathing deeply and taking small steps, for the footing was made uncertain by loose rock and evergreen debris. Creases in the land held tiny racing brooks, stunted willows, and aspens so slender and supple they looked like pale green flames shimmering on white wicks.

If there was a pass anywhere ahead, Willow saw no sign of it. The peak whose side they were climbing stretched up and up and up until it became swathed in mist. The mountain's face was seamed by avalanche chutes that were lined with dark, low-growing shrubs and aspen seedlings. Beneath the lid of clouds, other peaks were stacked nearby like cards tightly held in a gambler's fist.

There were no low places, no inviting valleys or divides winding between thrusts of stone, no visible breaks in the rocky ramparts. More and more often the route Caleb followed took them across patches of broken rock so barren that only avalanche weed grew, sending bright pink spikes lifting toward the overcast sky. Finally, there was rock alone, nothing but broken stone and a single clump of dark spruce and pale aspen ahead, growing in a sheltered fold of land.

Beneath Willow, Dove labored for breath. For the hundredth time, Willow bit back the desire to demand that the relentless climb end until Dove could breathe easily again.

Caleb isn't a cruel man. He can see how worn Dove is from carrying me. If he thought it was safe to stop, he would.

Willow repeated the words to herself for the next hour, which was how long it took the horses to struggle up the steep route to the small group of trees growing among the rocks. As soon as Caleb reached the grove, he dismounted, jerked off his boots, and pulled on knee-high moccasins.

By the time Dove caught up, Caleb had the repeating rifle free of its scabbard and was inspecting the firing mechanism, making certain no moisture had gotten in during the ride. His gloves were in his coat pocket. Despite the cold air, his bare fingers were swift and sure as he worked over the rifle. When he looked up, there was no more comfort in his eyes than there was in the chill gleam of the rifle barrel.

"How do your horses feel about gunfire?" he asked.

"They got used to it during the war. Are we finally stopping?"

"We don't have any choice. It took us half an hour to go three miles and gain five hundred feet of altitude. We've got a thousand feet higher to go. Without rest, your mares won't make it at all."

Willow didn't disagree.

"I'm going to watch our backtrail," Caleb continued. "Get some rest yourself. You look like a gust of wind would blow you away."

He walked off, moving over the loose rock without hesitation or noise, for the soft soles of his moccasins allowed him to feel if the footing was secure before he committed his weight to it. He walked until he reached a low pile of boulders that would both conceal him and give him a clear field of fire over the open parts of the trail below. He settled in behind the rocks, rested the rifle barrel in a notch between two boulders, and began scanning the landscape, sighting over the rifle barrel.

Fifteen minutes passed before he heard Willow's soft voice.

"Caleb? Where are you?"

"Over here," he replied.

Willow scrambled down into the boulders, only to find there was very little room in the stony nest. Caleb's wide shoulders all but filled the space.

"Why aren't you resting?" he asked.

"I thought you might be thirsty." Breathing quickly from the short walk, she squeezed in next to him and held out the canteen. "You didn't take time to drink."

He uncapped the canteen, lifted it, and tasted a tantalizing hint of peppermint. "You did."

"What?" Willow asked as she settled gingerly onto the rocky ground.

"You drank. I can taste it."

She gave him a startled look.

"Mint," he said simply.

Pink climbed up her cheeks when she realized what he meant. "I'm sorry. I didn't—"

He put the pad of his thumb against her lips, stopping her embarrassed apology. "I like the taste of you, Willow."

For a moment the silence was so intense she was certain Caleb could hear the wild beating of her heart. The corner of his mouth lifted in what could have been a smile. His touch became heavier, pressing against the inside of her lower lip in a caress that was as unexpected as it was sensual. Then his hand lifted, leaving her feeling disoriented. He brought his thumb to his lips, tasted it, and smiled.

"Mint."

Willow took a shaky breath and wondered at the feelings coursing through her. The white curve of Caleb's teeth against his black beard was unreasonably handsome. The gold in his eyes was a fire burning, watching her.

Caleb turned away and pulled the spyglass from his coat pocket, changing the direction of his thoughts in the most efficient way he could. Methodically, he began quartering the backtrail. After a few moments, his breath came out in a hissing curse.

Far below, a horseman was coming at rapid clip, taking the same way over the land that Caleb and Willow had. Even using the spyglass, the distance was so great that Caleb couldn't identify the man. Caleb waited. A second man came out of the forest. He, too, was riding a dark, rangy horse.

Caleb kept watching, but no other figures showed up in the magnified circle of the spyglass. Two men, two dark horses that showed signs of being ridden hard over a long distance. They were the same men he had seen last night. Caleb was as certain of it as he was of the smooth brass tube in his hand.

"The altitude has slowed them a little, but not enough," Caleb said.

"Altitude?"

"We're more than eight thousand feet high. That's why you're out of breath after a few steps. It gets to the horses the same way until they're used to it. Mine are mountain horses. So are theirs. Yours aren't."

"What are we going to do?"

Caleb lifted his rifle and sighted down its barrel. The men were still out of range. Even so, he didn't lower the rifle. He simply waited.

Willow saw a stillness come over Caleb, the in-gathering of muscle and concentration of a cat about to spring. Far below and off to the left, two riders were crossing the distant park at a hard canter. He levered a shell into the rifle's firing chamber and began tracking the second of the two riders.

"Are you going to shoot them without even finding out who they are?" Willow asked, her voice strained.

"I know who they are."

"But—"

"Look up that mountain," Caleb interrupted savagely. "Do you see any cover, any place to hide a person, much less seven horses, if someone starts shooting from below?"

"No," Willow said unhappily.

"Think about it, southern lady. Once we leave that grove, we're sitting ducks."

Willow laced her fingers together and held on hard, trying not to tremble while Caleb shifted position very slightly, never taking his eyes from the men below.

"How about it?" he asked without looking away from the men. "You want to take a chance on those two being God-fearing, church-going boys who just happened to be taking a long ride over a hard, little-known pass that leads to nothing but another long ride and another little-known pass?"

"No," she whispered.

Caleb smiled grimly. "Don't sound so unhappy, honey. At this range I'll be lucky to get close enough to scare them." He sighted on the second man but made no effort to take slack off the trigger. "Wish to hell Wolfe was here. That man is pure hell with a rifle."

A misty rain began to fall as the two riders vanished into the forest that ringed the park. If they followed the tracks, they would emerge again at the bottom of the slope in twenty minutes. Caleb lowered the rifle and turned to Willow.

"You better go back to the grove," he said. "If one of those men has a big-bore Sharps rifle, things could get real lively in these rocks."

"At this range?"

"I've seen men killed at six hundred yards with a big Sharps. I've heard of men killed at eight hundred yards."

"How far down is it to the park?" Willow asked.

"Less than a thousand feet straight down. Where they'll come out of the trees, they're maybe six hundred yards away. That wouldn't be a problem for

Wolfe, but I'm only middling good with a long gun. Get moving, honey."

Willow started to come to her feet, only to be yanked down by Caleb.

"Those damn fools are coming straight up! They must be afraid they'll lose us in the rain!"

The men burst out of the trees about nine hundred yards away, spurring their horses in great lunges, climbing diagonally across the mouth of an avalanche chute. Caleb tracked the second man with the rifle but did not shoot. They would have to criss-cross that chute, and others, several times before they gained the cover of the grove where seven horses were concealed. At a normal pace it would take the men half an hour to climb to where Caleb and Willow were concealed, yet the men were less than three thousand feet away as a rifle bullet flew, and they were closing fast.

"Keep your head down," Caleb ordered.

Crouched among the cold rocks, Willow watched the only thing she could see—Caleb Black. He was both motionless and relaxed, holding the rifle easily, waiting for the men to come closer. His eyes were those of a bird of prey, intent and clear. No tension showed in his hands or in his face. Willow wondered how many times he had waited like this during the war, utterly still, watching prey that were also men come closer with each instant.

Aiming low to compensate for the steep slope, Caleb squinted into the shifting veil of rain and squeezed the trigger. The rifle leaped in his hands. Before the report echoed away down the mountainside, he fired quickly, repeatedly, levering bullets into the firing chamber without drawing the rifle barrel off target.

The second man yelled and grabbed his right arm. The first man drew his rifle from its saddle scabbard, but was forced to drop the weapon and hang onto the saddle horn with both hands as his horse started plunging wildly down the slope. Bullets whined and ricocheted off stone, sending sharp rock chips flying around the horses' feet and stinging their bellies. Bucking, sliding on their hocks, fighting their riders every step of the way, the horses tried to bolt back down the mountainside.

Swearing beneath his breath because he had missed one of the men and failed to seriously wound the other, Caleb kept levering in bullets and firing. When a bullet whined off a nearby boulder, the uninjured rider spurred his horse savagely. It panicked, lost its footing, and rolled head over heels downhill. The rider didn't kick clear of the stirrups in time. When the horse regained its feet and plunged on down the mountainside, the rider stayed sprawled on the rocky slope. The second rider looked back but kept going, abandoning his partner to whatever fate awaited.

Caleb let out a long breath, sighted, and squeezed the trigger very gently. The rifle leaped. The fleeing rider pitched forward for an instant, then struggled upright once more. The forested flank of the mountain reached out, swallowing up horse and rider before Caleb could fire again. The skirmish had lasted less than a minute.

"Damnation."

Silence came, almost stunning in the aftermath of the rifle fire. Willow looked up and shook her head, dazed by the number of times Caleb had shot. She had heard of repeating rifles, but had never seen one in action. The amount of bullets one man could shoot in a short time was frightening.

"You're a one-man army with that rifle," she said faintly.

"Some godforsaken army," Caleb muttered, scowling bleakly down the slope as he methodically fed

shells into the rifle, replacing those he had used.
"Can't hit the broad side of a barn at six hundred
yards."

"In this light you'd be lucky to *see* the barn." Shifting so that she could look through a crack between
rocks, Willow peered downslope. "Looks like you hit
one of them."

"His stupidity laid him low, not me. Damn fool
spurred his horse when it was already scared enough
to jump over the moon. Horse went down and so did
he."

"Is he alive?"

Caleb shrugged and continued peering down the
mountainside over his rifle barrel, trying to pick out
any motion of a horse returning or a man moving up
to the edge of the forest to return Caleb's fire.

The drumroll of running horses drifted back up the
slope, the hoofbeats sounding thick and slurred in
the silence that had followed the sharp, distinct re-
ports of the rifle.

"Time to go," Caleb said.

"What about him?" Willow asked, looking at the
fallen rider.

"He's counting the wages of sin. Leave him to it."

7

CALEB led the way up and across the wet, rocky slope at a pace that was just short of suicidal. Even his big horses were breathing hard before they cleared the ridgeline and began winding down the other side. The forest grew higher on the far side of the mountain, embracing Caleb and Willow almost immediately. Spruce and fir became mixed once more with aspen. The rain diminished to nothing more than a wet whisper. Aspen trunks glowed with a ghostly radiance.

There were many possible paths off the mountain. Caleb ignored the obvious ones as he pressed on around the shoulder, zigzagging through the steepest parts, always descending. As he rode, he pulled out his father's journal and checked landmarks against those his father had noted.

When Caleb finally signalled a stop, Willow glanced numbly at the sun. It was several hours until sunset on what had become the longest day of her life. She had gone from exhaustion to a grim kind of indifference. It took her several minutes to realize that Caleb had vanished. She pulled the shotgun from its scabbard, clung to the saddlehorn, and waited for him to emerge from the shifting play of forest and clearings.

The pale, chill mist of the heights had given way to broken clouds. A restless wind cried softly through evergreens and made aspen quiver with a sound like distant rain. When the sun broke through the clouds, it burned with a pure, intense heat that soon had Willow removing her jacket, unlacing her buckskin shirt and furtively unbuttoning the soft red flannel beneath to allow the breeze to cool her.

The soft, eerie cry of Caleb's harmonica warned Willow that he had returned. Relieved, she put the shotgun back in the scabbard and urged Dove forward. Caleb emerged from the forest ahead, riding Trey. He had long since shed his shearling jacket and leather vest, and had unfastened several buttons on his wool shirt as well.

"If there's anyone around, he's leaving fewer tracks than a shadow," Caleb said. "Come on. According to Dad's journal, there's a good campsite just ahead."

"Are we really going to camp so early?" Willow asked, trying and failing to keep the hope from her voice.

"The Arabians are game, but they're not used to altitude. If we don't rest them, you'll be afoot by this time tomorrow. That would be a shame, because by this time tomorrow we're going to have God's own storm."

Willow measured the sky with dazed hazel eyes. It had looked a lot worse and only spit a few drops.

"It will rain, southern lady. If we were still a thousand feet higher, it would snow."

"Snow?" Willow asked, unconsciously flapping her buckskin shirt to allow more cooling air beneath.

"Snow," he repeated.

What Caleb didn't say was that they should push on without resting, for a storm could easily close any of the several passes between them and the San Juan region for a day or a week. But Willow looked too pale for Caleb's comfort, almost transparent, and there were deep lavender smudges beneath her eyes.

Reno has been waiting this long for my bullet, Caleb told himself silently. *He can wait awhile longer. Sure as hell it won't make any difference to Rebecca.*

Willow saw the suddenly grim line of Caleb's mouth and said no more about the weather. Sun or snow or rain, it didn't matter to her. The horses needed rest and so did she. She didn't know what Caleb was made of—rawhide and granite, most likely—but even he had to be feeling the strain of constant travel and little sleep.

Half an hour later Caleb led Willow into the big meadow his father had mentioned. Deer bounded away as the riders emerged from the forest into open space. Not until they were on the far side and concealed among trees once more did Caleb dismount and begin stripping gear from his horse.

From the corner of his eye he saw Willow painfully drag her leg over the saddle. He moved swiftly to her, knowing what was going to happen. Her legs buckled, his hands shot out, and he caught her just before she hit the ground.

"Easy does it," Caleb said, holding Willow upright with an arm around her waist and her weight braced against his hip. "Now try standing."

Slowly, Willow's legs accepted her weight.

"Walk for a bit," Caleb said.

Walking slowly, supporting Willow, he helped her to work out the cramps in her legs. After a few minutes, she was able to walk on her own.

"All right?" he asked, releasing her reluctantly.

"Yes," she said huskily. "Thank you."

She took a deep breath and started toward Dove. The hot golden light slanting between clouds made everything glow with an energy she wished she could share.

"I'll take care of Dove," Caleb said. "Picket your other mares along the edge of the meadow. Leave the stud loose. He'll be better than a hound for picking up scents, and he's not going anywhere those mares don't go."

By the time Willow was finished, Caleb had the rest of the horses stripped of gear and picketed in the grass. He went from horse to horse and poured a mound of grain near each one. Soon the sounds of strong teeth crunching hard kernels became as much a part of the meadow as the silky whisper of the small brook winding through grass a hundred feet away.

"Sit down and rest while I build a fire," Caleb said.

Willow let out a sound of relief and said, "I was afraid we were going to have another cold camp."

He smiled thinly. "Even if those gunnies had friends, no man's going to come over that mountain today, wondering every step of the way if I'm going to cut loose on him again."

Despite her fatigue, Willow picketed her horses and gathered enough dry wood for a fire before she allowed herself to rest. Caleb had put the saddles over a fallen log. She propped herself against the nearest saddle, sighed, and was asleep before she took another breath.

Caleb returned from the forest, saw that Willow was asleep, and covered her with a blanket to ward off the chill of the ground. She didn't awaken when he went into the forest once more and returned with a huge armload of springy evergreen boughs. Nor did she stir when he went into a nearby thicket of young evergreens, spread the boughs into a bed, and began tying the supple young trees overhead to form a living tent.

His big, lethally sharp knife quickly cut more

boughs to weave among the still-living branches, filling in holes until he had made a surprisingly watertight structure. The opening beneath was small, fragrant, and protected. One tarpaulin was lashed over the top of the living shelter. The other went over the cut boughs. He shook out the sole cotton flannel blanket as a sheet, added two heavy wool blankets on top, and the wilderness bed was complete.

When Caleb came outside again, Willow was still fast asleep.

"Willow," he said, sitting on his heels next to her.

She didn't stir.

Bending down slowly, Caleb brushed his lips over her cheek, inhaled deeply, and wondered how any woman who had spent as much time on hard trails as she had could still smell of rose petals.

"I'll be back," Caleb said as he stroked golden strands of hair away from Willow's eyes.

She sighed and turned toward his touch, curling trustingly against his hand. Slowly he gathered her into his arms and stood. The slight weight of her pierced him, reminding him of how small she was and how much had been demanded of her on the trail. He was as tired as he had been since the war. He could imagine how exhausted she must be.

Taking care not to awaken Willow, Caleb carried her into the fragrant shelter he had made.

"Sleep for a little while," he whispered.

He brushed the back of his fingers over her soft cheek and retreated from the shelter as silently as the sunlight sliding back up the mountain slopes.

MARVELOUS scents awakened Willow—bread and onions and trout and bacon and coffee all mixed together with evergreen resins and the coolness of a mountain evening.

"I'm dreaming," she muttered, rubbing her eyes.

She inhaled deeply. The enticing aromas remained.

"Do you want to eat or sleep?" Caleb asked from just beyond the shelter.

Willow's stomach growled loudly.

He laughed and went back to the fire. "Up and at 'em, honey."

A few moments later Willow emerged from the shelter. Overhead the sky was scarlet and gold. The surrounding peaks were a crystalline black with edges sharp enough to draw blood. The horses were grazing quietly at the fringe of the meadow. The only sound was the muted crackle of the small, carefully shielded fire.

Caleb handed Willow a battered tin plate and a tin fork with one bent tine. Startled, she looked at him.

"I know it's not very fancy for a southern lady," he began coolly, "but—"

"Oh, do hush up!" Willow interrupted. She took the plate and the fork and sat cross-legged near the fire. "I was just surprised to see a plate and fork. I didn't know you had anything but a knife longer than my forearm, a frying pan, and a little pot with a broken hinge for coffee. Suddenly, all kinds of things appear, forks and plates and evergreen tents."

"No point in getting out the cutlery for bread and bacon," Caleb said, amused without showing it. Politely, he offered her a tin cup. "Mind the rim. It will burn your soft little mouth."

Hazel eyes flashed with reflected firelight as Willow shot him an irritated look. "I've drunk from tin cups before."

"Didn't know you fancy southern women favored tin."

Whatever Willow had been going to say was lost when she saw the contents of the frying pan.

"Trout?" she said, hardly able to believe what she was seeing. "Where on earth did you get them?"

"Undercut bank at the far end of the meadow."

"I didn't know you brought a fishing rod."

"I didn't."

"Then how . . . ?"

"Little devils smelled that bacon grease and just jumped right into the pan."

Willow opened her mouth, closed it, and shook her head as she stared at the succulent, golden-brown fish. "Caleb Black, you are the most astonishing, *maddening* man."

Smiling slightly, he took the tin plate from her hand, bent over the skillet, and deftly used the tip of his big hunting knife to flip two fish onto her plate.

"Greens?" he asked.

Mutely, Willow nodded. He stacked some dandelion greens next to the trout.

"How about mountain onions and Indian celery?"

"Please," she said faintly.

The fish tasted even better than it smelled. Willow and Caleb ate quickly, before the descending night could steal warmth from the food. Despite her haste and head start, he finished before she did. He watched her delicate greed and smiled with the knowledge that he had given her an unexpected pleasure.

"Honey?" he asked when she set aside her plate.

"What?"

"Do you want honey on your bread?" he asked, grinning at her dazed look.

"I thought we ate it all."

"I found a honey tree. The bees had already bedded down for the night, so they didn't mind too much when I stole a bit of honeycomb."

"Did you get stung?" Willow asked instantly, searching Caleb's face.

"Once or twice."

With a small sound, she came to her knees beside Caleb. "Where?"

"Here and there," he said, shrugging.

Caleb felt Willow's fingers searching lightly over his bearded cheeks, his forehead, his neck, checking that he was all right. The concern in her expression made his breath stick in his throat. It had been a long, long time since anyone had worried about the small wounds that daily life left on his tough hide.

"Where?" she insisted.

"Neck and hand," he said huskily, watching her lips.

"Let me see."

Obediently, Caleb held out his left hand. Willow caught it between her own and leaned closer to the fire. There was a slight swelling among the crisp black hairs on the back of his hand.

"Show me the other sting," she said.

Without a word, Caleb unbuttoned his wool shirt and flipped the left side open. On the side of his neck, where the heavy line of his beard merged with the curling black hair of his chest, there was another small swelling.

"Lean down closer to the fire," Willow said. "You're so tall I can't see if the stinger is still in."

Caleb leaned closer. When he felt Willow's warm breath move across his skin, he was very tempted to grab her and show her the part of his body that was presently suffering a lot more discomfort than his neck.

"Does it hurt?" she asked.

His mouth crooked, but he shook his head slowly.

"I can't see a stinger." Willow looked up, rather startled to realize how close she was to Caleb. His eyes were only inches away and they reflected the golden leap of flames.

"Are you going to offer to kiss it and make it better?'' he asked, watching her with an intensity that was just short of demand.

Willow's cheeks reddened. "You're a little old for that, aren't you?"

"The day I'm too old for a woman's kiss, I hope they're reading scripture over my grave."

For an instant Caleb held Willow with the force of his eyes alone. She watched him in return, her eyes wide with what could have been desire or fear. Caleb waited for the space of a long breath before he released her by turning away. He had offered the sensual lure. She had refused it. As far as he was concerned, that ended the matter. Fancy lady or not, she had a right to choose her men.

"Go to bed, Willow."

Caleb's voice was as cool as the mountain wind. She blinked, surprised by the change from husky warmth to impersonal chill.

"Baking soda," she said.

"What?"

"Baking soda would help to ease the stings."

"I'd rather have your warm little tongue licking my wounds."

Willow's breath came in audibly.

"Go to bed, southern lady. Go *now*."

A trick of firelight made Caleb's eyes burn with a gold that was clearer and hotter than flames. Willow took one look and couldn't decide whether to run away from Caleb or toward him. The desire to step into his arms was so unnerving that she came to her feet and went the long way around the fire to the shelter, avoiding Caleb entirely.

But even when Willow was stretched out on the fragrant bed, she couldn't fall asleep. She kept hearing Caleb's words, kept seeing the passion burning in his eyes, kept feeling an answering passion burning deep within her own body. Lying quietly, listening to the night wind breathing freshness over the land, Willow wondered what would have happened if she had answered the sensual challenge in Caleb's eyes.

Just as Willow was sliding into sleep, the first soft, haunting notes of the harmonica shivered up toward the moon. She recognized the song instantly, a lament to a young man lost in war. The notes wept softly, grief transformed into music and played with piercing sweetness. Tears stung at the back of her eyes as she remembered summers past, a time when the Moran family house had rung with male laughter and her mother's happiness at being surrounded by her husband, her five tall sons, and a daughter with hair so gold as to make an angel weep with envy.

Other ballads followed "Danny Boy," old songs brought to America by Caleb's ancestors more than a century before, ballads and laments from England and Ireland, Scotland and Wales. Caleb knew them all. He breathed them into the night with a skill that held Willow motionless, enthralled. She could see him through the opening in the green canopy, his face lit from beneath by fire, shadows defining and enlarging him with each movement of his body.

As sleep slowly claimed Willow, Caleb became unearthly in her vision, powerful, an archangel whose harmonic voice was as pure as his body was compelling; but most compelling of all was the passionate promise burning within him, a dark fire reaching out to her, promising her heaven and Hell combined, two bodies burning in a single bright flame.

THE smell of rain and forest permeated everything. Water drummed down and ran off the tarpaulin Caleb had lashed over the evergreen boughs. There was enough room to sit up beneath the green canopy, but Caleb's head brushed the lowest boughs. Occasional gusts of wind made the forest moan and shook the limber roof of the shelter. So far it had held. Rivulets of rain crawled down several pine branches and dripped into the strategically placed tin cup, plate, and coffeepot. While neither Caleb nor Willow was wet, neither was particularly dry.

"Three of a kind," Caleb said, fanning his cards over his saddle, which was doing double duty as a table.

Willow frowned at her own cards. A black queen, a red jack, and three motley numbered cards frowned back at her.

"Nothing," she said. "I think I'm missing something about this game."

Caleb glanced at Willow from beneath black eyelashes as he gathered up the damp cards and shuffled with quick, deft motions.

"All you're missing is decent cards," he said, dealing rapidly. "I know you won't believe me, but usually beginners have all the luck."

"Oh, I'm having it. All bad." Willow picked up her cards, looked at them and laughed with genuine amusement. "How many do I have to keep?"

"At least two of them."

"That many, huh?"

A smile tugged at one corner of Caleb's mouth. A lot of women—and even more men—Caleb had played cards with would have been sulky at the run of bad luck Willow was having, but she wasn't pouting. She accepted the cards in the same way she had accepted the hard ride, bad weather, and uncertain shelter. Watching her, it was all Caleb could do not to reach out and lift her over the saddle and into his lap. The passion that was never far beneath his surface when she was nearby had become claws of need sinking into him, twisting with each breath he took, shaking him.

Setting his jaw against the fire burning in his blood, Caleb picked up his own cards.

"Eeny, meeny . . ." Willow said softly.

Caleb laughed despite the hardening of his body. Willow had proven to be a good trail companion, uncomplaining, with a whimsical sense of humor that kept taking him by surprise. She wasn't at all what he had expected of a spoiled fancy lady.

"That's no way to do it, honey."

"Nothing else has worked," Willow pointed out reasonably. She put three cards face down on the saddle. "Three more, please."

Shaking his head, Caleb dealt the cards she had requested and slipped the rejects onto the bottom of the deck.

Willow watched his deft hands with admiration. His coordination kept taking her unawares, for she kept expecting a man who was so obviously powerful to be somewhat clumsy. She picked up her cards, peeked at them, and tried to keep the poker face that Caleb had told her was necessary to a true understanding of the game.

"That bad, huh?" he asked sympathetically.

"It will cost you fifteen good pine needles to find out."

Smiling, remembering Willow's unbudging refusal to play for money, Caleb counted out fifteen needles from the mound in front of him.

"Call," he said.

"Seven, six," Willow said, laying out the red and black cards face up, "five, four, and two."

"I've got a pair, jack high."

"Is that better than what I have?"

"Honey, anything is better than what you have."

Caleb looked from his winning hand to her useless

cards. "You must be lucky at love, because you aren't worth two straws at cards."

"And you're very good." Willow lowered her lashes, watching him from beneath their fringed shelter as she asked casually, "Does that mean you're unlucky at love?"

"I would be, if there were such a thing. Another hand?"

For a moment Willow was too surprised to speak. "You mean you don't believe in love?"

"You mean you do?" he retorted dryly, shuffling the cards with a speed that blurred all the edges.

"What do you believe in, then?"

"Between a man and a woman?"

She nodded.

"Passion," Caleb said succinctly, feeling the red-hot claws of his own need raking him.

The cards arched beneath his fingers and interlaced in a blur of motion, sliding over one another only to be divided, arched, and interlaced again in a new way.

"Is that all? Just passion?" Willow asked, her voice almost a whisper.

"It's more than most men get from a woman." Caleb shrugged and began dealing cards. "Women want a man to take care of them. Men want a woman to warm their bed. Women call the arrangement love. Men call it by another name." He glanced up. "Don't give me that shocked look, *Mrs.* Moran. You know how the sex game is played as well as I do."

Willow hated the flush that heated her cheeks at the mention of her married state, but was unable to do anything to stem the guilty tide of color. In silence, she picked up her cards and opened them. She stared at the numbers and faces but saw nothing.

Overhead the rain stopped as suddenly as it had begun. The quiet was almost shocking. Wind came, shaking the shelter. With an abrupt motion Caleb emptied the contents of the tin cup into the coffeepot and placed the cup below the leak once more.

"How many?" he asked, his voice as hard as his body.

Blinking, Willow focused on Caleb as though she had never seen him before. "I beg your pardon?"

"How many cards do you want?" he asked impatiently.

"None," she said, putting her cards aside. "It's stopped raining. Are we going to get back on the trail?"

"Can't wait to see your . . . husband?"

"Yes," Willow whispered, closing her eyes, shutting out Caleb's contemptuous golden glance. "Yes, I want to see Matthew very much."

"I suppose he understands all about love." Caleb's voice was savage, condemning.

Willow's eyes opened and her breath came out as though at a blow. "Yes. Matthew loves me."

Caleb stared at Willow. There was no rush of blood to her cheeks, no refusal to meet his eyes. The mention of marriage might have made her blush, but she obviously was quite certain of one thing: Matthew Moran loved her.

The thought didn't comfort Caleb one bit.

"How long since you've seen him?" he asked.

"Too long."

"How long, fancy lady?" Caleb demanded. "A month? Six months? A year? More?" He barely restrained the question he really wanted to ask: *Where were you when Reno was seducing my innocent sister, planting his seed in her, leaving her to die bearing his bastard?*

But if Caleb asked that, Willow would have questions of her own. The answers would insure that she never told him where her fancy man was holed up, waiting for his fancy woman and a fortune in fancy horses to arrive.

Disgusted, Caleb threw in the cards he had just dealt.

Willow watched, but said nothing. She didn't understand what was riding Caleb, but she sensed the savagery in him with great clarity.

"Answer me," Caleb snarled.

"Why does it matter when I last saw Matthew?"

The slight trembling of Willow's hands belied the composure of her voice, but Caleb wasn't looking at her hands. He was looking at her mouth. Her lips were smooth and full, pink as her tongue. Their curves fascinated him. There were other curves he longed to touch, to taste, to test the softness of her breasts; but most of all he longed to strip off buckskin and flannel and explore the nest of golden hair that concealed her feminine secrets. The memory of that thick triangle pressing against her drenched pantelets had haunted him mercilessly.

In that instant Caleb knew if he stayed cooped up with Willow a minute longer in the enforced intimacy of the shelter, he was going to demand more than useless information from her soft lips. A few minutes ago she might have given him the kiss he hungered for, and more besides. But not now. Now she was almost frightened of him. Now she was longing for the fancy man who told her lies about love.

Caleb knew he had only himself to blame. He had let the hunger burning within him erode his self-control until he could barely call his body his own. That was stupid. Reno hadn't seduced his girls with the rough edge of his tongue—he had whispered loving lies while he unfastened laces and plundered the soft heat beneath. That was what Willow was missing, all the smooth lies and smoother manners of a gentleman.

If Caleb wanted to sheathe himself within Willow's body, he would have to control his savage anger at her lover. Then, maybe, Caleb would be able to control the passion that was eating into the very marrow of his bones.

With a muttered curse, he grabbed his hat and rifle and left the shelter in a coordinated rush of power. Behind him, Willow let out her breath slowly, wondering why the subject of marriage and Matthew Moran always put a razor edge on Caleb's temper.

"I'm going to look around," Caleb said from outside the shelter. "I'll be gone for several hours. Don't build a fire."

"All right," Willow answered.

She waited, listening, hardly daring to breathe, remembering the savagery of Caleb's voice. She heard nothing but the fitful wind unravelling the last of the storm. When she emerged tentatively from the shelter, she was alone and the sun was pouring a cataract of golden heat over the land. Clouds retreated with each passing minute, revealing newly whitened peaks.

"Caleb was right," Willow said aloud, hoping the sound of her own voice would hold loneliness at bay. "It snowed. But then, Caleb is always right, isn't he? That's why I hired him."

Willow shivered as she remembered Caleb's savagery when he questioned her about Matthew. It was as though the very fact of her brother's existence somehow offended Caleb.

"Not my brother," she corrected herself quickly. "My husband. I have to remember that. Matthew is my husband, not my brother."

Yet what Willow remembered was the intensity of Caleb's eyes when he watched her lick honey from her fingertip, and the huskiness of his voice when he asked her if she was going to kiss his small hurts and make them better. She had been tempted, so tempted, and he had seen that. He wanted her, she was drawn to him, and he thought she was married.

Scarlet burned suddenly from Willow's breasts to her hairline as she realized that he must think her a flirt at best, and at worst . . .

Fancy lady.

Willow took a deep, steadying breath. It would be for only a few more days. A week, perhaps. Then they would be among the five peaks and Matthew would find them and they could all laugh about her necessary disguise as a married woman. Until then, she needed the disguise more than ever.

Caleb was a wild, sweet fire in her blood.

8

With a curious, tingling shudder, Willow forced herself to think of something other than the man whose uncertain temper and crooked smile kept throwing her off balance. She concentrated on the sunlight beating heavily down all around her, stripping veils of mist from the wet land. Although the ground was cool, the air was rapidly becoming almost hot.

The horses had emerged from the cover of the forest and were grazing. They ate hungrily, looking up from time to time, but otherwise relaxed. Their calm told Willow that no one was nearby. For a few minutes she watched their coats steam in the rapidly heating air, reassured by the familiar presence of her Arabians. Within an hour the horses would be dry, and so would the meadow.

Willow went into the shelter and came out carrying the shotgun, a blanket, lavender soap, Caleb's cavalry shirt, and her clean camisole and pantelets. Watching Ishmael for any sign that she wasn't alone in the meadow, she went to the creek and followed it downstream from the camp until she found a patch of willow bushes growing right next to the water. Behind the screen of bushes she undressed until she wore only the scarlet flannel longjohns.

When Willow knelt and put her hand in the water, she barely bit back a shriek. The creek was colder than the streams she was accustomed to in West Virginia, much less one of the sun-warmed farm ponds where she had bathed whenever she could sneak away.

"The sun will warm you up," she told herself firmly. "Now get to it before Caleb comes back."

Willow temporized, washing in reverse of her usual order rather than stripping down right away. Still dressed, she wetted her hair and worked it into a lather. The soap fairly seemed to explode into bubbles when it hit the water. Very quickly she had lathered and rinsed her hair twice. Sitting on her heels, she wrung out her hair and shook it over her back to dry. Then she peeled off the cotton flannel and washed herself to the accompaniment of gasps and gritted teeth whenever cold water hit a particularly sensitive part of her body.

After blotting herself dry as best she could with the flannel, Willow stepped into her pantelets and camisole. She shook out Caleb's big shirt and pulled it on over her head, lifted out her hair, and settled into shivering herself warm. It took only a few minutes. She gathered everything she had brought and walked out of the willows, looking for a warm, sunny place along the brook to wash her clothes.

A hundred yards away, Ishmael's head came up and his ears pricked together as he saw Willow emerge from cover. He watched her walk along the stream for a minute, then went back to grazing. Certain that no one would be able to sneak up on her— except, perhaps, Caleb—Willow knelt near the water, set the shotgun within reach, and began washing her flannel underwear. When she was finished, she spread the flannel underwear on the meadow grass to dry.

The heat of the sun amazed her. Already the snowline was visibly melting up the mountain peaks, retreating with every passing minute. The air was almost hot. Its silky dryness was like a tonic after the days of overcast and rain. It was difficult for Willow to believe that she would be wanting heavy clothes when the sun went down. At the moment, even with wet hair, she was warm enough to consider peeling off Caleb's heavy wool shirt and lying down on a blanket in the sun while her hair dried. She compromised by unbuttoning one of the rows of buttons and allowing the cavalry shirt to flop open on the right side.

The horses continued to graze quietly, assuring Willow that she was alone in the meadow. She shook out the blanket, set the shotgun nearby, and began combing snarls out of her hip-length hair. It was a tedious job, but in time most of the water-darkened strands hung freely down her back. With a sigh of relief she stretched out on her stomach to let the sun complete its work of drying her hair. Then she would finish grooming the thick mass with her brush.

The light breeze, the hum of insects working over the meadow, the muted song of birds, and the hot sun combined to unravel Willow. With a long sigh, she slid into sleep.

When Ishmael nickered, she awoke with a start. Even as her hand closed around the shotgun, she recognized Caleb approaching her with long, easy strides. Hastily, she sat up and flipped the blanket across her legs. Her hair slid forward over her shoulders in an untamed fall of gold. Frantically, she groped around the blanket but couldn't find the brush and comb.

"Good thing nobody is nearby," Caleb said. "Between that red stallion and your underwear drying on the grass, it would take a blind man to overlook us."

"You didn't tell me to keep the horses in the forest," Willow muttered as she rearranged the blanket to cover her bare feet.

"I didn't tell you to keep your pants on, either."

Caleb's voice was neutral, giving no indication as to his mood. Willow looked cautiously at him through the screen of her dark amber eyelashes. His smile flashed crookedly against the black backdrop of his beard.

"Don't worry, honey. If I wanted the horses in the forest, I would have picketed them there myself. As for your clothes," he said, his eyes crinkling at the corners, "they don't stand out nearly as much as that red stud."

Relieved, Willow smiled up at Caleb. The day was too warm and too unexpectedly wonderful to spend arguing. His own smile widened as he bent and scooped up the brush and tortoiseshell comb that were peeking out from the meadow grass.

"Looking for these?" Caleb asked.

"Yes, thank you."

Instead of putting them in Willow's outstretched hand, he moved behind her, knelt, and calmly began combing her hair. After her first, startled reaction was ignored, she accepted the small intimacy.

For such a big man, Caleb's hands were light and surprisingly gentle. Patiently he worked the remaining snarls from Willow's long, sun-warmed hair. With an unconscious sigh of pleasure, she relaxed beneath his hands.

Caleb's eyes narrowed as he measured her response to his, but he made sure that Willow saw nothing of his response, for he didn't think he could conceal the hunger in his eyes and body. Delicately he drew the comb through the incandescent gold of her hair, easing out all tangles before he set the comb aside and switched to the brush without interrupting the slow rhythms of his hands moving over her hair.

"You're very good at this," Willow said after a time of hushed silence.

"I had a lot of practice when I was a boy. My mother had a hard time carrying a baby. Most of the time she was so ill she couldn't wash and comb out her own hair."

"You did it for her?"

Caleb's answer was a rumble of sound that had no meaning beyond agreement. "Mom had no daughters and no other living children until Rebecca."

"Your sister?"

"Yes, my baby sister. She was beautiful, as sleek and quick as a mink. All the boys wanted her, but she wouldn't have any part of them, until . . ."

Willow heard both sadness and rage in Caleb's voice and sensed that the girl called Rebecca hadn't made a happy choice in her man.

"I'm sorry," Willow whispered, touching Caleb's hand where it rested on her shoulder. "It must be very hard for you to be away from your family."

Caleb had no doubt that Willow meant every word she said. He also had no doubt that she made no connection between herself and a girl called Rebecca Black. When Caleb thought about it, he realized Willow's ignorance was hardly surprising. Reno wouldn't be likely to discuss one conquest with another.

Anger prowled in Caleb, but it was no competitor at the moment for the desire that permeated every bit of his big body. He lifted a fistful of Willow's thick hair and let it slide from his grip in a silky, golden waterfall. The scent of lavender drifted up to him. He knew that her clothes would smell of the same lavender soap she had used on her hair. He inhaled deeply, letting the fragrance expand through him. For some reason he liked lavender even better than the rose sachet Jessica Charteris preferred. Lavender refreshed his senses and tantalized them at the same time.

"My father was an Army surveyor," Caleb said almost absently as he watched the silken drift of Willow's hair down her back. "He was gone more than he was home. I did what I could to care for Mother. The part I liked best was brushing her hair. It was black and straight, like mine. Light used to make blue-white rainbows in it. I thought it was the softest, most beautiful thing in the world, until now."

Willow shivered as Caleb's palm moved caressingly from her forehead to her nape and burrowed beneath the thickness of her hair. His hand lifted and let the smooth strands slide away.

"Soft as a kitten's chin," he said huskily, "and the color of the summer sun. My mother used to read me fairy tales about princesses with hair like yours. I never believed them, until now. Touching your hair is like touching sunlight."

Caleb resumed brushing Willow's thick hair with slow sweeps of his hand. Strands of gold shifted and shimmered beneath his touch. As though alive, filaments of hair lifted and clung to his hands, silently asking that the gentle caresses continue. Strands followed his fingers, clung to his shoulders, and fanned across his chest in soft invitation. He fought against the temptation to unbutton his shirt and feel the silky touch on his bare skin. His shirt remained fastened, but he couldn't prevent himself from rubbing a handful of her fragrant hair against his cheek. He inhaled deeply, then forced his fingers to release the locks of hair.

"I think the t-tangles are out," Willow said hesitantly. "Should I get dressed now?"

The sensuous shiver in her voice made Caleb smile. "No hurry. We're not going anywhere today. I thought I'd catch another mess of trout and gather some more greens before the weather goes bad again."

"More rain?"

"Probably."

"When?"

"After sunset."

Willow sighed. "I was told the plains were dry."

"They are. You're in the mountains now. But compared to where you came from, it's plenty dry. That's why you keep licking your lips."

"I do?"

"You sure do, honey. If you're carrying any oil in that big old carpetbag of yours, you might put some on. Bacon grease works, but you get tired of the taste real fast."

For a few moments there was only the whisper of soft bristles moving through Willow's long hair. She closed her eyes and savored the unexpected luxury of having her hair brushed by someone other than herself. Then a thought struck her.

"How will you catch the trout?"

"Same way I did last night."

"How was that?"

"With my hands."

Willow turned and looked over her shoulder with wide hazel eyes. "You're teasing me."

"Maybe a little." Caleb's nostrils flared as he inhaled the scent of her once more. *But not as much as I'm teasing myself.* "Close your eyes, you're distracting me."

"If I close my eyes, will you tell me how you really catch trout?"

"Sure."

Long amber eyelashes lowered until they rested against Willow's smooth skin. Sunshine caught and tangled in the thick lashes, making tiny, iridescent flashes of light. Caleb watched, fascinated, wanting to run the tip of his tongue over the soft fringe.

"My eyes are closed," Willow pointed out when Caleb didn't speak.

"I noticed. How did you get such long eyelashes, honey?"

"I stole them from a calf."

He laughed softly, shaking his head at her quickness.

"Caleb," she said coaxingly, "how do you catch trout with your bare hands? I've never heard of anyone doing that."

"Not even Matthew Moran?"

She shook her head. "Not even Matt."

With a rumbling sound of satisfaction, Caleb resumed brushing Willow's hair, admiring its shine and softness. When he began to talk again, there was a subtle difference in his touch, a lingering over the nape of her neck, a tracing of the long tendrils that curled down her arm, a sensuous stroking down the length of her spine that encouraged her to arch against his palm like a cat.

"First of all," Caleb said deeply, "you have to find trout that haven't been scared out of their pretty little scales by a southern lady taking a bath in their parlor."

Willow laughed behind her hand.

"It's true," he said, tugging teasingly at a lock of hair. "Trout are like beautiful girls, flighty creatures that take a lot of soothing before they can be caught."

The brush moved from Willow's crown to her nape, followed by Caleb's hand. Long fingers eased beneath the heavy strands and skimmed over the curve of her neck. She shivered, wondering if the touch had been accidental. His fingers skimmed over her neck once more, tracing the hairline with a caress as light as a breath.

"So a man with trout on his mind walks softly and sort of eases up to the edge of the brook," Caleb continued, his voice as lazy and murmurous as the breeze. "Then he kneels down real slow and easy like, and slides his hand into the water behind a trout."

As Caleb spoke, his big hand gathered up the golden mass of Willow's hair and lifted so that he could brush from beneath. Some of the strands slipped away from his fingers, for the hair caught on the big buttons of the cavalry shirt she wore. Setting the brush aside, he began to gently untangle her shining hair from the buttons. No sooner did one strand come free than another slithered from his grasp and fell forward, becoming trapped and tangled on a button.

"Damn," Caleb said softly, using both hands to corral Willow's silky hair. "This isn't working. Lift your arms up, honey. Higher. That's it."

Caleb peeled the shirt from Willow's body so matter-of-factly that she didn't think to object until it was too late.

"Caleb, I don't—"

"Once your hand is in the water," Caleb continued, talking over Willow's words, "then you just stay real still for a time, as though you had nothing on your mind but sitting and dreaming by a meadow stream."

The brush glided through Willow's hair once more, sending shivers of pleasure over her scalp, shivers that were only increased by the soothing hand that followed each stroke of the brush. The strands that fell forward no longer tangled around buttons, but instead fanned in a golden veil over her camisole. The full curves of her breasts pressed up against the fine lace.

While Willow watched, tendrils of hair slid away from her breasts, leaving the peaks barely covered. She bit her lip, wondering if her hair concealed the outlines of her body enough for decency.

"It's all right," Caleb said softly, sensing the tension in Willow. He stroked the shining hair that fanned over her shoulders and back. "Your hair covers as much of you as my shirt did. Unless you're cold?"

She shook her head, making light ripple and twist sinuously through her hair. "The sun is almost hot."

"Yes, it is."

Caleb's voice was so low it was like a purr from a big cat, as much felt as heard. Without breaking rhythm, he continued brushing Willow's hair with slow, gentle movements until she sighed and relaxed once more, giving herself to a pleasure that was so acute it made sweet chills course over her skin.

"That feels so good," Willow whispered finally.

"To me, too," Caleb said, running his hand lightly down her hair. He laughed softly. "I think your hair likes me as much as I like it."

Willow made a questioning sound.

"Watch," he said.

The brush followed thick ribbons of hair that had fallen over Willow's right shoulder and fanned out over her breast.

"See?" He lifted the brush slowly. Shining strands of hair rose languidly, clinging to the brush and to the edge of his hand. "It's chasing me."

For an instant, Willow was too shocked to speak. The soft bristles of the brush moving lightly over her breast had stroked it into vivid life, causing a rush of sensation that left her weak. She closed her eyes as a curious heat radiated suddenly from the pit of her stomach. The sensation was both piercing and sweet, unlike anything she had ever known before.

"Let's see if the other side likes me as well," Caleb said in a low voice.

The brush stroked softly over Willow's left breast, which also was veiled by a fall of golden hair. When the brush lifted, filaments of bright hair followed, clinging to the brush and the male hand that held it.

"Yes," he said huskily, looking at the breast whose tight peak parted the golden veil of hair, "I believe it does."

Willow could say nothing at all. Her breath was lodged in her throat as another trembling rush of sensation claimed her. When Caleb heard the break in her breathing, his own body responded with a violent surge, his heartbeat deepening and quickening until he could count each pulse in the rigid flesh between his legs. He had expected Willow to leap up and push away his hands or to turn angrily on him for daring to touch her even with the brush.

He hadn't expected her breasts to blossom at a single touch until her nipples pouted in shades of pink beneath the nearly transparent camisole. The intense sensuality of her response was as startling as the depth of his own passion for her, a passion that shook him until he had to clench his fingers around the brush's slender handle or lose it to the wildness ripping through his body.

Unable to speak, barely able to breathe, Caleb forced himself to continue the slow, seductive rhythms of the brush moving over Willow's hair, caressing her scalp, her nape, the slender length of her back. He very much wanted to stroke the golden veil over her breasts again, but he didn't trust himself not to drop the pretense of the brush and slide his hands beneath her camisole until he could feel her hard nipples nuzzling against the exact center of his palms. He wanted that so much his hands shook.

But he knew it was too soon. Even the most trusting trout couldn't be taken by storm. Willow wasn't completely trusting. Caleb sensed the ambivalence in her quite clearly. If he brushed over her breasts right now she would flee. The certainty of her wariness was all that was keeping his hands where they were, stroking her back with slow sweeps that belied the passionate blaze of his narrowed eyes.

"Once your hand is in the water and things have settled down," Caleb said, "you begin easing closer to the trout. You do it so slowly the fish accepts your presence as natural. While you ease closer, you have to read the trout. Is it getting restless? Is it worried?"

"How can you tell what the trout is feeling?" Willow asked huskily.

"As my daddy used to say, you have to watch the wee beastie very, very carefully."

Willow smiled at the faint Scots burr in Caleb's voice. Soundlessly, she let out her pent-up breath and relaxed a bit more with each slow stroke of the brush.

"You see," he continued in a deep, lazy voice, "the trout has to think your hand is just a part of the stream, nothing more than a current flowing over her. If you move too quickly, the trout will flee. Then you have to start all over again. Patience is the key. That and the fact that trout just naturally love the feeling of the current stroking over their sleek bodies."

"Do they really?" Willow asked, her voice unusually husky.

"Why else would trout seek out the fastest currents and just hang there, transfixed, with water caressing them from all sides?"

The weight of Willow's hair lifted as Caleb began to brush from beneath once more. He caught up all the silky strands and twisted his wrist slowly, wrapping her hair around it. Frissons of pleasure moved over her when she felt the warmth of the sun on her bare nape.

"Think of it," Caleb whispered against Willow's neck. As he spoke he brushed his cheek very gently over her nape. "Suspended in rushing currents..."

At first, Willow thought it was her own soft brush whispering so delicately over her skin. Then she felt the warm rush of Caleb's breath and knew it was his beard caressing her.

"... all that sensitive skin being stroked all at once ... all over."

Willow's heart began beating so violently she was certain Caleb could hear it. He repeated the exquisite caress again, drawing a low sound from her.

The sound was like a knife slicing through Caleb's self-control. The tiny feminine cry could have been passion. It also could have been fear. He couldn't tell without touching her more intimately, and he was too good a hunter to do that just yet. If it was passion making her tremble, further seduction would only make her more eager. If it was fear, further seduction was in order.

No man ever made a meal of the trout that got away.

When Caleb released Willow's hair and began using the brush again, she was trembling too much to conceal it.

"Aren't the t-tangles gone?" she asked, shivering.

"Not quite, honey. We've got a few to work out yet. Then I'll braid it for you. One of the Army wives taught me a fancy French way to do it."

Willow made no more objections, because she didn't know quite what she should do. Caleb had done nothing that displeased her. Nor had he pressed her for any greater intimacy than that of simply combing her hair. There was another problem, too. If she stood up to leave, she would lose the cover of the blanket over her legs.

And, she admitted silently to herself, she would also lose the sheer pleasure of feeling Caleb's big, gentle hands smoothing over her hair, enjoying the caresses as much as she did.

Sighing, Willow again gave herself to the golden sensation of having his fingers trailing through her hair and tugging very gently, almost lovingly, on the strands. She no longer felt tense, for she was certain if she asked Caleb to stop, he would.

And knowing that, she felt no need to ask.

The uneasiness that had claimed Willow slid away, leaving behind a shimmering kind of peace that expanded with each slow movement of Caleb's hand over her hair. Closing her eyes, smiling, Willow wondered if the trout felt half so good while suspended in a stream's caressing currents.

"So after the trout accepts your hand as part of the water," she murmured, "then what?"

Caleb released his breath in a soundless rush of air. The relaxation of Willow's body told him that her previous trembling had been as much wariness as passion. The knowledge simultaneously chastened him and increased the intensity of his own desire. She was worried, uncertain, almost frightened, yet she could no more refuse his sensual lures than the trout could refuse the intimacy of the caressing currents.

"Then you slowly and carefully stroke the trout," Caleb said in a deep voice, setting aside the brush, "until it's bemused by pleasure."

"Is that possible?" Willow whispered. "Can you feel so much pleasure you forget to be afraid?"

"It's possible." Caleb gathered her hair again and slowly kissed the nape of her neck. "It just takes gentleness and patience."

He released her hair so that it fell over his own shoulder. Softly, slowly, as though he could absorb her through his palms, he ran his hands from her shoulders to her fingertips and back up again, this time stroking the sensitive inner skin of her arms.

"Caleb?" Willow whispered, trembling.

"It's all right, little trout." He lifted her, turning her until she faced him. His thumb skimmed over her lower lip, then pressed sensuously in a touch very like a kiss. "I'll be gentle as sunlight with you."

Luminous hazel eyes watched Caleb. Their beauty fascinated him, color shifting between splinters of blue and green and gold, never the same twice, more beautiful every time he looked.

"Are you afraid of me?" he asked huskily.

Willow's head moved in a slow negative that sent light twisting through her hair and desire twisting through the man who knelt so close to her.

"Some men are rough," Caleb said, lowering his mouth to Willow's, stopping a bare fraction from completing the caress. "I'm not one of them. I've never pushed a woman who didn't want me. I never will. Share a few kisses with me, southern lady. If you decide you don't want me, I'll let you go." He lowered his head a fraction more and whispered against her lips, "Do you believe me?"

The delicate caress of Caleb's breath sent shivers over Willow. "Yes," she sighed.

The sudden blaze of his eyes was unbearable to her. She lowered her lashes, shielding herself from the golden fire. When his lips brushed softly and repeatedly over hers, she trembled. The few times she had been kissed in the past had been nothing like this. The boys had been as eager as puppies, and as clumsy.

There was no clumsiness in Caleb's kiss, nor in the lean hands that held her face so gently she was barely aware of them. The brushing contact of his mouth over hers continued slowly, rhythmically, teaching her to anticipate the next warm pressure of his lips, the next shiver of delight when his mustache would stroke the increasingly sensitive peak of her upper lip.

When the anticipated pleasure didn't come, Willow opened her eyes and whispered Caleb's name.

"Yes?" he asked, forcing himself not to kiss the mouth that trembled so enticingly beneath his lips.

"Would you . . . kiss me again?"

"Those weren't kisses."

"They weren't?"

"No more than a handful of sunlight makes a whole day. Do you want me to kiss you?"

She nodded, sending fragrant, silky hair spilling over his hands.

Smiling, Caleb bent down to Willow once more. His lips brushed over hers again in the caress that had rapidly become addictive to her. Then the tip of his tongue slid between her trembling lips. Her breath came in with a tiny, shocked sound and she stiffened.

"Honey? I thought you wanted me to kiss you."

"I d-do."

Caleb searched Willow's eyes, wondering what was wrong. "Then why did you pull back?"

"I . . . I'm not used to kissing. It's been . . . years."

Black eyelashes swept down, shuttering the leap of passion in Caleb's eyes. The realization that Willow had been so long without a man's touch sent a deep shaft of satisfaction through him. Fancy woman she might be, but she wasn't indiscriminate with her favors.

"That's all right, honey. We'll take it slow and easy, as though it were the first time."

Caleb's long fingers slid more deeply into Willow's hair, seeking the warmth of her scalp, rubbing gently.

She sighed with pleasure. He caught the soft rush of her breath as he bent and began brushing his mouth slowly over hers, increasing the pressure by tiny increments until her lips were gently parted. This time when his tongue touched the peak of her mouth, she didn't withdraw. As he slowly and thoroughly traced the sensitive edge of her lips, she shivered with pleasure at the surprising caress. He repeated the exciting touch again before he dipped inside and skimmed the inner softness of her lips.

"Mint," he whispered against her mouth, smiling. "Share more of it with me."

She hesitated, then whispered, "How?"

"Lick your lips."

Automatically, Willow obeyed. She didn't understand the sudden narrowing of Caleb's golden eyes as he watched.

"Again."

As he spoke, he lowered his head until he could follow the hesitant progress of her tongue with his own. She trembled and her hands gripped the hard strength of his forearms, but she didn't withdraw.

"Mint," Caleb said in a low voice. Talons of passion sank into him, raking him with need. "God, I'll never taste mint again without remembering this. Lick my lips, sweet woman. I love the taste of you."

"Caleb," Willow whispered.

It was all she could say.

"Don't remember how?" he murmured. "It's all right. I don't mind showing you."

Lightly, he ran his tongue over Willow's trembling lips before he eased gently inside, stroking the soft inner surfaces of her smile in a lingering caress that taught Willow just how sensitive her lips could be. Motionless but for the wild beating of her heart, she wished the moment would never end.

And, for a time, it didn't.

"Your turn," Caleb said finally against Willow's mouth.

She made a low sound of disappointment that told Caleb just how much she had enjoyed being caressed by his tongue.

"Something wrong?" he teased.

"I didn't want the kiss to end," Willow admitted softly.

"That still wasn't what I'd call a kiss."

"It wasn't?"

"No." Caleb's mouth eased over Willow's for an instant. His tongue flicked out, tasting her. "But we're getting there, honey. We're getting there. Now lick my lips."

Hesitantly, Willow obeyed. At first she barely touched Caleb. The darting caresses could have been born from shyness or could have been the result of an experienced woman's knowledge of how to tease a hungry man. Motionless, Caleb waited with a hunter's patience, knowing that sensual teasing worked both ways with a girl as passionate as Willow.

And he had no doubt of her passion. The flashes of it she had revealed were a lure greater than her sun-bright hair and sweetly curving body. The passion in her called to him relentlessly, a siren song of ecstasy and release.

After a few quick touches, Willow grew bolder. Her tongue lingered, tracing Caleb's slow, lazy smile. She discovered that his lips were as smooth and warm as satin left in the sun. The rim of his mouth was as sensitive as her own, for she distinctly felt the shudder of response that went through him when she circled his lips with the tip of her tongue. The knowledge that she could affect his powerful body to that extent made something deep within her uncurl and stretch like a cat awakening. Sensations pierced her

as passion rose and prowled through her on unsheathed claws.

Without knowing it, Willow leaned closer to the
seductive strength and heat of the man who held her
face so gently between his hands. Her tongue caressed him again slowly, thoroughly, eased daringly
between his lips, learning the sleek resilience of his
inner surfaces, returning to trace again the intriguing
difference in textures, tasting him and herself at the
same time, the piquant flavor of mint intermingled
with a man's heat.

When Willow finally lifted her head, Caleb's eyes
were closed but for glittering slits of gold.

"Was that a kiss?" she whispered.

"Not quite," he said in a husky voice.

"Did I miss something?"

"Open your mouth and I'll show you."

"What?"

"That's it," he breathed. "Just like that."

With a smooth movement of his head, Caleb bent
and captured Willow's mouth. The tip of his tongue
skimmed the inner surfaces of her lips in a caress that
became more exciting each time she felt it. When his
tongue slid between her teeth and tasted her with a
new intimacy, she stiffened, then let out her breath
raggedly.

"Almost there," Caleb said, his mouth against Willow's. "Open more for me, honey. Let me taste that
sweet, teasing tongue of yours."

For an instant Willow hesitated, but the temptation
of Caleb's mouth overcame her shyness.

"A little more," he coaxed, looking down at her
deep rose lips with a hunger he couldn't conceal. "Just
a little more . . . yes, let me see you, taste you . . ."

Caleb's words ended in a groan as his mouth fitted
seamlessly over Willow's parted lips. The velvet penetration of his tongue was both a shock and a reve-

lation to her. The slow withdrawal followed by an even deeper penetration wrung a tiny cry from the back of her throat.

The sound made every muscle in Caleb's big body tighten. Slowly, thoroughly, he continued seducing Willow's mouth, teasing and caressing her tongue, luring her into his own mouth, showing her how exciting a kiss could be. The languid dance of seduction and retreat continued until Willow knew nothing but the frantic beating of her heart and the taste of Caleb spreading through her like fire after a lifetime of cold. She slid her hands from his forearms to his shoulders and from there around his neck, pulling him closer. His arms came around her in return, gathering her against his chest until her nipples nestled against hard muscle.

Pleasure rippled through Willow as her breasts tightened in a rush, making her tremble. The pressure of Caleb's hands increased, arching her more and more deeply into the embrace, shifting her against his body with sinuous motions. She made another sound of pleasure and instinctively opened her mouth farther, wanting more of his taste, his heat, the sweet friction of his tongue caressing her. The strength of him was an incredible lure, for he fitted perfectly against the untried hungers of her own body.

The kiss changed, deepening with each broken breath Willow took, each helpless movement of her body. Her sensuality seared through Caleb, shaking him. He had never known a woman to respond so completely to a kiss, a fire spiraling hotly upward, burning out of control. Nor had he known what intense passion he himself was capable of, fierce heat and hunger claiming him, shutting out the world.

Caleb forgot the game of seduction and retreat he had been playing, forgot caution, forgot everything but the girl twisting like fire in his arms, burning him alive. His hands kneaded from her back to her hips, ravishing and cherishing her in long strokes. His tongue mated with hers in wild, seething silence and his fingers sought the smoldering center of her.

The clothes Willow wore were no barrier to Caleb's passionate seeking, for her pantelets had no seam between her legs. With a thick sound of satisfaction, Caleb slid his fingers between layers of thin cotton. He caressed the soft, hot nest of hair at the apex of her thighs and then he touched the even softer, hotter flesh beneath.

Willow stiffened in shock. Reflexively she struggled against Caleb, clamping her legs together and grabbing his hand, trying to push him away. It was like trying to push away a mountain.

"No, Caleb, please don't!"

"It's all right," he said thickly. "I won't hurt you. You're so soft, so hot, perfect for me."

His hand flexed and his fingertips slid over her with shocking intimacy.

"No, you said just kisses. Oh God, Caleb, please, please, *no!*"

For an instant Caleb stared down into Willow's frantic face as they both measured the futility of her struggles against his much greater strength. Where he was touching her she was sultry, yielding, weeping passionately for him. The temptation to take her despite her words was so great that he could feel himself yielding, sinking into the silky fire of her body.

Willow sensed the overwhelming power of Caleb's body, looked at his savage gold eyes, and prayed that he was a man of his word.

"Caleb," she whispered. "You promised. Please. Stop."

Abruptly, Caleb pushed away and surged to his feet, furious with Willow for refusing what her body so plainly wanted and equally furious with himself for wanting her so much he had lost his head. For a long, crackling moment he looked at her.

"Fancy lady," he finally said through his teeth, "some day you'll be on your knees in front of me again—*but you won't be begging me to stop.*"

Caleb turned on his heel and walked away, leaving his flat, cold promise to echo in the silence.

9

As Caleb had predicted, rain came again to the mountains. The sound of it was welcomed by Willow, for the silence had become oppressive.

Caleb hadn't been in camp when she had finally gathered her dry clothes and her courage and had returned to the fire. All seven horses still grazed in the meadow, silently telling her that, wherever Caleb had gone, he would be back. The horses couldn't tell Willow when, however. She gathered edible greens in the meadow and tried to forget what it had been like to be kissed by Caleb Black until the world burst into fire and he was the burning center of it.

Forgetting was impossible. Flashes of memory and sensation splintered through Willow at odd moments, making her shiver with pleasure and yearning.

Rain began to fall while the last scarlet flush of evening still stained the western sky. Willow retreated to the shelter and changed into her trail clothes. She sat in the doorway and watched for a figure striding through the twilight rain. No one came. Finally she curled up across the entrance and fell asleep.

When Willow woke up, she was between the blankets and Caleb was sharpening his knife while chunks of meat roasted over the fire. The sky was iridescent with a pink, rain-scrubbed dawn. Though she made neither sound nor motion to tell Caleb that she was awake, somehow he knew. He turned and looked toward the shelter.

"Coffee's hot," he said, looking back at the whetstone in his hands. The big blade of his hunting knife flashed as he stroked it over the stone. "You've got fifteen minutes until we ride. Hear me?"

Willow's heart sank at the cold distance in his voice. "Yes, I hear you."

When she returned from the forest, Caleb handed her a stick with a chunk of roasted meat skewered on it. Saying nothing, he went back to honing his knife. Automatically, she bit into the meat.

"Fresh venison," Willow said, surprised.

Caleb grunted.

"But I didn't hear a shot," she pressed, wondering how far Caleb had walked to hunt deer. Gunfire carried for miles between the stone peaks.

"I didn't use a gun."

"Then how . . . ?" She glared at him. "Caleb Black, you aren't going to tell me you caught a deer the same way you caught those silly trout!"

"Not quite, southern lady." Steel sang huskily against stone. "I used the knife."

"You threw it?"

"That would be a damn fool thing to do, and despite the evidence yesterday, I'm not a damn fool."

Willow flushed and tried to apologize. "Caleb, I didn't mean—"

"I stalked the buck until I was close enough to cut

its throat," Caleb continued, ignoring her attempt to speak.

Her eyes widened in shock. "You what?"

"You heard me."

"But that's impossible."

"You keep telling yourself that while you eat your venison. But don't take too long over it. We've got a high pass to cross before it rains again."

Calmly, Caleb tested the knife's edge against the hair on his forearm. The blade was sharp enough to shave with. Satisfied, he returned the knife to its sheath, reached for the shotgun, and began methodically taking it apart and cleaning it.

Willow ate breakfast while she watched Caleb clean the shotgun, rifle, and six-gun. Clearly he was a man at home with the weapons. He worked quickly yet thoroughly, with an economy of motion that was fascinating to her. The skill, precision, and delicacy of his big hands made memories splinter inside her, showering her with sensations.

"Caleb," she began huskily.

"Southern lady, do you suppose you could be bothered to get off your rump and groom your own horse? The kisses were nice enough, but I'm still not standing in line to be your maid."

Caleb's voice stung like a whip, making Willow angry at herself and at him. "That's good, because I'm not standing in line for your kisses, either."

She dropped her half-eaten venison in the fire and stalked out to the meadow.

Willow made no attempt to speak to Caleb again. They left the meadow in a silence broken only by the creak of saddles and the rhythmic beating of hooves. An hour into the ride, he reined in at the top of a long rise and let the horses blow while he carefully searched the area ahead with his spyglass. Then he took out his journal and filled in more of the blank spaces on the map he had been keeping of their route since Canyon City. When he finished, Willow still hadn't come alongside. Impatiently he turned Trey and rode back to her.

"Come up where you can see," he said.

Willow urged Dove to the top of the ridge. The view from there was breathtaking. Willow sat in rapt silence, looking out over the land.

Before her, a clearing in the forest stretched for miles between widely separated ranges of mountains. Aspen and evergreens defined the creases of the land and the flanks of the mountains, but most of the open area was covered in grass and wild flowers. A cobalt blue river coiled lazily through the park. Beaver ponds shimmered in shades of emerald and blue. Towering above it all, dominating even the untouched magnificence of the sky, were dark, ice-shattered peaks. Snow frosted the higher altitudes, gradually thickening into the glittering white of year-round icefields.

"See over to the left, where those two peaks look like a dog with one chewed ear?" Caleb asked.

"Yes."

"I want you to ride along the left side of the park, heading for the peak that looks chewed. If you see anything you don't like, run for the forest. If anyone comes after you, use the shotgun on whatever is within range."

Willow looked from the mountains to the man who was sitting on his horse only a few feet away from her, yet even the remote peaks seemed closer.

"Where . . ." her voice tore. She cleared her throat and tried again, forcing herself to be calm when the thought of being abandoned made her shake. "After the peak, where do I go?"

The fear in Willow's voice was too raw to hide completely. Caleb heard it and knew what she was thinking.

"I'm not cutting and running," he said coldly. "Maybe that's how the men you're used to act, but I'm not one of your fancy men, am I? When I give my word I keep it."

Looking everywhere but at Caleb's savage yellow eyes, Willow nodded.

"When I was out hunting, I saw signs of a deer kill," Caleb continued in a clipped voice. "Maybe a day old, maybe more. Wolves had been at it, but I could tell it was killed by a man."

"Indians?"

"Renegades," Caleb said flatly. "Some horses were shod and some were barefoot. Only bunch I know like that are Comanchero 'traders'. Raiders is more like it. They have a lot of Taos lightning with them."

"What's that?"

"Tangle-leg, tarantula juice, booze," he explained impatiently.

"Oh, whiskey."

Caleb grunted. "Call it what you will, they had so much of it they left a half-inch in one of the bottles."

Willow frowned. She had heard of Comancheros, and none of what she had heard was good. They were indeed renegades of the worst sort—a mixture of white and Mexican outlaws, tribeless Indians, and halfbreeds who bowed to neither white nor Indian law.

"Don't Comancheros usually stay farther south?" she asked hopefully.

"Only when the Army chases them there. There's damn all worth stealing in the Mexican desert, and a lot of Comancheros looking to steal it. The Army has been too busy fighting rebels to waste any time on Indians and raiders, but now that the War Between the States is over, the Army is back. Things will get real lively before the Utes are herded onto some reservation. While the Army is busy, the Comancheros will scavenge around the edges like the coyotes they are."

Uneasily, Willow looked at the open space stretching before her, mile upon mile of beautiful grassland that must certainly be a natural gathering point for people riding through the rugged mountains, looking for easy passage.

"Pretty, isn't it?" Caleb asked, watching the land with a faint possessiveness. "You can't see it from here, but there's a year-round stream coming down off that rocky ridge. A man could put a house in over there and have a clear field of fire on three sides and country only a mountain goat could cross on the fourth. The water is sweet and plentiful."

The mixture of emotions in Caleb's voice made Willow turn from the land to him. He loved the land. Even as he described its dangers, his voice caressed its possibilities.

"If a man built his house in the right place, he wouldn't have to get shot to fill a bucket." Caleb continued. "Cattle could graze the high country in summer and hay could be cut from the lowlands for the winter. After a few years of hard work, a man would have himself as fine a spread as any Virginia gentleman ever did."

Willow looked at the country again, but this time through Caleb's eyes, seeing places to be ambushed or to hide, places that could be defended and others that would be easily overrun.

"Do you always think like that?" she asked.

"I've wanted to raise cattle for ten years. It's just a matter of finding the right place and getting the money to begin."

"No, I meant do you always think about fighting?"

Caleb gave Willow a sideways look that was part amusement and mostly disbelief. "Southern lady, anyone who wants to survive out here thinks like that.

It's second nature, like remembering landmarks in front *and* in back of you, because everything looks different going than it did coming. But coming or going, this is as pretty a land as God ever made, and wild enough to be home to the devil himself. If a man doesn't keep his eyes peeled and his ears pricked out here, he'll end up stone cold dead."

"Then why do you want to ranch here?"

Caleb's smile offered neither comfort nor real humor. "Back East and in California, other men already own the good land. Not here. Here a man can have as much good land as he's willing to fight for. I'm not a bad fighter, Willow, and not a bad hand with cattle, either."

"Is that what you want—to homestead land here and be a rancher?"

Caleb nodded absently, again watching the country rather than the woman who was watching him.

"You can find some mountains and parks like these a few days south of the San Juan country," he said. "The grazing is fine, but you'd be combing Apaches and Comanches out of your hair every sunrise, and your cattle would have more arrows than a porcupine has quills. Not much pleasure in that, or profit."

For the space of several breaths Willow looked at the land, then back at the hard-faced man who was watching every shift of breeze through forest and grass, his clear gaze sifting each motion to find one made by man. Or rather, men.

Comancheros.

Uneasiness prickled through Willow. She hadn't expected the West to be civilized, but she hadn't really understood what such a total lack of civilization meant, either. In some ways it was rather like being at war. Constant vigilance was needed, for inattention could be fatal. That didn't bother Willow greatly, for she had become used to living on edge during the war. She had become good at listening for sounds, at sleeping lightly, at sliding away into the forest with her mother at the first hint of danger.

But this wide, wild, extraordinary land wasn't like her farm. Here she was dependent on Caleb's strength, fighting skills, and knowledge in a way that frightened her.

He warned me it would be like this, Willow told herself. *He told me in plain English.*

She shivered as the echoes of a past conversation whispered through her mind once more. *Where I'm taking you there's no law at all. Out in those mountains a man takes care of himself because no one else will do it for him.*

And a woman? What does she do?

A woman finds a man tough enough to protect her and the kids she'll bear him.

It seemed far more than a handful of days since Willow had heard and disregarded Caleb's warning, thinking that whatever lay ahead couldn't be more dangerous than the war she had already survived. It seemed a lifetime since she had ridden out of Denver's rude comforts into a land that grew more wild with each westward step.

Yet, even knowing that, she wouldn't have traded one of those steps for the safety of the East she had left. Despite the danger, there was something in the wild horizons of the Rockies that lifted her heart and made her soul sing.

Willow closed her eyes and absorbed the small sounds of the land around her. One of the horses snorted and stamped. A saddle creaked as Caleb shifted his weight. A bird called off in the meadow. There was no smell of smoke, of sawn lumber, of turned earth. The breeze carried scents untainted by man, becoming a river of life rushing softly around her, caressing her.

"Damn it, Willow, I said I would be back. Don't you believe me?"

Startled, she opened her eyes. "Of course I believe you."

"Then what's wrong?"

"Nothing," she said, smiling almost sadly. "Not the way you mean. It's just that . . ." Her voice faded. "Suddenly I realized that I love this clean, wild land, even if it isn't very safe." She smiled with lips that wanted to tremble. "The idea takes a little getting used to."

Caleb studied Willow with a sudden, fierce intensity, but said only, "If you wanted to be safe, you should have stayed home."

"Yes," she whispered. "I know. Don't worry, Caleb. Whatever happens is on my head, not yours. I might not have known what I was coming to, but I knew what I was leaving behind."

Caleb waited.

Willow said nothing more. She simply looked out over the land and measured the bittersweet pleasure of having realized part of her dream of finding a new home, only to discover that the land might not be possible for a woman living alone. It wasn't like the more gently made country of her childhood. Yet the gentle land had been ravaged beyond her ability to bring it back.

"What are you thinking?" Caleb asked quietly.

"I was tired of the wounded, worn land," Willow said slowly. "I wanted to see the Mississippi rolling broad-shouldered down to an unknown ocean. I wanted to see a treeless plain stretching from horizon to horizon with buffalo a great brown river winding through shoulder-high grass. I wanted to see the Rockies thrown like a magnificent stone gauntlet across the plains."

Willow's voice faded as she thought of other things she had wanted, to see a face that was kin to her or at least not enemy, to see her favorite brother, to laugh with him, to remember a time when she wasn't alone. She wanted . . . She shook her head slowly, for she wanted things that had no words, simply a longing as deep as her soul and as endless as night.

Slowly, Willow let out her breath and accepted that, whatever happened, she was more alive here than she would have been in West Virginia. Nothing had ever called to her in quite the way the mountain landscape did, except the man who rode beside her. Like the mountain, Caleb was hard, unexpected, often baffling. And like the mountains, being with him offered moments of warmth and wild beauty. She turned and smiled gently at him.

"Go do what you must," Willow said softly. "I'm all right now."

Caleb hesitated before he pulled a big pocket watch from his pants and handed it to Willow. "Give me fifteen minutes head start. Then come on at a smart trot."

Willow's fingers tightened around the watch. The metal was smooth, burnished, and radiated the heat of Caleb's body into her cold hand. Memories exploded in her, memories of being kissed, of his beard brushing against her sensitive skin, of his powerful body molded to hers, of his hand between her legs, shocking and caressing her in the same searing instant. Sensations rippled through her, making her tremble.

To have come so close with both the land and the man, and then to know how easily both could be lost . . . Willow bit her lip and bowed her head.

"Don't worry," Caleb said, moved despite himself by Willow's fear and her fight against giving in to it. "I won't be far off. If you hear gunfire, go to ground and wait for me to find you."

"What if—what if you don't?"

"I will. I didn't live this long to be killed by some no-account, drunken Comanchero."

Caleb tugged his hat down and lifted the reins. His big horse moved off at a canter, leaving Willow alone. Motionless, she watched while Caleb cast for sign along the left side of the clearing, working back and forth until he vanished in a depression in the wide, gently rolling park. He reappeared a few minutes later, only to drop from sight once more.

When the fifteen minutes were up, Willow drew the shotgun from its scabbard, laid the weapon across her lap, and started down the lefthand side of the basin at a hard trot. The horses strung out behind her, prodded by Ishmael to keep the pace.

It was two hours before Caleb rejoined Willow and rode by her side through the grass at the edge of the forest. The land was still open, still spacious, a wide, wide river of grass flowing between lofty dams of stone.

"See anything?" she asked.

"Tracks," he said succinctly. "Four horses. One shod. They're either hunting deer, hunting us, or hunting someone else."

"How can you tell?"

"They were doing the same thing I was doing—casting around for sign."

"Where are they now?"

"They split two and two. One set of tracks cut to the left behind us. The other cut off to the right along a branch of the river. There's a good pass at the head of that branch. If it weren't for those two gunnies, I'd have brought us in that way. It's closer to where we're going. As it is, we'll go over the divide in a few days."

"The Great Divide?" Willow asked breathlessly.

Caleb smiled at her excitement. "Comancheros

crawling all over and you hardly turn a hair, but you get excited over one more mountain pass."

"All my life the rivers have gone to the Atlantic Ocean. To see water that's going to the Pacific . . ." Willow laughed with delight. "I know it's foolish, but I can't help it. I grew up with letters from my brothers telling me about China, where a whole city is made of dhows tied together in the harbor, and the Sandwich Isles, where the waves are bigger than the barn before the rebels burned it, and Australia, where there's an ocean reef bigger than the Thirteen Colonies put together, and all I ever saw was West Virginia sunrises, chickens scratching in the kitchen garden, and a haze over the hills."

Caleb grinned, intrigued by Willow's excitement. "Sounds like wanderlust runs in your family. No wonder you had the gumption to come looking for your fancy man when he wrote for you."

"I'd have come anyway," Willow admitted. "I couldn't bear home anymore. There was nothing left but memories of a better time."

Willow fell silent after that. Caleb didn't try to lure her into more conversation. It was safer that way, both for his alertness and for keeping the distance he knew was necessary between himself and Reno's woman. It was far too easy to like Willow, to enjoy her laughter and her silences, to remember what it had been like to feel her body soften and turn to warm, sweet honey in his arms.

Fancy woman. That's all she is. Sweet Jesus, why can't I remember that when I look at her? Why is she under my skin and in my blood?

The answer was as simple and as indelible as the instant his hand had slid between thin layers of cotton and felt the sultry woman heat of her licking over his fingertips. He had never had a woman want him that much, that fast, that hot. The memory of it hardened him in a bittersweet rush, leaving him achingly aware of just how much a man he could be with a woman like Willow Moran.

Caleb wrenched his attention from what he couldn't have to the huge mountain park spreading away on three sides. From time to time he slowed the pace to a walk and checked their position against the peaks. Once he took a compass, a pencil, and his father's frayed, leatherbound journal from his saddlebags. After a few minutes he drew out his own journal. He compared the compass readings with the lines he had written three years ago, compared his drawing with the peaks to the left, and nodded. Although he had not ridden this side of the peaks before, he knew where he was.

"Where are we headed?" Willow asked, coming alongside.

It was the first word either of them had spoken in several hours. Neither one had found the silence uncomfortable. They were accustomed to their own company.

"You tell me," Caleb said dryly. "The San Juans are south and west of us. We could go pretty much straight south between ranges for a few days and cut across just north of San Luis peak. Or we could go over the divide west of here and then go south. Or we could do a little of both."

"Which is quicker?"

He shrugged. "Going south might be easier but would take longer. Going west would be easy for a day, then there's a long climb over the divide and some zigzagging on the other side. Depends on whether your man really is on one of the Gunnison's tributaries or if maybe he's on the Animas or the Dolores or the San Miguel or any of ten other rivers worth naming."

Willow hesitated. "The Gunnison is the only river

Matt mentioned, but I'm not sure he's on a direct tributary. He did say there's a hot spring and a creek and a high, tiny valley surrounded by mountain peaks except for a really steep climb to the entrance."

Caleb made a sound of disgust. "You've just described the whole damned San Juan region. Mountains and hot springs. Hell, there are hot springs all around us now and we're not even there yet."

"What about the valley?"

"It's called a hanging valley and the Rockies are full of them."

"A hanging valley?" she asked, frowning. "What's that?"

"See that ridge off to the right, on the same line as the beaver pond?"

"Yes."

"Look straight up from there."

After a minute Willow said, "All I can see is a cascade jumping down the mountain."

"That's it. Hanging valleys are hidden, but the creeks that drain them aren't."

"I don't understand."

Caleb frowned. "It's like someone broke a valley in half or quarters, set each piece like a stairstep up the mountainside, and then strung them together with a creek. Since there's no exit or entrance to the valleys but a waterfall or a steep cascade, and they overhang the park below, they're called hanging valleys. Good places to graze cattle in the summer, if you can find a way to get cows into them. Hell in the winter, though. Snow comes early, piles deep, and stays late."

Willow thought about it, then shook her head. "That doesn't sound like Matt. He hated cold weather."

"Is he a farmer?"

"If he were, he would have stayed in West Virginia," Willow said dryly. "We—that is, the Moran family—owned several big farms before the war."

"Is he a cattleman?"

She shook her head.

"Trapper?"

She shook her head again.

Caleb grunted. "I hear there's gold in some of those high creeks."

Willow flinched.

"God above," Caleb said in disgust. "I should have known. Your fancy man is whoring after gold."

She said nothing.

"Well, that explains it," he muttered.

"What?"

"Why he left you," Caleb said succinctly. "A man obsessed by yellow metal doesn't give a damn for anything else—not wife, not child, nothing but the golden bitch."

And least of all would he care for an innocent girl who gave her love and her body with never a thought for the future, Caleb thought grimly. *Poor little Rebecca. She never had a chance.*

"Matt isn't like that," Willow said.

"Then why did he leave you alone so long that you forgot how to kiss a man? He should have come and gotten you when the war started," Caleb said flatly, "and you know it as well as I do."

There were other thoughts as well, ones he didn't dare speak aloud. *If Reno had been with Willow during the war, he wouldn't have been in New Mexico, seducing my sister. He would have had his own fancy lady to take care of his lusts.*

The condemnation in Caleb's face was clear to Willow. She flushed, but said nothing. If she had been Matt's wife, what Caleb said would have been true. But she was only Matt's sister. Like his brothers, Matt had been gone more than ten years with just a few brief visits in between travels. He had no ties to North or South. He was owned by his love of the uninhabited West and the gold that winked like captured sunlight in wild mountain streams.

Silence returned until Caleb reined in abruptly, brought the spyglass to his eye, and swore viciously under his breath. He scanned the countryside all around but saw no other men. The two he had spotted cantered toward him openly, making no attempt to conceal their presence.

"What is it?" Willow asked after a moment.

"Comancheros. Two of them. Get out the shotgun. Don't make a fuss about it, but keep it pointed between the two men. If they split up, you keep track of the one on the left. If he goes for a gun, give him both barrels and be quick about it. Hear me?"

"Yes," Willow said tightly. "But I—I've never shot a man."

Caleb's smile was like a knife sliding from its sheath. "Don't worry, southern lady. These aren't men. They're coyotes jumping around on their crooked hind legs."

He pulled the rifle from its saddle scabbard, slipped the thong from his six-shooter, and waited. Nothing else was said while they watched the riders grow from pea-sized dots to life size. Willow thought the Comancheros were going to gallop right over them, but at the last minute they reined in so sharply that their ponies sat hard on their hocks.

The ponies were small, unshod, and thin as slats. Despite that, they weren't sweating or breathing hard from their long gallop through the meadow. Like the horses, the men were small, wiry, tough, and of mixed blood. The men were also dirty, edgy, and heavily armed. The man on the right was blond and blue-eyed beneath months of grime. The man on the left was *mestizo*.

From twenty feet away, the blue-eyed man called out, "*Ola*, Man from Yuma."

"I see you, Nine Fingers," Caleb said. "You're a long way from where we last met."

The Comanchero smiled, revealing one tooth of gold above and one black gap below. He looked at Willow. The blunt lust in his eyes made her skin cold.

"How much for her?" Nine Fingers asked.

"She's not for sale."

"I'll give you a fat poke of gold."

"No."

Nine Fingers gave Willow another long appraisal. "Then how about I just rent her for a time?"

Caleb shifted slightly in the saddle. When Nine Fingers looked away from Willow, there was a six-shooter in Caleb's right hand and a rifle in his left. At this range, the pistol was the more deadly of the two weapons.

"You're a mite jumpy," Nine Fingers said.

"Yes."

Caleb's voice was mild despite the rage tightening his gut. No woman, even one who was no better than she had to be, deserved what was in Nine Fingers' pale blue eyes. The thought of the Comanchero even looking at Willow, much less touching her with his filthy hands, made Caleb's finger tighten on the six-gun's trigger.

"Well, I guess I would be edgy, too, was I riding shotgun on a prime piece of woman-flesh and seven prime pieces of horseflesh."

The other Comanchero spoke abruptly to Caleb. "You want Reno? I see him. I take you."

"No thanks. I'm on another job right now."

Nine Fingers laughed gutturally and said something to his friend about the Man from Yuma riding a yellow-haired pony harder and longer than a white-eyes fleeing Comancheros.

Caleb looked quickly at Willow, wondering if she understood the mixture of coarse Spanish and Indian words. Her expression hadn't changed.

"Seeing as how we're *amigos*, how about we ride that yellow pony for you," offered Nine Fingers in English, spurring his horse closer as he spoke. "Then you'll have time to chase Reno."

The sound of the revolver being cocked was startlingly clear. Nine Fingers yanked back on the reins. The other Comanchero spoke quickly.

"You no want shoot, Yuma man. Bad men near. Ver' bad. Hear gun and come hell-running you bet."

"That won't be your problem," Caleb said, looking at the two Comancheros. "You'll be dead before the first echo comes back from the mountain."

Nine Fingers smiled. "Short Dog is telling you the truth. Jed Slater is looking for you. He is purely pissed about the moniker you hung on his little brother. Kid Coyote." Nine Fingers laughed with real amusement. "Old Jed promised to send you to Hell."

Caleb shrugged. "He isn't the first."

"He's talking about a big bounty on your scalp."

"Coyotes talk a lot, too."

Nine Fingers kept talking. "Not like this. Every bounty hunter between here and the Sangre de Cristos will come a helling, hoping to lift your scalp. Four hundred Yankee dollars for the man that kills you. A thousand Yankee dollars for the man who brings you to Jed alive."

"You're welcome to try," Caleb said.

"Much money," Short Dog said.

"Much trouble," Caleb retorted. "Dead men spend no dollars."

Nine Fingers laughed deeply and looked at his companion. "*Es muy hombre, no?*"

Short Dog grunted and watched the barrel of the shotgun, which Willow had kept pointed between the two Comancheros. He urged his horse a few steps to the side. The shotgun barrel followed him.

"If Short Dog moves his hands, shoot him," Caleb said to Willow without looking away from Nine Fingers.

She said nothing. She simply cocked the shotgun with a quick motion that spoke of familiarity. The Comancheros traded glances.

"Now don't get your water hot," Nine Fingers said, watching Willow intently. "We're not hunting any tombstones. But think on this, little lady. If you come with us real easy like, we'll be real easy like with you. If you wait until your man's killed to be good to us, we won't be listening to your begging. We'll take you, strip you naked, and when we get tired of you we'll sell you to the highest bidder between here and Sonora."

Willow never looked away from Short Dog's hands.

Nine Fingers smiled reluctantly. "Takes orders good, don't she? I like that in a whore."

"Ride or die," Caleb said flatly.

"*Adios.*"

"The Comancheros spun their ponies on their hocks and galloped off in the direction they had come—the same direction Caleb and Willow had to go in order to cross over the Great Divide and pick up the trail into San Juan country.

Caleb watched until the Comancheros angled across to the righthand margin of the clearing and vanished into a fold in the rolling land. As he holstered his six-gun and put the thong in place, the sound of three, closely spaced pistol shots echoed back through the park. Caleb said a savage word under his breath and waited, listening intently. The distant, flat echo of triple rifle shots came from the right. Instants later, from behind and to the right, came the faint sound of more gunfire.

"That tears it," Caleb said. "Put the shotgun away and get ready to ride like the hounds of Hell are coming after us—because they will be as soon as Nine Fingers meets up with his friends."

10

For several miles Caleb kept the pace at a hard gallop, taking advantage of what cover the land provided and keeping a watch on the gently rolling parkland to the right. They splashed through several small and three large streams. At the fourth big stream he reined in, checked the compass, and turned west to follow the stream back to its source in the towering mountains.

Despite the new direction, for a time the land itself remained unchanged. There were still grassy, gently rolling rises, occasional pine and aspen groves, and snow-shrouded peaks in the distance. Gradually, it became clear that the stream Caleb had chosen to follow cut deeply into the mountain range. Forested mountains began to close in on both sides. In some places the width of the park shrank to less than a mile. At times the forest swept down in long ragged fringes that almost met, choking the meadow grasses.

Caleb slowed to a fast canter, a pace he held even after sweat darkened the horses' coats and lather began to appear in thin white streaks on shoulder and flank. The Montana horses were breathing deeply but easily. The Arabians found the pace harder to maintain. Dove began breathing audibly, great gulps of air that flared her nostrils as big as fists. Yet she kept running her heart out, spurred on by nothing more than Willow's voice talking softly in her ear, praising her.

After what seemed an eternity to Willow, Caleb allowed the horses to drop back to a walk. It wasn't kindness that forced the change, but necessity. The mountains were closing in once more and the land was rising so steeply beneath the horses' feet that anything more than a walk would be foolish unless the alternative was immediate death. It hadn't come to that yet, but he was betting it would.

"Get off," Caleb said, dismounting as he spoke. "We'll swap horses. Take a walk in the bushes if you need to. You won't get another chance until full dark."

Willow was more concerned with her tired mare than with herself. No sooner were Willow's feet on the ground than she yanked at the cinch and stripped off the saddle so that Dove could breathe more easily.

Caleb looked up, saw that Willow had taken care of Dove, and went to Deuce.

"Put your saddle on Ishmael," he said when she headed toward Penny, lugging the heavy saddle. "We've got a harder ride ahead of us than behind us."

Willow stopped and stared at Caleb in disbelief. "Don't you think we lost them?"

"No. I chose the closest pass out of that basin I know, but they're sure to know about it, too. I can't guarantee we'll get over the divide before they catch up. So all we can do is run and keep running. But your horses still aren't used to the altitude. The Comanchero horses are."

"We've been heading south, haven't we?"

Caleb nodded.

"The Comancheros rode south," she said.

"They sure did."

"What if we run into them before we even turn off for the pass?"

"Then we'll be flat out of luck."

Willow bit her lip. "But if we beat them to the pass trail, we'll be all right?"

"Unless they get there first."

"But how would they know we took a particular trail unless they came all the way back here and tracked us?"

"It's the only decent pass for sixty miles in any direction," Caleb said. "Even a drunken Comanchero can figure out where we're going to be. Up this creek about ten miles there's a place where another route comes in from the south and joins with the pass trail. We've got to beat them to that fork."

For an instant Willow closed her eyes. *Ten miles.* Her horses couldn't run for ten more miles. The Arabians were doing worse than Caleb's mounts even though they weren't carrying as much weight.

Caleb jerked the pack saddle off Deuce and put on the riding saddle, talking while he worked. "Problem is, if we run much more, we'll start losing the mares. Ishmael is stronger, so you'll ride him. If the mares can't keep up, they're on their own." Caleb looked at Willow, pinning her with the intensity of his golden eyes. "Tell me now, Willow. If there's no other way, which would you rather be—dead or with the Comancheros?"

Willow remembered Nine Fingers' pale blue eyes watching her. Bile rose in her throat.

"Dead," she said without hesitation.

For a long moment Caleb looked at her. She returned the look unflinchingly.

"So be it," Caleb said in a low voice. "You would

be dead pretty quick anyway. White women don't last more than a few months with Comancheros, especially blondes. Too many men lust after yellow hair. But the choice had to be yours."

Willow turned away, saying nothing. There was really nothing she could say.

When she came back from the forest, the horses were saddled. Dove was still breathing hard, but the sweat was drying on her body. Caleb was standing by Ishmael, waiting to help Willow mount.

"That's not necessary anymore," she said. "I can get on by myself."

"I know."

Caleb held out his hands, forming a stirrup for her. She stepped into it and was lifted into the saddle. For just a moment she felt his palm caress her calf gently, but the touch was so brief, and he turned away so quickly, she wondered if she had imagined it. His face had looked so grim.

"Caleb?"

He turned back toward her.

"No matter what happens," Willow said in a rush, "don't blame yourself. You warned me in Denver that my Arabians couldn't take the pace. You were right."

One long step brought Caleb back to Willow's side. "Come here," he said huskily.

When she bent down, his long fingers caught her face, held her for the space of a breath, and then he took her mouth in a swift, fierce kiss that ended before she could respond.

"Your horses have done just fine. In fact, they've been one hell of a surprise," Caleb said against Willow's lips. "And so have you. Stay right behind me, honey. Those are grand mares, but they aren't worth dying for."

Before Willow could say anything, Caleb released her and swung into the saddle. He lifted the reins and the big animal leaped into a canter. To Caleb's surprise, even without Ishmael's prodding, the mares clung like burrs to the stallion's flanks, running free as mustangs. If they lagged, Willow spoke to them and was answered by a flick of ears and a faster pace.

Many times in the next ten miles Caleb heard Willow calling to her Arabians and saw the mares respond, working harder to keep the punishing pace. As the miles raced by, he found himself praying that the mares wouldn't falter, for he finally understood why Willow had refused to leave them behind. There was a bond between Willow and the Arabians that couldn't be described. They would run themselves to death for her, with never a whip or a spur laid against their silky hides.

"Almost there," Caleb said, turning in the saddle until he could look at Willow. "See those trees? All we have to do is—"

Caleb's words ended abruptly as rifle fire shattered the mountain silence. Deuce stumbled and went down. Caleb grabbed his rifle and kicked free of the stirrups. Three more shots came in rapid succession, then it was quiet again but for the thunder of hooves as the Arabians swept by. Caleb dove behind a fallen tree as a fourth shot rang out.

Willow hauled hard on the reins, spinning Ishmael around so tightly that great chunks of earth flew from beneath his hooves. There was no time for thought, no time for planning, nothing but the knowledge that Caleb was afoot in a place where to be afoot was to die. She bent low over Ishmael's lathered neck and sent him back down the trail to Caleb, asking the stallion for everything he had. As the Arabian swept past the log, Willow called out to Caleb.

"Get on behind me!"

Rifle in his right hand, Caleb came up off the ground like a mountain cat. As Ishmael surged past,

Caleb grabbed the saddle horn with his free hand and leaped on behind Willow. Despite the much greater burden, the stallion hit his full pace within three long strides.

Willow expected bullets to shower around them, but nothing came except a drumroll of hooves as Ishmael raced past the confused mares, sweeping them up in his wake. Trey appeared alongside, running hard. When Caleb looked back, Deuce was on his feet again and running raggedly after his trail mate.

A rifle went off very close, making Willow cringe in the instant before she realized it was Caleb firing.

"Cut right!" he yelled.

Instantly, Willow reined the stallion hard to the right. No sooner had the horse set off on the new course than shots sizzled past, kicking up dirt where Ishmael would have been had he not been turned aside.

"Get to the top of that rise before they can reload!" shouted Caleb.

Bending low over Ishmael's lathered neck, Willow called to her straining stallion. He answered with a burst of speed despite the steepness of the way and the weight of two riders.

"I'll drop off at the top in the boulders," Caleb said. "Take the horses on into the trees. Hear me?"

"Yes," she said loudly.

"Just another hundred yards," Caleb said under his breath, looking at a clump of boulders that marked the end of the rise. "Run, you red demon."

Ishmael's steel-shod hooves dug into the slope, tearing out clots of earth as the stallion attacked the steep mountainside. By the time Ishmael surged over the top, the horse's breath was coming in labored groans.

Caleb dropped off and landed running, rifle in hand. He took cover among the boulders as a bullet whined off granite four feet away. Three more shots were fired, but none of the slugs came close enough for Caleb to hear where they hit.

"Too eager, boys," he muttered. "You have to take your time and aim. Especially when all you have are single-shot rifles."

Following his own advice, Caleb chose his target carefully from among the seven that were offered. An instant after he squeezed the trigger, he was rewarded by a scream of surprise and pain from down the slope as a Comanchero threw up his hands and fell from his horse. The other six scattered to either side, seeking cover in the meadow. Caleb stood up and fired shot after shot, knowing he would never have a better chance of shortening the odds.

But the range was five hundred yards and increasing with every second. In the end Caleb managed to hit only two more men before he had to take cover again himself. As he dropped behind the boulders he mentally counted the bullets left in the rifle. Five. He would have to let the remaining Comancheros get in damned close and then finish them off with the pistol. At least he could reload that weapon with bullets from his belt. And when he ran out of bullets for the six-gun, there was always his knife.

Caleb smiled sourly at his own thoughts. The raiders were greedy and over-eager, but not totally stupid. They wouldn't make things easy for him. Either they would wait until dark and rush him, or they would spread out and come in from all sides at once. They might easily have reinforcements on the way. Numbers, time, and geography were on the raiders' side. They had taken cover smack across the route to the only pass around.

Deuce's ringing whinny came up the slope and was answered by Trey. Like the Arabians, the Montana horses had been raised together. They would stick close to each other if they could. Trotting raggedly, Deuce struggled up the slope despite the bullet wound gleaming redly across his chest.

Caleb thought longingly of the extra ammunition tucked into the saddlebags that Deuce carried. He considered making an attempt to get into them, but discarded the idea. If he whistled the horse over, the raiders would guess he was going after more ammunition or weapons and would shoot Deuce dead before the horse got close. If he tried to get to Deuce, Caleb would be shot dead. The horse was a hundred yards wide of the boulders and there was nothing but grass for cover in between.

Caleb watched Deuce vanish into the trees, then turned his attention back to the raiders. Nothing was moving. The men had gone to ground in whatever cover they could find. Methodically, Caleb began checking the field of fire on all sides, sighting on possible bits of cover and gauging the range.

When Deuce limped up to his trail mate, Willow grabbed the reins and spoke soothingly to the frightened animal. As soon as Deuce would allow it, she unfastened the saddlebags, knowing that was where Caleb kept his spare ammunition. She wanted to loosen the cinch to ease Deuce's breathing, but was afraid to. They might have to mount up and ride with no warning.

Deuce was too edgy to allow Willow close to his chest, but she saw enough. The wound was shallow, as much a burn as a gouge. It was the swelling on the horse's left foreleg that spelled trouble. She doubted that Deuce would be able to carry a rider at all, much less one of Caleb's size.

Nor could the mares carry Caleb. Not right away. They were still breathing hard, trembling, all but run into the ground. Ishmael was hard used. So was Trey, but of them all, Trey was in the best shape.

Don't think about the horses, Willow told herself grimly. *You can't do anything for them now. What you can do is get these cartridges to Caleb.*

As Willow dug quickly through the heavy saddlebags, she found five boxes of ammunition. Two contained shotgun shells. Three contained cartridges, but one of the boxes had a different size of ammunition than the other two. She didn't know which would go with the rifle and which with Caleb's pistol. There was also the spyglass, a compass, and other miscellaneous personal items.

In the end Willow decided to take everything, not knowing what might be useful to Caleb. She grabbed the saddlebags, dragged them into place on her shoulder, picked up the shotgun, and walked cautiously to the edge of the trees. Caleb was a hundred feet away from her at almost the same elevation, separated from her by a low runoff channel. The distance was too great for her to throw a box of ammunition, much less the saddlebags. But if she crawled and was quick about it, she shouldn't be visible from below for more than a few seconds.

"Caleb," Willow called softly, "I'm coming in behind you."

He spun around, ready to tell her to do no such fool thing.

It was too late. She was on her hands and knees already, crawling toward him with no more cover around her than the low ditch could provide.

Swiftly, Caleb turned back and began firing at places where raiders had gone to ground, hoping to pin them down while Willow crossed the trough. Realizing what he was doing, Willow scrambled to her feet and raced toward the rocks. Just as she threw herself down beside Caleb, bullets began whining off the nearby boulders.

"You little fool!" Caleb said savagely. "You could have been killed!"

"I—" The need to breathe shut off Willow's words. Panting from a mixture of altitude, exertion, and fear, she fought for oxygen.

Caleb took the short-barrelled shotgun from Willow's hands, pointed it downslope, and waited for movement. When it came, he let go with both barrels. He didn't expect to kill anyone at that range, but he sure could raise welts on their hides with double-aught buckshot. At the very least, the Comancheros wouldn't stick their heads up for a minute or two.

When Caleb reached into the saddlebag for more shotgun shells, the correct box was thrust into his hands. He reloaded quickly, fired, reloaded, and glanced back to see how Willow was doing. She had two other boxes of ammunition out and opened, ready to be used, and was puzzling over how to reload his rifle. Though she tried to conceal it from him, her hands trembled when she wasn't actually using them.

"I'll do that," Caleb said. "Take the shotgun and sit with your back to me. If you see anyone sneaking up, don't waste time telling me about it. Just shoot."

Willow nodded and took the shotgun, relieved to have something to do with her hands. She sat cross-legged and looked from side to side, hoping she wouldn't see a man creeping up on them.

They aren't men. They're coyotes jumping around on their crooked hind legs.

Silently, Willow repeated Caleb's grim reassurance and watched for movement. At the back of her mind she counted the shells Caleb was loading into his rifle with a speed that spoke of great familiarity.

"You *are* a one-man army," she said finally.

"You're not half as surprised as those raiders were," Caleb said, smiling wolfishly. "They were sure they had me after I fired that one lone shot. It won't last, though. Sooner or later they'll find someone to sell them repeating rifles. Then the civilized folks will be in a hell of a mess."

Rifle fully loaded once more, Caleb shifted position until he could peer through a notch between two boulders. The raiders' wiry, ugly little ponies were scattered across the meadow, feeding eagerly, indifferent to the booming of guns around them.

"How bad is Deuce?" Caleb asked.

"He's burned across the chest. His left foreleg is swelling, probably strained when he fell. I don't think he'll be able to take a rider very far."

"You'd be surprised, honey. Is he bleeding much?"

"No."

"Any other horses hurt?"

"The mares are done," Willow said, trying to keep her voice as unemotional as Caleb's. "They'll follow as long as they can, but . . ."

A big hand squeezed Willow's shoulder gently. "What about Ishmael?"

"He's tired, but still strong enough to take me anywhere I tell him to go."

"That's one game stud," Caleb said admiringly. "Makes me understand why Wolfe is so set on mustangs."

"What do you mean?"

"Mustangs are descended from the Spanish horses, which came from Arabian stock. Don't judge all mustangs by those ponies out there. They're as mongrel as their riders. Tough, though. Damned tough. Give them a hatful of hay and less water and they'll go a hundred miles a day for weeks at a time."

While Caleb spoke, he reached into one of the saddlebags and came out with the spyglass. Methodically, he began covering the ground in front of him, quartering from side to side. The glass brought up each blade of grass, each shift from sun to shade, each suspicious bit of color or movement. Caleb looked up from the glass, then through it, mentally marking the spot of every raider the spyglass picked out.

The glass confirmed what Caleb had already suspected. The Comancheros were scattered out in such a way that there was little or no chance of sneaking through them to the pass trail—especially with seven tired horses.

Caleb turned and began studying the land behind him through the spyglass, seeking anything that looked like a possible route out or enemies sneaking up. He saw nothing human moving, even after several very careful sweeps. Yet something kept nagging at his mind, something about the shape of the land itself.

"Dad's journal," he whispered suddenly.

"What?"

"Switch places with me."

Willow scrambled around Caleb.

"If something starts moving downslope, shoot," he said.

While Willow kept an eye on the raiders, Caleb pulled his father's journal out of the saddlebags and flipped through the pages quickly. He studied first one page, then a second, then the first again, flipping back and forth and checking the peaks rising behind the boulders.

"There's another pass," Caleb said in a low voice, reading quickly. "It's a righteous bastard, eleven thousand feet and then some, but it can be climbed by a horse."

"Do the Comancheros know about it?"

"Doubt it. According to Dad, no one had used the route for a long time when he saw it. It's from the time before Indians had horses, when going twenty miles out of the way for an easier pass meant losing a lot of travel time."

The silence was destroyed by a single shot that whined off the rocks shielding them. Despite herself, Willow flinched and made a low sound.

"It's all right," Caleb said, setting aside the journal and sighting down the barrel of his rifle. "They just want to see if we're still awake up here."

The rifle leaped and a crack of sound made Willow flinch. Even before the echo reverberated, Caleb shot again and again, pouring bullets into the areas where he had seen raiders through the spyglass. He fed shells into the rifle in the pauses between shots, mentally thanking Winchester's cleverness in making a weapon that could be reloaded almost as fast as it could be fired.

Several choked screams told Caleb that his aim had been good. He kept firing until one of the raiders broke and ran for better cover. Carefully, Caleb shot once more. The runner took a step and fell face down. He didn't move again. Two shots came in return, but only two. The remaining Comancheros weren't in any hurry to collect the bounty on Caleb's scalp.

Sound cracked through the area, making Willow flinch in the instant before she realized that it was thunder rather than rifle fire rolling down the mountainside. Before she could take another breath, a barrage of water pelted down, announcing the beginning of the afternoon thunderstorms. Within minutes it was raining so hard that she couldn't see more than a hundred feet in any direction.

"Take the shotgun and run for the horses," Caleb said as he fired downslope once more, hoping to discourage the Comancheros from coming up the slope under the cover of rain.

"What about you?"

"*Run,*" he commanded.

Willow ran.

Caleb's shots rang out behind her, yet by the time Willow saw the horses, he had caught up and was running right beside her.

"Watch for raiders," Caleb said curtly.

While Willow watched their backtrail, Caleb yanked the riding saddle off Deuce, relieving the injured horse's burden. For a moment he considered using one of the mares as a pack animal, but a single look at their hanging heads and the lather dissolving on their coats beneath the driving rain told Caleb the mares were worse off than Deuce. Working quickly, he transferred as much equipment as he could to the saddlebags and bedrolls tied on behind the riding saddles. When he was finished, Deuce was carrying less than thirty pounds, none of it vital for their survival.

Caleb pulled on his shearling jacket and lifted Willow into Ishmael's saddle.

"It will be a hard, steady climb," he said in a low voice. "Stick with it even if Deuce and the mares don't. Promise me, Willow."

Biting her lower lip, Willow nodded.

Caleb reached up and brushed her cheek with his fingertips, leaving a trail of warmth in the cold rain. Then he swung up on Trey's back.

"I'm not going to stop short of the summit," he said. "We need every bit of daylight to get over that pass."

Even as Willow started to say something, Caleb merged with the rain and vanished. The horses filed out in the driving rain, with Deuce limping in the rear.

After the first thirty minutes, Willow stopped listening for Comancheros and looking over her shoulder every few minutes. After the first hour, she stopped checking to see that the Arabians were following. They were keeping up well enough, but Willow didn't know how much longer the mares would be able to go on. Despite the slow pace, they were breathing as though they had been trotting for hours. True to Caleb's prediction, Deuce kept on coming despite his game leg, walking quickly enough to overtake the slowest mare.

They climbed steadily, relentlessly, until Willow couldn't remember a time when the land hadn't tilted steeply in front of her. Willow alternated between a headache and a lightheadedness that made her fear for her health. Beneath heavy curtains of rain, the dark shape of spruce trees appeared more frequently among pines and aspen. Every few minutes she peered through the sheets of water to where Caleb was, clinging to his presence as the only certainty in a world gone the color of rain.

Thunder boomed occasionally, but no longer startled Willow. They forded a stream and climbed a forested, rolling ridge on the far side. Gradually the route leveled out somewhat, then ascended into another grassy park. A clean, racing creek boiled down the center of the clearing between shrub-covered banks. Caleb crossed the water and turned upstream. The land rose steadily beneath the horses' feet once more, making even a slow walk an effort.

Once, when it was very steep, Caleb dismounted. Willow followed suit before she led Ishmael toward the rain-shrouded figures ahead. After thirty feet she went to her knees and swayed dizzily.

Caleb appeared from the rain and caught Willow up in a hug. "You should be riding, honey. You're not used to the altitude."

"It didn't bother me—this much—in Denver," she panted.

"You were four thousand feet lower in Denver. We're almost two miles high here."

Willow looked at Caleb with dazed eyes. "No wonder—my horses—"

"Yes," he said. "But they keep on going just the same. Like you."

For the first time Willow noticed the bruise on his forehead.

"You're hurt!"

"I'm all right. You're dizzier than I am and there's not a mark on you."

The relief in Willow's hazel eyes was as transparent and intense as her concern had been. Caleb held her even closer, savoring her emotion. It had been a long, long time since anyone but Willow had worried about him.

"Thank you," he said finally.

"For what?"

"For coming back after me when bullets were flying and a lot of men would have cut and run. For having the sense to know I'd need the saddlebags and the courage to bring them to me. For laughing when other women would have cried or whined or yelled at me. For being a hell of a good trail partner."

Willow's eyes widened in the instant before she looked away from Caleb, feeling lightheaded again. The blaze of his whiskey-colored eyes warmed her as no fire could have.

"That's very kind of you," she said huskily.

"I'm not a kind man."

"Yes, you are. I know I've caused you trouble. Because of my stubbornness about the Arabians, you've had to risk your life again and again." Willow smiled wearily and glanced up at him from beneath her eyelashes. "So when I want to scream or yell or whine, I think of what it would be like without you and I keep my mouth closed."

Caleb laughed and held Willow even closer. He heard her ragged sigh, felt her body leaning trustingly against his, and tried not to think about a man called Reno.

She's far too good a woman for a rounder like Matthew Moran.

No sooner had the thought come than it crystallized into a vow within the silence of Caleb's mind. Willow's capacity for courage and loyalty and passion deserved better than a man who seduced and abandoned young girls. At the very least, Willow's deep sensuality deserved better than a man who left her alone for so long she forgot how to kiss.

But not how to respond. She hadn't forgotten that. The memory of her headlong passion and soft, sultry body was an ache and a wild hunger within Caleb.

No woman who loved another man could respond like that—so quick, so deep. She'll be mine before she sees her fancy man again. I'll seduce Willow so completely that when he's dead, she'll turn to me instead of mourning a fancy man who isn't worth a single one of her tears.

She can't love him. She simply can't.

Caleb bent and caught Willow's mouth beneath his own, sealing the silent vow. The kiss was unlike any he had ever given a woman, tender and yet so deeply passionate he felt as though he was sinking into Willow, sipping from her very soul. When he finally lifted his head once more, she was trembling. He carried her to Ishmael and put her in the saddle. The look he gave her was as intense as the kiss had been.

"Stay close to me," he said almost roughly.

Before Willow could answer, Caleb had turned away. He mounted Trey, turned the big horse upstream, and began leading the way toward the remote, difficult notch in the ramparts that his father had named Black Pass.

Wind moaned down from the unseen heights, ruffling the horse's long manes. Caleb knew what waited on the far side of the pass, for his father had fallen in love with the series of high valleys leading down into an immense park. The park was known to white men, for eventually it provided a much more accessible passage between high peaks and mountain ranges than Black Pass. The side valleys leading up to Black Pass were unknown to white men. Even Indians avoided them, for game could be found in far easier places. Ancient tribes, however, had used the pass for their own reasons. No man knew what those reasons were, but the ghostly trail still remained, whispering of men long dead.

Caleb turned aside from the stream, for beavers had built several dams, killing the pines and gnawing down the aspens for a thousand feet in all directions, turning the meadow to a shallow lake. Several creeks came in. A few miles beyond, another valley joined the first, isolating the ridge whose flank they had been following in order to stay beyond the reach of the bog that edged the beaver pond.

After an hour the beaver dams receded behind the horses. The meadow narrowed to no more than fifty yards across, then forty, then ten. The route climbed up, leaving the stream to cut its way through solid rock below them in a canyon far too steep for a horse. The forest thinned, vanished into a kind of scrub, then reappeared as they descended the shoulder of the mountain into another valley where they could walk beside the stream once more.

Soon the route began climbing again. Mountains closed in on either side and the land pitched up beneath the horses' hooves. The forest crowded in, but somehow Caleb always found a way around deadfalls and aspen groves where the trees were so tightly interwoven they offered no passage to a man, much less a horse. The sound of the stream became deepthroated and the way steep.

Caleb checked his compass every time a side creek

came in, searching for the brawling little ribbon of water that would lead to another, higher valley, and from there to yet another and another until finally the highest level of the notch was reached and the divide was crossed.

There were no pines now, only spruce, fir, aspen, and a stunted form of willow that grew in avalanche chutes and in the small, boggy meadows cut by the stream. Caleb sensed the increasing openness of the country around him, the falling away of lesser peaks and ridges as the horses climbed up the backbone of the continent. His father had said the view from the top was as breathtaking as the altitude. Caleb had no way to check his father's observation. Rain fell steadily, obscuring anything farther than a few hundred feet away.

Lightning danced on the heights of an invisible peak, sending thunder belling repeatedly down the mountain, violent cannonades that sounded like explosions and rifle fire mixed together. Heads down, ears back, the horses walked into the teeth of the storm with tall, dark evergreens whipping and moaning overhead. The surrounding forest shielded them from the worst of the wind, but not from the ice-tipped rain that gradually turned to sleet.

They climbed with the violence of the storm all around them, sound and light hammering down until Willow screamed in fear but the storm drowned even that, leaving her feeling as though she were suspended in a cauldron of sound so overwhelming it became a punishing kind of silence. The air thinned until she was breathless just sitting on Ishmael and doing nothing more than hanging on with hands numbed by wet and cold.

And still the trail climbed. Sleet slowly was transformed into fat white flakes of snow swirling on the wind like petticoats of icy lace. Thunder came less frequently, at a greater and greater distance, finally becoming a muttering of the air, as much sensed as heard. Snow fell until it was ankle deep. The stream took on a dark, oily sheen.

Caleb checked his compass, turned Trey to the left, and began a long, ascending diagonal across the mountainside. In the fresh snow, the ancient, abandoned trail gleamed in a different shade of white than the snow falling on ground that had never been disturbed by the passage of man. Caleb looked at the ghostly thread snaking away to the overhanging clouds and wondered if any of the horses had the strength to take it.

The aspen vanished first, then the fir, then the spruce, until the forest was nothing more than a black-and-white fringe licking down sheltered ravines that lay a thousand feet down the mountain. Caleb and Willow were suspended between a mercury sky and a white ground. Veils of snow lifted and rippled, sporadically concealing and revealing the sweeping landscape. Far below, the creek was a black ribbon coiling through a steep, narrow, snow-choked ravine.

Gusts of wind tore aside the falling snow, unveiling a lid of clouds across rugged mountains whose very tops were still hidden in mist. For the first time Caleb saw an end to the climb . . . but not soon. There was at least another mile to go, another thousand feet to climb on a ghost trail slanting across broken rock, clawing up and up until finally the last ice-shattered ridge was climbed and melted snow flowed west, not east.

Caleb reined in and dismounted. Ishmael and Deuce were within two hundred feet of him. The mares were more spread out as they struggled upward. The last two mares were lost in the veil of snow that the others had climbed free of. Caleb waited, but no more Arabians appeared. Then the wind wailed and pushed aside more curtains of snow, revealing two mares a mile below, laboring slowly up the trail.

Ishmael walked the last few yards to Trey, then stood head down, blowing hard, fighting for each breath in the thin air. Caleb helped Willow down, supporting her with one arm while he loosened the saddle cinch. When the wind was still, steam peeled away from the horses in great plumes and the rasp of their labored breathing was loud.

"I'll—walk," Willow said.

"Not yet."

Caleb swung Willow up onto Trey, tied Ishmael on a long rope, and fastened it to Trey's saddle. Caleb took the reins and began walking up the trail, leading the big horse. Willow looked over her shoulder, saw Ishmael following and Deuce limping not far behind, and prayed that the mares would be able to keep going.

The route became steeper, the snow deeper, until Caleb was sinking in to his knees at each step. The horses were no better off. Every few hundred feet Caleb stopped and let the horses blow. Even Trey was feeling it now. He was breathing like a horse that had been run hard and long. Willow couldn't bear to listen. She knew her weight was making it worse. Despite the stabbing pain in her head and the nausea that stirred in her stomach, she started to dismount.

"Stay put," Caleb said curtly. "Trey is a lot—stronger than you are."

Caleb's words were spaced for the quick, deep breaths that still couldn't satisfy his body's hunger for oxygen. He was accustomed to altitude, but not to being more than eleven thousand feet high. The thin air and days of hard riding had worn him down as surely as it had the horses.

By the time they reached the base of the last, steep pitch, Caleb was stopping to catch his breath every thirty feet and the horses were strung out for miles down the trail. The clouds had unravelled into separate patches nestling between ridges. In the distance, rich gold light glistened where the late afternoon sun poured into valleys between cloud-capped peaks.

Trey stood with his head down, his breath groaning harshly, his sides heaving. He might be able to walk farther, but not carrying even so light a weight as Willow. Caleb loosened the cinch and pulled Willow from the saddle. He put the heavy saddlebags and bedroll over his left shoulder, supported Willow with his right arm, and began to walk up the trail. He paused only once, sending a shrill whistle over his shoulder. Trey lifted his head and reluctantly began walking once more.

Wind had blown away the snow to reveal the rocky bones of the mountain itself. The rocks were dark, almost black, shattered by the weight of time and ice. The ghostly trail vanished, but there was no doubt of their destination. Caleb fixed his eyes on the barren ridge rising in front of him, blocking out half the sky. He barely noticed the receding clouds and the thick golden light washing over the land.

Willow tried to walk alone. She managed it for twenty breaths, then sixty, then a hundred. She thought she was still walking when she felt Caleb's arm tighten around her waist, all but lifting her. Vaguely she realized that she would have fallen without his support. She tried to apologize.

"Don't talk," he gasped. "Walk."

After several racking breaths, Willow managed to take a few more steps. Caleb stayed beside her, breathing hard, supporting her, urging her on. Together they struggled up the steep, stony ridge, hearing nothing but their own pounding heartbeats and the rasp of their overworked lungs. Every few minutes, Caleb would pause long enough to send another shrill whistle back down the trail, calling to Trey and Deuce, who had outpaced all the mares.

Caleb shifted the saddlebags and bedroll to his other shoulder, caught Willow up again, and resumed walking. He stopped for breath every thirty steps, then every twenty, but even that wasn't enough for Willow. The long days of riding, the uncertainty, the fight with the Comancheros, the altitude, everything had combined to rob her of strength.

Grimly, Willow struggled onward, trying not to lean on Caleb. It was impossible. Without his strength she wouldn't have been able to stand.

"Almost—there," Caleb said.

Willow didn't answer. She couldn't. Her steps were only inches apart, more stumbling than true walking.

Caleb looked up at the route ahead and remembered with unnatural clarity the words his father had written in his journal to describe Black Pass: *Steep, rough, and colder than a witch's tit. But the pass is there all right, for any man with spine to take her. Up and over the Continental Divide, climbing until you're looking in God's eye, high enough to hear angels sing, if you can hear anything but your heart pounding and your breath sawing.*

Without warning, Caleb and Willow were there, standing on the brink of heaven, heart pounding and breath sawing and angels singing all around. Caleb's arm loosened around Willow, allowing her to slip to the ground. He dropped the saddlebags and bedroll next to her, sank down, and pulled her against his chest.

She slumped gratefully against him. For a long time she fought desperately for breath. Finally her breathing slowed. She realized that Caleb was cradling her, gently stroking her hair and cheeks, telling her again and again that the worst was over . . . they had finally reached the highest point in the pass. She gave a long, shuddering sigh and opened her eyes.

Caleb saw the color returning to Willow's skin and felt a relief so great it was almost pain. He gathered her even closer, shifting around until she was looking toward the setting sun. The clouds were all but gone, reduced to incandescent golden banners flying from the highest peaks. The snow that had fallen was already melting, threading back down the mountain peak in silent black tears.

"Look," Caleb said, pointing.

Willow looked at a hand-sized patch of snow that blazed nearby in the dying sun, weeping tears of gold. She watched a drop form and slowly separate from the still-frozen snow, falling away in the first instant of its long journey back to the sea.

The water was flowing west, toward the setting sun.

11

WILLOW awoke with the sun in her face and the sound of Ishmael's frantic whinny ringing in her ears. Heart pounding, she sat up suddenly. It took her a moment to remember where she was—in a tiny hanging valley on the western slope of the Great Divide. The whole valley was barely three hundred acres of grass surrounded on three sides by steep, forested ridges. The fourth side fell away so sharply that the stream was as much a waterfall as a cascade.

"Caleb?"

No one answered Willow's call. Belatedly, she remembered that Caleb had left long before first light, riding Trey and seeking the four mares that hadn't found their way into the valley by moonrise. She had wanted to go with him, but had fallen after she took three steps. He had carried her back to the blankets. She had dreamed she was following him and had wept each time she awakened to find herself alone and her mares lost.

Now Willow could sleep no more. She crawled out of the bedroll, picked up the shotgun Caleb had left for her, and went to see what was bothering Ishmael. The angle of the sun told her that it was mid-afternoon. She had slept all night and most of a day.

Ishmael snorted and tugged against his picket rope, whinnying wildly.

"Take it easy, boy," Willow said, glancing in the direction the stallion was staring. "What is it?"

The stallion's call split the silence again.

Riding on the wind came an answering cry. A few minutes later three of the missing mares walked wearily into the meadow. Willow took the stallion off the picket rope and led him to a rock. Shotgun in hand, she leaped from the rock onto the stallion's bare back. Instants later, he was cantering eagerly toward the mares, nickering a welcome. Willow stared at the forest beyond the three mares but saw no sign of Caleb, his big Montana horse, or Dove, the only mare still missing.

With rising uneasiness, Willow waited while Ishmael sniffed over the mares, assuring himself that they were indeed the same ones he had lost. After a few moments, the mares began cropping grass ravenously, ignoring the delighted stallion.

"Ishmael, that's enough. Let's go see what happened to Caleb."

Willow had no sooner reached the edge of the meadow when Ishmael's ears pricked and he whinnied softly. An answering whinny came from the forest. Trey trotted into the open. A page from Caleb's journal had been torn out and tied to the saddle horn. Willow worked the paper free and opened it.

I'm walking Dove in. The other mares perked up and started tugging to be free as soon as they got below nine thousand feet. They were headed in the right direction so I turned them loose, and Trey, too. Give them some grain.

Dove is done in, but still game. I'll stay with her as long as she's standing.

Tears scalded Willow's cheeks at the thought of her tired mare. Dove, more than any of the horses, had borne Willow's weight through the long days on the trail. That was why she was so exhausted now.

A glance at the angle of the sun told Willow she had better get to work despite the tiredness that sapped her strength. The valley was more than eight thousand feet high—lower than Black Pass, but nowhere near as low as she was accustomed to. She led Trey to the campsite, stripped gear from him, and turned him loose in the meadow. While she poured out grain for the horses, he rolled in the thick grass, drank deeply from the stream, and fell to eating grain as though starved. She knew how the horse felt. It had been more than a day since she had eaten, and then it had been only a bit of jerky.

Caleb would be ravenous when he returned, for he had taken no food with him.

Working as quickly as she could, stopping from time to time to catch her breath, Willow dragged the saddles and packs in under the overhanging cliff that protected the campsite on one side. She dragged downed wood into camp, started a fire, rigged a tripod for cooking, fetched water, and felt as though she had been running uphill carrying a pack. She had long since abandoned her heavy jacket and Levis. Now she unlaced the buckskin shirt, unbuttoned the flannel beneath, and thought longingly of a bath. But there were too many other things to be done and not enough time before the sun set behind the looming peaks.

Just as the last shaft of light abandoned the high valley, Caleb and Dove emerged in the meadow, startling deer that had drifted out of cover to feed near the horses. After a few seconds the deer resumed browsing. It had been so long since they had been hunted by man they had lost much of their fear of humans.

Dove didn't notice the deer or anything but the grass and water. She nudged Caleb's hand, asking to be released from the pressure on the halter that had kept her walking long after she wanted to stop. Caleb stroked her neck, spoke softly to her, and released her to join the other mares.

Willow grabbed the canteen, poured in coffee, snatched up a handful of fresh biscuits, and hurried across the meadow. She was breathless by the time she reached Caleb, who had just finished pouring out some grain for Dove.

"Is she all right?" Willow asked.

"Played out, but nothing that rest and food won't cure. Her breathing doesn't rattle, so her wind wasn't broken."

"Thank God," breathed Willow. She held out the canteen and biscuits. "Here. You must be starved. Thank you for getting the mares. I dreamed I was going back for them, but when I woke up I was still here and I didn't know how I could—"

Caleb drew Willow close and kissed her. When he straightened, he was smiling despite the exhaustion that lined his face. He made a sound of enjoyment and licked his lips.

"You taste like coffee and biscuits," he said teasingly. "And something else . . ."

"Venison stew," she admitted, laughing despite the color flooding her cheeks. "I cooked up what was left."

"You taste like heaven," he corrected, brushing his lips over her mouth again. "Sheer, sweet heaven."

Caleb stretched and yawned, trying to revive himself. Willow uncapped the canteen and held it out. The rich aroma of coffee drifted up. He took the canteen and drank deeply. The liquid was strong and black and hot enough to steam. He made a thick sound of pleasure and drank again, feeling warmth expand through him like a second sunrise. He took a biscuit, popped it whole into his mouth, and chewed. Two more biscuits disappeared in the same manner, to be washed down by more coffee.

"Come to camp," Willow said softly. Her clear hazel eyes measured Caleb's exhaustion in the slowing of his reflexes and the darkness beneath his tawny eyes. "You've barely slept in days. Eat some hot stew and sleep. I'll stand guard."

"No need," he said, yawning again. "See those deer?"

She nodded.

"We're the first people they've ever seen," Caleb said.

"But I saw the marks of other fires against the cliff."

"They burned a long, long time ago, before the Spanish brought horses. At least, that's what my daddy figured, and he knew more about Indians and wild land than any man alive." Caleb's eyes searched the heights that all but surrounded the small valley. "He figured he was the only man in centuries to see this place."

"Why did the Indians abandon it?"

"Horses, I imagine. From what I read in the journal, the trail out of here is almost as rough as the one over the top. Fine for a man on foot who's used to altitude, but damned hard on a horse." Caleb smiled crookedly. "It's quicker and a damn sight easier to use lower passes and let a horse do the work. Man is a lazy creature, given the chance."

"You aren't," Willow said. "If it weren't for you, my mares would be stranded in the rocks on the other side of the pass."

"They came too far to let them go," Caleb said simply. "How is Deuce?"

"He must have strained his left foreleg when he went down after being shot. It's swollen below the knee."

"Is he putting weight on it?"

"He favors it, but he moves more easily since I bound it with cloth from my riding habit."

Caleb grunted. "Best use for the damn thing. What about the bullet burn?"

"I was afraid it would be infected, but it looks as clean as that brook going through the meadow."

"Daddy was right about that, too," Caleb said, yawning again. "Not much gets infected up here. Something about the thin air, I guess, or the lack of human beings. How much of that stew did you leave for me?"

"About two quarts."

"I'll eat slowly so you can cook more."

She smiled and took his hand, leading him toward the campsite. "I made lots and lots of biscuits."

In camp, Willow watched from the corner of her eye as Caleb made short work of the stew, biscuits, coffee, and wild greens.

"No trout?" he asked lazily, mopping up the last bit of gravy with the last biscuit.

Willow smiled and shook her head. "They all ran from me."

"Guess I'll just have to teach you how to catch them all over again, won't I?"

Color burned on Willow's cheeks as she remembered the last time Caleb had told her how to catch trout.

"Don't worry, honey," he said, stretching out on the bedroll. "Right now I'm too done in to sneak up on my own shadow."

Caleb was asleep before he took another breath. Willow waited until he was sleeping too deeply to be disturbed. Then she pulled off his boots, eased his gunbelt and hunting knife off his hips, and covered him with the thick blankets. She wrapped up the gunbelt and placed it within reach, exactly as he would have done if he hadn't been too tired.

Willow put the shotgun close to her side of the bed and crawled in next to Caleb. Even though the sun had been gone from the valley floor less than half an hour, it was already chilly. The heat radiating from Caleb was wonderful, luring Willow closer and closer until she sighed and relaxed against his big body. He shifted, drawing her even more tightly against himself, holding her as though he, too, was cold. Smiling, holding him in return, Willow fell asleep with the familiar feel of Caleb's heartbeat beneath her cheek.

WILLOW awakened on her side, tucked spoon fashion against Caleb, her head on his upper arm, his chest warming her back, her bottom snug in the cradle of his thighs . . . and one of her breasts cupped in his right hand, which had slid between buckskin and flannel to seek the silky warmth beneath.

When Willow realized the intimacy of Caleb's touch, her heart turned over. She froze, caught between the knowledge that she should retreat and the pleasure of lying so close with Caleb while sunshine poured into the tiny valley, filling it to overflowing with golden light.

After a few minutes, Willow's heartbeat settled down, but not the sensations that glittered over her without warning, shortening her breathing and tightening the breast within Caleb's grasp until the hard nipple nuzzled against the center of his broad palm. An odd ache claimed her, a desire to arch against his palm like a cat being stroked. The feeling was so strong and so unexpected that she held her breath, wondering what was wrong with her. She tried to ease free of his hand without disturbing him, but he was too deeply tangled in her clothes.

Half awakened by Willow's cautious retreat, Caleb made a low, sleepy sound and gathered her more closely against himself. His free hand moved, seeking the warmth and silk of her body but settling for the soft weight of her other breast muffled beneath layers of clothes.

Willow's breath wedged firmly in her throat as she felt herself cupped and cuddled through clothing until that breast, too, tightened in an aching rush. She shivered, fighting the desire to twist slowly against Caleb's hands, increasing the pressure of his touch on her breasts.

I must be losing my mind, Willow thought, shivering.

Breathing shallowly, not wanting to move for fear of waking Caleb and embarrassing both of them, Willow lay stiffly and waited for the normal movements Caleb made while asleep to remove her from the unintentional, sensual cage of his embrace.

Release didn't come. Tension did. Unable to bear it any longer, Willow eased the blanket off her body as the first step toward freeing herself. But removing the blanket was a mistake. The sight of one of Caleb's big hands on her breast and the other hand buried deep between rawhide laces and through a gap in her flannel top made Willow forget to breathe. Frantically she closed her eyes. After the first rush of embarrassment passed, she opened her eyes again.

Nothing had changed. The contrast between his tan hand and the whiteness of her own skin was as vivid as before. The difference between the lean strength of his fingers and the soft fullness of her breast was still . . .

Exciting.

I am losing my mind.

Willow told herself she should either get out of bed

or pull the blanket up once more and spare herself the sight of Caleb's hand tangled so intimately in her clothes. She did neither. She simply lay motionless except for the ripples of sensation washing through her with each breath, each unintentional stirring of her breasts against Caleb's hands.

A bird called sweet melodies from the rocks and was answered from the far side of the meadow. A breeze brushed through tall grass, making a sound like spirits breathing. Sunlight caressed the land as surely as Willow was being caressed with every breath she took. Caleb shifted again, drawing her even closer, cupping his hand more deeply around her naked breast beneath her clothes.

Air came from Willow's lungs in a rush. Very carefully, she eased Caleb's right hand from her chest to her buckskin-clad hip. Then she slid her own hand inside her bodice in an attempt to remove Caleb's other hand without awakening him. There simply wasn't enough room for her hand as well as his inside the closely fitting buckskin.

Holding her breath, she picked the buckskin laces free of their holes and unfastened the flannel top beneath until it was completely open. The buckskin lacings, however, opened only to her ribs, which left her little maneuvering room. It would have to be enough.

Slowly, Willow slid her fingers over Caleb's hand and tugged ever so gently. His hand moved against her naked breast, sending his hard palm rubbing over her nipple. A burst of heat licked through her, making her breath catch in a tiny moan. Her back arched in sensual reflex, repeating the caress, caressing his hand in turn. Biting her lower lip, Willow pulled gently at Caleb's hand again, trying to free herself without awakening him. He muttered sleepily and tightened his grip on her once again, trapping her taut nipple between his fingers.

The small, ragged sound Willow made brought Caleb fully awake. He felt the lithe curve of her body snugged against his own, the fullness of her hip beneath one of his hands and the naked silk of her breast nestled in his other. Smiling, he flexed both hands, enjoying the very feminine feel of Willow's body.

"Caleb?" Willow asked fearfully, a bare thread of sound. "You—you aren't awake, are you?"

"I'm getting there."

The heat of her blush was so violent he felt it suffuse her breasts.

"I didn't mean to awaken you," she whispered. "I—I was just trying to—to move your hand."

"This one?" Caleb asked, spreading his hand over her buttock and squeezing gently, deeply.

Willow's breath broke. "No—I mean, yes, but mostly the other one."

"The other one?" Caleb smiled into her hair. "Where is it? I can't see."

"I can, and that's the problem." Willow heard her own words and wanted to groan.

"You can, huh? So tell me where it is."

"Caleb Black, you know very well where your hand is!"

"How could I? It's asleep," he lied, smiling and searching through Willow's hair for the sensitive nape of her neck. "So I can't move it until I know where it is. Tell me, honey."

"On my—on my—" Her voice broke.

"Shoulder?" Caleb offered.

She shook her head.

Willow's hair slid aside, revealing her nape. His mouth settled over it, kissing gently, nibbling softly. He felt every bit of the sensual shivering that ran through her body. An answering heat flowed through him. He had never held a woman who was so responsive to his least caress.

"Is my hand on your ribs?" Caleb asked deeply, running his teeth over Willow's nape again, feeling her shiver, wanting to groan with the sweet agony of his own need.

"N-not my ribs," she whispered, barely able to think.

"Your waist?"

But this time Willow couldn't speak at all, for Caleb's teeth had closed on her nape in a tender, fierce caress that made thought impossible. She closed her eyes and tried not to cry out with the surprise and pleasure coiling through her, tightening her whole body. When his fingers closed delicately on her nipple, plucking the taut flesh, she moaned.

"Now I see what the problem is," Caleb said, propping himself on his elbow so that he could look over Willow's shoulder.

"What?" she whispered.

"This." His hand flexed beneath her clothes and her back arched. "See? We're all tangled in your clothes. Lie still, honey. I'll get us free."

Holding her breath and blushing, Willow watched Caleb with smoky hazel eyes and waited. His hand moved beneath the flannel, cupping all of her breast while his thumb drew lazy circles around her nipple. Her whole body stiffened.

"Easy, honey," he murmured. "Am I hurting you?"

Willow made an odd sound at the back of her throat when his thumb rubbed the hard peak of her breast. He smiled and rubbed again, loving the velvet hardness that rose so eagerly to his touch.

"Almost free," Caleb said. Slowly, he shifted Willow onto her back, caressing her with slow sweeps of his thumb. "Gently, honey, just a little more and you'll be free. Shift your shoulder a little. Yes, like that. Now take a slow, deep breath. That's it." A shudder ran through his body as he looked down at her uncovered breast. "God, you're beautiful, as perfect as a rosebud."

Caleb bent down to Willow's breast, turning his head slowly from side to side, letting the coarse silk of his beard caress her soft flesh, tightening her nipple even more. She gasped and grabbed his head.

"Yes," he said thickly. "Show me what you want."

Shocked and embarrassed, she tried to tug his head away, but her motions caused her erect nipple to brush against his lips.

"Yes," he said. "That's what I want, too."

Caleb took the tip of Willow's breast into his mouth as his hands tightened, making it impossible for her to move away while he caressed her with tongue and teeth. A strange, wild sensation speared through Willow, drawing a choked cry from her.

"Honey?" Caleb asked huskily, looking up. "Did I hurt you?"

"We shouldn't—shouldn't be doing this."

Caleb closed his eyes and fought the denial surging through him, a denial as fierce as the hunger he had for the girl whose breast lay against his lips.

"Did I hurt you?" he asked again.

As he spoke, he blew on the nipple that was still glistening from his mouth. The soft rush of air over Willow's breast made her stomach tighten. Her hips moved in a reflexive response she didn't understand.

Caleb did.

"Tell me, Willow." He kissed the tight rosebud he had drawn from her breast. "Did I hurt you?"

Willow tried to speak but couldn't. She shook her head.

"Did you like it?" he asked.

Heat suffused her face. She turned her head against his chest, hiding from him.

Very gently, Caleb smoothed his bearded cheek over her breast once more before he turned away, not certain if his discipline would stand against the sight of her bare, soft breast nestled between buckskin folds, her nipple hard and rosy with the heat of his mouth.

"It's all right, honey. I won't force you."

Caleb got up and went to the fire. After a few minutes, Willow joined him. They ate breakfast in a silence that wasn't quite uncomfortable. He didn't mention the morning intimacy of the bed. Nor would he let her talk about it. He was afraid she would try to refuse him the honey and cream of her body in the future. He wouldn't—couldn't—let that happen.

Shy, wary little trout. It's been so long since she has felt a man's touch. All I need is patience and she'll swim right into my hands. I've always been told I'm a patient man. Why is it so hard to be patient with her?

Why is it so hard, period? Caleb asked himself impatiently. *I'll be lucky to stand up straight all day.*

Willow watched Caleb shyly from beneath her lashes as he moved around the camp, putting the supplies back into pack sacks, checking cinches and headstalls, making certain that the long ride hadn't frayed anything other than flesh and bone. When he walked out into the meadow with a new bag of grain, she went beside him.

A whistle brought Trey trotting and Deuce limping up for inspection. Caleb poured out two mounds of grain and worked over his horses while they ate, checking hooves and hide for damage, talking soothingly the whole time, praising his horses' stamina and gentle temper. Willow watched, fascinated by Caleb's easy strength and masculine grace. The restraint and precision of his hands also fascinated her. He was so gentle that Deuce didn't even flinch when his wound was checked, yet Caleb did a thorough job of inspection.

"Still clean," Caleb said quietly. He stroked the horse's muscular shoulder, feeling the roughness of hair where lather had run and dried more than once. "I'd groom you, boy, but I suspect you would rather be left alone for a day or two. Don't blame you a bit. That was one hell of a trail."

One of the mares caught the scent of grain on the wind and trotted up, nickering softly. Caleb smiled and tugged gently on her forelock.

"Hello, Penny. Feeling better after a night of eating?" he asked.

Penny nudged the grain sack pointedly.

Willow laughed. "Quit torturing her. She knows what's waiting for her."

Caleb gave Willow a sideways look and a slow smile.

"Waiting just makes it better, didn't you know?"

Wisely, Willow kept her mouth shut, but nothing she did could conceal her blush. She shivered as she recalled the passion she had tasted that morning.

Ishmael cantered across the valley toward them. His ears were erect, his stride easy and even, his body supple.

"He looks good," Caleb said.

"He's breathing a bit too hard."

"Altitude. He'll be fine in a week or two."

"It's getting from here to there that bothers me," Willow admitted, sighing and rubbing her temples.

Caleb began pouring out more mounds of grain as the Arabians closed in, lured by the rich aroma.

"We'll take it easy until you're used to the altitude," he said.

"Only twelve hours a day on the trail instead of eighteen?" Willow muttered beneath her breath.

But Caleb heard. His hearing was as acute as a

deer's. He glanced up and saw Willow standing with her eyes closed, rubbing her temples. He shook out a few more kernels of grain, tied the top with a leather thong, and set the burlap bag aside before he went back to Willow.

"Headache?" he asked quietly.

She lowered her hands almost guiltily. "Just a little. It's much better than it was in the pass."

"Here. Let me."

Whatever objections Willow might have had vanished at the slow, circular motion of Caleb's thumbs on her temples.

"Relax if you can," he said. "The tighter your muscles are, the more it hurts."

Willow made a small sound that was more an expression of enjoyment than a word as Caleb slid his fingers over her head and massaged her scalp, loosening knots she didn't even know she had. Strong, gentle, skillful, his hands rubbed away pain until she sagged with relief. With small pressures of his fingertips, he urged her closer until she was all but leaning against him. Her forehead dipped farther and farther, finally coming to rest against his breastbone.

Belatedly, Willow realized that Caleb had opened his shirt against the heat of the mountain sun. Her forehead was resting on his bare, warm flesh. The dark thatch of hair on his chest tickled her nose and mouth. When she breathed in, the scent of wool shirt and horse and man filled her senses. She sighed and rubbed her face against him, liking the feel of his masculine textures on her cheek.

"That feels so good," Willow said, moving her head slowly, increasing the pressure of Caleb's hands rubbing away pain.

"Good," he said, enjoying the warmth of her breath against his bare skin.

For a time there was silence. Then Willow sighed again and spoke.

"I'll never be able to repay you."

He laughed. "I'll let you rub my head in return."

"I meant for my mares. Thank you, Caleb."

"They were too good to lose over something that wasn't their fault."

"I know," she said simply. "It was mine."

Caleb smoothed the back of his fingers over Willow's temples. "You didn't build these mountains, honey. God did."

She smiled sadly. "But I hired a mountain guide and then refused to listen to his advice. I came very close to killing my beautiful mares who had done nothing except follow where I led them. They would have died if you hadn't gone back for them. I couldn't have done it. I tried, but . . ." Her voice broke.

"Hush, honey. It's not your fault."

She shook her head and whispered, "I wasn't strong enough. You were. You didn't have to go after them, but you went anyway, even though you'd had hardly any sleep in days."

Caleb's hands hesitated on Willow's temples, then he resumed slowly stroking her forehead. Her willingness to accept responsibility for the choices she made continued to surprise him. He had known few men and fewer women who didn't pass the blame when things turned out badly and grab the praise when things went well.

The longer Caleb was around Willow, the more he realized she was accustomed to taking care of herself and anyone else who was nearby. She was a far cry from the spoiled southern lady he had first thought her to be.

God must have been asleep when He let Willow go to a heel like Reno. She's too damn good for him. She can't know what Reno's like or she never would have given herself to him. I'll be doing her a favor when I bury that son of a bitch.

She'll be my woman before she sees him again. I'm not leaving this valley until Willow is mine in a way that nothing can change, not even the death of her fancy man.

"Thank you for my mares, Caleb," Willow repeated quietly, resting her head against his chest. "I owe you more than I can ever repay."

"Willow," Caleb whispered.

She opened her eyes and tilted her head back until she could see him. The glints of color in her hazel depths had never seemed more beautiful to Caleb than at that moment.

"You saved my life when Deuce was shot," he said. "You brought me ammunition and fought beside me afterward. You don't owe me anything at all."

"And how many times have you saved my life since we left Denver?"

"That's different."

"It is?"

"Yes." Caleb bent and brushed a kiss over Willow's lips. "That's what you hired me to do."

"You're very good at your work . . . and at other things as well."

Willow had been thinking of his care for the horses, but the instant the words were out of her mouth, she thought of other things he was breathtakingly good at. Color flooded her cheeks.

Caleb smiled crookedly and teased her lips with the tip of his tongue. "Really?" he asked. "What things are those?"

"You know very well what they are," she muttered.

"No, I don't," he said, shaking his head. The motion brushed kisses over her mouth. "Tell me."

Willow looked away and wished she would learn to think before she spoke. She had never been particularly impulsive before she met Caleb. But since she had met him, she was forever admitting to things that made her blush.

"I bet it's that I'm good at finding riding clothes for you in the middle of nowhere," Caleb suggested.

Willow's lips quirked in a small smile. She looked up at Caleb through long, dark amber eyelashes. "That's one of the things."

"And finding saddles."

Her smiled widened. "Yes."

"And catching trout."

Color stained her cheekbones.

"Is that it, Willow?" Caleb asked. His hands moved from her temples to just below her ribs. His muscles shifted and flexed as he lifted her slowly until she was at eye level. "Is that one of the things you think I'm good at? Catching trout?"

She nodded and said huskily, "You're especially good at that."

For the space of several heartbeats Caleb looked hungrily at Willow's full pink lips. Then he bent and took them in a swift, searing kiss that made her stiffen in surprise. His tongue slid between her lips to the smooth surface of her clenched teeth.

"Open for me," he whispered. "Let me taste all that warm honey."

He nipped at her lower lip. When she gasped in surprise, he twisted his head and took her mouth, teasing her tongue with his own until she trembled between his hands. At last, she sighed and touched her tongue lightly, shyly along his, returning the kiss. Willow's odd combination of reticence and response reminded Caleb of his promise to himself—that the next time he kissed Willow, it would be because she asked for him.

But he hadn't been able to wait. Slowly, reluctantly, cursing the passion Willow aroused so effortlessly in him, Caleb lifted his head. When he opened his eyes, she was watching his lips with wonder.

"Is kissing one of the things I'm good at?" Caleb asked hungrily.

Willow turned a shade of pink that was as deep as her lips. "Caleb!"

"If I'm not good, tell me what I'm doing wrong. I want to please you, Willow. I want to pleasure you all the way to your soul. I want that," he whispered against her mouth, "very much."

The trembling of Willow's lips beneath his own as she whispered his name was the sweetest thing Caleb had ever felt. Despite the hunger that poured in hot waves through his body, he made the kiss gentle, undemanding, taking nothing that she didn't first give to him.

The chaste kiss surprised Willow, for she could feel the passionate tension in Caleb's hard body. His restraint also reassured her, just as his willingness to stop touching her earlier had. Nor had he seemed angry when he stopped this morning. He had been angry the other time, when he had combed her hair and kissed her so deeply and touched the soft flesh no man had ever touched before. Stopping then had made him furious.

But not today. Today, Caleb wasn't angry at all. Today, sunlight and honey ran in Willow's veins.

Her hands went from the flexed strength of Caleb's biceps to his shoulders. The wool of his shirt no longer pleased her fingers. She sought the living warmth beneath and sighed with pleasure to find it. Catlike, she kneaded his muscles, enjoying the feeling of the hair that grew in black swirls over his chest.

Caleb waited for Willow to open her lips, offering a more passionate kiss, but he waited in vain. She gave back a kiss as chaste as he had given to her, then she sighed and stroked and petted him until he wanted to groan. The feel of her delicate hands on his skin was setting him on fire, as was the obvious enjoyment she took in his body.

Yet she made no move to deepen the kiss, to join her mouth with his once again in a prelude to a more intimate kind of mating.

Puzzled, Caleb wondered if Reno was the kind of man who liked to hurt women in bed. That would explain Willow's instant fear when she had felt Caleb's hand between her legs, but it wouldn't explain Rebecca's persistence in protecting her lover's identity. Rebecca had been cossetted and frankly spoiled. She had been full of mischief and love and life. A man who was cruel to her would never have won her heart, her chastity, and her loyalty. She would have required a gentleman before she gave herself.

Abruptly Caleb realized that he was no one's definition of a gentleman, especially at the moment. He smelled of horses and hard work and clothes that had been worn too long. Willow didn't. She smelled of lavender and meadow grass and sunshine. No wonder she was reluctant to get closer to him. Now that Caleb thought about it, he wasn't real crazy about being close to himself, either.

"I'm good at something else, too," Caleb said, lowering Willow to the ground and stepping back from her. "I'm a very special kind of water dowser."

"You are?"

He made a rumbling sound of agreement. "I can find hot springs almost anywhere."

The possibilities widened Willow's eyes and distracted her from the disappointment of being released from Caleb's arms so quickly.

"You can find hot water? Even here?"

"Especially here. My sixth sense tells me there's a hot spring just off the head of the valley, and the pool is big enough to float in."

She smiled, remembering the journal Caleb's father

had kept of his travels in the West. "You're a wonder, Caleb Black."

"Actually, I'm kind of slow to figure some things out, but I'm learning."

"Want to flip a coin?"

He blinked. "Whatever for?"

"To see who gets the first bath."

Caleb caught himself just before he said something foolish about bathing together. *Remember the trout. Slow and sweet and easy. No sudden moves. No impatience. All the time in the world.*

"You go first, honey. I'll groom the horses."

"That isn't fair to you."

"I like working with horses."

"Then I'll wash our clothes. Deal?" Willow asked, holding out her hand.

Caleb took it, brought it to his lips, and gently bit the pad of flesh at the base of Willow's thumb. "Deal."

He released her hand and began unbuttoning his shirt.

"What are you doing?" she asked.

"Taking off my clothes. Unless you planned to wash them with me still inside . . . ?"

"Er, no."

But the thought intrigued Willow. It showed in the deepening of color on her face. Caleb smiled and pulled off his shirt, enjoying the widening of Willow's eyes and the flush in her cheeks when she looked at him. She might have been reluctant to make love with him, even afraid, but she made no effort to hide her approval of him as a man. It was one of the many paradoxes about Willow that both lured and baffled Caleb.

Curious about her response, Caleb began unfastening his pants. Willow made a shocked sound and jerked her glance back up to his face.

"Same problem as with the shirt," Caleb said blandly.

Willow swallowed hard and said, "I'll get you a blanket."

She turned and ran across the grass toward camp with Caleb's deep laughter following her every step of the way.

12

WILLOW floated in the warm pool, wondering if she had died and gone to heaven despite her unangelic nature. Thirty feet above her, water gushed out from a crack in the black rock of the mountainside. The crack ran in a steeply narrowing V that ended in a waterfall. At the top of the V, the water seethed with steam. By the time it leaped and cascaded into the deep pool, the water had cooled enough not to scald naked skin. To Willow's surprise, the pool had proved to be sweet rather than sulphurous.

"Caleb is indeed a very special kind of dowser," Willow said softly to the pool. "If Matt found a valley like this, it's no wonder he never came back to the farm. All we had were cool creeks and sun-warmed, mud-bottomed ponds."

The nearby aspen and evergreens made murmurous sounds of agreement, whispering to Willow of the seductive, savage beauty of the western land. She whispered back, but it was Caleb she was thinking of, not the land. The thought of the liberties she had allowed him made her blush . . . and the passion he had tapped within her made her ache.

"What has he done to me?" Willow whispered, shivering, remembering.

"Not enough," she answered herself softly. "Dear God, not nearly enough."

If Caleb hadn't been so gentle with her, Willow would have been frightened by her own thoughts, by her own hungers, by the desire to lie in the midst of clean, seething water and feel Caleb's hands on her, touching her everywhere the water did.

A sweet arrow of sensation shot through Willow's body, charging her as though it was Caleb's mouth rather than warm water caressing her breasts. She trembled again, but not from fear. Once the shock of newness had worn off, she very much enjoyed the feelings he called from her body.

"I could say no to a man who was cruel or cowardly or stupid or selfish," Willow whispered to the pool. "But Caleb is none of those things. He's a hard man, but a soft man wouldn't last very long out here. And Caleb is no harder than he has to be. He takes no pleasure in gunfights and killing. He treats his horses kindly. Not once has he used a whip or sharp spurs.

"He didn't think much of me when he first met me," Willow admitted softly to the steaming water, "but he wasn't rough with me even then. And he was kind to Widow Sorenson, though I suspect Eddy is her paramour. Caleb must know, yet he defended both of them when they couldn't defend themselves.

"But most important," Willow said, shivering again, remembering, "no matter how hot his blood was running, Caleb hasn't taken me when other men would have. Other than that first time, he wasn't even angry when I said no. He's a gentleman even when I'm not quite a lady."

Willow was relieved at Caleb's self-control. She still felt cold when she remembered the barely leashed fury in his eyes when she had begged him not to touch her so intimately.

Fancy lady, some day you'll be on your knees in front of me again—but you won't be begging me to stop.

She had never seen a man so angry and yet so much in control of himself. She was grateful for that steel discipline of his. It allowed her to venture into the sweet, seething waters of passion without fear of drowning.

Yet even the thought of drowning in Caleb's arms pierced Willow with a pleasure that was also pain, the ache of hunger awakened and teased but not soothed by his smile, his hands, his mouth moving over her, burning through her inhibitions to the deep passion beneath. She wanted more of his kisses, his caresses, his taste, the intense sensuality that burned beneath his control.

Unable to bear her own thoughts any longer, Willow rolled over and lowered her feet to the rocky bottom of the pool. The water came up to her chin. Slowly, she half-swam, half-walked the short distance to shore, seeking the long ledge of rock that ran down into the pool. After a brief search, her toes found the ledge. It was warm and nearly smooth from the restless water rushing over it. The stone itself was clean, scrubbed by the constant turmoil of water leaping down the dark cliff into the pool.

After wringing out her hair and blotting herself dry, Willow dressed in the camisole and pantelets she had brought to the pool. Other than the faded, everyday dress she had stuffed into the carpetbag at the last minute—a dress she had worn so often she couldn't bear the sight of it—the fine cotton underwear was the only clothing she had that was clean. She didn't even have Caleb's shirt to pull on over the thin cotton, for the shirt was spread out in the meadow to dry along with the rest of the clothes she had washed.

Willow shook out the cotton blanket she and Caleb had been using as a sheet and wrapped it around herself, securing it under her arms. Holding it up like a narrow skirt, she picked her way through a hundred feet of forest to the meadow where Caleb was grooming the horses, wearing one of the heavy blankets around his hips.

At least, Willow hoped he was wearing a blanket. As hot as the day was, she wouldn't have blamed him for stripping to his underwear.

What underwear? I washed it all and spread it out in the meadow.

The thought of encountering Caleb naked among the horses was both daunting and . . . exciting.

Willow's damp hair felt cool on her flushed cheeks as she walked out into the meadow, taking care to stay in plain sight. The horses' heads came up as they spotted her. Ishmael nickered, catching the familiar scent of lavender on the breeze.

Caleb gave the stallion's back another stroke of the brush before he bent down and retrieved the blanket he had thrown off as soon as Willow had vanished into the forest that fringed the meadow. He wrapped the blanket around his hips and went back to grooming the stallion. It wasn't Caleb's modesty he was interested in preserving, it was Willow's. She had blushed like a virgin at the sight of his naked chest. She would go scarlet to her heels if she saw the rest of him bare.

"Your turn for a bath," Willow said as she walked up to Caleb.

He nodded, but didn't stop grooming Ishmael.

Willow tried not to admire Caleb's powerful shoulders, long arms, and the tapering of his body into narrow hips. As he brushed the red stallion, she also tried not to stare at the supple flex and play of skin and muscle, and the wedge of chest hair that tapered down to a finger's width at his flat navel, then flared once more where the blanket rode low on his hips.

She tried not to stare, but she didn't succeed. When she realized that he was watching her watching him, she looked away hastily.

"I don't mind," Caleb said.

"What?"

"I don't mind having you look at me."

As Caleb spoke, he realized it was the simple truth. He never would have guessed how satisfying it could be to have a woman look at him shyly with admiration and sensual hunger in her eyes. Perhaps it was because the few women he had known were older widows to whom a man's body was nothing remarkable. They had enjoyed his strength around the house and praised his self-control in bed, but they had never looked at him the way Willow was looking, as though the sun rose and set in his eyes and the moon lay cupped in his hands.

"In fact," Caleb said, "I like having you look at me. It makes me feel like a special kind of man."

"You are," Willow said simply.

His crooked smile flashed briefly as he shook his head. "I'm just a man, honey. Smarter than some, dumber than others, and harder than most."

"I think you're special," she whispered.

Caleb heard the soft words. His hand ceased making slow, sweeping strokes over Ishmael's back. "You're the special one, Willow." Before she could speak, he slapped the stallion's rump. "Go back to eating, horse. A bit of fat wouldn't do you any harm."

Ishmael trotted off to count his mares and remind them of his muscular presence. Watching, Caleb said quietly, "You better keep track of them, son. They're as spirited as they are graceful. Tough, too. I don't know of any flatland horses that could have stood up to what those mares did."

"They were bred for stamina, loyalty, and courage," Willow said.

"How did the Arabs manage that?"

"With rather brutal pragmatism," she answered, watching her mares ignore the strutting stallion. "For century after century, the sheiks rounded up all the brood mares and drove them out into the desert without water. They kept going until the mares were mad with thirst, then they were driven toward an oasis."

Caleb looked from Ishmael to Willow, caught by the husky intensity of her voice as she spoke of the horses she loved.

"When the mares scented water, they began to run," Willow said. "When they were within a hundred yards of water, the battle horns were blown. Only the mares that turned away from water and ran back to their masters were bred."

Caleb looked back at the Arabians for a long moment, measuring the results of the sheiks' harsh method of determining which mares were worthy of breeding. The test might have been brutal, but the results were extraordinary. Even worn to the point of gauntness by hundreds of miles of hard trail, the mares were still elegant, still alert, still responsive. If Willow saddled one of the mares and pointed it back toward the pass, the mare would go until she dropped.

The Arabians were like their mistress in that. No give up in them. Caleb liked that in a horse. He respected it in a man. He valued it in a woman above all else.

"Maybe the sheiks had the right idea," he said.

"Hard on the mares," Willow said dryly.

Caleb smiled and changed the subject. "You ever shave a man?"

"Lots of times."

"Good. Bring my razor to the pool in about ten

minutes," he said. Abruptly, Caleb turned away, wondering why it irritated him that Willow had shaved men before when it worked to his convenience now. "I put a real edge on the blade, so be careful of your fingers."

"And your face?" she suggested innocently.

Caleb smiled in spite of his irritation. He looked back over his shoulder at the girl standing in the meadow wearing little more than long hair and a thin cotton blanket.

"If you don't cut me," he said, "I'll brush your hair dry for you."

Before Willow could answer, Caleb turned again, walking swiftly toward the trees. She stared at his retreating back, her thoughts scattering at the idea of shaving a naked man in a warm pool.

That wasn't what he meant, Willow assured herself. *Was it?*

She went toward camp, stopping long enough to turn over the clothes that were drying in the meadow. She had to shoo Trey away from her Levis—the tall gelding apparently was intrigued by the scent of freshly washed clothes. Willow felt the same way herself. Whether denim or wool or flannel, the cloth smelled of sunshine and meadow and a hint of lavender. She inhaled deeply, loving the mixture of fragrances.

By the time Willow got to camp, found the folding razor, and crossed the meadow again, more than ten minutes had passed. She hurried barefoot through the forest, watching for stones beneath the thick carpet of pine needles. When she saw the pool glimmering through the trees, she stopped.

Caleb was still in the water.

"Caleb?" she called. "Are you ready?"

"Sure. Come to the far side of the pool."

With slowing steps, Willow approached the pool.

Caleb was sitting at the opposite side of the pool, where a ledge formed an uneven kind of bench. Just behind him, the runoff from the hidden hot spring cascaded into the pool, sending water seething and swirling up to his breastbone.

"Don't you want to get out?" she asked.

"I wouldn't mind, but you would probably blush to your heels," Caleb said calmly.

"Oh." Willow's breath caught. "Should I go away until you can put the blanket back on?" she asked quickly.

"Don't bother. The water covers more of me than the blanket did."

Willow tried to speak but her voice had dried up. She took a slow breath. "Caleb?"

"Hmm?"

"I've never been around a . . ." Her voice died as she remembered she was supposed to be a married woman. If she told Caleb she had never been close to a naked man, he would wonder what kind of a marriage she had. "That is, it's been a long time since I . . ."

"Shaved a man?" Caleb finished for her. "Don't worry, honey. I'll hold real still."

Uncertainly, Willow stood at the edge of the pool and nibbled on her lower lip. Caleb waited, seeing her ambivalence in the way she held her body. She was poised to flee, yet she was watching him with an expression close to yearning.

Wary little trout. She senses me coming closer and closer and knows she should swim away. But she likes the feel of my hands on her body too well.

God, so do I.

What did that bastard Reno do to make her so skittish of a man?

"Quit torturing your lip, honey," Caleb said finally. "I didn't mean to crowd you. Just leave the razor. I'll shave myself. It won't be the first time."

"But there's no mirror."

"I'll find a quiet piece of water."

"My—my hands are shaking," Willow said, wanting to explain why she wasn't going to shave him.

"I can see that. Go on back to camp. I'll be along in a few minutes."

She drew a deep breath, but couldn't bring herself to leave. She wanted to stay too much. Lifting the blanket, looking only at her feet, she waded across the tepid creek that flowed from the pool into the meadow. Under Caleb's watchful eyes, she picked her way around the pool until she could place the folding razor within reach of his long arm. Telling herself she shouldn't look, but unable to keep from a single swift glance, she realized that Caleb was right. The water covered more of him than the blanket had.

Most of the time.

But sometimes, for just an instant, the froth would swirl away and offer a tantalizing glimpse of the man beneath the seething silver water. Before Willow could realize what she had seen, the currents would shift again, concealing everything but Caleb's wide shoulders rising above the pool.

Slowly, Willow settled by the edge of the water, rearranging the blanket so that she could sit without revealing more than her naked feet. After a moment of taut silence, Caleb reached for the soap he had brought and began lathering his wet beard. When he finished, he held his hand out for the razor. Willow put half of the folding blade in his hand, but held onto the other half.

"If you trust me not to cut you, I would like to shave you."

Caleb closed his eyes, afraid that Willow would see the stark hunger in them. "I'd like that."

"I don't think I can reach you from here. Can you move closer to the edge?"

"Not without making you blush." He hesitated before adding matter-of-factly, "There's room for you to stand near me, if you don't mind getting wet again. Your hair will cover whatever the water doesn't."

Willow looked at Caleb. His eyes were closed and his body was relaxed on the wide ledge, as though the hot water had unravelled the constant vigilance that was so much a part of him. Reassured by his casual acceptance of the situation, she pulled her hair forward until it covered her breasts, took off the blanket, and set it beyond the reach of the dancing water. Carefully, she eased into the pool. She had bathed on the other side, where the pool deepened gradually. It got deep very quickly here.

Her foot slipped and she made a startled sound. Instantly, Caleb's hands closed around her waist.

"Hang on," he said. He lifted Willow and settled her sideways across his knees, shifted his grip, and held her out in front of him. "There's another ledge of rock somewhere close to my feet. Find it?"

After a moment of fishing around with her toes, Willow nodded, looking everywhere but at Caleb. The instant of feeling his bare legs beneath her wet bottom had doubled her heartbeat.

"Can you stand?" he asked.

Willow tried, but the water was almost up to her breasts and quite turbulent, for she was in the direct flow of the cascade. After a few attempts, she managed to brace herself against the stone ledge and between Caleb's knees.

"All right?" Caleb asked.

"I think so."

He smiled slightly, settled back, and closed his eyes. "Make damn sure, honey. I only have one throat."

Willow laughed and felt better. Caleb was so matter-of-fact about the situation that she felt foolish being nervous.

"Hold still now," she cautioned.

As it had been during the battle with the Comancheros, once Willow had a task for her hands, they stopped trembling. She shaved Caleb with quick, deft motions, washing the blade after each stroke. The lather vanished within seconds, torn apart by the currents that boiled softly throughout the pool.

Caleb sat motionless, but not from fear of being cut. He was afraid if he moved it would be to grab the trout that had so nearly come within his reach. The knowledge of his own nakedness and Willow's body so close by aroused him violently. The gentleness of her hands caring for him was also arousing, but in a different way. It brought a feeling of being cherished that strengthened rather than weakened his self-control.

"Almost done," Willow said, rinsing the razor. "You want to keep your mustache, don't you?"

"Damn straight," he said dryly.

"Good. I like the feel of it on my skin," she said, concentrating on her work rather than her words. "There. That's it. All clean."

She rinsed the razor, folded it, and looked up into the tawny blaze of Caleb's eyes. He took the razor and set it on a rock without looking away from Willow.

"Do you really?" he asked, his voice deep.

"Do I what?"

"Like the feel of my mustache on your skin?"

Willow heard the echo of her own incautious words. Color stained her cheekbones. "Close your eyes."

"Why? I've seen you blush before."

"I'm going to rinse off your face."

Cupping her palms, she tried to bring warm water to his cheeks, but more water drained away than touched him.

"Here," Caleb said. He put his hands beneath Willow's, then lowered them until they were a few inches beneath the water. He bent his head and moved his face from side to side, stroking his cheeks against her hands. When the last of the lather was gone, he took her hands from the water and kissed the center of her palms. "Thank you, Willow. No woman has ever cared enough to shave me."

Of their own accord, Willow's fingers moved from Caleb's face to his hair, tangling softly in the thick, damp strands. "I'll cut your hair, too, if you like."

"I'd rather you let me kiss you. Will you do that?" he asked.

She smiled. "Yes, I think I will. I like your kisses, Caleb. I like them very much."

A faint shudder went through him. "That's a dangerous thing to say to me."

"Why?"

"Come here and I'll tell you."

Willow leaned closer, only to lose her footing on the lower ledge. It didn't matter. Caleb's hands had already closed around her. He leaned forward, holding her upright in the seething water. The brush of his mustache across her lips made her shiver with anticipation.

"I want to taste you," he said against her mouth. "Let me in, honey. Let me kiss you the way we both want it."

His teeth closed on Willow's lower lip in a caress that was both sensuous demand and sensual plea. She made a small sound and opened her mouth, wanting the kiss as much as he did. The slow penetration and retreat of his tongue made her hands clench on his arms. She wanted more of his taste, of his caresses, of him. She wanted to be as close to him as the untamed pool.

With a small, hungry sound, Willow gave back the kiss in the only way she knew, the way Caleb had taught her, a teasing dance of tongue against tongue, warmth against warmth, hunger stroking hunger until they were locked together in mutual exploration and demand. Vaguely she sensed herself being lifted and turned until she was astride his legs, but her only thought was to lure him even more completely into the kiss, wanting to become so much a part of him that the kiss would never end.

Slowly, gently, relentlessly, Caleb separated himself from the embrace. Fighting for the control he had felt slipping away with each honeyed stroke of Willow's tongue, he looked at her with a raw hunger he couldn't conceal.

"Willow," he said hoarsely. "My God . . ."

Shuddering, Caleb closed his eyes against the picture she made, her lips reddened by the passionate kiss, her hair floating in golden streams around both of them, her breasts revealed through the wet lace of her camisole, her back arched over his arm, her long legs astride his. The memory of how her pantelets opened went through him in a savage stroke of need. If he moved forward just a few inches, he would be brushing unhindered against the thatch of golden hair.

As Willow's glance followed Caleb's, she realized that she might as well be naked from the waist up. From the waist down she was concealed as he was. Most of the time. She looked down, then glanced up in shock when the hard proof of his passion was revealed by a shift of the current.

"Easy, honey, don't panic now. I won't do anything you don't want me to. Hell," Caleb said roughly, "just kissing you is hotter than having another woman.

You go to my head faster than whiskey."

Willow took a breath, saw the narrowing of Caleb's eyes as he watched her breasts, and remembered how it had felt to have his hands and mouth caressing her. She knew he had also enjoyed it, yet he made no move toward her now. He simply held her and looked at her with a hunger that made her weak. Despite his obvious need, he was in control of himself.

I won't do anything you don't want me to.

With a virgin's serene misunderstanding of the power of passion, Willow decided that she could venture more deeply into the compelling currents that swirled between her and Caleb.

"Does that mean you want to kiss me again?" she asked, her eyes luminous.

"Yes," he said, drawing her slowly near, "I want to kiss you, Willow."

She tangled her fingers in his hair with a hunger she didn't understand, impatient to feel the intimacy of his kiss once more. All he did was brush his open mouth over her, caressing her without claiming her, tasting her eyebrows and hair and cheeks, but not the lips that trembled with desire.

"Caleb," she said finally, "I thought you wanted to kiss me."

"I am kissing you."

"Yes, and it's very nice, but that kind of kissing makes me, well, restless."

He smiled slowly. "Does it?"

The very male smile sent another lash of restlessness through Willow.

"You're teasing me," she accused.

"God, honey, I sure hope so."

"But why?"

"Because I've never known anything sweeter than holding you like this with the water all wild around us. So if you want more than I'm giving you, you'll have to spell it out for me. I don't want to scare you away, Willow. I don't want this to end for a long, long time."

"I don't want it to end, either," she admitted, tracing the line of Caleb's jaw to his chin, nuzzling the newly revealed dimple with her fingertip, then sliding down to test again the power and resilience of his shoulder. "You feel so good."

Caleb closed his eyes and wondered how much he could take before he lost control and frightened Willow away.

"Tell me, honey. Tell me what you want."

She looked at the harsh lines of his face, felt the tension drawing his body taut, and whispered. "Don't you know?"

His eyes opened. The passion in their depths was like twin candle flames burning. Carefully, he bent down and bit her lower lip, making her shiver and arch closer to him, her breasts brushing his chest and her hips so close that he felt control slipping away again. Ruthlessly, he clamped down on the hunger that made his whole body rigid.

"I know what you want, but I don't know how much," Caleb said, biting Willow's lower lip again. "If you're too shy to tell me, show me. Do whatever you want to me, however you want it. Anything, honey. Everything."

The temptation was extraordinary, the lure irresistible. She rose to it gracefully, coming closer to the instant when escape would be not only impossible, but unwelcome.

"Whatever I want?" Willow asked huskily.

"However you want it."

"I want it . . . all," she whispered, looking at Caleb's mouth.

With a groan, he pulled her closer and gave her what she had asked for, taking her mouth even as she took his. The kiss was like the pool itself, hot and constantly changing, teaching her how intimate a kiss could be. She pulled herself closer and yet closer to Caleb's body, making soft sounds and flexing her hands rhythmically on his arms, testing his male strength with a hunger she couldn't explain.

Restlessly, Willow combed her fingers through the dark hair on Caleb's chest. When she brushed over his nipples his kiss deepened even more. Instinctively, she returned to the sensitive nubs again, intrigued by both the changing texture and the tangible response she drew from him.

Then Willow felt Caleb's hands on her own breasts, felt him coaxing her nipples taut. Sensual lightning coursed through her body, making her moan. When his hands released her, she made a hoarse sound of disappointment.

"What?" he said against her mouth. "Tell me, Willow."

"Again." The word was broken, as hungry as the pink nipples pressing against the fragile fabric of her camisole. "Oh, Caleb, *again*."

Long fingers moved over the ribbons on Willow's camisole. The transparent cloth parted, floating up on the seething water.

"Lift up your hair, honey."

She gathered up the floating strands and pulled them behind her head. When her arms lifted, her breasts were visible through the turbulent water. Caleb's eyes narrowed hungrily as he looked at her. His lips parted, showing the white edge of his teeth, and she knew that he wanted to kiss her again, differently. She remembered how it had been to feel his tongue teasing her breasts, his teeth gently caressing, his mouth tugging on her as she changed to meet the sweet demands he made.

"Caleb," Willow said huskily.

He looked up, afraid he would find fear in her eyes. Instead he found fire.

"Will you . . . kiss me the way you did this morning?" she asked.

Slowly, Caleb's hands tightened, lifting Willow from the water until one of her breasts brushed against his mustache. He felt the shivering that went through her, tightening her nipple until it nuzzled against his lips. His tongue flicked out, circled her, drew her in, loved her until her breath broke and her fingers dug heedlessly into his shoulders. He smiled and closed his teeth around her with exquisite care. She gasped as she arched against him, twisting slowly, knowing only his mouth and the wild singing of passion deep within her body.

Caleb ached to tangle his fingers in the dark gold at the apex of Willow's thighs, to test the sleek depths of her, to know if she needed him as much as he needed her. But when he had touched her like that before, she had panicked and begged him to stop. Now she was on her knees in front of him, astride the clenched power of his thighs, her hips moving with the rhythms of his mouth on her breast. Now he couldn't bear to have her turn away.

His teeth closed gently on her velvet nipple once more, making her cry out with pleasure. He released her and looked at the transformation passion had wrought in her body. Her breathing was as rapid as his, her creamy breasts were flushed with heat and the loving marks of his mouth, her lips were red, trembling, and her pupils had dilated until her eyes were nearly black.

She was the most beautiful thing he had ever seen.

"C-Caleb?"

He closed his eyes because he could not bear to look at Willow any longer without touching the silky flesh hidden between her legs.

"I—I want—more. But I don't know—what." Willow shivered with soft violence. "Help me, Caleb. *Help me.*"

His eyes opened and a stillness came over him as he realized that Willow was telling the simple truth. She was stretched on a rack of passion and had no idea how to find release.

"The kind of touch you want from me made you panic once before."

Caleb saw the moment of understanding break over Willow, saw her shudder and close her eyes. For the space of a long breath they remained closed. Then she took her hands, put them over his, and slowly pulled them down her body, drawing them from her breasts to her waist, skimming the deeply indented curves of her torso. Just below her navel, she lost her courage.

"Stay with me," Caleb said against Willow's mouth when she would have lifted her hands from his. "That way I'll know you want it, too."

Her hands rested over his as he slowly eased his palms down her body, seeking the womanly fullness of her hips. The frail cotton of her pantelets was little barrier to his touch. He filled his hands with her round curves and squeezed. She gasped and shivered violently.

"Frightened?" he asked softly.

"It feels . . . strange."

"Bad?"

"No, it just makes me ache in the oddest places."

"Does it? Where?"

Willow's breath thickened into a soft moan as Caleb's big hands flexed again, making her very aware of the luxuriant flare of her own hips.

"Is that where you ache?" he asked, smiling slightly.

She shook her head.

"Where, honey?"

Willow bit her lip and looked at Caleb, torn between passion and embarrassment. "Don't you know?"

"I'm beginning to think I don't know much about you at all," he admitted in a low voice. His hands flexed and his whole body clenched at the passion coursing visibly through Willow in response to his touch. "Where does it ache, little one? If you're too shy to tell me, take my hand and show me."

For a moment, Willow didn't think she had the courage to do even that. Then currents swirled and tugged at her, sending a glittering burst of sensation through the pit of her stomach, leaving behind a redoubled ache. She took one of Caleb's big hands and slowly brought it from her hip to her navel and from there to the warm, water-washed triangle at the apex of her thighs.

"There?" Caleb asked softly.

Willow tried to look at him but couldn't. She closed her eyes and nodded. His palm covered her as his long fingers sought the opening in the pantelets and curled down between her legs, gently seeking her softest flesh, finding it, holding her so close that not even the seething waters of the pool came between them. Her breathing unravelled in a low moan. Instinctively, she tried to protect her tender flesh by closing her legs. It was impossible. She was kneeling astride his thighs, balancing herself by holding onto his shoulders.

"Easy, little love. I won't hurt you."

Willow barely heard Caleb's low voice. His hand was moving slowly, both soothing her and increasing the sensual ache. Bright splinters of sensation raced up from his touch, driving away her uncertainty, leaving only a stark pleasure that shortened her breath. Then she felt the tender probing of his finger and stiffened as though he had laid a whip across her bare flesh.

"*Caleb.*"

He clenched his jaw and closed his eyes, forcing himself to withdraw from the sleek feminine heat he had just discovered. But he couldn't force himself to release Willow completely. She felt too good against the palm of his hand, too soft, too hot. Nor could he prevent the languid, caressing movements of his fingers that made her even softer, hotter. Without meaning to, he probed very lightly. She shuddered but didn't withdraw.

"Do you want me to stop?" Caleb asked, his voice rough with passion and restraint.

Willow's only answer was a moan as something deep inside her tightened and then tightened again, making her body twist slowly against Caleb's touch.

"Willow?"

"I don't know the words for what I want," she said raggedly. "But I like having you touch me. I like feeling you against me . . . inside me. Do you like it, too, being inside me?"

Caleb fought a silent, savage battle with his body. All that enabled him to keep his self-control was the near certainty that Willow wasn't what he had thought her to be.

"Yes, I like it," he said almost roughly. "But I thought you didn't. You went stiff."

Willow heard the hunger and restraint in his voice, and something more, an uncertainty she had never heard before from him. She looked at Caleb with luminous hazel eyes.

"I couldn't help what I did," she admitted. "Being touched like that . . ."

"Did I hurt you?"

She shook her head. "It was just unexpected."

"Did you like it?"

"Yes," Willow said. "It sent heat all through me, everywhere, but especially where you're holding me now. I love your hands, Caleb. They're a beautiful fire on my body."

He tried to speak but couldn't. A hammer blow of passion shook him, taking him right up to the edge of ecstasy and leaving him there, shaking. He had never lost control with a woman, but he was a heartbeat away from it now.

"Hold onto me, Willow. Hold on hard. I'm going to touch you again. There's something I have to know."

Willow started to ask what Caleb meant, but the movement of his hand took her breath away. Tenderly, relentlessly, two fingers pressed into her tight, sleek center. Her nails dug suddenly into his bare shoulders. At first Caleb thought he was hurting Willow. Then he felt her shiver, felt the sultry pulses of her pleasure. He smiled through clenched teeth and probed lightly, seeking her depths. He was barred from them by the taut, frail barrier of her maidenhead.

Breath hissed through Caleb's clenched teeth at the proof of Willow's innocence. He knew he should withdraw from her, leaving her virginity intact if not untouched.

And he knew he could not force himself to withdraw.

The certainty that Willow was no man's fancy lady made it impossible for Caleb to release her. She hadn't known a man's kiss, hadn't known the touch of a man's hands on her breasts, hadn't known the tender, savage fires of passion. Yet she knelt nearly naked in front of him now, accepting his presence within her innocence, and her softness caressed him in return, urging him to explore more deeply the secrets only he had ever touched.

She was his, only his, and he should not take her.

"Willow."

Her name was as much a groan as a word, but she understood. She made a murmurous sound that was pleasure and questioning combined.

"You're a virgin," Caleb said simply.

Willow opened her mouth. Nothing came out but a gasp of pleasure when he moved within her.

"I—that is—" She shuddered and threw back her head, forgetting what she had been going to say.

"Don't bother trying to deny it. I'm touching the proof of your chastity right now." Caleb's eyes opened. Passion made them almost opaque, like hammered gold. His voice was as rough as his touch was gentle. "What is he to you?"

"Who?"

"Matthew Moran."

Willow blinked and tried to gather her thoughts. "My brother. Matt is my brother."

Caleb went utterly still for an instant before breath rushed out of him as though at a body blow. Killing Willow's fancy man was one thing. Killing her brother was entirely another.

Willow would never forgive him.

Her brother. Rebecca's seducer, the man who murdered my sister as surely as if he had put a gun to her head and pulled the trigger.

Willow's brother!

Closing his eyes, shutting out Willow, Caleb tried to ease the strident demands of the hunger clawing at his body so that he could think. All he could do was scream silently inside his mind at the savage trick of fate that finally had given him a woman whose passions ran as strong and deep and hot as his own, only to make it impossible to have her, leaving him empty in ways he had never been empty before.

Slowly, Caleb began withdrawing from Willow's body, feeling as though he were being torn in two, yet knowing if he took her, she would hate herself when she saw him standing over her brother's body.

Her brother's killer.

Her lover.

Willow.

Caleb didn't know he had spoken her name aloud until he felt the warm rush of Willow's breath over her lips.

"It's all right," she said urgently. "I understand. I finally understand." Her kisses were quick, biting, almost frantic as she felt Caleb's touch sliding from her body, setting her afire all over again even as he withdrew. "Listen to me," she said, her voice shaking. "You told me that one day I would be on my knees in front of you, only I wouldn't be begging you to stop. You were right. I'm begging you now, Caleb. Don't stop. If you stop touching me, I'll die. Please, Caleb. I'm beg—"

With an anguished sound, Caleb took Willow's mouth, stilling the pleas that were too painful for him to hear any longer. He kissed her deeply, wanting to sink so completely into her that she would never be able to turn her back on him, no matter what he did, no matter who died.

The kiss wasn't enough. It would never be enough. Willow knew it as well as Caleb did. Her hand went down his body, blindly seeking to complete the joining he had prepared her for. Slender fingers found Caleb, measured him, approved him with an honesty that nearly undid him. He shook with the force of the passion raging through his body, demanding to be freed of all restraint.

With a thick sound of need, Caleb put his hand over Willow's as he pulled her down onto his thighs, pressing his aching flesh against her, gently parting the soft folds of skin and touching even softer flesh, pushing a finger's width into her before control returned and he forced himself to stop.

But he could not force himself to withdraw.

"Willow," Caleb said hoarsely. "Push me away."

She curled her hand around him, but not to follow his command. The pressure of his hard flesh just inside her body was delicious. She wanted more of him, not less. She settled more completely over him and instinctively drew up her knees, pushing him a bit more deeply into her body.

"No!" Caleb said, clenching his hands around Willow's narrow waist, stilling her motions. "If I take your innocence, someday you'll hate yourself as much as you'll hate me."

Eyes closed, she shivered and pressed harder, taking more of him.

"Oh God," he groaned. "Willow, don't."

"I can't help it. I've needed you all my life and I didn't even know it. I love you, Caleb Black." She leaned forward and kissed him, wanting him. "I love you."

Agony twisted through Caleb, tearing him until he wanted to scream his protest at the casual cruelty of life. Willow loved him . . . and as soon as he found Reno, love would become hate.

But it was too late for regrets, too late for explanations, too late for anything except the sweet violence of passion claiming them.

"Open your eyes, Willow. I want to see you. I want to remember what it was like to be loved by you, because sure as sunrise, someday you'll hate me."

Caleb's voice was hoarse beyond recognition. Willow's eyes opened slowly. They were luminous with love, smoky with passion. She watched his eyes as he pressed more deeply into her. He wanted to ask if he was hurting her, but he had no voice. He had taken women with affection, with gentleness, with pleasure, yet never before had he felt the shattering intimacy of joining himself with a woman in the way he was joining with Willow now—openly, watching her as she watched him, seeing and feeling the exact instant when he transformed her body from virgin to woman, hearing her soft cries as he filled her completely, knowing each elemental shivering of passion through her as though it were his own body shivering.

He would have spoken to her then, told her how beautiful she was, how much the gift of her innocence meant to him, but he couldn't breathe. She was sleek and tight around him, and the honey of her passion was hotter than the pool. He rocked gently against her, heard her breath break, and forced himself to be still.

"Am I hurting you?" Caleb asked in a low voice.

"No," Willow said. "It's good—so good. Like flying. Like riding fire. Oh God—I can't bear it. Don't stop—don't ever stop!"

Willow's broken words took the world away, leaving only the fire of passion consuming both of them. Caleb found her mouth in a kiss that was both tender and yet demanded her very soul. His fingers sank deeply into her hips, squeezing, feeling the hidden shuddering of her response tugging at him, stripping away his control one hot pulse at a time. Blindly, he searched through the wet silk of her hair, seeking her most sensitive flesh, discovering it taut and full. He caught the sleek nub between his fingers, rubbing as he rocked against her, harder and deeper each time.

Caleb's name was torn from Willow's throat as passion wracked her. Her anguished cry seared through him, driving him more deeply into her, taking both of them more deeply into the heart of fire. He drank her cries as he wanted to drink the passion coursing through her, to know every bit of her, to sink into her soul. Knowing he should hold back, yet needing her too much to control the full force of his passion, he stroked her soft flesh hungrily, relentlessly, demanding everything she could give to him.

"Forgive me, love," Caleb groaned even as he stroked Willow again, dragging fresh cries from her lips. "I can't stop. It's never been like this. I can't—stop."

Willow's back arched and Caleb's name came from her lips with every rapid breath she took, every motion he made. Suddenly the pleasure became too much to bear, the rack of passion too tight to endure any longer. She cried out for release from the sensual vise that was almost pain.

And then release came, consuming her more deeply than pleasure had, ecstasy shaking her until she wept.

Willow's broken cries stripped away the last vestige of Caleb's control. He drove into her again and again while the sweet violence of release consumed him as completely as it had her. With a harsh, exultant shout he spent himself repeatedly inside her soft, shivering body.

And then he held her, rocked her, crying her name in silence, unable to believe he had seduced the innocent sister of the man he had vowed to kill.

13

"**A**RE you all right?" Caleb asked finally, afraid to open his eyes and see how much pain his unbridled passion had caused Willow.

Reluctant to disturb the golden aftermath of ecstasy, she made a murmurous sound and rubbed her cheek languidly against Caleb's chest.

"Willow?"

She tilted her face back until she could see her lover's tawny eyes.

"Forgive me," Caleb said in a raw voice. "I didn't mean to hurt you." He shook his head in a gesture of bafflement. "I've never lost control like that."

Willow's slow, womanly smile made heat slide impossibly through Caleb's veins.

"If you're waiting for me to berate you, you'll wait a long, long time," she said, kissing his shoulder, smiling.

A strong finger tilted Willow's chin up until Caleb could look directly into her eyes. He saw no pain, no shadows, nothing but the radiance of a woman who had found completion in the elemental union of male and female.

"I didn't hurt you?"

"Well, you almost did at first. You're, er . . ."

"Too rough," he said bluntly.

Willow gave him a surprised look. "That wasn't what I meant."

He waited.

"Caleb," she said in exasperation, "you must have noticed that you're a big man. Big hands, big feet, big shoulders, big . . . just big, that's all."

He saw the red staining Willow's cheeks and the laughter lurking in her beautiful hazel eyes. His heart ached at the thought of hurting her in any way at all. Gently, he kissed her lips and wished that she were anyone except Reno's sister—even a fancy lady who had known many men.

But Willow had been a virgin, and she would always be Reno's sister.

No point moaning over spilled milk, Caleb told himself grimly. *What's done is done and I wouldn't undo it even if I could. I'll die remembering what it was like to take Willow, to hear her sweet cries, to feel her release tugging at me. A virgin, and she burned me alive.*

Maybe I'll get lucky. Maybe that son of a bitch will be killed by Indians or break his neck looking for gold. Maybe he'll be dead before I find him.

The thought was like a balm spreading through Caleb. But life hadn't taught him to believe in the easiest solution to any problem. It had taught him to do what had to be done, because too many people just looked away and left the dirty work for other people to take care of.

People like Caleb Black, who knew that the simple justice of an eye for an eye was never simple and rarely just, but the alternative was a West where the weak went unprotected and unavenged, a West where men without conscience preyed upon those least able to defend themselves.

If Reno isn't dead before I get to him, he soon will be. Or I will be. Or both.

Caleb gathered Willow close and held her, simply held her, for his thoughts were tearing at him.

"What's wrong?" she asked. "Didn't you enjoy what we did?"

He smiled sadly and buried his face in lavender-scented hair. "If I'd enjoyed it any more, I'd have died."

Willow laughed, but there was a catch in her voice. "Yes, it was like that, wasn't it? Dying, but not quite. Being reborn, but not the same." Her arms tightened around Caleb. "I'll never be the same again. You're part of me now."

"Remember that," he said, holding her hard, his voice rough. "Remember that when you look at me and see the man who took your innocence. I should have controlled myself. I didn't. I couldn't. I've never been like that with a woman. I'm sorry, Willow."

"I'm not. I love you."

Willow held her breath, wanting to hear him say he loved her. All that came was the steamy whispering of the water around their joined bodies as Caleb turned his head and claimed her mouth in a kiss that was both tender and so intense that it left Willow shaken.

"Someday you'll remember having said that, and you'll wish you had held your tongue," Caleb said quietly. "But I'm glad to hear it. I'm glad to know I pleased you."

Fear squeezed Willow's heart, draining some of the radiance from her. "Caleb, what's wrong? I don't understand."

"I know." He took a deep breath and tried to tell Willow about his dead sister and the man who had seduced her, but Caleb could no more force himself to speak and destroy the light in Willow's eyes than he had been able to prevent himself from taking the gift of her untouched body. "After we find your brother, you'll understand."

The questions Willow would have asked were scattered by Caleb's kiss. She didn't understand the yearning in him, or the darkness. She didn't understand the unhappiness she sensed in him when she spoke of love, yet she knew all of those things existed as surely as did the stirring of his body within hers once more.

What Willow did understand was that she wanted to bring Caleb ease and laughter, to be the sunrise banishing darkness from his life.

Reluctantly, Caleb ended the kiss. "If you don't get off my lap," he said, biting Willow's lips just a bit fiercely, "my good intentions will go to Hell in a handcart."

"What good intentions?"

"I'm trying not to seduce you again."

"Ever?" Willow asked, unable to conceal her dismay.

Caleb closed his eyes and silently conceded that it would be better if he never pressed into Willow's soft body again, sinking into her, losing himself in the baffling, overwhelming currents of passion that flowed between the two of them. But the thought of never taking her again was unbearable. He had never known anyone like Willow. She satisfied him as no other woman ever had, teaching him how hungry he had been before he had found her.

And he had just begun to plumb the depths of the passion in her.

"I'm trying not to seduce you right now," Caleb said, his voice thick.

"Why?"

"It's too soon for you. I don't want to hurt you."

Willow smiled slightly. "You aren't hurting me."

"I'm not moving in you, either. But I will be real quick if you don't get up."

Caleb put his hands around Willow's waist and began lifting her from his lap. The feel of her gliding over his hardening flesh took his breath away. He heard her stifled gasp and his hands tightened, testing the sleek resilience of her waist. The gasp became a throaty sound of pleasure.

"Stop it," Caleb said, bending until he could bite the smooth skin of Willow's shoulder.

"Stop what?" she murmured as she threaded her fingers through his hair.

"Making me want to stay in this pool and take you until I'm so weak I drown."

"Weak?" Slender hands kneaded Caleb's shoulders and the thick muscles of his biceps. "You feel about as weak as a mountain."

"Didn't you know? Being with a woman weakens a man."

Willow laughed and moved her hips, frankly measuring him. "Do tell. When?"

His breath came in hard.

"When does it weaken you?" she repeated as she moved her hips again.

Caleb's slow smile made Willow shiver with anticipation.

"You'll be the first to know," he promised. Then he set his teeth and lifted her free of his aroused flesh, biting back a groan as he did so. "After you, the water feels cold."

When Willow understood the meaning of his words, she took a quick, broken breath. "And I feel empty. Is it—is it natural to want you like that, to want to stay that way forever?"

Caleb's tawny eyes changed as the heat of his body redoubled, set afire by the knowledge that Willow truly enjoyed having him inside her.

"How did you stay innocent so long?" he asked.

"I didn't feel this way with other men. Only you," Willow said simply. "Even my fiancé. When Steven held my hand or kissed my cheek, it was nice, but it didn't make my heart run away and my chest so tight I couldn't breathe."

"Your fiancé?" Caleb said harshly. "Are you engaged?"

"He died three years ago."

Visibly, Caleb relaxed. "The war?"

Willow nodded.

"Do you still love him?"

"No. I know now that I never loved him. Not really. Not the way I love—"

Caleb's quick, fierce kiss shut off Willow's words. "Out of the water, woman. My good intentions are shrinking by the second."

"Shrinking? I would have said the opposite," she muttered beneath her breath.

There was a crack of surprised laughter from Caleb, followed by a single word. "Out!"

He emphasized his command by putting his hand on Willow's smooth bottom and giving her a boost. Just as his palm fell away, his touch changed to a caress that traced the shadowed curve between her hips.

Breathlessly, Willow scrambled out of the warm water and picked up the cotton blanket she had left on the rocks. She turned around just as Caleb emerged from the pool. Silver rivulets poured from his body, highlighting every texture of his masculinity. The blunt thrust of his arousal was startling.

"Too late to run now," Caleb said dryly, watching Willow's eyes widen as she measured him. "We fitted together like a hand in a velvet glove and you loved every bit of it."

She swallowed, flushed scarlet, and said in a faint

voice, "I'm sorry. I didn't mean to stare at you."

"You're still staring."

"Oh." Guiltily, she closed her eyes.

Caleb took a step forward, bent, and kissed Willow's cheek lightly. "Look all you like. I'm just teasing you. You're so sweet to tease. Like licking honey." He leaned over, scooped up his razor and his own blanket, and held out his free hand to her. "Come on. I promised to brush your hair dry."

Her eyes opened. "And you always keep your promises, don't you?"

"Always. Even the ones I don't want to." Caleb's mouth flattened into a grim line. "Especially those."

An eye for an eye.

"You don't have to brush my hair if you don't want to," Willow said hesitantly. "I know it's a lot of trouble getting all the tangles out."

Caleb smiled and threaded his fingers more deeply between hers. "I love brushing your hair. It's like brushing sunlight." He saw her shiver and squeezed her hand. "Come on. It's warmer in the meadow."

Ishmael's head came up the instant they stepped from the cover of the trees out onto the grass. The stallion watched for a few moments before he returned to eating.

"He's wary for a horse that's never run wild," Caleb said.

"That wariness saved my life during the war. He'd smell the soldiers coming and set up a ruckus. Mama and I would run for the forest if she was well enough, or the cellar if she wasn't."

Caleb's hand tightened. He brought Willow's fingers to his mouth and stroked across them with his mustache.

"I don't like thinking about you being in danger, being hurt, being scared, being hungry." He hesitated, baffled by the fierce protectiveness he felt toward Willow. "It unsettles me."

"Lots of women had a worse time of it than I did. I was lucky. The only soldier who ever found me looked the other way."

"Maybe he had a sister."

Something in Caleb's voice reminded Willow that he, too, had a sister. "Maybe he did. Like you."

"Rebecca is dead."

Willow flinched at the barely repressed savagery she sensed beneath Caleb's words. "I'm sorry."

"She was seduced and then abandoned by a man. I went out looking for her lover to bring him back to marry her. She died of childbed fever. Her baby girl died a few hours later. I didn't find out for a month."

"Dear God," Willow said. "I'm so sorry, Caleb."

He looked down into her clear, compassionate eyes and wondered what she would say if he told her that the baby who had died was her niece.

"I swore to kill him," Caleb said evenly. "When I find him, I will."

Willow looked at the bleak expression in Caleb's eyes and had no doubt that he would do just that. She remembered her first impression of Caleb. Dangerous. And her second. An implacable, dark angel of justice.

Eye for eye, tooth for tooth, life for life.

A chill moved over Willow's skin, roughening it. There was an intensity and a power in Caleb that was almost frightening.

"You're shivering," Caleb said, frowning. He wrapped his blanket around Willow's shoulders, led her across the meadow, and spread the cotton blanket she was carrying. "Lie down here. You'll be warmer next to the grass where the breeze can't get to you. I'll get your brush and comb."

Caleb left before Willow could tell him that she wasn't cold, not in the way that he had meant. After a moment, she stretched out on her stomach on the blanket, trying not to think about the sister Caleb had lost and the man he had sworn to kill because of it.

Very soon, Willow realized Caleb had been right about getting warmer out of reach of the breeze. Before he had gone the hundred feet to camp, she pulled off the wool blanket and tossed it aside. The fine cotton and lace of her underwear dried quickly in the direct sun. Within minutes, heat infused her, making her feel languorous. She stretched luxuriantly, smiling at the sheer pleasure of being alive.

"You look like a kitten that's just discovered cream," Caleb said.

"That's what I feel like," Willow admitted.

She opened her eyes as Caleb knelt beside her. A single glance told her that he was still as naked as the sunlight, still powerful, still potent. When her eyes returned to his, the smile he gave her was both amused and rueful.

"You have a pronounced effect on me," he said.

"I noticed."

"Not frightened anymore?"

She shook her head.

"Embarrassed?"

"Well . . ." But she was unable to deny the blush that crept up her body.

Caleb laughed softly and brushed the back of his fingers over Willow's flushed cheek. "You'll get used to me, little one. Just like I've gotten used to being naked with you."

She gave him a puzzled look.

"In some ways," he admitted, "I'm as new to this kind of play as you are."

Willow blinked. "You are?"

Caleb hesitated, wondering how to explain something he wasn't sure he understood himself. He wanted Willow to know this was the first time he had found a woman whose sensuality increased and enhanced his own, each driving the other higher and then higher, teaching and learning with every touch, every cry, every kiss.

"None of the women I've known made me want to be buck naked with them in a sunny meadow," Caleb said finally. "I doubt if any of them would have wanted to be naked with me. Not one of them could make me hard with a look, a word, a casual touch." He made a baffled sound and added ruefully, "It's damned unsettling, if you want the truth. You reach places inside me I didn't know were there."

"You do the same to me."

Willow's husky admission made Caleb want to ravish and cherish her at the same instant. The force of the conflicting urges held him motionless. Letting out his breath in a soundless curse, he picked up the wool blanket and began drying Willow's hair, working quickly yet gently, touching her in the only way he would permit himself.

Soon Willow's hair was lying in a rippling, shining fan over her shoulders. Long after the strands were dry, Caleb continued brushing, sifting through her hair, loving the feel of it caressing the sensitive skin between his fingers as he worked.

"You have the most beautiful hair," Caleb said, finally setting aside the brush.

Willow sighed and stirred, sitting up with a fluid movement, her legs curled to one side. The wild electricity of her hair made it cling to her even as it divided over her breasts and fell to her hips. Caleb stroked a flyaway handful back from her face. She kissed the masculine fingers that were gently tangled in the golden strands.

"Thank you." She smiled, remembering what he had once said. "In spite of your disdain at the idea, I think you would make a wonderful lady's maid."

Caleb's smile flashed beneath his mustache. "Southern lady. My God, what a surprise you were," he said huskily.

"Not southern," Willow said. Then she looked down at the fine lace clinging to her body, clothing whose dampness emphasized rather than concealed her breasts, her waist, the shadowed secrets at the apex of her thighs. "And not a lady."

"Hush," Caleb said, putting his fingers across Willow's mouth. "What happened wasn't your doing. It was mine. But I can't feel ashamed of what we did. It was too good for shame or regrets. Even if I could give you back your innocence, I wouldn't. I've never been given a gift half so sweet. Don't belittle yourself because of it."

Willow's smile was as beautiful and haunting as her eyes watching the man she loved, the man who had yet to talk of love to her. Yet Caleb was very gentle with her despite the harshness she knew he was capable of, a dark angel of justice, dangerous, deadly.

But not with her. Whether he ever spoke of love or not, he cherished her.

Willow kissed Caleb's fingers and admitted to herself that he was right about what they had shared. She should be embarrassed to remember their intimacy, to look at his nakedness, to sense with such clarity her own nudity beneath the flimsy lace. But she wasn't embarrassed. She had never felt more alive and yet more at peace than she did with Caleb. There was a rightness in being his woman that went to her very soul.

"I wouldn't take my innocence back," Willow whispered, kissing the calloused masculine fingers that were pressed against her lips. "I would never find a better man to give it to than you."

The lines in Caleb's face tightened as he heard Willow's soft words and felt the warmth of her lips whispering kisses against his hand.

"How do you feel?" he asked. "Still cold?"

Willow shook her head. Golden hair rippled and shimmered, falling over his hand like captive sunlight.

"No aches and pains?"

Despite the heightened color in Willow's cheeks, her slight smile was as old as Eve. "No pains."

"No aches, either?"

"None that can't be cured. What about you? Do you ache?"

As Willow spoke, her hand moved beneath a veil of golden hair until she could touch the blunt masculine flesh between Caleb's thighs. He jerked reflexively at the caress and his breath hissed between his teeth. Startled, Willow snatched back her hand.

"I'm sorry," she said quickly. "I didn't mean to hurt you."

Caleb let his breath out, trying to still the violent beating of his heart. "You didn't hurt me."

"You—moved."

"Have you ever been so close to a lightning bolt that you could feel currents racing through you? That's what it felt like when you touched me. Only it was pleasure racing through me, not pain, and the force of it surprised me."

Willow's eyes widened.

Caleb smiled despite the fire still coursing through him. "Go ahead, honey. Explore. You won't take me by surprise again."

"I don't want to hurt you," she said hesitantly.

"Then you better pet me again, because I want those soft hands on me so much I ache."

Willow looked from Caleb's rather fierce smile down the length of his body. He was kneeling beside her, facing her, sitting on his heels, his thighs flexed to take his weight. The long, powerful muscles of his legs stood out in relief. So did the quintessentially male flesh that was so responsive to her touch. She could count his heartbeats without even resting her fingers against him.

Despite their recent intimacy, in many ways Caleb's body was still a mystery to her. Hesitantly, Willow allowed her hand to settle on his thigh, curious about the elemental differences between male and female. The hair on his legs was thick, black, shiny, hot from the sun. His skin was warm and supple, and the muscle beneath was shockingly hard. His skin was darker than her own, though much lighter than the skin on his chest.

"You work stripped to the waist, don't you?" Willow asked without looking up.

"Sometimes."

Caleb's voice was thickened by desire. He was discovering that being looked at by Willow was almost as arousing as being petted by her. The sensuality, curiosity, and approval in her eyes made him feel as tall as a mountain. And as hard.

"But never all the way naked," Willow said, noting the fine pale skin sunlight had never touched before now.

"I told you, honey. In some ways this is as new to me as it is to you."

She smiled. "I like that. I like knowing I'm touching you in ways no one else ever has."

"You're barely touching me at all," Caleb pointed out hungrily, "but you're right just the same. No one has ever been like you, Willow. You make it all new."

Smiling, watching Caleb's face, Willow traced the thick upper muscle of his thigh with her fingertips. She saw the narrowing of his eyes, felt the tightening of his legs, heard the swift intake of his breath as she came closer and closer to the hard reality of his desire.

Her fingers tested the thick cushion of hair that surrounded his very different flesh. Hesitantly, then with greater assurance, she stroked the length of him, enjoying the heat and shifting masculine textures. When she reached the blunt tip, she made a surprised, approving sound.

"No wonder you didn't hurt me. You feel like satin, all warm and sleek and smooth."

Caleb's answer was a groan and a wild wave of desire hammering through his veins. If he hadn't already been on his knees, Willow's words and the skimming caress of her fingers would have brought him down. He couldn't prevent the potent response of his body, the silky residue glistening on her fingertips in stark testimony to the uncontrollable passion she called from him.

Willow's hand stilled.

"I'm sorry," Caleb said huskily. "I didn't mean to shock you."

"You didn't," she murmured.

"I sure as hell shocked myself," he said.

Willow glanced up at him, surprised.

"I'm not used to losing control like that," he said bluntly.

"Oh."

"I'm not used to this at all."

"Do you . . ." She hesitated. "Do you like having me touch you?"

Caleb smiled. "What do you think?"

Willow let her breath out in a rushing sigh. "I think I've never touched anything quite so fascinating. You make me shameless, Caleb. And I don't even care."

He bent down and kissed her gently. "There's no need for shame between us. Shame is for people who cheat and steal and destroy. Being together like this is part of creation, and it's good."

"Yes," she whispered. "It's good. Lock and key.

Woman and man. Two halves of a beautiful whole. All my life I've known that without really *knowing*." Willow smiled at Caleb. "How dull the world would have been if male and female were the same."

Caleb laughed, then his breath caught as one of Willow's slender hands glided between his legs, seeking more of the primal differences between male and female. Enjoying her open curiosity, Caleb shifted, allowing her to find what she sought. He was rewarded by a gentle exploration that brought him to the brink of losing control once more. He groaned, trying to stifle the overwhelming pulses of ecstasy. He was only partially successful.

With a soft sound, Willow touched the liquid silk of passion once more.

"How long," she asked softly, "do you think it would take you to get used to losing control?"

"I don't know," he admitted in a rueful voice, "but I get the feeling you're planning on finding out."

"Do you mind?" Willow's voice was as gentle as her fingers curling around him, exploring and memorizing him with slow movements of her hand even as she cupped him in her palm. "I'm discovering that I like touching you where you're most a man. I like seeing your eyes narrow and your whole body tighten as you fight against losing control. You're so strong, Caleb. I love that strength."

One of Willow's fingertips skimmed the blunt satin flesh whose smoothness and taut heat fascinated her. A sultry drop formed beneath her touch. She shivered visibly as her own body secretly answered. Her hands moved lovingly, cradling him, testing him, teasing him, admiring him.

Caleb shuddered in response to Willow's honest sensuality. A lightning stroke of desire surged through him. He heard her quickened breath and felt her fingertips gliding over his hot flesh, enjoying the result of the silky pulse that had escaped his control.

"Do you mind?" she asked again.

"Touch me any way you like. Let me touch you in the same way," Caleb said, words pouring recklessly from his lips as hungers he had never known existed were called from him by Willow's hands. "Let me show you everything I ever wanted with a woman. And then let me give you things you can't even imagine with a man."

"Yes," Willow whispered, drawing her nails very lightly down his straining flesh. "As long as I can keep touching you."

Caleb made a thick sound while her hand moved warmly, pleasuring him, enjoying him with an honesty that aroused him to the point of agony.

"If you keep that up, I'll lose control," Caleb said almost roughly. "Is that what you want?"

Willow looked at his tawny eyes, felt his power, sensed the life coursing through the flesh she held so intimately, and realized that she wanted him in just that way. "Is that kind of pleasure . . . allowed?"

Caleb met Willow's luminous, smoky glance and knew with a distant sense of shock that he was going to give her what she wanted. Her sensuality burned through his self-control in ways that would have angered him if her honesty hadn't disarmed him so completely at the same time.

"Curious little cat," Caleb said huskily. "Go ahead. It's just as well."

"What do you mean?"

His laugh was too short, too hard. "Feel me, honey. I want you like Hell on fire, but it's too soon for you to take me again. I'd hurt you."

Willow looked from the topaz blaze of Caleb's eyes to the hungry flesh she was stroking. He was hard, hot, full, and she could feel his heartbeat pulsing heavily.

"As for what's allowed," Caleb said, "I never was a man for fences and foolish rules. Anything you want is allowed. I mean it, Willow. Anything."

"Even this?" she asked, giving in to the temptation that had become unbearable.

She bent down, sending her hair sliding across his naked legs and the far more sensitive flesh she was cradling in her hands. The cool golden strands were in violent contrast to Caleb's own heat, but nothing was as stark as the searing instant when her lips parted and the tip of her tongue caressed the same satin texture that had so intrigued her fingers.

"You're even smoother than I thought you would be," Willow whispered as she straightened.

Taken by surprise once again, Caleb fought for control of his own body. The wild little caress was the last thing he had expected from Willow. It slid past all his defenses, leaving him completely naked in her hands. He felt the first shuddering pulses of release tear through his body. With a low sound he gave himself to ecstasy and to the girl who was watching him with wonder in her eyes.

When Caleb could breathe once more, he brought Willow's hands up his body and kissed them.

"Now you know," he said.

Willow's smile was another kind of caress. "Yes."

"And now it's my turn to know you in the same way."

Her eyes widened. "I don't understand."

"You will."

One of Caleb's hands touched Willow's mouth, sealing in her questions with a sensual pressure before sliding down to the hollow of her throat. The rapid beating of her pulse was evidence that pleasuring him had excited her. His hand slid under golden strands of hair until it rested between the smooth rise of her breasts.

"No objections?" he asked softly.

Willow shook her head, making light shimmer through her hair.

Caleb's other hand eased beneath Willow's hair. When he began sliding the camisole from her body, she made no protest. As the fine lace floated to the ground, he looked at her openly, approving of her, feeling a fierce satisfaction when her nipples became tight pink buds in response to his glance.

"What are you thinking?" Caleb asked.

Once it would have embarrassed Willow to answer, but no more. Caleb had given himself to her without restraint or hesitation. She could do no less with him.

"I was thinking of being kissed," she said simply.

"Here?" He touched the velvet tip of one breast.

Willow trembled as pleasure showered through her. "Yes."

"And here?"

The other peak hardened beneath his touch.

"Yes," she whispered.

"I'm thinking about it, too."

Caleb bent and kissed Willow's breasts, brushing his mustache across her slowly, repeatedly, enjoying the breaking of her breath at each caress. His long fingers stroked her waist, then retreated down her body, taking the last of her clothing.

"I'm thinking about kissing you here, too," Caleb said, pressing a fingertip lightly into her navel.

The unexpected caress sent a sunburst of sensations radiating from the pit of Willow's stomach. Her breath came in with a surprised gasp. Caleb's hand slid lower, drawing a shivering sound from her. She was soft, sultry, welcoming.

"And here."

Willow made a breathless sound that was pleasure and surprise combined.

"Open for me," he whispered, bending down,

touching his tongue to her navel.

The gentle brush of Caleb's fingertips between her thighs was exquisite. Willow gave a ragged little sigh and shifted her legs, allowing him more freedom. The gliding, probing intimacy of his finger made her gasp. The liquid ease of his penetration was a sweet revelation for both of them.

"Hot little cat," Caleb said, biting her belly gently. "I can feel how much you liked making me lose control. I'm going to enjoy doing the same to you."

Gently, Caleb bore Willow back onto the blanket until she was lying down once more.

"Tell me if I hurt you," he said, easing deeply into her. "You're so small . . ."

Willow shuddered.

"Did that hurt?" he asked.

"No."

"You trembled."

"I was remembering."

"What?"

"You. Inside me."

Caleb smiled and bit Willow a little less gently, drawing another small cry from her. His thumb moved and splinters of fire pierced her, melting her in a shimmering rush. She felt the spreading warmth of her response and stiffened in shock.

"Caleb, I didn't mean to—"

"It's all right," he interrupted, laughing softly to feel the heat of Willow's pleasure on his hand. "It happened in the pool, too, but you couldn't feel it. I could, though. It drove me right over the edge."

He smoothed his cheek against the golden thatch that shielded her softness.

"Open more for me," Caleb whispered.

Willow's legs shifted again, making room for him to kneel between them. A hard thumb circled the satin knot of nerves that was no longer hidden. Streamers of pleasure burst through her, making her cry out. When he lifted his thumb, she moaned a protest. He smiled and redoubled his touch inside her, pressing sensually, teasing her with the memory of what it had been like to be filled completely. The heat of her response spilled between them.

"That's it, little cat," Caleb said, bending down to Willow. "Tell me you like my hands as much as I liked yours."

His tongue circled the satin nub, touching her with a whip of fire. The caress excited her beyond bearing. Pleasure burst again, a hot rain that she shared helplessly with him.

"Sweet woman," he said, tasting her.

"Caleb," she said urgently, for the tension in her was becoming unbearable. "I—"

Pleasure burst within Willow again, taking her voice. Caleb made a low sound of satisfaction and encouragement, asking for more of her response, luring her closer and closer to the brink of ecstasy with each sultry flick of his tongue, enjoying her in a way he had never enjoyed a woman before. His teeth closed gently on the violently sensitive nub, holding her captive for silky caresses that were like nothing she had ever imagined.

Suddenly, Willow knew what it felt like to be touched by lightning. A sound of anguished pleasure was torn from her as her whole body tightened. She called Caleb's name again and was answered by a caress whose intimacy ripped away the world, hurtling her into wild ecstasy.

After a few more moments, Caleb reluctantly released Willow's shivering flesh and kissed a path up her body. Her eyes opened, dazed by the pleasure whose aftermath was still rippling through her in ever widening rings.

"Such beautiful eyes," Caleb said. "Beautiful

mouth, beautiful breasts, beautiful . . . woman."

Willow saw the luminous approval in Caleb's glance and shivered again. She slid her arms around him, urging him to press full length against her, needing to feel him along her whole body. Understanding her need, for it was also his own, he braced his weight on his elbows and lowered himself until he touched every inch of her.

Sighing, Willow hugged Caleb even closer, quivering with every other breath, still captive to the ecstasy he had given her. The weight and textures of his body covering hers felt incredibly good. Without thinking, she rubbed against him, liking the heat and strength of him. He eased more of his weight onto her, no longer trying to keep her from feeling all of him. When she sensed the hard masculine need in him, her breath came in swiftly.

"You have the damnedest effect on me," Caleb said, his voice gritty and rueful. "So stop wriggling and hug me until it goes away."

"Is that the way it works?"

"I don't know. I've never had this problem before."

"You haven't?"

"No," he admitted, biting Willow's ear delicately. "Just with you."

Willow gasped and tightened her grip on his big body. The heat and power in Caleb sent pleasure rippling through her once more. Instinctively, she shifted, wanting to bring him even closer. He tried to throttle a groan but was only partially successful.

"Caleb?" she asked huskily.

"Hold still, honey."

"I have a better idea."

Willow's legs shifted again, separating until she could feel the blunt thrust of his hunger pressing against her. She moved her hips slowly, wanting a different kind of closeness. The sound of Caleb's breath hissing out told her that he was as aware of her welcoming, sultry core as she was.

"Damn it, Willow. I don't want to hurt you."

"Does the key hurt the lock?" she whispered.

"Not when they're made for each other. Were you made for me, little cat?"

"Yes," she said huskily. "Only for you. Take what's yours, Caleb. Give me what is mine."

For a long, burning moment he looked down into Willow's hazel eyes, in thrall to her honesty. Certainty condensed within him, the realization that he could no more turn away from her than a river could run back from the sea.

Caleb breathed Willow's name as he bent to kiss her. Slowly he claimed what was his and gave what was hers, merging their bodies a shimmering fraction at a time, feeling the sharing all the way to his soul. The breath came out of her in a long, rippling sigh that was his name. He wanted to ask if he was hurting her, but before he could find the words, her body answered. The tiny, secret contractions of her pleasure urged him deeper, gilding him with her response. He answered with a silky pulse that mingled his essence with hers, easing his way even more until their joining was deep and complete.

The feeling was exquisite. Willow's eyes opened as she felt herself coming slowly undone, ecstasy stealing through her. She whispered Caleb's name, trying to tell him of the beauty he was giving her, but she knew no words to describe the transformation taking place in her body. His kiss told her that he understood, that he was being transformed as surely as she was. She heard her own name breathed against her lips, sensed the pulses of his ecstasy rippling through his body into hers.

The knowledge that Caleb was coming undone as slowly and completely as she was sent another shimmering tide through Willow, consuming her and him as well, fusing them in a union that was both primitive and sublime. Neither knew where self ended and other began, for there was no self, no other, simply an incandescent whole where once two halves had been.

14

"**H**ow is he?" Willow asked.

"Good as new. All Deuce needed was some time doing nothing except eating his fool head off."

Caleb slapped Deuce on his haunch, sending the big horse trotting into the meadow's evening silence once more. The bullet wound had healed cleanly. The strained foreleg had taken longer, but now there was no hesitation in the horse's stride.

"He's moving well," she said. "Not a bit of a limp anymore."

The unhappiness in Willow's voice was at odds with her words, but Caleb understood what she meant. He felt the same way. The eighteen days he had spent with her in the hidden valley was as close to heaven as he ever expected to come. Now that Deuce was sound again and the Arabians were better accustomed to high altitude, there was no excuse to linger.

"We can stay longer," Caleb said abruptly, speaking aloud the thought that had haunted him more and more frequently since he had discovered Willow's innocence. "We don't have to go haring off after your damned brother. If we were meant to find him, we'll find him no matter where we are. And if we weren't meant to find him, so be it."

Willow flinched at the hard edge to Caleb's voice. She had grown accustomed to his laughter, his gentleness, and his unbridled sensuality. Not once in the past eighteen days had she seen the bleak archangel that was also part of him. She had almost forgotten it was there.

"If it were just me, I'd never leave this valley," Willow said unhappily. "But Matt must need help or he wouldn't have written to his brothers. It was just his bad luck that no one was left at home except me." She smiled at Caleb and added in a soft voice, "But it was my good luck, because it led me to you."

Caleb closed his eyes and tried to control the unreasonable anger snaking through his veins—anger at Willow, at himself, and most of all at the simple fact that once Reno was found, Willow was irretrievably lost.

"I'd rather stay in Eden," Caleb said roughly.

"So would I, my love," she said, going to him. "So would I."

Willow slid her arms around Caleb and held him, savoring the familiar warmth and strength of him. His arms closed around her a little fiercely, lifting her off her feet. He kissed her hard and deep before he set her firmly on the ground once more and pinned her with a glance so savage she made a sound of protest.

"Remember," Caleb said harshly, "you were the one who wanted to go looking for him. I was willing to leave it to God."

"What do you mean?"

Caleb's smile was as thin and fierce as the blade of the big knife he always wore, but he said nothing more.

"Caleb?" she asked fearfully.

"Dig out your map, southern lady."

She flinched at the tone of his voice and at the nickname he hadn't used since they had come to the valley. "My map?"

"The one you have hidden somewhere in that big carpetbag," Caleb said, turning away from Willow, walking back toward camp.

"How did you know?" she asked, dazed.

"Easy. Gold-hunting fools always draw maps for other fools to follow."

The savagery in Caleb's voice startled Willow. She stared after him uncertainly before she followed.

When she arrived in camp, Caleb was stirring the ashes of their breakfast fire. He didn't even look up as she went to the unwieldy carpetbag that was her only luggage and began rummaging through its contents. He didn't look at her when she ripped apart a section of lining and withdrew a folded piece of paper. He didn't look at her at all until she walked slowly up to the fire, map in hand.

"I would have showed you sooner," Willow said quietly, "but the map really isn't much help."

Caleb gave her a sideways glance that could have peeled bark from a living tree. "You didn't trust me and we both know it."

Color flared on her cheekbones. "It wasn't my secret to tell. It was Matt's, and he said not to show the map to anyone. But I'm showing it to you now." She thrust the paper into his hands. "Here. Look at it. You won't find much I didn't already tell you. Matt never was a trusting kind of person. He made it so no one could steal the map and get any use of it. Unfortunately, I can't get much use of it either."

Saying nothing, Caleb took the map, opened it, and glanced quickly over the paper. The major landmarks were easy enough to recognize, the rivers and the clustered mountains of the San Juan country. Various passes into the heart of the country were marked, but no one pass was preferred over another. Whether someone started in California, Mexico, Canada, or east of the Mississippi, routes into the San Juans had been laid out to follow.

Caleb looked at Willow questioningly.

"Matt didn't know for sure where anyone was," she explained. "The letter came to our biggest farm with instructions to forward it wherever the Moran brothers were. I copied the letter and sent it to the last address I had for each of my brothers."

"Where was that?"

"Australia, California, the Sandwich Isles, and China. But that information was years old. They could be anywhere now, even back in America."

Caleb raised his eyebrows and looked again at the map. He grunted. "Your brother is a good hand at drawing maps." Caleb frowned. "But he left off one detail. Where the hell is his base camp?"

"It isn't marked as far as I could see." Willow took a deep breath. "I think Matt was so cautious because he found gold."

"I expect so. Some damn fool usually does."

Willow stared, unable to believe the indifference in Caleb's voice. "Do you have something against finding gold?"

He shrugged. "I'd rather raise cattle. When the going gets rough, you can eat them. You can't eat gold."

"You can use it to buy food," Willow pointed out rather tartly.

"Sure. Unless you get yourself shot in the back by some gunnie who figures it's easier to jump your claim than to stake his own." Cold topaz eyes pinned Willow. "I've seen gold camps. They have the stink of Hell about them. Nothing but greed and killing and whores."

"Matthew isn't like that. He's every bit as decent as you are."

Caleb said nothing, but his mouth thinned at being compared to the man who had seduced and abandoned Rebecca. He stared broodingly at the map. At one point, deep in the heart of the San Juans, five meticulously drawn triangles had been placed to indicate various mountain peaks. Despite the fact that there were many more mountains in the area, no more triangles appeared.

Across the map was written, *Make a fire and I'll come.* Beneath it was a line of Spanish. Caleb translated it silently. *Three points, two halves, one gathering.*

Willow stepped close and saw that he was looking at the writing.

"That was another thing I couldn't figure out," Willow said. "Why would Matt write the line in Spanish?"

"Do you know Spanish?"

"No."

"Maybe that's why," Caleb said flatly.

He looked at the triangles again. Willow followed his intent, tawny glance.

"Where are we supposed to build the fire?" she asked after a minute. "Any one of those triangles could be his camp."

"One is as useless as another. Those are mountain peaks, not camps. We could look for five years and never find anything but rough country."

"You needn't sound so happy about it," Willow grumbled. "Why don't you want to find Matt?"

Caleb looked at her almost fiercely before he spoke. "That's rough country. Let me take you back to Wolfe Lonetree. He'll protect you and the Arabians while I look for your brother."

"If I'm not along, you'll never get close to Matt. If he doesn't want to be found, you have a better chance of catching moonlight on water than catching him."

Caleb bit back a curse. That was exactly what it had been like chasing Reno—trying to catch moonlight on water.

But then I didn't know where the son of a bitch was. Now I do.

Willow frowned over the map. "I can't understand why Matt didn't leave better clues. He isn't a careless kind of person. He was the one who taught me how to navigate by the stars, taking readings and drawing lines and making angles of intersection." She bit her lower lip. "All I can figure is if we light a fire at any one of those five peaks, he'll be able to see us. You know the country. You can find a place that can be seen for a long way and we'll light a fire and—"

"Get our fool heads shot off," Caleb said flatly, interrupting Willow. "Nobody lights a signal fire in that country unless he's looking to get his scalp lifted. Your brother knows it, too, or he would have been dead long ago."

"But then why did he say it?"

"It's a trap."

"That doesn't make sense. Matt wouldn't want to hurt his brothers."

"Are your brothers fools?"

Willow laughed. "Hardly. Matt is the youngest. He learned a lot of what he knows from his older brothers."

"Then none of your brothers would be damn fool enough to light a fire in Indian country and wait like a staked goat for whatever came."

Willow wanted to argue, but knew it would do no good. Caleb was right. None of the Moran brothers would be that foolish.

"A trap," she said unhappily.

"Like you said, your brother is a careful man."

"Then we'll just have to climb each peak until we find his camp," Willow said, taking the map from Caleb.

He heard the determination in her voice and knew she wouldn't stop seeking her brother until she found him or died trying. Reno had written for help and Willow had answered in the only way she could.

"You're going to find your brother come Hell or high water, is that it?"

"If you were me, would you do any less?" she asked, wondering at the tangible hostility in Caleb every time her brother was mentioned.

Caleb closed his eyes and tasted the pain that the future would bring, Willow's screams echoing as she watched her beloved brother and the man she loved face each other over drawn weapons, gunfire echoing and death coming down like thunder.

Be sure you've got a good reason to draw on Reno, because a second after you do, both of you are likely to be dead.

"So be it," Caleb said bleakly.

Fear went through Willow like black lightning. "Caleb?" she asked shakily. "What is it? What's wrong?"

He didn't answer. He went to his saddlebags, pulled out his journal, a pencil, and a ruler, and came back to where Willow waited, map in hand and fear in her heart. Saying nothing, he took the map, spread it on his journal, and began drawing lines.

"What are you doing?" she asked finally.

"Finding your goddamned brother."

Willow winced. "But how?"

"He's a careful kind of man. He was real careful how he drew these triangles, even though he stood them every which way on the paper."

"I don't understand."

"The triangles are all the same kind, with one angle

of ninety degrees and two angles of forty-five degrees.''

Willow stared at the triangles and saw that Caleb was right.

"If you cut the ninety degree angle in two and drop a line down through the base, you get two equal triangles," Caleb said, working swiftly as he talked.

"So?"

"So if you lay a ruler along that dividing line and draw it out to the edges of the map, and you do it for each triangle, all the lines should intersect somewhere. 'Three points, two halves, one gathering.' It should be about—"

"There!" Willow interrupted, pointing to the map where line after line had crossed. "Caleb, you've done it! That's where Matt is!"

Caleb said nothing. He simply noted the area of intersection in relation to landmarks both in his mind and on the map, and then threw the paper into the fire. Willow made a startled sound as flames bit ravenously into the map. Before she could move to prevent it, the paper writhed and curled and turned to ash.

"Good thing your Arabians are in good shape," Caleb said tightly. "We've got Hell's own ride ahead."

He looked from the fire to Willow. In the twilight her eyes were mysterious, the color of autumn rain. The thought of losing her was a knife turning in him. Silently, he held out his hand to her. She took it without hesitation, not understanding the darkness she saw in him, but knowing that he needed her. When he drew her closer, she came willingly, needing him in the same way. For long minutes, they held each other, neither moving except to cling more tightly, as though they expected to be torn apart in the next instant.

"Love," Willow whispered finally, looking up at Caleb. "What's wrong?"

His only answer was a kiss that didn't end until he was deep inside her and she was shivering with the fulfillment that grew more consuming each time he came to her. After he sipped the ecstatic tears from her lashes, he began all over again, taking and giving and sharing until there was no yesterday, no tomorrow, nothing but the timeless instant when two became one.

When Willow fell asleep, she was still joined with Caleb. For a long time he listened to her slow breaths, felt her small stirrings, watched moonlight glow on her cheeks. When he could bear it no longer, he closed his eyes and fell asleep, praying that Reno was already dead.

WILLOW stood in the stirrups and looked over Ishmael's pricked ears. The land fell away before her in so many shades of green she couldn't find names to describe all of them. The countryside was neither flat nor truly mountainous. Although distant clusters of high peaks jutted sporadically from the horizon, the land between the clusters was mile upon mile of rumpled forest and grassland, as though a huge patchwork quilt had been thrown over an uneven floor. The wrinkles were long, high ridges where pine and aspen and scrub oak grew. The troughs between wrinkles were equally long, wide parks where rivers ran.

Taking a deep breath, Willow tasted the freshness of the air, grateful that she had finally adapted to the altitude. Caleb had told her that even at its lowest point, the land was nearly seven thousand feet high. Many of the peaks were twice that height. It was like riding on the green roof of the world with stone chimneys rising in the distance. The sense of openness was exhilarating.

Nowhere could be seen smoke, buildings, rutted roads, fences, or any permanent sign of man. Yet men were out there, somewhere. Caleb had seen tracks in places where mountains pinched the grassland into divides that were natural funnels for travelers. Some of the tracks had been headed north or east. Most of them hadn't. Most of them were headed toward the San Juans.

"That's where we're going," Caleb said, pointing. "The farthest peaks you can see."

From where Willow was, the cluster of mountains looked rather like a low, spiky, purple crown set with fractured pearls. The country between her and the San Juans was as wild as it was beautiful.

"How long will it take us to get there?" she asked, having learned that travel time rather than distance was the only measure that counted in the West.

"Two days if we could ride directly. As it is, we'll be lucky to do it in four."

"Why?"

"Indians," Caleb said. "The Utes are damn tired of tripping over white men every time they turn around. Then there's always Slater and his bunch."

"Don't you think we lost them?"

"It's hard to lose someone who knows where you're going," Caleb said sardonically.

"Won't they give up after not finding any of our tracks for almost three weeks?"

"Would you give up?" he asked.

Willow looked away from the bleak clarity of Caleb's eyes. Although he hadn't mentioned abandoning the hunt again, she knew he wanted to. Yet when she asked why, he changed the subject with an abruptness that stung.

"Jed Slater is riding a grudge," Caleb said, looking

away from Willow. "He's the kind of man who will ride it until he dies or I do."

"Is that why you don't want to find Matt?" Willow asked, remembering the older Slater brother's reputation as a gunman. "Because you know Slater will be looking for you in the same place?"

Caleb gave Willow a hooded glance. "Only a fool hunts trouble. Enough of it comes without looking for more."

He kicked Deuce lightly, sending the horse trotting down into the long, winding park that eventually would descend to a grassy valley thousands of feet below their present elevation. Unhappily, Willow looked at Caleb's broad back vanishing down the trail and wished she had phrased her question more tactfully. No man liked admitting that he was looking for ways to avoid a fight.

Frowning, Willow urged Ishmael forward, thinking about the man she loved rather than the route ahead. Caleb had been withdrawn since they had left the little valley yesterday. He had kept to a hard pace, his whole manner that of a man getting through a distasteful task as quickly as possible. And never once, either in the valley or after it, had he spoken of what would happen between the two of them after they found her brother. Never once had Caleb said that he loved her, that he wanted to marry her, that he even wanted to be with her after his promise to guide her to her brother had been kept.

Yet Willow had awakened this morning to find Caleb looking at her with a yearning that was so great it had made her heart turn over. Then he had gotten up without a word, leaving her with tears standing in her eyes and fear coiling coldly in her stomach.

The memory haunted Willow throughout the long day, prickling her skin like an icy rash, making the beauty of the land bittersweet.

The long descent from the high country ended as many others had, in a wide valley that wound between ranges of mountains. Their route took them along a river that was rarely more than a hundred feet across. The water was clear, clean, and swift. Aspen and a tree that looked like a poplar grew along the river's edge, spreading masses of shivering silver-green leaves across the sky. Flowers of every hue winked and flirted among the grasses, telling of a spring that was not yet spent.

As always, the sun was hot. Willow was wearing only Levis and the buckskin shirt with most of its laces undone. The flannel underwear that had felt so good in the higher country was now folded and rolled into a blanket behind her saddle, along with the heavy wool jacket. The silver murmuring of the river had become a siren song promising cool, pure water to ease her growing thirst.

Just when Willow was certain Caleb was going to go past supper without stopping, he reined in, dismounted, and walked back to her.

"We'll rest here for a bit."

Willow began to dismount, only to be plucked from Ishmael's back. Caleb lowered her slowly to the ground, letting her slide down his front. The look in his eyes and the frank arousal of his body made her heartbeat double. The uneasiness that had haunted her all day was replaced by a giddy sense of relief and a glittering rush of anticipation. Heat rippled through her, transforming her. In the space of a few breaths her body changed, preparing itself for the joining to come.

"Rest?" Willow asked, smiling, wanting so much to take the darkness from Caleb's eyes. One of her hands drifted down his body. "Are you sure that's all you had in mind?"

His breath came in swiftly. "I thought I might catch some trout for supper."

"You might," she agreed. Her hand moved slowly, measuring and pleasuring him in the same motion, glorying in the answering blaze of his eyes, all darkness gone. "Depends on the bait. Or is it the pole?"

"You," he said huskily, "are one sassy little trout."

"But I rise to your bait every time."

"No, honey. I rise to yours."

Willow's soft laugh was as sensual as the slow movement of her hand. "Shall we argue about it?"

His answering smile was lazy and hungry at the same time. "Yes, I think we shall." Long fingers worked over the fastening of her Levis. "Two falls out of three?"

"You're bigger than I am," she pointed out.

"Harder, too." Caleb's hand slid between layers of cloth. "But it's too late to get cold feet now."

The only answer Willow could make was a throaty sound of pleasure as his long fingers touched her. He knelt quickly, stripping away her boots and Levis. He had no patience for his own clothes. He simply unfastened his pants and pulled her to the ground astride him, wild with a need he couldn't control.

"God," he groaned when he teased and tested her, "you're softer every time. Hotter. Sweeter."

Willow tried to answer, but the feel of Caleb thrusting deeply into her body took away her breath. The hunger in him was almost violent, as though he must have all of her, know all of her, touch all of her in some elemental way. The first shattering wave of pleasure hit her as soon as they were fully joined, but it was the desperate need in him that stripped away the world, leaving only Caleb and the ecstasy that destroyed and created her in the same endless instant. Small cries rippled from her as she surrendered body and soul to the man she loved.

The depth and quickness of Willow's response was as exciting to Caleb as the heat of her body melting around him, telling him that she was his woman, only his. It was what he needed, what he had sought through the long hours in which he had circled and circled the dilemma of Reno Moran and found no solution, no reprieve except this, the joining that was unlike anything Caleb had ever known. The passion in Willow was as hot as the sun and as deep as time, an intensity of feeling that reached down into his soul.

And soon she would hate him with a passion as deep as her love.

Willow's name came from Caleb's lips as a broken cry, for the passion he had called from her had claimed him as well, giving him more completely to her with each raking pulse of ecstasy, an elemental surrender of self that was not unlike her own.

He held her, praying that Reno would never be found . . . and knowing he would.

"MORE tracks?" Willow asked.

Caleb nodded. He hadn't shaved since they left the hidden valley, but even six days of beard stubble couldn't hide his grim expression.

"Shod?"

He nodded again.

"How many horses?"

Though Willow's voice was no more than a thread of sound, Caleb heard. Sometimes he thought he could hear her in the silence of his mind, a woman crying passion, crying love, crying grief, crying hate.

"No less than twelve horses," Caleb said roughly, preferring the unhappy truth of enemies to the thoughts that stalked him no matter how ruthlessly he shoved them aside. "No more than sixteen. Hard to tell. They weren't picketed separately."

Willow frowned and looked around. The days of

cautious, relentless travel had brought them among
the splendor of the San Juan mountains. At present,
she and Caleb were in the midst of a high, grassy
basin that was perhaps two miles across and circled
by snowy peaks of breathtaking size and ruggedness.
Slender aspen grew in the rolling folds of the basin,
providing cover for deer and for people such as Willow and Caleb, who had no desire to be spotted from
nearby peaks or ridges.

But the basin would soon be transformed as all
other parks and meadows had been transformed by
the rising of the land. Rugged peaks would close in,
the meadows would shrink, and the creeks would
race between dark walls of stone until a higher
meadow was reached, a smaller meadow, and the
cycle would be repeated again and again until they
came to the headwaters of a tiny brook at the apex of
yet another pass. Then the route would begin to descend, repeating the cycle in reverse, creeks becoming
rivers and meadows becoming huge parks once more.

"Is there another pass we could take?" Willow
asked.

"There's always another pass somewhere."

She bit her lower lip. "But not nearby, is that it?"

"That's it. We'd have to backtrack a few hours to
where the creek forked. Then we'd have to go three
days out of our way to come in from the other side
of that mountain." Caleb jerked his thumb over his
shoulder, looked at Willow, and waited.

"Are we close to Matt?" she asked finally.

"If he drew the map right and we read it right,
yes."

"While you were scouting ahead, I thought I heard
gunfire," she said.

"You've got good ears," Caleb said. Nothing in his
tone revealed that he had been hoping she hadn't
heard the shots.

"Was it you?" she asked.

"No."

"Matt?"

"Doubt it. More likely someone from Slater's bunch saw a deer. A bunch of armed men don't need to worry overmuch about attracting Utes by shooting fresh meat."

"Matt is alone."

"He's used to it."

"I heard five shots. How many does it take to kill one deer?"

Caleb said nothing. He knew that more than one or two shots usually meant a fight, not a hunt.

"Matt might be hurt," Willow said urgently. "Caleb, we have to find him!"

"More likely we'll find Slater's bunch if we head up that draw," Caleb said, his voice flat. But even as he spoke, he was reining his horse around, heading into the canyon that rose on either side of the river. "I'll ride ahead. You keep that shotgun handy. Unless we have Satan's own luck, we're going to need it."

Despite Caleb's grim warning, they found nothing that afternoon but tracks. The land began rising slowly beneath their feet. The river became faster, more narrow, more rocky, and mountains crowded in on both sides. Willow could tell from the horses' breathing that the altitude was higher than the little valley had been, and they were climbing higher with each step.

The water course they had been following forked as the land rose once more. The tracks of shod horses followed the right fork. Caleb took the left, for it led toward the place where five lines had intersected on the map that he had burned to ash, wishing that he could burn the past with it.

But burning all the bitter yesterdays wasn't possible.

So be it.

The words were like rifle fire in Caleb's mind. Their echo came back as Wolfe's warning.

You hear me, amigo? You and Reno are too well matched.

And Caleb's own answer, the only one there could be, eye for eye, tooth for tooth, life for life, the past echoing into the present, the savage circle complete.

So be it.

Except that it could not be. Caleb could not leave Willow alone in the mountains, no one to protect her, a woman abandoned unwillingly by her man, but abandoned just the same. . . .

Will she die the way Rebecca did, in agony and exhaustion, bearing her lover's dying child?

Eye for eye, tooth for tooth, life for life.

Bile rose behind Caleb's clenched teeth as he rebelled against the very idea of hurting Willow. He could not do that to the girl whose only sin was to love too much. She had done nothing to earn such betrayal.

Nor had Rebecca. Yet betrayal had come, and agony, and death. The man who had brought disaster to her walked free, able to seduce another innocent, abandon her, and create another savage circle of betrayal and vengeance.

In an anguish that grew greater with each step forward, Caleb searched for a way out of the trap of duty and desire and death. He found none except to let the seducer live, and in so doing condemn some unknown girl to a seduction and abandonment she had done nothing to earn, and then another girl, and then another; for a man's desire rose with the sun and set only in the dark warmth of a woman's body.

As Caleb rode into the dark canyon, he wondered how he could let Reno live and still call himself a man.

15

WALLS of rock loomed on either side of the narrow cleft, blocking out all but a thin swath of sky overhead. High above, the mountain peak was still washed with clear sunlight, but in the bottom of the ravine dark forerunners of night flowed out of every crevice. The dense shadows were exactly what Caleb had been seeking. He dismounted and went back to Willow.

"No fire," he said in a low voice.

Willow nodded her understanding. She had heard the gunfire clearly half an hour before. Two rifle shots. It was impossible to determine the direction of the shots, for the sounds had echoed off stone walls too many times before reaching her ears.

"How close?" Willow asked quietly.

Caleb knew she was asking about the shots they both had heard. He looked up at the rim of the gully and shrugged. "Could be the next ravine over. Could be a mile across the basin and up on another peak. Sound carries real well up here."

While Caleb picketed the horses fifty feet downstream, Willow rinsed the canteen in the tiny brook that leaped and foamed from a notch high in the rock wall. The water was so cold it made her hands ache. A chill wind blew down the gully from the hidden peak, making her shiver despite her heavy wool jacket.

"I've never felt water so cold," Willow said as she handed Caleb the canteen. "It made my teeth ache."

"Meltwater," Caleb said briefly. He took Willow's hands and rubbed them between his own, warming them. "Damn near ice. There's a snowfield at the top of that notch." He breathed heat over her fingers before he opened his shearling jacket, pulled her hands inside, and smiled down at her. "Better?"

"Much."

Willow smiled and made a murmurous sound of approval as she smoothed her hands over Caleb's warm chest. Within a few moments, she had picked apart the button just above his belt buckle and eased one hand inside to rest against the heat of his skin. His breath hissed in as her fingers tangled gently in the line of hair that ran down his torso.

"You're better than any fire," Willow whispered as she turned her hand over to warm the other side. "Heat but no smoke to give us away."

"Keep that up and there might be."

"Really?" she asked softly, laughing up at him. "Where?"

"Don't tempt me, honey."

"Why not? I'm so very good at it."

Caleb's eyes narrowed and his heart beat with redoubled force. In the sudden, hushed silence between Caleb and Willow, the sound of the tiny creek was like a river, but it wasn't loud enough to cover the break in his breathing when her cool fingers dipped below his belt. The width of the gunbelt defeated her attempts to touch him.

Smiling, Caleb removed his gunbelt and big knife

and set them aside. "Try it now."

Willow nibbled at the dimple in his chin and the beard stubble that had grown once more. He caught her teasing lips in a hard kiss that made him forget for a few moments the bleak future that was coming closer with every moment they looked for Reno. When her cool fingers slipped inside the waistband of his pants, Caleb made a hungry sound.

"Much, much better," she said approvingly as she ran her fingernails down the long muscles of his torso.

"I've got an idea for making it even better."

Caleb smiled as he unfastened Willow's coat and tugged at buckskin laces until he could ease his fingers between folds of cloth and buttons to brush the silky flesh beneath. Her breath caught, broke, then came out in a rush of pleasure.

Yet Willow's greatest pleasure was in watching Caleb respond to her. She loved seeing the darkness and tension of his expression change as the result of her touch. She loved taking shadows from his eyes, replacing them with fire. She loved caressing him, feeling his body change. She loved bringing him laughter and release. She loved . . . Caleb.

And someday soon he would realize that he loved her in return. Willow was certain of it. No man could come to a woman with such intense passion, such overwhelming tenderness, and not love her at least a little.

Smiling, watching Caleb, Willow stood on tiptoe, asking for his mouth, needing to taste him once more, to have the small consummation of his kiss. With a growling sound, he took what she offered and gave what she needed, joining their mouths hungrily.

"Well," said a sardonic male voice behind Willow, "now I know what you were doing for the weeks you were missing."

It was too late to reach for the gunbelt and Caleb knew it.

"Matt?" Willow cried, spinning around, facing the voice.

The man had come from downwind of the horses, taking Willow and Caleb by surprise. She peered into the shadows, then made a choked sound and ran into the stranger's arms.

"Matt!" she said in delight, hugging him. "Oh, Matt, is it really you?"

"It's really me, Willy." Reno hugged her in return, but there was anger as well as relief in his expression. After a few moments, he set her aside and measured the tall, hard-faced man who was at the moment flipping a gunbelt into place around his hips. "Caleb Black."

Caleb didn't acknowledge the question buried in the two words. He simply settled his gunbelt with a smooth movement and faced the bitter future. "Matthew Moran."

Reno's pale green eyes narrowed at the bleak hatred in Caleb's voice and at the violence implicit in the other man's stance —legs braced slightly apart, hands loose and relaxed at his sides, ready to draw the sixgun whose thong had already been slipped off.

"Looks like Wolfe was wrong about you," Reno said bitterly. "But much as I'd like to beat the hell out of you for turning my sister into a—"

"Don't say it," Caleb interrupted in a voice as savage as the light in his eyes. *"Don't even think it."*

With dawning horror, Willow watched the two men she loved. She tried to speak, but the words stuck in her throat. She had expected joy, not anger, when she met her brother once more.

"Matt?" she asked finally, looking at the brother who was as tall as Caleb, as strong, and every bit as furious. "What's wrong?"

"Are you married to him?" Reno demanded.

The cold chill of the wind reminded Willow that her jacket was undone. She buttoned it and held her head high despite the flush spreading hotly across her cheekbones.

"No," she said.

"Are you promised?"

Angrily, Caleb started to speak.

She cut him off. "No."

"Christ. And you ask me what's wrong. What happened to you, Willy? What will Mama say when she knows—"

"Mama's dead."

Reno's eyes widened, then closed. "When?"

"Before the war ended."

"How?" he asked roughly.

"She never was very strong. After Papa was killed, she just gave up."

"Where are Rafe and—"

"I don't know," Willow said harshly, interrupting. "I haven't seen any of my brothers for years. The only family I really had was my memory."

The expression on Reno's face changed, all anger draining out, leaving only sadness. He reached for his sister again, folding her into his arms. Putting his cheek against Willow's hair, he rocked her gently.

"I'm sorry, Willy," he said. "I'm so damned sorry. If I'd known, I would have come back. You shouldn't have had to face it alone."

With a choked sound, Willow threw her arms around Reno and held on. Caleb watched through slitted eyes, remembering the instant when a half-asleep girl had reached for him.

Matt, oh Matt, is it really you? I've been so lonely. . . .

After a long time, Reno released his sister, blotted her eyes with his dark bandanna, and kissed her cheek. Then he looked over her head at Caleb.

"You and I will talk later," Reno promised flatly. "Right now there are ten men out there, and they're aching to get their hands on me, Willow, and that sorrel stallion of hers. They'd like a piece of your hide, too, but they're going to have to stand in line. I have first call."

"You won't have to call. I'll be stepping on your heels every inch of the way."

Reno's left eyebrow rose in a dark arc, but he said nothing, even when Willow went back to Caleb, took his right hand in hers, and kissed its broad palm before lacing her fingers deeply through his. She opened her mouth to say something, but before she could speak, Ishmael's head came up. Ears pricked, nostrils flared, the stallion drank the wind coming down the small, brush-choked ravine.

Caleb's right hand jerked, but his fingers were tangled with Willow's. Reno had no such problem. With shocking speed a gun appeared in his left hand. Willow stared, unable to believe what she had seen. One instant Reno had been standing with his hand at his side. The next instant, there was a cocked gun in it. She had seen nothing but a blur between.

"Matt . . . ?" she whispered, stunned.

Reno made a curt gesture with his right hand, silencing his sister. Slowly, he started forward. Caleb's hand shot out, restraining Reno.

"No shooting," Caleb said, his voice a bare thread of sound. "There's a quieter way."

He pulled off his boots, drew his long knife, and glided into the brush on stocking feet with the muscular silence of a cougar.

A movement from Willow caught Reno's eye. He watched as she picked up a shotgun and came to stand with her back to him. Together they waited for Caleb's return, each one guarding a different route out of the ravine.

The long minutes of waiting gave Reno plenty of time to realize how many ways his sister had changed. The girl he remembered was a laughing, teasing whirlwind who had looked to her older brothers to protect her from their father's uncertain temper. The sister who stood with her back to him was an unsmiling woman prepared to fight for her own life. And her man's.

Willow never knew how long it was before the ghostly cry of a wolf sifted through the ravine, announcing Caleb's return. She faced toward the sound just as he stepped from cover. Swiftly, she went to him, her eyes going over him like hands. When she saw the blood on his coat, she made a low sound.

"Easy, honey. I'm all right," Caleb said, taking the shotgun from her suddenly shaking hands.

"Blood," she said.

"Not mine." He bent and kissed Willow fiercely, holding her. "Not mine."

She nodded to show that she understood, and she clung to him.

Reno's pale green eyes missed none of the currents surging between his sister and the grim-faced man who was holding her with surprising tenderness. Reluctantly, Reno conceded that Wolfe had been right— Caleb was a hard man, even a ruthless one, but he was careful of those who were weaker than himself.

"All clear," Caleb said to Reno over Willow's head.

Reno arched a dark eyebrow. "How many?"

"Just one. I was going to let him go, but he picked up the track of the horses."

Willow didn't ask what had happened. She had no doubt as to the man's fate.

"Recognize him?" Reno asked.

Caleb nodded. "I had words with him in Denver. He made his choice. So be it."

A half-amused, half-feral smile crossed Reno's

mouth. "Wolfe was right about that, too."

"What?"

"You're an Old Testament kind of man. Was it Kid Coyote out there?"

"No. Just some no-account claim jumper from California."

A sudden stillness came over Reno. "Claim jumper?"

"As ever was." The smile on Caleb's mouth was like the blade of a drawn knife. "I suppose he had a notion about some fool finding gold up here."

Reno gave Willow a cool glance. "You told him."

"She didn't have to," Caleb said curtly. "Only one reason a man risks his butt up on these peaks. The golden whore."

"There's nothing base about gold," Reno countered softly, his voice low and his eyes vivid against his tanned face. "Indians believed gold came from the sun god's tears. I'm inclined to agree with them."

Caleb made a disgusted sound. "More likely the water came from lower down the body." He looked at Willow. "Sorry, honey. I know you're tired, but we better find another camp. I stripped the claim-jumper's horse and sent it off on down the mountain at a run, but Jed Slater is a good tracker. Sooner or later he'll catch us unless we keep moving or a good rain comes."

"It won't rain tonight," Reno said.

"Maybe by morning," Caleb said, looking at the sky.

"Maybe." Reno shrugged. "Nothing to do for it either way except get out of here. I have a camp nearby. We'll wait for Wolfe there."

"What's Wolfe doing up here?"

"He got to fretting about the odds against you," Reno said. "About three weeks ago he turned up at my camp and told me you were bringing my 'wife' to me and might need all the help you could get."

Silently Caleb absorbed the fact that Wolfe had known where Matt Moran was holed up and had said nothing to Caleb.

You're too evenly matched.

Grimly, Caleb admitted that Wolfe had been right about that. Reno was as quick and cool on the draw as any man Caleb had ever seen. The chance of either one of them surviving a duel in any shape to help Willow get out of the mountains was damned slim.

And if they died, she died. Only not quickly, not cleanly. Willow would die cruelly at the hands of outlaws who cared nothing for her laughter, her quick wit, her courage.

"Where's Wolfe now?" Caleb asked.

"Out there, dogging Slater. Wolfe figured if Slater found you before I did, you'd need help. If he'd known that you were going to take advantage of Willow's innocence . . ." Reno bit back an ugly word and looked at the gun in his hand. "Wolfe would have come looking for you with a whip. He was so sure you were an honorable, decent man. First time I've known him to be wrong."

Willow's breath came in harshly, but before she could speak, Caleb did.

"You've got no call throwing stones on the subject of seducing innocent girls and you goddamned well know it," Caleb said savagely to Reno. "Now, are we going to get out of here or are you planning on waiting for Slater to find us and start shooting us like fish in a barrel? Or maybe you're planning on using that gun on me right now and to hell with Willow's safety?"

Reno returned the six-gun to its holster with an effortless motion. "I'll wait. Slater won't. Let's ride."

RENO's temporary camp was so well concealed by the land itself that Willow wondered

how he had ever found it in the first place. The narrow, spruce- and aspen-choked ravine that opened
onto a swiftly racing creek looked impassable. Nor
was there any obvious reason to force a passage into
the ravine. There were many such blind gullies on
the mountainside, places where water flowed only
at the peak of the snowmelt or after an especially
heavy storm. There was nothing about this particular
ravine that looked any different. There was certainly
no reason to think that it eventually opened onto a
high, small bench where part of the mountainside had
slumped away from the main mass of stone.

Before entering the ravine, they had walked the
horses in the icy mountain stream for more than a
quarter mile, hoping to throw off any trackers. Nothing could entirely conceal the passage of the eight
horses, however, except time and a good rain.

There was no trail into the ravine, no broken brush
or scarred trees to mark the passage of man. Reno
dismounted from his horse and went to the mouth
of the ravine. There he untied thongs that had been
subtly weaving together two spruce trees. The trunks
of the spruce grew almost parallel to the ground, legacy of the crushing weight of winter's deep snow. As
soon as the thongs were released, branches sprang
apart, revealing a dim passageway into the ravine.

"You'll have to walk the rest of the way," Reno
said.

Caleb dismounted and went to help Willow. Before
he could, Reno had already handed her down from
the saddle. It wasn't the first time Reno had moved
to stand between his sister and the man who was
obviously her lover rather than her husband.

Caleb's mouth thinned to a grim line, but he said
nothing. He didn't want Willow to be present when
he and Reno thrashed out the subject of sisters and
seducers.

Eye for eye, tooth for tooth.

Unfortunately, the rough justice in the situation didn't make Caleb feel any better about his position as a seducer.

I'm begging you now, Caleb. Don't stop. If you stop touching me I'll die.

He wondered if it had been that way for Rebecca, a hunger so deep that she begged for Reno. Had Reno tried to pull back from Rebecca, only to find that he could not?

Willow. Push me away. Oh, God. Willow, don't.

I can't help it. I've needed you all my life and didn't know it. I love you, Caleb. I love you.

Caleb closed his eyes and bowed his head as memories sleeted through him, heaven and Hell entwined.

Am I hurting you?

No. It's good—so good. Like flying. Like riding fire. Don't stop—don't ever stop.

And he hadn't.

When his eyes opened, Reno was watching him, noting Caleb's fist clenched so hard on the reins that the leather buckled, seeing the savage, whiskey-colored eyes where ecstasy and anguish were interlocked like flame and shadow.

Curtly, Reno gestured for Caleb to begin leading the horses through the narrow passage.

When all the horses were in the tiny valley, Caleb and Reno returned to remove what evidence they could of the passage of so many horses. By the time they got back to camp, it was dusk. Willow was just picketing the last horse in the valley's deep grass. When Caleb and Reno walked into camp, she was struck by the similarity between the two men. Both were broad-shouldered, both were long-limbed, and both moved with the muscular coordination of healthy animals.

The memory of Reno's speed with a gun returned

to Willow, telling her that the two men were alike in one other way as well. They both were dangerous.

It frightened her.

"Caleb," Willow said, "I'm worried about the shoes on my Arabians. Would you check them for me?"

Surprise showed briefly on Caleb's face, but he said nothing. Although he always helped with Willow's horses, it was the first time she had asked him to do so.

"Sure." Caleb glanced swiftly at Reno, then returned his attention to Willow. He smoothed the back of his fingers lightly down her cheek. "I won't be far, honey. If you get tired of the company, come and get me."

She smiled despite her fear. "I'll be all right."

Reno waited until Caleb was out of earshot before he turned to his sister.

"All right, Willy. What the hell happened?"

The icy green of her brother's eyes told Willow how much of his rage he had been concealing. Numbly, she wondered how to begin.

"Remember the summer evenings?" Willow asked finally, her voice low and husky. "Remember the dinners when the table was crowded with food and the air was filled with talking, and you and Rafe would see which one of you could make me giggle first? Remember the sound of crickets and the smell of new-mown hay?"

"Willy—"

She continued talking right over Reno's attempt to interrupt. "Remember the warm nights when the men of the family sat on the veranda and talked about blooded horses and field crops and faraway places and I would sneak out and sit and listen and everyone would pretend I wasn't there because girls weren't supposed to care about horses and crops and faraway places?"

"What does that have to do with—"

"Do you remember?" Willow asked in a voice that trembled with suppressed emotion.

"Hell, yes, I remember."

"That's all I had. Remembering. Memories and a box full of Yankee notes and Confederate scrip that was worthless except for starting fires. The moon still rose, but the hayfields and white-fenced paddocks were gone. The veranda and house burned one winter night. The little church where Mama and Papa were married and we were all baptised burned, too, nothing left but crooked headstones looking like ghosts rising out of the weeds."

"Willy," Reno began unhappily, but she wouldn't let him talk.

"No. Let me finish, Matthew. I couldn't live on memories. I'm a girl, but I have dreams, too. I'd saved all your letters. When the last one came, asking for help, I sold what was left of the ruined land, wrote to Mr. Edwards, and headed West. There was just enough money for the trip. Caleb Black agreed to be my guide to the San Juans." She smiled sadly. "But I can't pay him the fifty dollars I promised."

"Is that what happened? Did you sell yourself just to—" Reno began, his voice harsh.

"No!" Willow interrupted. Then, more calmly, "No." She closed her eyes for a moment before she opened them and faced her brother unflinchingly. "I wish Caleb could have come courting me on a West Virginia farm. He would have complimented Papa on his blooded horses and Mama on her spinet playing and me on my pies. After dinner Caleb would have sat on the veranda to talk with my brothers about crops and horses and weather . . . "

Reno started to speak, only to find he had no words to equal the yearning in Willow's eyes.

"But it wasn't to be," she said. "Mama and Papa

are dead, all but a few of the horses are gone, the land is laid waste, and my brothers are scattered across the face of the earth."

Reno reached out toward Willow, only to have her step beyond his reach.

"I don't know what the future holds for me," she said in a low voice. "But I know this. If I must, I'll walk away from the past like a snake shedding skin. All of the past, Matthew. Even you."

"Willy . . ." Reno whispered, holding out his arms. "Don't back away from me."

With a choked sound, Willow went to her brother, returning his hug as fiercely as he gave it.

"It will be all right," Reno said, closing his eyes, concealing the cold purpose in them. "Everything will be all right, Willy. I'll see to it."

When Caleb came back to camp, he found Willow putting out the last of the venison jerky they had made during their stay in the small, distant valley. Reno picked up a piece, chewed it, and made a sound of surprise.

"Venison."

Willow nodded. "We smoked it in the valley while Deuce healed up."

"I'm surprised Caleb risked shooting a deer."

"I didn't," Caleb said from behind Reno. "I stalked it, then cut its throat."

Reno turned with a swiftness that was startling. His left eyebrow raised in dark surprise. "You're real quiet on your feet for a man your size. I'll keep it in mind."

"Why?" Willow asked tartly. "You're not a deer."

The smile Reno showed Caleb wasn't comforting. Nor was it meant to be. But when Reno turned back to Willow, his smile gentled.

"Go ahead and make a small fire," Reno said. "It's been too long since I've had a good biscuit. Even

when you were a kid, you made the best biscuits I
ever ate."

"Are you sure?" Willow asked, looking up.

"Darned sure. I used to come in from the fields for
supper, sniffing the wind like one of Papa's hounds.
If I smelled biscuits, I'd run to the kitchen and hide
a hatful of them before Rafe came in. I never could
eat as much as he could at one sitting."

Willow laughed, remembering. Then her laughter
stilled as she remembered other times that were gone
and the people who were gone with them. "I meant,
are you sure about the fire. Is it safe?"

"Tonight it's safe enough. Tomorrow night?" Reno
shrugged. "Make a lot of biscuits, Willy. It could be
a while before we have another fire."

"All right."

Saying nothing to one another, Caleb and Reno
watched Willow work over the fire. When the food
was ready, both men ate quickly, neatly, leaving nothing behind. Afterward, when Reno started to ask
about family things, Caleb got up and went out from
the small fire to make a bed. The muted voices of
brother and sister followed him into the darkness,
soft laughter and murmured words remembering a
time that would never come again.

The knowledge of how much Willow loved her
handsome, green-eyed brother was a chill spreading
through Caleb's blood, quenching his hope that she
would understand what he must do. Willow had
never seen the careless side of Reno, the side that
took his ease at the cost of weaker people. Nor had
Wolfe seen that part of Reno. Only Rebecca had, and
she had paid for the bitter knowledge with her life
and that of her baby girl.

Grimly, Caleb cut and piled spruce boughs, making
a mattress behind a windbreak of low-growing fir. At
some point, he became aware of the silence of the

night, no voices murmuring, only the wind and the tiny brook. Instants later, he sensed Reno moving almost soundlessly toward him.

Caleb turned with the swift, lethal silence of a striking snake. Reno stood in the moonlight at the edge of the meadow, looking at the bed Caleb had made.

"Where are you sleeping?" Reno asked coolly.

"Here."

"You don't look like a man who needs a mattress."

"Willow likes them. Underneath all that determination, she's a soft little thing."

Even moonlight couldn't blur the lines of anger on Reno's face. "Don't push me, you son of a bitch."

Caleb's smile was savage. "If you don't like being pushed, get out of my way." He glided closer, his walk soundless, predatory. "I was hoping Willow would be asleep before we had our talk, but so be it."

"I should kill you."

"You could try," Caleb offered.

His voice seethed with barely repressed violence. The thought of a rank seducer such as Reno being protective of his own little sister's virtue made Caleb furious. But he could say nothing, for Reno was only reacting as Caleb had when it was his own sister's virtue under discussion.

In any case, Caleb had already returned the favor, seducing Reno's innocent little sister.

Eye for eye, tooth for tooth, life for life.

The thought didn't comfort Caleb.

Reno watched Caleb with eyes turned silver by the cold moon. "A shot will bring Slater down on us like a cold rain," Reno said.

"That's why you're still alive. I don't want Willow put at risk for a snake like you."

The flat hatred in Caleb's voice shocked Reno. It puzzled him, too.

"I know why I'd like to kill you," Reno said slowly, "but I don't know why you want to kill me. It's more than Willow, isn't it?"

"Yes." Then Caleb's breath came in hard as he realized that wasn't true. Not any longer. He had very little time left with Willow. He would fight for every minute of it any way he could and every way he had to, short of endangering her. "Don't stand between me and Willow, Reno. You'll only get hurt and that will hurt her. But she's my woman. If she wants to sleep next to me, she will."

Willow's voice called softly from the fire. "Caleb? Matt? Is something wrong with the horses?"

"They're fine, honey," Caleb called in return.

"Are you too tired to play the harmonica? Matt has a wonderful voice."

"I'll be glad to play for you."

Reno gave Caleb a glittering look of frustration and said in a low voice, "When she's asleep, we'll talk."

"Count on it."

Caleb brushed past Reno and walked toward the tiny fire and the girl who stood smiling and holding out her hands, watching him with a combination of worry and relief in her eyes. She was uneasy whenever her brother and Caleb were alone.

"Are you sure you aren't too tired?" Willow asked Caleb.

He brushed a quick, fierce kiss over her lips. "I'm never too tired to please you."

Willow clung to him and whispered hurriedly, "Matt means well. Please don't be angry."

After a gentle squeeze, Caleb released Willow and sat a few feet back from the fire. Before she could say anything else, the haunting notes of an old ballad lifted softly above the flames, a song telling of a young girl's certainty that she had discovered the love of her life.

After the first few seconds, Caleb faltered. He hadn't known what he was going to play until he heard the notes. His heart contracted at the cruel trick his mind had played. The song had been one of Rebecca's favorites, for the words told of a girl newly in love and thinking of the future that soon would be hers.

I know where I'm going.

I know who's going with me.

Willow and Matt sang a harmony that was all the sweeter for its simplicity. The beauty of Willow's voice surprised Caleb, for she had never sung when he played the harmonica in the valley. She had simply curled up next to him and stared into the fire with a dreamy smile of pleasure on her lips.

The next song Caleb played was also a ballad of love, but the woman walked away, leaving the man to face a future that held nothing of children or a woman's softness. In the third ballad it was the man who was inconstant, the woman who mourned. Without hesitation, Reno and Willow sang each song, their voices blending effortlessly, for the Moran family had spent many a cold winter night singing in front of a fire.

But both sister and brother gradually stopped singing halfway through the fourth song, the lament of a man torn between duty and love, damned no matter which way he turned. The harmonica's supple voice wept over choices in chords no human voice could match.

Willow listened and felt chills coursing over her skin. She had heard the song many times before, had sung it often herself as a girl, and she had smiled, for the tragic words only made her own life more sweet by contrast. But this time when the final note shivered into silence, there was no laughter in her. Tears glistened in Willow's eyelashes and made thin silver trails down her cheeks.

Silently, Caleb stood and held out his hand to her. She stood and took it without a word. Relief coursed through him. Only then did he realize how afraid he had been that Willow wouldn't come to him in the presence of her brother.

"Good night, Matt," Willow said.

Reno nodded curtly, for he didn't trust himself to speak. If he hadn't seen the naked love in Willow's eyes when she looked at Caleb, Reno would have gone for the other man's throat. But the love was there beyond any doubt. It might enrage Reno that Willow was no longer innocent, but there was nothing he could do to change it. Nor did he want to destroy her happiness, for there had been little of it for her in the past years.

Abruptly, Reno had some sympathy for the man in the ballad, caught between duty and love. Reno, too, was between a rock and a hard place, nowhere to turn, no comfort possible.

Caleb stood by the bed he had made and listened for a long moment. He heard no sound behind them. Reno was a man of his word—he wouldn't force the issue until after Willow was asleep.

"It's all right," Willow said as she took off her boots and jacket and slid beneath the blankets. "Matt isn't pleased, but he accepted it."

"I don't think so, little one," Caleb said as he stretched out beneath the blankets.

But when Willow would have spoken, he took her mouth in a possession that was as gentle as it was complete. When he finally lifted his head, it was only to return again and again, as though she was a spring and he was a man who had spent too long without water.

"Caleb," she whispered, trembling. "What is it? What's wrong?"

His only answer was another haunting kiss, then another, until Willow forgot the question. She could feel only the restraint and hunger warring for control of Caleb's body. He held her lightly, sheltering her rather than demanding anything of her. With every kiss he knew he should stop. He didn't want Reno looking at Willow in the morning, knowing she had coupled with Caleb the night before. He didn't want Willow shamed.

Yet he wanted her more than he ever had before.

Finally, Caleb lifted his head a fraction, just enough so that he could talk without losing contact with Willow's lips. "We should sleep."

"Sooner or later, yes."

"Willow," Caleb whispered, sliding his hands down her body, wanting her too much to deny himself. "Do you want me?"

"Yes," she breathed into his mouth. "I'll always want you, Caleb. I love you."

Willow's words ended in a soft, low sound of pleasure as Caleb claimed her mouth once more. Despite the hard urgency she felt in his body, the kiss was tender, slow, a sweet consummation that foreshadowed the deeper joining to come. His hands moved over her, taking away clothes, bringing the greater warmth of his palms caressing her. It was the same for his own body, his own clothes pushed away by her hands, her skin hot and smooth against his.

Familiar, ever-new sensations whispered through Willow, the exciting heat of Caleb's kiss, the silken rasp of his beard against her thighs, the exquisite caresses within her, his mouth consuming her. When he asked for her melting passion, she gave it, bathing both of them in the fire he called from her with each touch, each intimate glide of tongue and fingertips.

When she could bear no more, she gave herself to ecstasy. He put his hand over her mouth, stilling her small wild cries of completion.

Finally Caleb lifted his palm, kissing Willow gently but making no move to join his body with hers.

"Caleb," Willow whispered. "Don't you want me?"

"I—"

His breath broke as Willow's hands found him and held him as gently captive as she herself had been held.

"You always surprise me," she whispered, gliding down his length. "So smooth. So hard."

"And you so soft." His fingertips caressed her sultry, responsive flesh, loving her. "I want you, Willow. More each time. *I want you.*"

Shivering with pleasure, Willow watched the moonlit face of the man she loved as he took the gift of her body, giving his own in return until they were fully joined.

"Better each time," Caleb whispered.

With each slow movement he felt the fine shivering of his lover, a trembling, radiating anticipation that was also his own. He felt her warm breath against his mouth, tasted her sweet kiss, saw her eyes watching him in a silver haze of passion, and sensed the tension gathering in her body once more. Despite the cruel claws of need raking him, he moved gently inside her, rocking slowly, wanting to give her more pleasure than she had ever known in his embrace.

The soft sounds Willow made went no farther than Caleb's mouth as she unravelled beneath him, captive to ecstasy once more. He continued moving slowly, rocking, caressing her with his whole body, loving her gently, relentlessly, sending streamers of fire radiating up through flesh that was still shivering from a tender storm of fulfillment.

"Caleb," she whispered. "I—" Her back arched as

pleasure speared through her.

"Again," Caleb whispered. "Again, Willow. Until there is nothing else but you and me. No brothers. No sisters. No yesterday. No tomorrow. Just us and the kind of pleasure you can die of."

Willow's eyes opened as a sweet violence consumed her. She tried to speak but could not. She had no voice, no thought, no yesterday, no tomorrow, nothing but Caleb and the kind of pleasure she could die of.

16

WILLOW stirred, awakened from her dreams by the absence of Caleb's warmth. Sleepily, she sat up. Just as she was going to call his name, she heard his voice from the direction of the campfire where her brother had made his bed. Reno's voice answered. Neither man sounded friendly.

Adrenaline went through Willow in a wild rush, sweeping away all chance of going back to sleep. She began dressing quickly, fearful of the argument that might develop if she left Caleb and her brother alone.

"You took your damned time," Reno said.

"I wanted to be sure."

"I'll bet." Reno's voice was sarcastic. "Is she finally asleep?"

"Keep your voice down if you want her to stay that way."

"Don't tell me what to do, you son of a bitch. I don't take orders from the likes of you."

"When it comes to Willow, you do," Caleb said, his voice as hard as Reno's had been.

Reno moved abruptly, a man composed of midnight and the slicing silver light of the moon. Every muscle in his body was poised to strike at Caleb.

"You better plan on getting Willow to a preacher real quick," Reno snarled. "If you don't like that idea, you can reach for that six-gun you're wearing. Frankly, I'd rather you went for the gun."

"Don't be a damned fool," Caleb said coldly. "At the first shot, Slater's bunch would be all over us like a rash. Even if we're quiet as stone, we've left tracks from here to Hell and back. Slater's no fool. He's getting closer to us all the time. It's going to take at least two of us to shoot our way free of him."

"That will be my problem, not yours. You'll be dead."

"What about Willow?" Caleb demanded. "Do you know what Slater's bunch would do to her?"

"Same thing you did."

Fury snaked through Caleb's body, testing his self-control. "I didn't rape Willow. She wanted it just as much as I did."

Reno's breath came in hard and fast. "Shut your foul mouth."

"No," Caleb said in a flat voice. "I'm tired of listening to you carry on as though you never lay with a girl."

"I never seduced a virgin!"

"Liar."

Caleb took a single, predatory step toward the other man before he brought himself under control once more.

"My sister was just as innocent as Willow," Caleb said in a low, savage voice. "You seduced my sister, you left her, and she spent her days crying and watching the road, waiting for the man who said he loved her and would come and marry her. He didn't come back and he sure as hell didn't love her. All he loved was the pleasure he got between her legs, and any woman could give him that. When gold fever called, he left her and never looked back."

Ten feet away from the men, Willow stood frozen in darkness, her hand jammed in her mouth so that she wouldn't cry out from the pain that grew greater with every word she overheard.

You seduced my sister, you left her....

He sure as hell didn't love her. All he loved was the pleasure he got between her legs, and any woman could give him that.

"My sister died after giving birth to your bastard," Caleb said, and his eyes promised vengeance for that death.

Reno saw the barely controlled rage in Caleb and had no doubt that the other man was telling what he believed to be the truth.

Reno also had no doubt that it wasn't the truth.

"When?" he asked flatly.

"Last year."

"Where?"

"Listen, you—"

"Where?" demanded Reno, cutting Caleb off.

What Reno really wanted to know was the girl's name, but he knew if he asked, Caleb would reach for his gun. A minute ago, Reno would have been glad to provoke the fight.

But not now.

Caleb was right. As long as Slater and his men were around, the real loser in any fight would be Willow.

"Arizona Territory," Caleb said, biting off each word.

Reno's eyes widened in surprise as he put facts together. "You're the Man from Yuma."

"Dead right, Reno. I've been hunting you for a long time."

Willow flinched at the hatred in Caleb's voice. She remembered something Eddy had said, something about letting Caleb know if he heard anything about a man called Reno. A new fear grew in Willow, a fear so great she could barely breathe.

Had Caleb known all along that her brother was called Reno? Was that why Caleb had seduced her? Eye for eye . . .

The thought went through Willow with an agony as great as her love. She prayed that Caleb hadn't known her brother's nickname before tonight.

"You're dead wrong, Yuma man. I never touched your sister. Marty did, though. He was crazy for her."

There was a taut silence as the two men measured each other across the ashes of a dead campfire. The temptation to believe Reno was so great that it shook Caleb, telling him how much he didn't want to kill Willow's brother.

"Who," Caleb asked softly, "is Marty?"

"Martin Busher, my partner. At least he was until he met Becky Black. I saw the way things were going and drifted."

"Where is he now?"

"Dead."

The breath came out of Caleb in a long sigh. "Are you certain?"

"He was supposed to meet up with me here about eight months ago," Reno said. "We were going prospecting. He never showed up. I waited two weeks, then went prospecting on my own. I figured he got married and settled down." Reno's expression changed, hardening. "One day I heard shots. I went to take a look. When I got there, the fight was over. Marty was dead."

"Utes?"

"Probably. None of the horses wore shoes."

Caleb hesitated before he very slowly reached into his pocket with his left hand, making certain that every motion was illuminated by moonlight.

"Don't get edgy, Reno. This isn't my shooting hand. I've got something I want you to look at."

Reputation and observation had told Reno that Caleb was indeed a right-handed shooter, but Reno watched very carefully just the same. More than one man had died watching the wrong hand.

All that came from Caleb's pocket was a gold locket. He flicked it open, using his left thumbnail.

"Strike a match," Caleb said.

Reno did, using his right hand, for he was a left-handed shooter.

Gold metal shone brightly, reflecting the flare of the match. Willow saw the locket, remembered Caleb showing it to her, asking her if the people inside were her "husband's" parents. Fear filled her, choking her. With a tiny sound, she did what she had done during the war when she had hidden and men had drawn so near that fear threatened to overwhelm her; she bit into her hand until physical pain restored her self-control.

"Recognize them?" Caleb asked.

A quick glance was all Reno spared. It was all he needed. "Must be Marty's folks."

"Must be? Why?"

"Ears," Reno said succinctly. "Marty could put a milk pitcher to shame."

A muffled sound that was part laughter and part relief came from Caleb, but he still didn't understand what had happened to put him on the trail of the wrong man.

"When I asked Becky who the father was," Caleb said slowly, "she told me a man called Reno, a man whose real name was Matthew Moran."

The words echoed in Willow's head, her worst fears calmly spoken by the man she loved.

The man who didn't love her.

The man who had been hunting Matthew Moran, nicknamed Reno. But Caleb hadn't found Reno. So

Caleb used what he did find, which was a girl who could lead him to Reno.

A chill shook Willow as she understood that Caleb was indeed what he had seemed in Denver, a dark angel of retribution.

Eye for eye, tooth for tooth.

Sister for sister.

The vague salt and copper taste of blood spread through Willow's mouth, but the pain of her hand was nothing compared to the bleak realization that she had been seduced in order to balance the merciless scales of a justice that was as hard as Caleb Black.

"Becky said her man gave her the locket when he rode out to make their fortune in gold."

Reno hissed a word under his breath. "Your sister lied about me, Yuma man."

"I'm beginning to think so," Caleb agreed calmly, "but why?"

"What were you going to do when you found your sister's seducer?"

"Beat the living hell out of him, then stand him up in front of a preacher with Rebecca," Caleb said.

Reno smiled grimly. "My sentiments exactly. Did she know what you were going to do?"

"She knew me."

"Then she was probably trying to protect her man, such as he was. Marty couldn't have been more than seventeen. He was a good kid, but he wasn't up to your weight in any kind of fight." Reno smiled savagely. "I am. I know just what to do with a man who forces himself on an innocent girl."

"I didn't force Willow and you know it."

"Like hell, Yuma man. You were alone with her. She was at your mercy and you—"

"Tell him, Willow," Caleb interrupted, his voice like a whip.

Without looking away from Reno, Caleb held out his left hand to the girl who had been standing motionless in darkness, trying not to make a sound. Caleb had wanted to spare Willow this, but it was too late now.

"Tell your brother how it was between us right from the start," Caleb said.

"Get away from him, Willy."

Without a word to either man, Willow lowered her hand from her mouth and walked forward until her boots crunched among the ashes of the dead campfire. Ignoring Caleb's outstretched hand until he slowly withdrew it, she stood between the men, looking at neither of them, touching neither of them. A single drop of blood slid down her hand like a black tear in the moonlight.

It would be as close to crying as she came. Tears came from hope or fear, and Willow felt neither. Not anymore. All she felt was cold.

"Willy?" Reno asked quietly, worried by his sister's eerie calm.

"I begged for him to take me."

For a moment, the meaning of Willow's words escaped both men. They were too shocked by her voice to get past it to the words. The huskiness and subtle laughter that was so much a part of her voice was gone. In its place was nothing at all, a flatness of tone that was barely human.

"I can't believe it, Willy. You weren't raised to—"

"No more," Caleb said, cutting across Reno's words. "You asked, she answered, and that's the end of it."

Gently, Caleb stroked Willow's hair, silently urging her closer to him. She remained motionless, as though nothing more than moonlight was touching her. Long fingers brushed over her cheek. She turned away. With a whispered curse, Caleb dropped his hand and turned back to her brother.

"You can climb down off your high horse," Caleb said roughly to Reno. "I'll marry Willow as soon as we can find a preacher."

Silence stretched, then snapped with Reno's long sigh. His body shifted subtly, coming off the fine edge of battle readiness. His left hand curled into a fist, then relaxed.

"Damn good thing, Yuma man."

Willow saw the change in Reno as he relaxed. She remembered the speed with which her brother had drawn his gun, and understood why Caleb had agreed to marry her. Fury uncurled in her body, an emotion as cold as her passion had been hot.

"Good?" Willow repeated softly. "A liar will marry me rather than face my brother—who happens to be a gunfighter called Reno—and that's good?"

Abruptly, tension arced through Reno again. "Are you saying Caleb lied his way into your bed?"

"How did I lie to you?" Caleb asked simultaneously. His voice was soft but it nonetheless overrode Reno's question. "Tell me, Willow. Tell me how I seduced you with lies. Did I promise to marry you?"

The sound Willow made could hardly be called laughter, but it was. "No. No promises."

"Did I tell you all the lies about love and forever after that a man bent on seduction uses?"

Willow's breath came in harshly. "No. No words of love and forever after."

"Then how did I lie to you? *Tell me.*"

The sound of Willow swallowing against the tension in her throat was painful to hear. Her eyelashes closed, but it was only for an instant. Caleb was right and they both knew it. He hadn't had to lie. She had fallen into his hands like a peach all flushed and hot from the sun. The ease of the conquest must have surprised him. No wonder he thought she was a fancy lady.

For him, she was.

"You didn't tell me you were hunting my brother," Willow said at last, not looking at Caleb.

"I thought you were Reno's fancy lady," Caleb said roughly. "You were my best hope of avenging Rebecca. Your brother is a hard man to track down. I didn't like using a woman to get to Reno, but given the same circumstances, I'd do the same thing again."

Willow turned and looked at Caleb for the first time since she had walked out of one kind of darkness and into another kind, one whose end she couldn't see.

"I hope Marty lied to your sister," Willow said, her voice as soft and cold as snow. "I hope she heard a thousand loving lies from her man. I hope she died believing each one of them. It would make the memories less . . . shameful."

"There's no shame in what we did," Caleb said furiously, feeling his self-control evaporating with each word Willow said. She had always had that effect on him, making a shambles of the defenses that other people found so solid. "We aren't the first man and woman in creation who couldn't wait for a preacher to put the seal on their marriage."

"What marriage?" she asked.

"The one that will take place as soon as we get the hell out of here," he retorted.

"Yuma man, I'm not marrying you."

Caleb was too surprised to say anything.

Reno wasn't. "You can marry him or you can bury him. Your choice, Willy."

Caleb gave Reno a hard look, but when Caleb spoke, his voice was reasonable. "Bullets aren't like words. You can't take them back when you've gotten over your anger."

For a few moments Willow continued to stare

through Caleb as though he didn't exist. Finally, her breath came out in a long rush. "Yes. My brother is blindingly quick with his belt gun, isn't he?"

That wasn't what Caleb had meant, but he was too disturbed by the quality of Willow's voice to protest. Her voice belonged to someone much older and much less gentle than the girl who unravelled so sweetly and so completely in his arms.

"He's quick enough," Caleb said evenly.

Silence stretched as Willow looked at the big man she had loved before she ever really knew him. But as much as the mistake hurt, she knew it was her own doing, not Caleb's. He may have abetted her ignorance, but he didn't create it. He hadn't lied to her. He hadn't needed to.

She had lied so successfully to herself.

Silly little trout, not knowing the difference between lust and love, mistaking a backwater swirl for the river of life itself.

Willow closed her eyes and saw again the stunning instant when Reno's gun had simply appeared in his hand. There had been no warning, no hesitation, nothing but speed and a cold steel weapon poised to kill.

Her fingers clenched together, fingers interlaced. The small wound across the back of her hand protested and wept another black tear. Willow barely felt it. Her thoughts were too painful to allow for anything except the silent scream raking at her throat.

Caleb doesn't love me but he'll marry me rather than face my brother's gun.

Caleb, who had saved Willow's life more than once on the long way to the San Juans. Caleb, who hadn't forced her into his becoming his fancy lady. If anything, she had forced him, tempting him in ways she hadn't even understood at the time.

Of course Caleb doesn't love me. An Old Testament kind

of man doesn't love a fancy lady. He uses her, though . . .
the pleasure he finds between her legs.

The memory of her own wanton sensuality washed through Willow in a scalding tide of humiliation that receded slowly, leaving her skin as cold and colorless as her voice.

"Well, Willy," Reno said impatiently. "What will it be? A wedding or a funeral?"

Willow knew she had to choose, but there was no choice she could live with. She couldn't condemn Caleb to death at her brother's hands. She couldn't condemn herself to life with a man who at best saw her as a duty he had acquired on the way to avenging his sister's death. And at worst . . .

Fancy lady.

At worst, Willow would condemn herself to marrying a man who had nothing but contempt for her and a lust that could be slaked between any woman's legs.

Slowly, Willow opened her eyes and looked from the brother who didn't understand her to the man who didn't love her.

"I'll do what I must," Willow said.

Caleb looked at her sharply, sensing the leashed turmoil beneath the quiet words.

But Reno simply nodded, satisfied. "Nearest preacher is at the fort over the divide." He smiled at his sister. "I'll stand up for you, Willy, even though it will cost me most of a summer's digging."

"That's not necessary," she said.

"My pleasure."

"Pleasure?" Willow's voice made the men exchange uneasy glances. "There is no pleasure in a wedding performed under threat of a six-gun. That's why you're giving up your summer of digging, *Reno*. You want to make sure the wedding takes place."

"You're wrong, Willy."

She looked at her brother as though she had never seen him before. "How can you be so sure? What makes you think that Caleb won't just leave me and ride on as soon as he's out of range of your gun?"

"What kind of man do you think I am?" Caleb demanded angrily.

"Old Testament," Willow said succinctly. "You owe me nothing. I'm no kin to you. I was simply a means to an end. An eye for an eye and a virgin sister for a virgin sister. The fact that you seduced the wrong man's sister is a trifle that I'm certain God will forgive. Your intentions were pure. Justice without mercy. Retribution."

"I didn't take you for revenge," Caleb said between his teeth, "and you damn well know it. I wanted you!"

"Not as much as I wanted you."

Willow. Push me away.

Though neither spoke aloud, the memory of Caleb's words lay between them. The memory of what had happened next also lay between them, Willow's eagerness to complete the union, her body tempting him unbearably, her voice telling him how much she loved him.

"Willow," Caleb whispered, reaching toward her.

Silently, she stepped just beyond his reach.

Caleb dropped his hand and turned to Reno. "I'm marrying your sister. You have my word on it."

"I never doubted it," Reno said calmly. "We'll leave during the next storm. That way I might be able to keep this place a secret long enough to file a claim on it."

Moonlight glinted in Caleb's eyes as he looked at the sky. "It might storm sometime tomorrow. Hard to tell with a sky like this."

Willow looked at Caleb and then at Reno. She said nothing because she didn't trust herself to say anything more without revealing that she had no intention of marrying him. Nor did she intend to cause the funeral her brother was so eager to enforce.

"Come on, honey," Caleb said gently, holding out his hand once more. "If we're going to ride out tomorrow, you need to rest."

Willow took another step backward, away from the man holding out his hand to her.

"Willy, you're being foolish," Reno said in an impatient voice. "Caleb seduced you, he's marrying you, and that's the way it ought to be."

"No, it isn't." Willow focused beyond the two men. "A marriage ought to come from love, not duty."

Reno made a sound of amusement and disgust. "A woman taught me back in West Virginia that love is for boys and girls who aren't grown up enough to know any better. Caleb is a man. He knows his duty. It's time you learned yours, Willy. You danced the tune and now it's time to pay the piper."

"Yes," she whispered, accepting the outcome of her own choices, shivering as a chill roughened her skin. "I understand."

"Good," Reno said, relieved. He stepped forward and hugged her. The embrace was awkward because she was stiff, unmoving. "Come on, Willy," he coaxed. "Don't sulk. If you didn't have a lot of feeling for Caleb, you wouldn't have become his woman. If he didn't want you, he wouldn't have taken you. Now you're getting married. What's so awful about that?"

Willow turned and looked at her brother.

When Reno saw her face, his eyes narrowed. "Willy?"

"Tell me," she said softly, "how would you feel if our positions were reversed? How would you feel knowing that your bride came to you because the only other choice was certain death?"

Reno's mouth opened, but he was too shocked to say anything.

Caleb's low, savage cursing was the only answer Willow got. It was enough.

"Yes. That's a fair summary of how I feel." Willow stepped away from both men. She wrapped her arms around herself, noticing for the first time how cold she was without her jacket. "Excuse me. I have things to do. I wouldn't want to be caught unprepared if a storm blows up unexpectedly."

"I'll help you," Caleb said.

"No."

"Damn it—" began Caleb.

"Yes," Willow interrupted bleakly. "Damn it. Damn it straight to Hell."

Silently, both men watched as Willow walked into the night. When they could neither see nor hear her anymore, Reno let out a long breath.

"Good thing she wasn't packing a gun," he said. "She'd have gone for it." Reno shook his head. "And it's a good thing she thinks she loves you, Yuma man. Otherwise she'd cut your throat while you slept."

Caleb shook his head. "If that's what she wanted, Willow would take me head on and wide awake, even knowing she would lose. There's no quit in her. I admire that, even though it would be a lot easier sometimes if she was meek."

Reno shook his head in amazement. "She was such a sweet little girl, all smiles and mischief and golden hair."

"Sweet little girls have to be packed in cotton and put on a high shelf if they're going to stay sweet." Caleb looked out into the darkness that had swallowed Willow. "I'd rather have a woman who won't fold up the first time life gets hard. I'd rather have a woman who makes choices and doesn't whine if things don't turn out the way she expected. I'd rather have a woman's passion than a little girl's sweet smiles. I'd rather have . . . Willow."

"You've got her." Reno smiled slightly. "She's mad as a cat in a bathtub right now, but she'll come around and make the best of it. She doesn't have any choice and she knows it."

"I'd rather she came to me willingly."

"From what I've gathered, lack of willingness on her part hasn't been a problem for you," Reno said sardonically.

Caleb turned so swiftly on Reno that he instinctively tensed.

"Preacher or no preacher, Willow is my *wife*," Caleb said savagely. "She came to me as innocent as any woman ever came to a man. If you do anything to make her feel ashamed, you'll get the fight you've been begging for. You've got my word on that."

Reno's left eyebrow climbed in a black arc as the flat promise in Caleb's voice sank in. After a moment, Reno laughed softly and held out his hand. "Welcome to the family, brother. I'm glad Willow found herself a man she won't have to apologize for when fighting time comes around."

Grimly, Caleb smiled and he shook hands. "Don't worry, Reno. If you ever need another gun, you just send word. I'll be there come Hell or high water."

"Well, there's one fight coming I won't have to send word on. Hope to Hell Wolfe is around somewhere. Two guns against Slater's bunch isn't enough."

"It might be if you have a repeating rifle."

"Wolfe told me about that fancy long gun of yours. Said you can load and fire damn near at the same time."

Caleb nodded.

"Have to get me one of those," Reno said. "Wish I had one now."

"So do I. Is there another way out of here?"

"Maybe. Depends on the horses you're riding. Look here . . ."

Reno hunkered down on his heels and began drawing in the ashes with a twig. The passage of the stick left a dim white line through the darker ashes on the surface of the fire as Reno talked in a low voice about the valley and the mountainside.

Across the small valley, Willow froze, listening as hard as she could. She hadn't been able to hear the individual words while Caleb and Reno spoke, but she had been able to distinguish voices from the random whisper of wind and the rush of the creek. The abrupt lack of conversation made her fear it wouldn't be long until Caleb came back to bed. She wanted to be somewhere else before that happened.

Hurriedly, Willow tore a blank page from Caleb's journal and stuffed it into her jacket pocket with the pencil she had already taken. She kept the journal as well, for it had Caleb's carefully drawn map of all the rugged country they had covered, as well as the easier passes they hadn't taken. Between that and her ability to read the stars, she should be able to find her way back over the mountains, even though she would be traveling at night to avoid attracting attention.

Willow walked toward the horses, dragging her saddle and a hastily made bedroll behind her. One big jacket pocket was filled with venison jerky, which was all she would have to eat until she reached Canyon City. The prospect of short rations didn't bother Willow nearly as much as the fact that she would have to leave her mares behind. She simply hadn't the skill to hide them and herself as well. They would be better off with Caleb, who had cared enough for the Arabians to ignore his own exhaustion and go back over the divide to rescue the four mares.

The breeze shifted, bringing with it the murmur of male voices from the campsite. Willow relaxed slightly, knowing that she had a few more minutes before Caleb came after her. She wished she could be gone before Caleb sought her out, but that would be too dangerous. If only a few minutes separated them, he would come after her and catch her. She needed time to put enough distance between them that chasing her would be futile.

Ishmael scented Willow and nickered softly. She put down the saddle and quickly opened the bedroll as though she planned to sleep in the meadow with her horses. The blankets were lumpy with the various things she had between the layers, but she doubted Caleb would notice in the dark. Her carpetbag would have been too obvious, so she had left it behind.

Willow sat down and wrote quickly, saying what had to be said despite the pain it cost.

> *Matt, I'm sorry I'm not the innocent girl you remembered. Forcing Caleb to marry me won't change what happened.*
> *Don't come after me. Let me shed the past and start all over again as a widow. I won't be the first such widow, and I won't be the last.*
> *If you ever see our brothers, tell them I think of them often and remember them with love.*

Willow paused, her courage faltering at the thought of what she had to say next. But it must be done. Caleb must understand that he had no duty to her.

> *Caleb, take your pick of the mares as payment for bringing me to my brother. Please take the other three to Wolfe Lonetree. He can have one if he'll care for the other two until I can come for them.*

*If you do that, you have no other duty toward me.
We are both free to begin over again.*

After a few minutes, Willow went out among the
horses, silently saying good-bye. The mares took the
nighttime visitation with the same gentle spirit they
took everything that came to them from their mistress. Tears burned behind Willow's eyes as she felt
the velvet muzzles snuffling over her, nudging her,
asking to be petted and loved.

*Caleb will take good care of you. Better than I could.
He's strong enough to get you to safe pastures.*

Ishmael's head came up and he nickered softly,
looking into the night past Willow's shoulder. She
turned around slowly, knowing who would be
there.

"It's too late to start sleeping apart," Caleb said,
gesturing toward the place where Willow had left her
bedroll and her saddle at its head as a pillow.

Willow shrugged, not trusting her voice.

"Come back to bed with me, honey. Nothing has
changed."

She shook her head with a weariness that was apparent even in the moon's pale light.

Caleb's hand shot out, catching Willow's arm as
she turned away. Willow made a startled sound. She
had forgotten how quick he could be.

"Please don't touch me." Willow's words were un-
inflected, remote.

Caleb's eyelids flickered at the distance in Willow's
voice, but he didn't release her. "You're my wife."

"I'm your whore."

His breath came in with a ripping sound. His other
hand shot out. He pulled her close, imprisoning her
in his arms, wishing there were sunlight so he could
see her eyes.

And then Caleb saw Willow's eyes, and wished the moon were less bright.

Her eyes were no more alive than her voice. A fine tremor moved through her body as she stood within his arms. Once that trembling would have signalled the depth of her passion for him. Now it signalled a terrible combination of shame and acceptance.

"You're not my whore," Caleb said in a savage voice. "You were never my whore!"

"Fancy lady. Whore. Call it what you will. It doesn't change what happened, what I am." Willow turned away as much as Caleb would allow her. "Let go of me."

"No," he said, and pulled her tight against his body.

Caleb's flat refusal was unexpected, as was the arousal he made no effort to hide.

Willow was shocked. She hadn't expected him to require her presence in his bed tonight. She hadn't really believed that he thought of her as his whore.

She had been wrong. But then, she had been wrong about him before.

"I see," Willow said. She forced her hands between their bodies and began unbuttoning her jacket with fingers that shook. "You want to rut between my legs again."

His hand came down hard across her mouth. "*Stop it*. You're my woman, not my whore, and you god-damned well know it!"

Caleb's eyes were narrow slices of silver in the moonlight. His mouth was a black line. His face was utterly savage.

Willow could see the rage in Caleb, taste it, feel it. He was more angry than she had ever known any man to be. Without warning, he moved his hand and replaced it with his mouth. He was so quick that she had no chance. She was held within the fierce cage of his arms, no way to turn, no escape, nothing but the urgent pressure of his mouth breaking open hers, leaving her defenseless against his kiss.

Motionless, Willow waited for the intimate thrust of Caleb's tongue. It didn't come. Instead his mouth gentled and his tongue coaxed hers in a sweet seduction that was more threatening than any forced claiming would have been. It was the same with his hands sliding softly over her body, spreading pleasure in their wake, making her tremble.

Despair washed through Willow. Caleb knew her too well. Helplessly her nails bit into his upper arms as the wildness in her sensed the outlet he was offering and clamored for release.

"Yes," Caleb said savagely, biting Willow's neck with fierce restraint as he felt the sleek pain of her nails. "Come to me. You're hurt and angry and don't know what to do. Take it out on me, Willow. I'm not afraid of the passion in you. Let it free."

The realization that Caleb knew about the wildness that seethed beneath her unnatural calm wrenched a sound of despair from Willow's lips.

"Stop, please, stop," she begged in a shaking voice. "Leave me some pride, Yuma man. Even a whore needs a little pride."

A chill went over Caleb. "Stop staying that. Do you hear me? *You're not a whore*."

"Prove it! Let me sleep where I like. Let me sleep alone!"

There was a silence that stretched until Willow wanted to scream. The only signs of her turmoil were the tremors that shook her randomly. None of the emotion showed on her face. She simply watched Caleb with the eyes of a stranger as she waited to find out whether she was woman or whore.

And he knew it.

"Sleep where you please whenever you please,"

he said coldly. "I'm damned sick of being treated like a conscienceless seducer by you and your brother."

Abruptly, Caleb released Willow and stepped back.

"Let me know when you get over your sulking and want to be treated like my woman. Then I'll let you know if I still feel like being your man."

17

NOT until Willow was miles beyond the valley's narrow entrance did she dismount and remove the shreds of her riding habit from Ishmael's feet. The stallion snorted as the last thong was taken off and the scraps of material fell away. He stamped impatiently.

"I know," Willow said quietly, stroking Ishmael's neck, soothing her edgy horse. "The rags bothered you, but they kept your hooves from making noise on the rocks."

Unhappily, she looked at the sky. Dawn lay just over the eastern horizon, bleaching stars from the night. She wished she could simply go to ground and hide for the day, but that would be certain disaster. It was much too close to the valley for her to be safe. She had to ride fast and hard through the day and the next night as well.

Tomorrow at dawn she would be able to picket Ishmael in some secluded meadow and sleep at his feet. Tomorrow, but not today.

Willow got back in the saddle and rode on down the mountainside, leaving the hidden valley farther behind with each moment. Around her the land slowly condensed from the night, revealing the silhouettes of distant peaks against the pale sky, and a mixture of grassland and forest nearby. She kept Ishmael just on the margin of the forest, where there was enough open space for speedy travel and enough cover nearby if she needed it.

The heavy shotgun lay across Willow's thighs. It made for awkward riding at times, but she had discovered during the long night that she liked the feel of the smooth wooden stock and the reassurance of the twin barrels loaded and ready to fire.

Ishmael's head turned suddenly to the left as he looked across the grassland to a place where a brook flowed between ridges on the way to joining a larger creek. The stallion's ears pricked forward and his nostrils flared deeply as he tested the wind.

Without hesitation, Willow turned the stallion hard to the right, fleeing whatever he had scented, heading for the cover of the forest. Heart beating double time, she guided the stallion deeper into cover. When the trees were so close around her that the horse had difficulty walking—and she had difficulty ducking branches—she turned and urged Ishmael on a track parallel to the one they had abandoned.

No matter how carefully Willow listened, she heard nothing but the creak of her saddle, the muffled rhythm of Ishmael's hooves on evergreen needles, and the soft sighing of wind. Gradually, the forest thinned to scattered groves and then scattered trees, and finally nothing but meadow grass, wildflowers, and willows growing on the margins of the stream. The park was at least a mile across at its narrowest and went on for five miles. It was more a basin than a river valley.

The route the journal indicated took her the full length of the grassland. Part of it could be taken along the edge of the forest. Most of it could not. The beginning was the worst. There would be two miles without any real cover.

Willow tightened her grip on the shotgun and the reins as she listened intently and watched the grassland for signs of life. It was difficult to see much in the dim, featureless pre-dawn light. Several shadows that were the size of deer moved slowly along the margin of meadow and trees. Nothing else moved but grass stirred by the wind. It was so quiet she could hear the high, wild cry of an eagle as it flew toward dawn, searching for the first kill of the day. Willow inhaled deeply. There was no smoke in the air, no obvious sign of other people, nothing but an eerie prickling on the back of her neck.

Suddenly, Ishmael shied and snorted. Willow didn't know whether the stallion was sensing her own uneasiness or if he scented some other horse on the wind.

"Easy, boy," she murmured. "I don't like that open space either, but there's no other way. Let's get it over with before the sun clears the peaks."

A touch of Willow's heels moved Ishmael into a canter. Though smaller than Caleb's Montana horses, the Arabian had a long, hungry stride.

A shout came from the forest behind and to Willow's left.

That can't be Caleb. After what he said last night, he wouldn't follow me. And even if Matt made Caleb come along, it's barely dawn. He and Matt are just getting up. Besides, the shout came from the wrong direction for the valley.

Another shout came. Willow looked over her shoulder. Four riders were coming toward her. Their horses were big, dark, long-legged bays. They came closer to her with each stride.

Willow lifted the reins and spoke to the stallion.

Instantly, his canter shifted into a gallop. After a few hundred yards she looked over her shoulder. The riders were following, their horses running hard.

Clutching the shotgun, Willow bent low over Ishmael's neck and spoke to him again, asking for more speed. His stride lengthened as he began to gallop in earnest, running close to the land, flattened out except for the elegant red banner of his raised tail.

Grass and bushes whipped by in a blur. Wind tore tears from Willow's eyes and tried to drag the breath from her throat. Ishmael's hooves made a continuous drumroll of sound. The pace was far too fast for the uncertain light, and too demanding on the stallion's strength, but there was no choice. She had to outrun the other horses.

Willow settled even closer to Ishmael's neck, balancing her weight over his driving shoulders where she would be the least burden to him. The shotgun made the position awkward for horse and rider both. After several tries, Willow managed to jam the gun into its saddle scabbard.

When she judged that a mile had gone by, Willow looked over her shoulder. Fear squeezed her heart. The four horses had drawn closer. As she turned around, wind ripped her hat from her head and quickly unravelled her hair until it streamed out behind like a ghostly flag. Blinking fiercely to clear her eyes of wind-caused tears, Willow leaned even farther toward, holding the reins only inches from the bit, burying her cheek against Ishmael's hot neck.

As the second mile flew by, the Arabian slowly began pulling away from the pursuing horses. When the men realized it, they started firing.

The fierce pace and the vague light helped Willow. She heard the shots over Ishmael's deep, hard breathing and the thunder of his hooves, but no bullets came close. Flattening against the stallion's sweaty neck,

Willow praised him and encouraged him while another mile raced by and dawn turned nearby peaks to burning gold.

The creek came out of nowhere, hidden by a fold in the grassland. Willow caught no more than a glimpse of the barrier of rock and water that had been thrown without warning across Ishmael's path. She clung like a pale shadow as the horse's whole body bunched in mid-stride, twisted, and then released in a gigantic spring that left the gully behind.

Caught off-stride by having to jump without warning, the stallion stumbled as he landed. Willow braced her feet in the stirrups and hauled up on the reins, lifting Ishmael's head and literally pulling him back into balance. Catlike, he collected himself and within seconds was running flat out again.

Willow threw a quick glance over her shoulder. The pursuers were falling off the pace. One of the horses had given up entirely. They had been faster than the stallion over the first mile, had held their own for a second mile, but they had lacked the Arabian's stamina for the long, grinding miles after that.

Relief washed over Willow in a wave that was almost dizzying. She turned back and leaned lower along the stallion's straining neck. Her voice praised him, telling him how he was running the other horses right into the ground. Ishmael's ears flickered back and forth, listening to his rider's words. Though the Arabian was breathing hard, his stride was still even. He hadn't come to the end of his strength yet, but he would soon. She could only hope that the other horses would be far behind by the time Ishmael could run no more.

As the fourth mile whipped by, a volley of shots came from behind Willow. She looked over her shoulder. All but one of the horses had given up. It had the long, racy look of a Thoroughbred. If it were indeed a racehorse, it wasn't used to races that went on for miles. It, too, was falling off the pace, but slowly.

And it took the gully like the Irish hunter it was.

Talking over the thunder of Ishmael's hooves, Willow asked for more of the stallion's strength. His ears flicked and his neck stretched out a bit more. Willow flattened out with him, crying from more than the wind. She knew she was running her horse far too hard, too fast, too long. She also knew that she had no choice but to ask Ishmael for his last ounce of strength.

By the time the fifth mile went by, the stallion's breath was sawing in and out of his mouth and lather covered much of his red body, but his stride was still hard and rhythmic. Fearful of what she would see, Willow waited as long as she could before she wiped her eyes on her forearm and looked over her shoulder.

The other horse was falling away rapidly, no longer able to run.

Willow wept with relief and pulled Ishmael back to a slower gallop, easing the strain on his heart and lungs. The long meadow swept past on either side, then bent around a tongue of stone thrusting down from the mountain. No one followed her into the sweeping curve. She pulled lightly on the reins again, slowing Ishmael even more.

And then she pulled back so hard that the stallion reared up and slid on his hocks.

In the first clear light of day, five horsemen were spread across the meadow in front of Willow, closing in on her at a run. Turning around and running from them was futile. Even if Ishmael could take another long race, it would only carry them back to the enemies he had just outrun. Escape to either side wasn't possible, for the meadow was being pinched between the high, steep walls as the stream descended, eating through the mountain.

Willow did the only thing she could. She yanked out the shotgun and urged Ishmael into a hard gallop once more. Hair streaming out behind her like a golden flag, she raced the stallion toward the men who were closing in on her.

CALEB saw the flattened grass where Willow's bedroll had been, counted horses in the gray light, and felt adrenaline rush through his veins.

She couldn't have run off. We'd have heard her.

Just as he turned away, he saw the pale flash of paper tied to a bush. He stripped off the note, read it, and felt as though he had been dropped in icewater.

Willow had gone alone into the night rather than face a dawn that held Caleb Black.

"Find her?" Reno asked as he watched Caleb stalk toward him.

"She took Ishmael and rode out last night," Caleb said flatly.

"We'd have heard her," Reno said immediately. "She must be hiding in the trees."

"Her stud's gone and so is she. She wrapped her horse's hooves in cloth," Caleb said. He knelt, wrapped up his bedroll, and tied it behind the saddle he had used as a pillow.

"She left a note dividing up her mares."

"But why?" Reno asked.

"She loves those mares like a mother loves her kids, but she hates me more. She'd ride through Hell itself to get away from me."

"Willy's not a fool," Reno said. "Where does she think she's going? She doesn't know these mountains."

"She took my shotgun and my journal." As Caleb

talked, he pulled two boxes of ammunition from a saddlebag and shoved them into the pockets of his shearling coat. "Getting lost will be the least of her problems."

"Slater," Reno said, shocked. "She knows he's out there somewhere. My God. What the hell did you do to Willow last night?"

"I was a *gentleman*," Caleb said savagely. "She told me she wanted to sleep alone. I let her. But don't worry, Reno. I'll never be that stupid again."

As sunlight brushed the highest peak, Caleb's whistle shredded the dawn silence. Two dark horses trotted toward him. He grabbed a bridle, saddle, and saddlebags and headed for Trey as Reno turned and ran back to his own camp. He reappeared a moment later with a bridle in one hand and a saddle thrown over his shoulder.

A short time later, Caleb and Reno emerged from the thicket that protected the entrance to the little valley. Reno didn't bother to tie the branches together behind them. He simply vaulted into the saddle and began looking for signs. Caleb was ahead of him. He made a sharp gesture, then turned and trotted downstream, making no effort to hide his tracks in the water.

Reno didn't object. Concealing the location of his valley was the least of their problems at the moment. Finding Willow before Slater did was all that mattered. Their best hope was that Willow had been traveling by moonlight and trying to be quiet. Caleb and Reno were traveling in better light and didn't give a damn who knew about it. They should overtake her quickly.

Suddenly Caleb reined in and held up his hand in a signal for silence. Both men stood in the stirrups, turning their heads slowly, trying to decide if they really had heard rifle shots, and if so, from which direction.

The sound of a ragged volley came from down below, followed by the boom of a double-barrelled shotgun.

Ruthlessly Caleb spurred Trey, sending the big horse hurtling down the trail at a breakneck pace. Reno was right on his heels. Both men had their rifles out and little hope of getting anywhere in time to use them. The shots had come from downhill and miles away. By the time Caleb and Reno got there, nothing would be left but tracks and spent shells.

Wolfe Lonetree was waiting for them just where the big meadow began. His horse blocked the tracks made by Ishmael while Willow had looked over the grass for the signs of man.

"Slater's bunch has the girl and the red stud about five miles down the trail," he said to Caleb and Reno. "She's not hurt and not likely to be hurt for a bit. Slater is trying to get her to tell where you are, but if we come charging up, he'll cut her throat just to spite you. You know his reputation."

"Yes," Caleb said in a clipped voice. "I know it. Can you get us close to where he's holding Willow?"

Wolfe nodded and reined his horse into the meadow. The mare was an odd blue-gray with black mane and tail, a color found in mustangs that were throwbacks to their Spanish ancestors. Three abreast, the horses cantered across the grassland on a long diagonal that finally brought them to a fringe of forest. Once there, they reined in to a walk, resting the horses for whatever might come. Without making a fuss about it, Wolfe made certain his horse was between Reno and Caleb. Speculatively, Wolfe's indigo eyes went from one man to the other, trying to figure out if Caleb knew who Willow's husband really was.

After a moment, Wolfe said dryly to Reno, "You must be Matthew Moran."

"Most people call him Reno," Caleb said, but his eyes never stopped searching the land ahead.

Wolfe smiled slightly and relaxed. "I always have. Didn't know you were married, Reno."

"Willy is my sister," Reno said. "She's going to be Caleb's wife."

Deep blue eyes went from Caleb to Reno and back to Caleb again. "Wife," Wolfe repeated softly.

Caleb nodded.

"Well, if ever a woman could put a bridle on you, that blond warrior I saw this morning would be the one."

"You saw her?" Caleb demanded.

"See that bald knob up there?" Wolfe asked, pointing.

Across the grass and about a thousand feet higher up, there was a stony knob.

"I see it," he said curtly.

"I was sitting up there with my binoculars, keeping an eye on Slater's bunch," Wolfe said. "The girl was a few hundred yards out in the meadow when she saw Jed Slater and some of his men break cover behind her. She didn't waste time wringing her hands. She sent that red stud of hers into a dead run. Slater was on that big racehorse of his."

Unhappily, Reno shook his head and said something beneath his breath.

"Then she never had a chance," Caleb said aloud.

"That's what Slater thought, too," Wolfe said. "He let that big horse run. A mile later he had cut Willow's lead to a hundred yards. Two miles later he was working hard to stay even. Three miles later he was losing ground. He tried shooting, but it was too late."

"I'll kill him," Caleb said.

Wolfe slanted the other man a sideways look.

"Wouldn't surprise me. God knows he's earned it."

"Is that when Slater caught Willy?" Reno asked. "Did she pull up when he started shooting?"

Wolfe shook his head. "Hell, no. She kept that red horse at a dead run every foot of the way, shots or no shots. They jumped a hidden gully that had to be every bit of twenty feet across. The stud nearly went down on the other side, but she hauled him back onto his feet and had him collected and running again in nothing flat. And they just kept on running. Never seen anything like it."

"What?" Reno asked.

"That red stud," Wolfe said simply. "Your sister ran him flat out for more than five miles. She never raised a whip, never beat him with her heels, never did one damn thing but stick to his neck like a burr. Slater's big horse is game, but he just didn't have the heart of that little red stud."

"Then how did Slater catch her?" Caleb demanded.

"He didn't. He had split his bunch to look for sign. Half of them were in front of her. She came around a curve in the meadow and there they were." Wolf looked at Caleb suddenly. "Are you sure you want to marry her?"

"Dead sure."

"Damn. I've got to tell you, Cal, if it were anyone but you, I'd make a run at her myself."

Caleb threw Wolfe a narrow look. "Forget it."

Wolfe's smile flashed against his dark features. "Don't blame you a bit. That's one hell of a girl. She saw the men in front of her and pulled her horse right back onto his hocks. By the time he got four hooves on the ground again, she had seen her best chance and she took it." Wolfe shook his head, remembering. "She aimed that red stud for the biggest gap in the horsemen, yanked out her shotgun, and headed for the men at a dead run."

Reno looked shocked. "Willow did that?"

Wolfe nodded, then glanced at Caleb. "You don't look surprised."

"I'm not. When the Comancheros jumped us, my horse went down. Willow turned around and came back for me and damn the rifle fire."

"I can see how that would put a man in a marrying frame of mind," Wolfe said, smiling. "Just watching her take on Slater's bunch gave me a few ideas in that direction. Those London ladies I met were as lovely as dawn, and would have lasted just about as long out here."

"Willow did fine as soon as I got her some decent clothes," Caleb said.

"Thought I recognized those buckskins," Wolfe said. "It took Slater's men a minute to figure out it was a girl riding up. Once they did, they sort of settled back, expecting it to end without a fuss. By the time they got their rifles out she was on top of them. They fired a couple of rounds to turn her, she fired back, and one of the men grabbed her right out of the saddle when the stud ran by."

Caleb's hand tightened on the rifle stock. "Did he hurt her?"

"Not as much as she hurt him," Wolfe said, satisfaction in every syllable. "He might as well have grabbed a wildcat. By the time I got down off that rock and up to the men, Willow was hog-tied on the ground and the man who had caught her didn't have enough skin left on his face to be worth shaving."

Wolfe didn't mention that Willow looked a little worse for wear, too, her pale cheeks showing the clear imprints of a man's hand.

"Then Slater came up and started asking questions about you," Wolfe continued, glancing at Caleb.

"Willow said she didn't know where you were, that she was lost."

"Did Slater believe her?" Reno asked.

Unhappily, Wolfe took off his hat, ran his fingers through hair as thick and black as night, and snapped his hat back into place. "No. He found a book of some kind she was carrying. Seems there was a map and a lot of notes in it."

"My journal," Caleb said. "She took it."

Wolfe's eyes narrowed, but he asked no questions despite his curiosity. "Slater told her to point out where she had been. She looked him right in the eye and told him she couldn't read. He threw the journal in her face and told her she had until the horses were cooled out to learn."

"How much time do we have left?" Reno asked.

Silently Wolfe scanned the countryside and the angle of the sun. "Maybe another hour. Those horses were lathered from their fetlocks to their ears. That's why I took a chance and came looking for you. If I hadn't found you in five more minutes, I was going back."

Caleb's mouth flattened. He knew what Wolfe wasn't saying—Jed Slater was a man accustomed to getting what he wanted in the most efficient manner possible. His reputation for applied cruelty had been earned during a particularly cruel war.

Wolfe looked at Caleb's harsh expression and knew what the other man was thinking. Hesitating, knowing he shouldn't, Wolfe nonetheless found himself asking the question that had eaten at him since the first moment he had realized who Slater's men were pursuing.

"How did you get separated from Willow?" Wolfe asked.

Caleb said nothing.

Reno swore and admitted, "She wrapped her stud's

feet in cloth and sneaked out of the valley."

There was silence while Wolfe thought about what Reno had said.

"She got past both of you," Wolfe said finally.

"Yes."

"Be damned." He sighed. "Any idea why she took off?"

Reno didn't wait for Caleb to speak. "Willow thinks Caleb seduced her to get even for me seducing Caleb's sister."

"Bloody hell," Wolfe said, shocked into using a kind of English he had sworn to forget. "Why did—"

"The horses have rested enough," Caleb interrupted. "Let's ride."

Without waiting to see if the other men would follow, Caleb touched spurs to his horse, sending it forward at a fast canter. A minute later, Wolfe passed him, taking the lead. Nothing more was said until Wolfe signalled for a halt.

"We have to leave the horses here," Wolfe said.

While Reno tied the horses out of sight, Caleb pulled off his boots and switched to moccasins. Wolfe started up the steep shoulder of a ridge that poked out into the grassland. When all three men were belly down just below the crest, they took off their hats and crawled up the last few feet.

Slater's camp was at the bottom of the slope, a thousand feet away. There was little cover on the slope itself, for it was too steep and too rocky for anything to survive except bits of grass and scattered, very stunted trees. The only other approach to the camp was up a grassy meadow where ten hobbled horses were grazing and five horses were being slowly walked while lather dried after their long, exhausting run.

Ishmael was one of the horses. Though they had

been walked for half an hour already, it would be at least another half hour before they were cool enough to be turned out with the other horses. Then Slater would come back and begin questioning Willow.

Before that happened, Willow had to be gone.

Taking care that no sunlight flashed off the spyglass, Caleb searched until he found Willow. She was off to one side of the camp, tied hand and foot among the supplies. Her arms were pulled awkwardly behind her back. A rope went from her wrists, around a waist-high stump, and from there to her ankles.

Ten feet behind her, a man lay propped against a saddle, cutting his fingernails with a pocket knife. His face looked like he had tangled with a wildcat.

Willow straightened. The movement caught Caleb's eye. For a moment, the hair on her cheeks slid aside, revealing the livid marks of a man's hand. A stillness came over Caleb for the space of one breath, two, three. He took a long look at the guard. Only then did Caleb resume quartering the area around Slater's camp, marking out the positions of other men, of available cover, of possible ambush sites.

While Caleb used the spyglass, Wolfe talked in a low voice that carried no farther than the men who were stretched out on either side of him. "If Slater follows his wartime practice, there will be a man guarding Willow and another guard about thirty yards out from camp where you'd least expect it. At the first sign of trouble, both guards will shoot Willow."

"I saw a man in the rocks off to the right," Caleb said softly. "I'll take care of him on the way in." He collapsed the spyglass and handed it to Reno. "Same for the man close to her, the one with the scratched face. I'll take particularly good care of him."

Reno scanned the slope and the approaches to the

camp while Caleb took off his heavy coat and made certain his six-gun was secured in the holster.

"You can't get close to them without being spotted," Reno said finally, lowering the spyglass. "And if you shoot them, Willow will be the next to die. We'll have to wait until dark."

"Slater isn't a patient man," Caleb said. "I'm not going to sit here and watch him ask questions and then cut her to ribbons with his steel-tipped quirt when she doesn't answer. That's what he did in Mexico when a woman wouldn't tell him where her husband was."

Wolfe's powerful hand clamped around Reno's arm, holding him down when he would have surged upright. "Easy, Reno. Cal likes it even less than you do, but he's right. If anyone can get Willow out of that camp alive, he can."

"Here," Caleb said, handing over his rifle to Wolfe. "Cartridges are in my jacket pocket. At this range, the gun pulls about a half-inch to the left. Willow and I might be in your line of fire for the first fifty feet. After that, I'm taking her up the ravine at the rear of camp. When we're over the top, we'll go to ground and wait for you to bring the horses to us."

Wolfe nodded and began sighting over the rifle, getting the feel of the new weapon.

Caleb turned to Reno. "How quiet are you on a stalk?"

"He's better than most and not as good as you," Wolfe said before Reno could answer. "But then, neither am I, and I was raised among the Cheyenne."

Caleb grunted. "Reno, you can stay up here with your rifle or you can come part of the way with me and we'll find out how slick you really are with that six-gun."

Reno smiled wolfishly. "I'll be stepping on your

heels every bit of the way."

He was talking to himself. Caleb was already moving. Stalking human game took time, and they had damn little of that left before Slater came back into camp.

WILLOW looked out from behind her screen of hair, saw that the horses were still being walked, and went back to trying to get out of the ropes that bound her. Desperate to be free, yet worried about attracting attention from her guard, she jerked and yanked at the bonds under cover of her long hair. Pain raked up from her wrists. Fear helped her to ignore the hurt. She never wanted to see the cruel promise in Slater's eyes again. The Comanchero Nine Fingers had made her feel unclean.

Slater horrified her.

Despite Willow's efforts, the ropes felt no looser now than they had when she first began twisting her wrists until the skin was rubbed raw. Fighting the despair that threatened to overwhelm her, she jerked first one wrist, then the other, hoping if she made herself bleed, her wrists and hands would be slippery enough to evade the tight bonds.

A glance at the guard told Willow that he must have finished hacking at his fingernails. He was lying on his back, his mouth open, dead asleep.

Willow began yanking openly on her bonds, taking advantage of the guard's midday nap.

"Don't move, honey. I don't want to cut you."

For an instant, Willow thought she had gone mad and was hearing things. Then she felt her bonds giving way and had to bite back a cry of relief and joy.

"Ease your ankles around to the right," Caleb said in a voice that was barely audible.

There was a soft rustling sound as Willow inched

her feet around toward the back of the stump. For a moment she felt a sensation of pressure on her ankles, followed by a slight rocking motion. The rope at her ankles fell away.

"Back up slowly until you're behind the stump. No! Don't watch the camp. That's my job. You watch what you're doing."

Willow scooted in slow motion until the stump was between her and the camp. Caleb was lying on his stomach, his body flat to the ground.

"Lie down real slow and crawl like a snake past me toward that little crease in the grass. See it?"

She nodded, lay down, and began wriggling along Caleb's length. When her head drew even with his chest, he gave her more terse directions, his voice so low she wondered if she was really hearing the words at all.

"The crease leads to a gully that's about a foot deep. Go left and keep snaking along uphill until you get to the rocks. Your brother is on the left, behind them. Whatever you do, *keep down*. Reno and Wolfe will have to shoot over us if we're spotted."

Willow wanted to ask questions, but a look at the bleak yellow clarity of Caleb's eyes closed her throat. She ducked her head and pushed herself forward on her stomach, feeling as exposed as an egg on a fence rail. Each time she looked up to see how far she was from the gully, it seemed that she had made no progress at all. But if she started to go faster, Caleb's hand clamped around her ankle, forcing her to go so slowly she wanted to scream with frustration and fear.

When Willow finally reached the gully, she discovered that it provided scant cover. Less than a foot deep, with wide, shallow, gently sloping sides, the gully was little better than grass when it came to hiding Willow and Caleb. The rocks he had mentioned were more than a hundred feet away. Willow put her cheek close to the ground and pushed herself along with arms that were trembling from the strain of moving so slowly and so awkwardly.

They were fifty feet from the rocks when one of Slater's men glanced over and discovered Willow was missing.

18

THE shout of discovery was cut off in mid-cry when Wolfe opened up with Caleb's rifle, raking the camp with bullets. Caleb threw himself over Willow, protecting her in the only way he could. Fifty feet up the ravine, Reno began firing his six-gun. The bullets came so rapidly it was hard to separate the sound of each shot. Other shots came from the camp, pistols and rifles all mixed together in an unholy barrage.

Flattened against the earth, frightened, barely able to breathe, Willow felt Caleb's big body jerk and heard him curse. More shouts came, more gunfire, bullets whining and thudding into the ground nearby, but she could see nothing, for Caleb covered her completely.

Abruptly, Reno's six-gun fell silent. The repeating rifle didn't. It continued to lay down a withering hail of bullets.

"Run for it!" Reno shouted.

The words had barely registered on Willow when Caleb yanked her upright and half-carried, half-dragged her toward the rocks. Reno was crouched to one side of the shallow gully, slamming a second, fully loaded cylinder into his revolver. Willow and Caleb hurtled past Reno as the repeating rifle finally fell silent.

Immediately, Reno opened fire once more, giving Wolfe time to reload. This time the shots came more slowly as Reno coolly picked off men who were foolish enough to stick up their heads to see what was happening. The range was extreme for a handgun, but Reno was extremely good with the weapon.

"Up that ravine," Caleb said curtly to Willow as he stood behind her and pointed her toward a dry watercourse that angled away from the ridge where Wolfe was. "When you reach the trees, go about a hundred feet, then get behind some cover and stay there until we catch up. Now *run*."

Willow scrambled forward just as the repeating rifle began firing once more. Caleb waited to see if she would keep going as directed. To his surprise, she did. He turned and started giving terse orders to Reno.

"I'll keep them down while you reload," Caleb said, "but you damn well better be able to do it on the run."

"You're wounded," Reno said without looking away from the camp. "I'll stay."

"It's not my shooting arm. Get going."

Reno spotted a man's boot poking out from among the supplies in the camp. "All right. Get ready."

While Caleb drew his six-gun, Reno sighted on the nearly hidden boot. He squeezed off his last shot, turned, and began shucking spent cases from his six-gun as he ran up the ravine after Willow.

Caleb had already chosen his target. As soon as Reno turned toward the ravine, Caleb opened fire. The bullet sent one of Slater's men scrambling for a better hiding spot. From the far side of the camp, someone opened up on them with a rifle. The rapid barking of the shots told Caleb it was a repeating rifle. Bullets whined and sang off the rock just below him. Instantly, return fire came from Wolfe's position, forcing the other rifleman to keep his head down.

Another rifle opened up. It, too, was a repeating rifle. Caleb squeezed off two more shots and counted the times the other rifles fired without pausing. Eight for one, nine for the other. They weren't the same model or kind as his own rifle, which meant Slater's men carried less in the magazine and were much slower to reload.

"Ready!" called Reno.

Caleb turned and ran as fast as he could up the ravine. He didn't bother trying to reload while he went, for his left hand was slippery with blood. He passed Reno, went on another hundred feet, reloaded, and yelled at Reno to withdraw. Working together smoothly, both retreated into the cover of the trees.

Willow was nowhere in sight.

"Find her and get her over the rise," Caleb said curtly to Reno. "It opens out on the other side. Wolfe will be able to bring the horses right to you."

"What about you?"

"I'll cover your backtrail until you get Willow over the rise. Now move!"

There was no time to waste arguing and Reno knew it. They had taken Slater by surprise. That advantage was rapidly evaporating. Slater's repeating rifles weren't as good as the one Wolfe was using, but there were two rifles against one. There were also ten men, minus the two guards and whatever Wolfe had done in the way of damage.

However Reno added it up, the advantage was on Slater's side.

Reno turned and raced into the trees, calling softly

to his sister. Willow stood up a hundred feet ahead of him. He ran to her and hustled her up the ravine much as Caleb had—half-dragging and half-carrying her. By the time they reached its head and climbed out into an area of mixed grass and trees, she was breathing as hard as she had going over the Great Divide. Reno was breathing almost as hard.

"Stand with your back to me and keep your eyes open," Reno ordered.

Fighting for breath, Willow watched uneasily, her glance darting from shadow to shadow. Nothing was visible but clumps of aspen and patches of grass, the forerunners of the basin that lapped at the forested peaks. Gradually her breathing slowed. Time crawled while she strained to separate natural sounds from those that might be made by men sneaking up on her. In the distance she heard rifle fire, but no six-guns.

Finally a wolf's harmonic cry floated up from behind Willow.

"Don't shoot!" she said urgently. "It's Caleb!"

"I never shoot at anything I can't see," Reno said calmly. "Come on in, Yuma man. Willy, watch the damned meadow!"

Hastily, she turned around and looked at the empty land, feeling her brother's back like a wall behind her.

It's just as well, Willow told herself unhappily. *I don't really want to see Caleb look at me with those cold yellow eyes and know that duty made him risk his life for me.*

The thought of how exposed he had been coming into camp chilled her. She hadn't even had time to thank him but that, too, was just as well. From the look in his eyes back at the valley, he didn't want anything at all from her.

Let me know when you feel like being treated like my woman. Then I'll let you know if I still feel like being your man.

"Anyone coming?" Reno asked.

"No," Caleb and Willow said simultaneously.

"Good. How do you feel about blood, Willy? Does it make you faint?"

"Not since I turned thirteen."

"Then switch places and go to work patching up your future husband while I watch the meadow."

For an instant, Willow didn't understand. When she did, she spun around and stared at Caleb, who was standing less than two feet away from her. The breath rushed out of her with a low sound as she saw blood spreading in a ragged, crimson sleeve down his left arm.

"Caleb, my God . . ." she said shakily.

"Don't faint, southern lady. You're no use to me passed out on the ground."

The clipped words restored Willow's control as nothing else could have. She stepped forward and looked at his arm, for it was preferable to the savage clarity of his eyes.

"Here," Caleb said. He reached behind his back, where he had moved his knife sheath to make crawling easier. "You'll need this."

With a hand that trembled, Willow took the big knife. When she saw the blood on it, she looked up quickly at Caleb, wondering if he had another wound she couldn't see.

"Not my blood," Caleb said.

Willow drew a deep breath and said nothing.

"Disappointed?" he asked sardonically.

She flinched subtly, then took a firm grasp on the knife and put the tip of the blade beneath his cuff. "Hold still."

"Don't worry, southern lady. I'm not going to give you an excuse to cut me up any worse than I already am."

The fabric gave way easily before the lethally sharp

knife. Willow peeled the sleeve aside to reveal the wound high on Caleb's arm. Her teeth sank into her lower lip as she saw the crimson stripe where a bullet had gouged a furrow across his bicep.

"Oh, Caleb," she whispered. "I'm sorry."

"You ought to be," he said flatly. "You and your girlish notions about love damn near got us all killed."

Willow looked at Caleb, then looked away quickly. His eyes were those of a bird of prey, intent and merciless. He had never looked more like what he was . . . dark angel of retribution.

Nothing had changed. Nothing would. Nothing *could*. She had fallen in love with a man who knew only the cold balance of right and wrong, duty and necessity. But she had her own ideas of right and wrong, duty and necessity. None of them included forcing a man into marriage simply because her brother was appallingly quick with his six-gun.

"You aren't the only one with a sense of duty," Willow said. She turned to Caleb's other arm and slipped the knife beneath the cuff. When she spoke, her voice was as raw as the sound of the cloth being ripped into strips with vicious jerks of her hands. "I couldn't stand by and watch you being forced into marriage with me just because Matt happens to be so damned quick with his gun!"

"Forced into marriage because of your brother's gun," Caleb said coldly. "Nice to know you think I'm a coward as well as the kind of conscienceless seducer who would turn an innocent girl into a whore."

"Seducer? Don't be ridiculous," Willow said, clipping each syllable as she wrapped Caleb's wound with a gentleness that was at odds with her voice. "Before you ever kissed me, I wanted you until I couldn't take a breath without wondering if the air had touched you first."

Caleb's body tightened as though he had been cut with a whip.

"I'm sorry," Willow said quickly, thinking she had been too rough in bandaging his wound. "I didn't mean to hurt you. As for being a coward," she continued as she carefully tied the bandage in place, "anyone who has the nerve to crawl into Jed Slater's camp in full daylight isn't a coward. You're simply too pragmatic to walk into certain death and too much a man to run away. That left marriage." She stepped back from Caleb. "That should do it."

"Does that mean you're finished tearing strips?" Reno asked dryly, turning around, facing them. "If so, it's time to—*Slater!*"

Before the cry left Reno's lips, Caleb spun around and drew his gun in a single, fluid motion that was so quick the eye couldn't truly follow it. Thunder erupted on Willow's right and then on her left as first Caleb and then Reno emptied their guns into the two men who were sixty feet away, creeping from the ravine to the edge of the grass, seeking a clear shot between the trees.

The sheer speed of Caleb's and Reno's response surprised the Slater brothers. Their aim was shattered as they fired quickly on the way to seeking better cover. But there was no cover within reach. Caleb and Reno were as accurate as they were fast. Realizing it, Jed Slater turned and fired even as bullets cut him down.

It wasn't the men he aimed at, but Willow.

A blinding pain burst in Willow's head, driving her to her knees. Darkness spiraled down from the sky, whirling around her. She heard Caleb's voice calling her name as she reached out to him, needing him as the solid center of a world that was spinning blackly around her. She felt the strength of his arms supporting her, but even his power couldn't hold the unnatural night at bay.

Willow was still trying to say Caleb's name when midnight condensed in a soundless rush, claiming her.

Caleb felt the sudden slackness of Willow's body, saw the blood welling from beneath her bright hair, and called her name in a voice that tore at his throat.

There was no answer. He hadn't expected one. With fingers that shook, he probed gently around the bloody wound. Then he cradled her against his body and grieved in the dry, wrenching silence of a man who had never permitted himself to cry.

WHEN Wolfe rode into camp, the first thing he saw was Reno and Caleb sitting thirty feet away in the midst of sun-dappled shadows. Willow lay between the two men. Caleb flashed a quick look at Wolfe and the horses, then turned back to Willow as though afraid she would slip away unless he watched her every instant. Her hand lay between his. He stroked the smooth skin, trying to reassure both Willow and himself that she was still alive.

After a long look at his sister, Reno stood and walked to where Wolfe waited.

"I heard the gunfire. Was Willow hit?" Wolfe asked as he dismounted.

"Yes."

"Bad?"

"We don't know. Her pulse is strong and steady, but she's unconscious."

Wolfe's dark eyes closed briefly. He turned and gave a brooding look to the girl who lay too quietly and the man who sat next to her, stroking her hand with a tenderness Wolfe wouldn't have believed if he hadn't seen it.

"What happened?" Wolfe said, turning away, feeling as though he had intruded on Caleb's privacy.

"Slater and his kid brother came up the ravine after us. They were sixty feet away when I spotted them." Reno's voice was heavy and worn. "Willow was fixing Caleb's arm. There was no time to get her out of the way. When Jed Slater knew he was finished, he shot her. May God damn his soul to Hell."

"Amen." Wolfe sighed. "What about Kid Coyote?"

"Dead."

Reno looked past Wolfe to the horses he was leading. Ishmael was among them. His head was high and his walk was strong. Other than a coat dulled by dried lather, the horse looked no worse for his long run.

"Thanks for fetching the stud," Reno said, his voice husky with all that had not been said. "He's a particular favorite of hers."

"No thanks needed. I would have killed every outlaw in the camp to get my hands on that red stallion," Wolfe said calmly. He waited, but Reno didn't say anything more about what they were facing with Willow's wound. "Did she bleed too much? Is that why she's unconscious?"

Reno hesitated, then made an oddly helpless gesture with his left hand. "It's a head wound. Caleb said the wound is shallow. He said he's seen men walk around with a bullet in their head until the wound closed." With a weary curse, Reno added, "He also said he's seen men die without ever waking up, and their wounds were as shallow as hers."

Wolfe swore softly and snapped the reins between his fingers as though they were a man's neck. "Looks like we better make camp here."

"It's too close to Slater's bunch."

"They're through," Wolfe said flatly. "That repeating rifle of Caleb's is a real ring-tailed wonder. You don't need to take it off your shoulder to reload it. You just stuff the bullets in the side and keep on shooting. It beat hell out of the two repeating rifles Slater had."

"Only because you were the one doing the shooting," Reno said. "I've never seen your equal with a long gun."

"Nor yours with a six-gun. Except, maybe, Caleb Black."

Reno's smile flickered sadly. "That Yuma man is quick, all right. I had to step around Willow to shoot. By the time I did, Caleb had emptied his revolver. He's as smart as he is quick. He saw right off that Kid Coyote was slow and scared, so he put six bullets in Jed Slater and left the Kid for me."

Wolfe nodded. "I've seen Caleb shoot. Not often, mind you, but when he does, he gets the job done. Glad the two of you sorted out your differences short of drawing your guns."

Reno pinned Wolfe with a pale green glance. "Caleb and I didn't get off to a friendly start, but that's a damn good man over there, and he's tearing himself up, blaming himself for what happened to Willy. That's pure foolishness. It's not his fault Jed Slater was snake-mean and tough enough to take six bullets and still shoot back." Reno made an angry gesture with his hand. "But Caleb won't listen to me. Can you talk sense to him?"

"I'll try, but I doubt it. I've discovered men aren't real reasonable where their women are concerned. Especially men like Caleb Black. Still water runs deep and quiet and looks real easy, but God help the fool who tries to make it run in a different course."

Wolfe walked over to where Willow lay. When Caleb looked up, Wolfe's throat tightened over protests he couldn't voice. Caleb looked like a man who no longer believed in anything, even Hell.

"What can I do?" Wolfe asked quietly.

"Get her mares," Caleb said, looking back at Willow. The back of his fingers caressed her cheek as lightly as a breath. "When she wakes up, I want her to see all her horses cropping grass nearby. I want her to open her eyes and see . . ."

Caleb's voice frayed into silence. Wolfe put his hand on the other man's right shoulder, squeezed, and turned away without saying anything. There were no words that could put the light back in Caleb's eyes.

Caleb didn't look up when Wolfe rode out. He didn't look up when Reno made an oversized bed of evergreen boughs. But when Reno would have moved Willow, Caleb pushed the other man's hands away and lifted Willow despite his wound. The pain in his arm simply didn't matter except to tell Caleb he was still alive and Willow wasn't, not quite.

"I'm going up on that rise," Reno said. "I'll be able to guard better from up there."

Caleb nodded without looking up. Gently, he put Willow on the bed, pulled the blanket over her once more, and lay down next to her. His fingertips sought her wrist again, needing the reassurance of her pulse. Its steady, strong beat was all that stood between Caleb and the kind of darkness he hadn't known existed until he had turned at the sound of Willow's cry and seen her falling.

But Willow had known such darkness existed. He had seen it in her eyes last night, when she stood in the moonlight and called herself his whore. He had been furious that she could so belittle herself and him and what they had shared. She had been furious in just the same way, a rage as deep as the passion they had shared.

Yet underneath all the hurt, all the rage, Caleb had heard Willow calling his name in silence, asking why something that had begun in such beauty had ended in such terrible darkness. He had been asking the same thing since he had known she was Reno's sister.

No answer had come to Caleb, only a pain that grew greater with each breath, each shared touch, each instant of knowing that eventually love would end and hatred begin.

And it had.

Reflexively, Caleb closed his eyes as though that would somehow erase the painful memories. It didn't. He kept hearing Willow's husky voice calling his name, haunting echo of a love lost before it could be truly found.

Caleb, what's wrong? Caleb? What happened? Why won't you answer me? Caleb? Caleb!

Then he realized that it was Willow, not memory, calling his name.

"Caleb."

Slowly he opened his eyes, afraid to believe he wasn't dreaming.

Willow looked at Caleb anxiously, her heart turning over at the expression on his face. Even as she winced at the headache that had come from nowhere, she touched his cheek with trembling fingertips, wanting to soothe the pain she saw in his eyes.

"You're hurt," Willow said, seeing the bloody bandage as though for the first time.

"I was shot." Caleb looked at her intently, wondering at the concern in her, the emotion that made her look at him as though the past night had never happened. "So were you."

Hazel eyes widened, revealing every shade of blue and green, amber and gray. Caleb felt his tension ease even more when both pupils contracted evenly in response to the increased light. The men who had died of their head wounds hadn't been able to respond to light with both eyes.

"Shot?" she asked. "How? When? I don't remember."

"Don't try to sit up," he said, but it was too late.

A low sound came from Willow. Caleb caught her and eased her back down onto the bed.

"My head hurts."

"Running into a bullet will do that." He kissed her very gently and stroked her cheek. When she didn't withdraw, but instead turned her face toward his caress, he felt a relief so great it was dizzying. He brushed his lips over hers and whispered, "Lie still, love. You're weak as a kitten."

"When did all this happen?"

Caleb looked at his watch and couldn't believe so little time had passed. He felt as though he had spent months watching Willow's unnatural sleep.

"Less than an hour ago," he said.

She frowned, trying to remember. "Matt? Is Matt all right? Are you?"

"Your brother is up on the hill guarding us. My wound isn't worth mentioning. Wolfe is getting your mares. He brought Ishmael back, too. Everything is fine. Except you. How much do you remember?"

Caleb couldn't quite keep the hope from his voice. Amnesia sometimes followed head wounds. He would give a great deal if Willow could forget what had happened last night.

He knew the exact instant when Willow remembered. The light and loving concern left her eyes. Very slowly, she turned her face away so that his fingers were no longer touching her cheek.

"I remember riding out on Ishmael rather than have you marry me under the threat of Matt's gun," she said finally.

"Yes, I can see you remember that. Anything else?" Caleb asked tonelessly.

Willow frowned and lifted her hands to her temples, trying to rub away the pain. "I remember running Ishmael much too long, too hard."

"Ishmael came through it just fine. Jed Slater didn't have any use for people in general and women in particular, but he was the finest horseman Kentucky ever raised. He cooled out Ishmael personally. Do you remember anything else?"

"Fighting the man who grabbed me. It didn't work. He slapped me so hard I couldn't see or hear."

Caleb's jaw tightened. "You clawed him pretty good just the same."

"Yes, I remember his face. He was the one guarding me." Willow's expression changed as she recalled the blood on Caleb's knife. "I thought he was taking a nap, but he wasn't, was he?"

"What else do you remember?"

"You," Willow said simply. "You cut me free, crawled behind me out of camp, and when the shooting started, you covered me with your own body." She looked at him through the thick amber screen of her eyelashes. "That's when you were wounded, wasn't it? I felt you jerk."

"Do you remember anything else?"

"I'm sorry, Caleb," she whispered, ignoring his attempt to change the subject. "I never meant for you to be hurt. I was the seducer, not the seduced. I knew Matt wouldn't see it that way and I didn't want him to shoot you for a seduction that was my fault, not yours, so I left. My brother is so fast with—"

Willow's words were chopped off as her breath came in with a harsh sound. She remembered seeing Caleb turn and draw his gun in a flashing instant and thunder rolling, and it had happened all at once, all of a piece.

"You're as fast as my brother."

"Maybe, but probably not," Caleb said evenly. "In any case, fast doesn't always count. What counts is hitting what you shoot at and being willing to take a bullet in return."

"You did."

"So did Jed Slater. He's lucky he died. I would have hung him for what he did to you."

Willow sighed and pursued the only subject that mattered to her. "You aren't afraid of Matt's gun, so why did you agree to marry me rather than face him?"

"I didn't want to kill someone you loved," Caleb said simply. "You loved your brother. You said you loved me. One of us would have been killed, Willow. Probably both. That's what happens when well-matched men are stupid enough or unlucky enough to meet over drawn guns. Since I planned on marrying you anyway, it seemed foolish to fight Reno over it. I'd just as soon your brother was alive to give you away."

"When . . ." Willow swallowed dryly. "When did you figure out how good Matt was with his gun?"

"The minute Becky said the name Reno. Your brother has earned a reputation as a bad man in a fight. He's never hunted that reputation, but that didn't keep people from talking. Wolfe warned me, too. He said Reno and I would likely kill each other."

"You knew all this and you went after Matt anyway?"

Caleb frowned down at Willow. "Of course. If I turned my back and walked away, who else would see that no more innocent girls were seduced and abandoned to die birthing Reno's bastards?"

"Matt would never do such a thing!"

"I know. Now. And I won't do it, either. We're getting married, Willow."

"You didn't seduce me!" she said through clenched teeth.

"Horseshit," Caleb said roughly. Then he touched Willow's cheek in silent apology. "Honey, no man ever crept up on a girl's blind side as carefully as I did on yours. Your combination of innocence and passion made me ache until I thought I would go crazy. I was determined to have you, but I was even more determined to make you ask for me. My pride couldn't take the thought of anyone saying that I had taken you against your will."

"So that's why you told me to push you away," Willow said in a faint voice, understanding too late.

"That's *not* why," Caleb said in a low voice. "I had just learned you were the sister of the man I had vowed to kill. I knew if I took you, you would hate yourself as much as you hated me when you faced me over Reno's dead body. I didn't want that, but I wanted you so much I couldn't force myself to turn away."

Willow's eyes widened in shock as she understood what Caleb had tried to spare her . . . but even his formidable self-control hadn't prevented him from taking her.

"That's when I told you to push me away," Caleb whispered, "when I knew you were Reno's sister. The thought of you hating me ripped me apart, but I didn't know what I could do to stop it. I couldn't live with myself if I let Reno go on and seduce other girls. Yet I wanted you so much I couldn't let you go. No matter what choice I made, I lost."

Understanding wrenched Willow as she remembered facing the choice of marrying a man who didn't love her or watching the man she loved die beneath her brother's gun. Neither choice had been bearable, so she had simply walked away, leaving both choices behind. Caleb hadn't had even that unhappy escape. Duty or desire or death had made a complete, seamless trap. No room to plead or hide. No way to be free. No way to change what would happen. No way to live with what would happen.

Willow didn't know what she would have done if there had been no escape for her. She made a low sound, caught in the painful understanding that Caleb had paid a high price for the passion she had created in him.

Long fingers touched Willow's cheek again, then withdrew because Caleb feared her reaction.

"I took you because I couldn't stop myself," Caleb admitted, his voice husky. "I held nothing back from you. I couldn't. I've never been with a woman like that, passion and peace and laughter all mixed together. You taught me how much I had been missing. *And I knew every instant of every hour I was with you that I was going to lose you as soon as I found Reno.*"

Caleb fought against the emotion closing his throat and burning his eyes like naked flame. He took a slow breath, trying to ease the brutal tension in his body. It was futile. The tension had never been wholly banished since he had known that Willow was Reno's sister.

"Then you called yourself my whore," he whispered, "as though what we had was nothing more than two strangers rutting in the dark. Yet to me what we had was . . . beautiful."

Willow felt the tension in Caleb's fingers, a fine trembling that rippled from him to her, telling her of the turmoil beneath his controlled surface.

"So I gave you what you wanted," Caleb said. "I left you to sleep alone, a woman not a whore. And when I woke up, I found out that even though I hadn't killed your brother, you still hated me so much you would rather ride into certain death than marry me."

"That's not true!" Willow said, sitting up. There was an instant of lancing pain that made her wince, but it passed quickly, submerged in the urgency of making Caleb understand. "I wasn't planning on dying. I just didn't want to spend my life living with a man who thought all that existed between a man and a woman was a simple trade—she scratches his itch and he gives her marriage or a handful of silver, depending on what kind of woman she is. That way of thinking makes all women the same kind. Whores."

As Caleb sat up, he struggled for the self-control he had always taken for granted before he met Willow Moran. Very gently, he turned her face against his neck, embracing her without hurting her.

"I never thought of you that way," Caleb said after a moment, his voice hoarse. "When you gave yourself to me . . ." His voice faded, then returned, even more ragged than it had been before. "It was the most beautiful gift I've ever been given. I had nothing to give you in return but the ugly choices that were tearing me apart. My only hope of changing those choices was to give you a pleasure so great that you wouldn't be able to hate me, no matter what happened after I found your brother."

Caleb forced himself to breathe deeply, evenly. It didn't work. The raw pain he felt was slipping out of control.

"When I discovered Reno hadn't seduced my sister, I thought God had heard my prayers. I was free of the trap. But you hated me anyway." Caleb drew a tight breath as his voice broke. He closed his eyes and fought to finish saying what had to be said before he lost the ability to speak at all. "You could be carrying my baby right now. I can't let you go off alone and pretend to be a widow. We're getting married. We owe it to the baby we might have created. Accept it, Willow. Don't fight me anymore. You'll only hurt yourself."

"Duty," Willow said, trying and failing to keep the bitterness from her voice. "Damn duty," she whispered despairingly. "A whole lifetime of cold duty. I didn't want that. That's why I rode out. I wanted so much more from my marriage than duty."

A small shudder went through Caleb, control slipping away, his voice roughening even more. "I'm sorry, Willow. I wanted so much more, too. I wanted to sleep with you in my arms and wake up to your smile. I wanted to see love in your eyes when you looked at me. I wanted to build a house for you and give you babies. I wanted a passion so deep that I'd sink into your soul the same way you had sunk into mine. I wanted . . . everything."

"So did I," she whispered.

"We could still have it," Caleb said against her hair. "Can't you forgive me and learn to love me again? I need that, Willow. I love you so much I can't even breathe."

She flinched and wanted to scream at having to listen to duty masquerading as love, but she hadn't the strength to scream. She hadn't even the strength to sit upright without leaning against the man who had always been stronger than she was, harder, needing nothing but himself and his God and duty.

"Don't." Willow sighed wearily. "You don't have to tell me sweet, loving lies to get me into your bed. I'm not an innocent girl anymore. I'm a—"

"No more, Willow," Caleb interrupted in a low voice. "I won't have you call yourself a whore again. I know you hate me. I know I never should have seduced you, but I can't go back and change what happened. All I can do is live with it and try not to hurt you anymore."

"Duty," she summarized.

"Damn duty," Caleb said, shaking. *"I love you."*

Willow felt a single drop on her cheek and shuddered. She had thought herself beyond tears. Even as she lifted her hand to wipe away the evidence of her despair, she realized that it wasn't her tear that burned against her skin.

Hesitantly, afraid to believe, she touched her trembling hand to Caleb's cheek. His tears scalded her, burning through her hurt and confusion to the truth beneath. A sense of duty could force a man to avenge his sister at the risk of his own life. Duty could force him to risk his life to rescue Willow. Duty could force him to marry the girl he had seduced.

But not even duty could force tears from a man as hard as Caleb Black.

With a sound of wonder, Willow rested her cheek against Caleb's, then turned and kissed him, tasting the bittersweet tears that were his and her own combined. It was the same for their whispered phrases, two voices combined in discovery and joy, a man and a woman bound to one another by the irresistible passion known as love.

Epilogue

WIND from the mountain peaks rushed cool and sweet over the land, setting yellow aspen leaves to dancing. Ishmael's head came up and his nostrils flared as he caught the familiar scent of the man and woman who walked together into the meadow. Behind them, at the edge of the forest, a large log house and barn gleamed in golden shades of unweathered wood. Window glass from Denver sparkled like jewels in the sun, a wedding gift from Wolfe.

Ishmael watched Caleb and Willow approach for a moment longer before the horse lowered his head, snorted, and resumed cropping the rich grass of high-country autumn. Around him grazed four Arabian mares whose bodies shielded and nurtured the foals they would bear in the spring. Nearby, tall Montana mares with rangy lines and deep chests grazed in the lush basin. They, too, would bear foals when winter released the country from its white embrace. Cattle grazed at the south end of the winding meadow, their bodies fat and sleek with the bounty of Colorado grass. Long rows of meadow hay lay drying in the sun, sending the fragrance of a captive sun across the land.

Caleb lifted Willow over the brook that sang down from the forested canyon at the end of the basin. Smiling, she wound her arms lightly around his neck and watched the tawny eyes of the man she loved. A circle of gold gleamed on her left hand. The ring was made from nuggets Reno had found in a high, hidden valley.

"And by next year," Caleb continued, brushing his lips over his wife's, "the home pasture should be fenced. Until then, Ishmael will have to keep an eye on his mares."

"He's done a good job so far," Willow said.

Caleb grinned. "I can't argue that. My Montana mares might have been bigger than what he was used to, but it didn't put that stud off his stride a bit."

Willow tried not to laugh, but the gleam of amusement in her husband's eyes was too beguiling. Laughing softly, she kissed the line of his jaw.

"Will it put you off your stride when I get big?" she asked against his skin.

Caleb went very still and his arms tightened. "Are you going to get big?"

"Come spring, I suspect I'll be as big as any of the mares."

"Are you certain?" he asked, trying and failing to keep the concern from his voice as he remembered his sister.

"I'm strong," Willow whispered. "Don't worry, love."

Joy and fear were mixed in the tawny intensity of Caleb's glance as he looked at the woman who had become the center of his life.

"I'll be with you," he said simply.

* * *

AND he was.

Their first child was born when high-country streams ran full with the wild rush of spring. Like the brothers and sisters who followed, he grew tall and strong and straight, fed by the clean western land and the love that wove brightly between Caleb and Willow Black.